Krewe of Hunters
Compilation

About Heather Graham

Heather Graham has been writing for many years and actually has published nearly 200 titles. So, for this page, we'll concentrate on the Krewe of Hunters.

They include:

Phantom Evil
Heart of Evil
Sacred Evil
The Evil Inside
The Unseen
The Unholy
The Unspoken
The Uninvited
The Night is Watching
The Night is Alive
The Night is Forever
The Cursed
The Hexed
The Betrayed
The Silenced
The Forgotten
The Hidden

Actually, though, Adam Harrison—responsible for putting the Krewe together, first appeared in a book called Haunted. He also appeared in Nightwalker and has walk-ons in a few other books. For more ghostly novels, readers might enjoy the Flynn Brothers Trilogy—Deadly Night, Deadly Harvest, and Deadly Gift, or the Key West Trilogy—Ghost Moon, Ghost Shadow, and Ghost Night.

The Vampire Series (now under Heather Graham/ previously Shannon Drake) Beneath a Blood Red Moon, When Darkness Falls,

Deep Midnight, Realm of Shadows, The Awakening, Dead by Dusk, Blood Red, Kiss of Darkness, and From Dust to Dust.

For more info, please visit her web page, http://www.theoriginalheathergraham.com or stop by on Facebook.

Krewe of Hunters Compilation

3 Stories by
By Heather Graham

1001 Dark Nights

EVIL EYE
CONCEPTS

Krewe of Hunters Compilation
3 Stories by
Heather Graham
ISBN: 978-1-945920-61-5
1001 Dark Nights

Published by Evil Eye Concepts, Incorporated

Sign up for the 1001 Dark Nights Newsletter
and be entered to win a Tiffany Key necklace.

There's a new contest every month!

Visit www.1001DarkNights.com/key/ to subscribe

As a bonus, all subscribers will receive a free
1001 Dark Nights story
The First Night
by Lexi Blake & M.J. Rose

Table of Contents

One Thousand and One Dark Nights

Once upon a time, in the future…

*I was a student fascinated with stories and learning.
I studied philosophy, poetry, history, the occult, and
the art and science of love and magic. I had a vast
library at my father's home and collected thousands
of volumes of fantastic tales.*

*I learned all about ancient races and bygone
times. About myths and legends and dreams of all
people through the millennium. And the more I read
the stronger my imagination grew until I discovered
that I was able to travel into the stories... to actually
become part of them.*

*I wish I could say that I listened to my teacher
and respected my gift, as I ought to have. If I had, I
would not be telling you this tale now.
But I was foolhardy and confused, showing off
with bravery.*

*One afternoon, curious about the myth of the
Arabian Nights, I traveled back to ancient Persia to
see for myself if it was true that every day Shahryar
(Persian: شهریار, "king") married a new virgin, and then
sent yesterday's wife to be beheaded. It was written
and I had read, that by the time he met Scheherazade,
the vizier's daughter, he'd killed one thousand
women.*

Something went wrong with my efforts. I arrived in the midst of the story and somehow exchanged places with Scheherazade – a phenomena that had never occurred before and that still to this day, I cannot explain.

Now I am trapped in that ancient past. I have taken on Scheherazade's life and the only way I can protect myself and stay alive is to do what she did to protect herself and stay alive.

Every night the King calls for me and listens as I spin tales. And when the evening ends and dawn breaks, I stop at a point that leaves him breathless and yearning for more. And so the King spares my life for one more day, so that he might hear the rest of my dark tale.

As soon as I finish a story... I begin a new one... like the one that you, dear reader, have before you now.

On the Krewe of Hunters
By Heather Graham

I've always been fascinated by both history and stories that had elements that were eerie and made us wonder what truly goes on, what is the human soul—and is there life after death? When I was young, I devoured gothic novels and became a fan of Washington Irving, Edgar Allan Poe, Bram Stoker's *Dracula* and Mary Shelley's *Frankenstein*.

And with years passing—for some of us earlier in life and others later—we lose people. When we lose people, we have to believe that we'll see them again, that there is a Heaven or an afterlife. Sometimes, it's the only true comfort we have. I think it's a beautiful part of us—the love we can have for others. But it also allows for pain so deep it can't be endured unless we have that belief that we can and will meet again.

Having grown up with a Scottish father and an Irish mother, I naturally spent some time in church learning the Nicene Creed—in which we vow that we believe in the Holy Ghost.

I suppose people with very mathematical and scientific minds can easily explain away such things as "death" experiences shared by many who technically died on operating tables before being brought back. "Neurons snapping in the brain," is one explanation I've heard.

But I sadly lack a scientific brain and my math is pathetic, so I choose to believe that all things may be possible.

Have I ever sat down with a ghost myself? No.

But I have been many places where it's easy to imagine that the dead might linger. I've heard of many strange tales. And I love the chance that when a loved one needs to be soothed, when a right must be avenged, a ghost—or perhaps the strength and energy of the human soul—might remain.

Thus the Krewe.

Who better than an offshoot of a crime-fighting agency to help these wronged individuals—far too, well, *dead*, themselves—who wish to set the record straight?

I've had incredible chances myself to do wonderful things and while I haven't met a ghost, I have certainly been places where the very air around you feels different. Walking through the Tower of London, stepping into Westminster Cathedral—or standing at dusk on one of the hallowed fields of Gettysburg, you can easily feel seeped with history and the lives that went before us.

I've enjoyed working on the Krewe novels, setting them various places I've loved myself. Each year, a group of writers takes the Lizzie Borden house for a night. For promo, I've done a documented séance at the House of the Seven Gables. I've been on expeditions with ghost "hunters" on the Queen Mary, the Spanish Military Hospital, the Myrtles Plantation, and many more wonderful locations where history, time, and place took their toll on men and women.

Wonderfully fun things happen. The incredible owner of the Lizzie Borden Bed and Breakfast and Museum, has restored the house to as close to the way it looked the fateful day that Lizzie herself either did—or didn't—take an ax (or hatchet!) and give her mother forty whacks. (It was really somewhere between 18 and 20, but that doesn't work well in a rhyme!) One year, the Biography Channel was filming there and my newly graduated Cal-Arts actress daughter, Chynna Skye, played Lizzie Borden for the Biography Channel—and hacked me to pieces as Abby Borden. (What a charming mother/daughter shot, right?) I've stayed at the 17hundred90 Inn in Savannah in the room from which their resident ghost, Anne, pitched to her death. The management there has a wonderful sense of humor—they have a mannequin of Anne in one of the windows, waving to those on the tours that go by. We also happened to follow a then young recording and television star's stay in the room. She left the inn a letter, telling them that Anne had been in her luggage, messing up all her packing. Having spent time with ghost trackers who did seek the logical explanation first, all I could think was, "But did you look for the note from the TSA?"

A favorite occasion was at the Spanish Military Hospital in St. Augustine where, watching the cameras set up by my friends, the Peace River Ghost Trackers, I was certain I saw a ghost. But good ghost trackers are out to find the solid solution to a "haunting" first—it was pointed out to me that I was seeing Scott's shadow as he moved across the room.

While Adam Harrison first makes his appearance in *Haunted*, the Krewe of Hunters series actually begins with *Phantom Evil*, taking place in one of my favorite cities in the world, New Orleans, Louisiana. I have put on a writers' conference there every year since the awful summer of storms and flooding decimated the city. There are few places in the world with an aura of "faded elegance," of the past being an integral part of the present. There are tales of courage there, of tragedy, and of adventure. The cemeteries stir the imaginations of the most solid thinkers. There are many ghosts with the right to be truly furious at their earthly fates—not to mention some of the most delicious food in the world!

Jane Everett and Sloan Trent first meet during a wicked season of murder at an old theater in Arizona reminiscent of the Bird Cage. The Wild, Wild, West certainly had its share of violence and intrigue as well. Cultures came together and clashed, miners sought treasure, and the ever-present human panorama of life went on—including love gone wrong, hatred, jealousy, and greed.

And where ghosts might well linger. If they exist, of course.

For this story—while thankfully, nothing went wrong and it was an incredibly beautiful day!—I have chosen a castle in New England and the seed of its imagining came from a real wedding—my son's.

Yes, in America, we have castles. That's because we've had men who lived with massive fortunes and could indulge their whims and have them brought over—brick by brick or stone by stone—from a

European country. And there's just something about a castle...

So many things can go wrong at a wedding. What with dresses, a wedding party, nervous brides, nervous grooms, bad caterers, and so on.

But what could be worse than the minister—dead on the morning of the nuptials?

Crimson Twilight

Dedication

For Franci Naulin and D.J. Davant

Yevgeniya Yeretskaya and Derek Pozzessere

and

Alicia Ibarra and Robert Rosello

And to all kinds of different, beautiful—wonderful weddings!

Chapter One

.

"I say we fool around again," Sloan Trent said.

Jane Everett smiled.

They'd spent the night before fooling around—even though it had been their wedding eve— so she assumed they'd fool around again a great deal tonight.

Which was nothing new for them.

They'd finally made it out of the shower and into clothing and were ready to head downstairs. But Sloan was still in an amorous mood. He drew her to him, kissed her neck just below her ear, and whispered, "There's so much time in life that we can't fool around... so you have to fool around when the fooling around is good, right?" He had that way of whispering against her ear. His breath was hot and moist and somehow had a way of creating little fires that trickled down into her sex, generating an instant burst of desire.

"We've just showered," she reminded him.

"Showers can be fun, too."

"We're supposed to be meeting up with Kelsey and Logan and seeing a bit of the castle before we get ready for the ceremony."

"You never know. Maybe Logan and Kelsey are fooling around and showering, too?"

He pressed his lips to her throat and her collarbone, drawing her closer, making the spoon of their bodies into something erotic.

She wasn't sure what would have happened if it hadn't been for the scream.

More a shriek!

Long, loud, piercing, horrible.

They broke apart, both of them making mad leaps for the Glock firearms they were never without, racing out of their room to the upper landing of the castle's staircase. Of all the things Jane hadn't expected as her wedding approached, it was for the minister to be found dead—neck broken, eyes-wide-open—at the first floor landing of Castle Cadawil. Logan Raintree and Kelsey O'Brien, their co-workers and witnesses for the wedding, rushed up close behind them.

They all paused, assessing the situation, then raced down.

Reverend Marty MacDonald lay on his back, head twisted at that angle which clearly defined death, his legs still on the steps, arms extended as if he'd tried to fly. Sloan looked at her, shaking his head sadly. She felt as if all the air had been sucked from her lungs. Her blood began to run cold. Her first thought was for Marty MacDonald. She didn't know him that well. She'd met and hired him here, on the New England coast, just a month ago when she'd first seen the castle. She and Sloan had been talking about what to do and how and when to marry, and it had suddenly seemed right.

But now. The poor man!

Her next thought was—

Oh, God! What did this say for their lives together? What kind of an omen—

"Tripped?" Logan Raintree suggested, studying the dead man and the stairs.

Logan was the leader of the Texas Krewe of Hunters—the mini-division within their special unit of the FBI. Many of their fellow agents liked to attach the word "special" with a mocking innuendo, but for the most part the Bureau looked upon them with a fair amount of respect. They were known for coming up with results. Jane had known Logan a long time. They were both Texans and had worked with Texas law enforcement before they'd joined on with the Krewe.

Kelsey had come into it as a U.S. Marshal. She'd been working in Key West, her home stomping grounds, until she'd been called to Texas on a serial murder case. She and Logan had been a twosome ever since.

One weekend they'd slipped away and quietly married. They told no one and it had become a pool in the home office, had they or hadn't they? If so, when?

Sloan had profited $120 with his guess. Sloan wasn't a Texan, though he, too, had worked there. Jane had met Sloan in Arizona during the curious case of the deaths at the Gilded Lily. He'd been acting-sheriff there at the time. Six-foot-four, broad-shouldered, wearing a badge and a Stetson, he'd been pretty appealing. That case put some distance and resentment between them, until solving it drew them together in a way that would never end.

"Tripped?" Logan said again, and she caught the question in his voice.

Logan and Sloan, and all of the members of the Krewe, worked well together. Logan and Sloan both had Native American mixes in their backgrounds, which brought a sense and respect for all beliefs and all possibilities.

Jane loved that about both men.

Of course, she loved Kelsey, too. She'd known Kelsey her whole life. Having grown up in the Florida Keys, Kelsey also had a keen interest in everyone and everything. She was bright, blonde, and beautiful, ready to tackle anything.

"So it appears," Kelsey murmured.

"Did you see anyone?" Sloan asked the maid, whose horrified scream had alerted them all.

The maid shook her head.

"I'm trying to picture," Sloan said, "how he tripped and ended up here, as he is."

"He had to have come down from far up," Kelsey noted.

Sloan rose and started up the winding stone stairway. "He'd have had to have tripped at the top of the stairs, rolled, and actually tumbled down to this position."

"Anyone can trip," Kelsey said, laying a hand on Jane's arm. "I'm so sorry."

Jane closed her eyes for a minute. She wanted to believe it. Tripped. A sad accident. Marty MacDonald had been a loner, a bachelor without any exes to mourn him and no children or grandchildren to miss their dad or grandpa. But did that mitigate a human life?

The housekeeper who'd screamed was still standing, staring down at the corpse through glazed eyes, her mouth locked into a circle of horror.

Jane felt frozen herself.

They were used to finding the dead. That was their job. Called in when unexplained deaths and circumstances came about. But this was her minister—the man who was to have married her and Sloan. She didn't move. The others still seemed to have their wits about them. She heard Sloan dialing 911 and speaking in low, even tones to the dispatch officer. Soon, there would be sirens. A medical examiner would arrive. The police would question them all. Naturally, it looked like an accidental death. But Jane always doubted accidental death.

But that was in her nature.

Would the police doubt so, too?

She felt a sense of hysteria rising inside her. She could wind up in an interrogation room on the other side of the table. *Did you do this? I think I know what happened,*" a hard-boiled detective right out of some dime novel would demand. He'd be wearing a Dick Tracey hat and trench coat. *"What was it? You were afraid of commitment. Afraid of marriage. You don't really love that poor bastard, Sloan, do you? You didn't think you'd get away with killing the rugged cowboy type of man he is. Tall, strong, always impossibly right. So you killed the minister. Pushed a poor innocent man of God right down the stairs!"*

Whoa.

Double whoa.

She didn't feel that way. She'd never felt for anyone like she did for Sloan. She was in love with his mind, his smile, his voice. The way he was with her, and the way he was with the world. They shared that weirdness of their special ability to speak with the dead. They also shared a need to use their gift in the best way. She definitely loved him physically. He was rugged and weathered, a cowboy, tall and broad-shouldered, everything a Texas girl might have dreamed about. He had dark hair, light eyes, sun-bronzed features, and a smile that could change the world.

Except that he wasn't smiling now.

"You just now found him?" Sloan asked the maid.

The woman didn't respond.

"Ms. Martin," Sloan pressed.

Jane had noticed the maid's nametag too, identifying her as Phoebe

Martin. At last, the woman blinked, focused, and turned to Sloan, nodding sadly, like a child admitting an obvious but unhappy fact.

"Is anyone else here?" Sloan asked her. "I mean, besides you, me, Logan, Kelsey, and Jane?" He pointed around to all of them, using their first names. That was a way to make her feel comfortable, as if she were one with them. In situations like this, people spoke way more easily to authorities when they felt as if they were conversing with friends.

The maid, an attractive young blonde woman of about twenty-seven or so, shook her head. "Right here, no. I didn't see anybody. I was coming from the kitchen and saw him lying here. But, yes, yes, of course, others are around. They're always around. The castle is never left empty. The caretaker, Mr. Green, is somewhere about."

"Anyone else?" Jane prodded gently.

Ms. Martin nodded solemnly. "Mrs. Avery is in her office along with Scully Adair, her assistant. And the chef came in about an hour or so ago. So did two of the cooks. Lila and Sonia are here. They're with housekeeping."

Jane knew that Mrs. Denise Avery managed the castle. She'd dealt with the woman to rent the rooms they'd taken for the weekend, including the chapel and ballroom. The castle was actually owned by a descendant of Emil Roth, the eccentric millionaire who, in the late 1850s, had the building disassembled in Wales and brought to the coastline of New England. The owner, another Emil Roth, had been born with more money than he'd been able to waste. The Roth family had made their fortune in steel, then banking. The current Roth was gone, Jane had been told, to Africa on a big game photography hunt. Mrs. Avery was a distant relative herself. And while the current Emil Roth spent money, Mrs. Avery tried to make it.

"Miss Martin, perhaps you could gather them all here, in the foyer," Sloan suggested.

"Gather them," she repeated.

"Yes, please, would you?" Jane prodded.

"The police and the coroner will arrive any minute and everyone should be here when they do," Sloan said.

Phoebe Martin looked at them at last. "Police?"

"A man is dead," he said. "Yes, the police."

"But… he… fell," she said.

"Possibly," Logan said.

"Probably," Jane said firmly.

Phoebe's eyes widened still further. "Pushed!"

"No. All we know is that he's dead," Jane said. "The local police need to come and the death investigated. The medical examiner or the coroner must come, too."

"Pushed!" Phoebe said again.

"There is that possibility," Kelsey said. She glanced at Jane and grimaced sorrowfully. "But, he probably just fell. No one was there, right? We were all in our rooms, you just came to the landing and found him, and the others are in their offices or on the grounds working. Poor man! He fell, and no one was here. But we still have to have the police."

"The ghost did it!" Phoebe declared.

"Ghosts are seldom vicious," Kelsey said.

Phoebe's gaze latched onto Kelsey. "How would you know? Ghosts can be horribly malicious. Ripping off sheets. Throwing coffee pods all around. Oh, you don't know! It was *her*, I'm telling you. She did it!"

Phoebe was pointing. It seemed she was pointing straight at Jane.

"What?" Jane demanded, her voice a squeak rather than the dignified question she'd intended.

But then she saw that they were all looking behind her at the painting on the wall.

She'd noted it before, of course. Just about a month earlier while driving through the area after a situation in the Northeast, she'd seen the castle. It was open three days a week for tours, and she'd been there for the Saturday afternoon event. Mrs. Avery had led the tour and introduced them to Elizabeth Roth via the painting, a young woman who'd lost her fiancé on the eve of their wedding. Elizabeth, the daughter of the house, had been found dead of an overdose of laudanum on the day her wedding should have taken place. It was said that she was often seen in the halls of the castle, wringing her hands as she paced, praying for the return of her lover.

She was beautiful. Rich waves of auburn hair billowed around her face, with soft tendrils curling about her forehead. Her features were fine and delicate and even ethereal. The painting appeared to be that of a ghost, and yet, Mrs. Avery had assured, it had been done from life by the artist Robichaux who'd been a friend of the family. Perhaps he'd sensed the doom that was to be her future. John McCawley, her groom, had been killed the night before the intended nuptials, hunting in the nearby woods.

"Miss Martin, you're suggesting that Elizabeth Roth did this?" Sloan asked quietly.

Phoebe nodded solemnly. "There have been other deaths over the years. On this staircase. Why do you think we're not booked solidly for weddings?"

Sloan looked over at Jane. She stared back at him with her eyes widening. No, she had to admit, she hadn't done much research on the castle. It had just been beautiful and available, perfect for the two of them. Or so she had thought.

A wry half-smile played lightly on Sloan's lips. An assuring smile, she thought. One that conveyed what she already knew. Ghosts don't stay behind to kill. And something else. They both knew they would be together always, whether this turned out to be the wonderful event of a wedding or not.

"Someone else died here? On these steps?" Sloan asked.

Phoebe looked at Jane. "Last time, it was the bride."

Sloan stared at Jane again. She widened her eyes and gave her head a little shake. Another point she had not thought about either.

"What happened?" Logan asked.

"The bride fell. She tumbled down the stairs. The police said that she tripped on her dress and fell. She died in a pool of white. It was terrible!" Phoebe said.

"It doesn't seem to be a particularly dangerous staircase," Kelsey murmured.

Jane looked down again at Marty MacDonald, dead at the foot of the stairs, his eyes still open in horror. As if he'd seen something awful. His murderer? Or something else? Why the hell would anyone have murdered the man? She realized that Sloan was watching her, frowning, aware of how upset she was. Or maybe relieved? Last time, it had been the bride to die. Sloan gave her a warning look filled with empathy. One that said this was sad, but there was no reason to believe it was anything other than a tragic accident.

"It has to be the ghost. It has to be," Phoebe whispered.

He gave his attention back to Phoebe Martin.

"Must be a powerful ghost," he suggested, not arguing with Phoebe but trying to get her to converse, without really stating anything they knew about the ghost world. "The reverend was not a small man. Assuming that they exist, I'm sure that ghosts do have certain powers. But, personally, I do find it unlikely that the ghost of Elizabeth Roth pushed a man down the stairs."

"You don't know our ghosts," Phoebe said, sounding a little desperate. "Maybe it wasn't Elizabeth. Maybe it was John McCawley, her fiancé. Oh! Maybe his hunting accident wasn't so accidental. Maybe he's seeking revenge!"

There was no painting anywhere of John McCawley, but then, he hadn't lived to become a member of the family and only family members, Mrs. Avery had assured Jane, were pictured on the walls.

"Most likely the poor Reverend MacDonald tripped," Sloan said. "But that's still a sad, accidental death. I believe we should gather everyone on the property here. The police will be arriving soon," Sloan said.

"Of course. I'll gather the others," Phoebe said.

But before she could scamper off, a man in his late-twenties with sandy blond hair, a trifle long, dressed in a tailored shirt and jacket reminiscent of Lord Byron, appeared at the landing.

"What in the devil? What's going on down there?"

Miss Martin didn't scream in terror again. She gaped in astonishment, staring upward.

"Mr. Roth!" she strangled out.

Jane arched her neck to get a better look at the man. Mrs. Avery had informed her that the owner would be gone for the duration of time they were at the castle. He'd supposedly left several weeks ago.

"Hello, Miss Martin," he said gravely.

"Hello," he said to the others, coming down the stairs and carefully avoiding the fallen dead man. He seemed justly appalled by the corpse, sadness, confusion, and horror appearing in his expression as he looked at the dead man.

"Mr. Roth?" Jane asked.

He nodded. "How do you do? Yes, I know. I'm not supposed to be here. And I'm so sorry. Poor man. Do you have any idea… the banister is safe, the carpeting is… secure. I've had engineers in here to make sure that it's safe. But, poor, poor fellow! He must have fallen. Are the police coming?"

"On their way," Kelsey said.

"It's just a normal stairway," Emil Roth murmured, looking up the stairs again. "How does it happen?" The question seemed to be retrospective.

"Mr. Roth, we just heard that a woman died here in the same way. Is that true?" Sloan asked.

Roth nodded, disturbed as he looked down again, then away, as if he couldn't bear to look at the dead man. "Can we do something? Put a sheet on him, something?"

"What about others?" Logan asked. "Dying here."

Roth looked at Logan. "Sir, many died over the years, I believe. It was the Cadawil family home in Wales and the family died out. And here, my parents both died in the room I now keep. Of natural causes. A child in the 1880s died of consumption or tuberculosis. Only Elizabeth Roth died by her own hand. Yes, we had a tragic accident the last time we agreed to have a wedding here. The bride died. A terrible, incredibly sad accident. Oh, Lord. I just wish that we could cover him up!"

"Not until the police arrive," Sloan said. "Best to leave him for the authorities."

Phoebe was still just standing.

"Miss Martin, if you'll gather the others, please?" Logan said gently.

Phoebe moved at last, walking slowly away at first, staring at them all, then turning to run as if banshees were at her heels.

Jane heard the first siren.

She was surprised when Emil Roth looked straight into her eyes. He seemed to study her as if he saw something remarkable.

"How?" he repeated, and then he said, "Why?"

The sound of his voice seemed to echo a sickness within him.

The police arrived. Two officers in uniform preceded a pair of detectives, one grizzled and graying in a tweed coat, the other younger in a stylish jacket. Sloan, closest to the door where they were entering, stepped forward and introduced himself and the others with a minimum of words and explained the situation. A Detective Forester, the older man, asked them all to step away. A younger detective, Flick, began the process of having the uniform officers tape off the scene. Everyone was led through the foyer to the Great Hall. They sat and Jane explained that the minister had been there to officiate at her wedding to Sloan. Emil Roth began to explain that he'd been in Europe planning for an extended stay in Africa but that a stomach bug had soured that prospect, so he'd returned late last night, entering through his private entry at the rear of the castle, where once upon a time guests of the family had arrived via their carriages or on horseback.

The others at the castle were herded into the Grand Hall and introduced themselves. Mrs. Avery, the iron matron in perfect appearance and coiffure. Scully Adair, her young redheaded assistant. Chef Bo Gerard, fortyish and plump, like a man who enjoyed his own creations. Two young cooks, Harry Taubolt and Devon Richard—both lean young men in their twenties who'd not yet enjoyed too much of their own cooking. Sonia Anderson and Lila Adkins, the other maids, young and attractive, like Phoebe.

None of them had been near the foyer, they said.

They were all astounded and saddened by the death of the minister. A few mentioned Cally Thorpe, the young woman who'd died in her bridal gown, tripping down the stairs too. Everyone seemed convinced that it was an accident caused by the ghost of Elizabeth Roth. The medical examiner arrived and while he said he'd have to perform an autopsy, it did appear that the minister had simply missed a step near the second floor landing and tragically broken his neck.

"Sad," Detective Forester said. "Ladies and gentlemen, there will be an autopsy, of course, and I may need to speak to all of you again, but—"

His voice trailed as his younger partner entered from the foyer and whispered something to him. He suddenly studied the four agents.

"You're Feds?" he demanded.

Logan nodded.

"And you're here for a wedding?" Forester asked.

He seemed irritated. But, obviously, they hadn't come to solve any mysteries since they'd been here already when the death had occurred.

"We're here for our wedding," Jane said. "I love the castle. It's beautiful."

"So you're responsible for the minister being here?" Forester asked.

"Yes," she told him.

He stared at her as if it were entirely her fault.

Then Scully Adair, Mrs. Avery's pretty redheaded assistant, stood up, seemingly anguished. "It's not Miss Everett's fault that this happened. It's the castle's fault. It's true! People can't be married here. It was crazy to think that we could plan a wedding. Something bad was destined to happen."

"Oh, rubbish!" Mrs. Avery protested. "Sit down, Scully. That's rot and foolishness. The poor man had an accident. Miss Everett," she said, looking at Jane. "Not to worry. We can find you another minister."

Jane was appalled by the suggestion. Mrs. Avery made it sound as if a caterer had backed out of making a wedding cake. A man was dead!

"The ghosts did it," Phoebe said.

"Ghosts!" Forester let out a snort of derision and stood. "I believe the medical examiner has taken the body. I have a crime scene unit checking out the stairway, but then there will be hundreds of prints on the banister." He paused and looked around again at all of them. "None of you saw or heard a thing, right?"

"Not until I found him," Phoebe said.

"And then she screamed, and we came running," Sloan said.

Forester nodded. "All right, then, I'll be in touch. We'll be awaiting the M.E.'s report, but I believe we're looking at a tragic accident."

Jane knew what his next words would be.

"None of you leaves town, though. Yeah, I know it's cliché, but that's the way it is. I want to be able to contact each and every one of you easily over the next few days."

He stared at Sloan, Logan, Kelsey, and Jane.

"Especially you Feds."

Chapter Two

For a long moment, Sloan Trent had simply sat beside Jane when the meeting had ended and others, except for Kelsey and Logan, had moved on. Then Sloan had held Jane close in silence. The bond between them remained. Nothing, he thought, could ever break that. And then they sat together with Kelsey and Logan. Maybe they were all still a little numb. They'd come for such a joyous occasion.

"We *can* find a... a..." Kelsey began, but then she paused and Sloan wondered what she had been about to say. *Another minister?* Or, perhaps *a living minister?*

The body of Reverend MacDonald was gone—taken to the morgue. Mrs. Avery had retired to her office. Chef and the cooks had presumably headed to the kitchen. Mr. Green had gone back to the groundskeeper's lodge and the maids were cleaning the rooms above.

"I'm not sure that this is what we want for the memory anymore," Sloan said, slipping his arm around Jane's shoulder. She was handling it well, he thought.

Or maybe not.

She seemed stricken. But Jane was strong. She'd proven that so many times. Of course, this was different. She'd planned the perfect small wedding for them in a beautiful place with just a few close friends. The ceremony had never meant that much to him. If she'd wanted a big wedding, fine. If she'd wanted to walk into city hall and say a few words, that would have been fine, too.

He knew that he loved her. No, that was truly a mild concept for the way he felt about her. He'd known what people might refer to as "the good, the bad, and the ugly" in life. He'd experienced a few one-night stands, never knowing if they were good women or not. He'd had relationships with really fine people. But he'd never been with anyone like Jane. Smart, funny, beautiful. And she'd be just as beautiful to him in fifty years. She had the most unusual eyes, not brown or hazel, more a true amber. When she looked at him with those eyes, he saw the world and everything he wanted in life within them. The idea that someone else completed him as a whole seemed cliché, and yet he woke each day happy she was in his life. He worked well with her. They trusted one another with no question. Their commitment was complete. And it didn't matter to him a bit if it was legal. But since they did both believe in God, along with the basic tenets of goodness associated with most religions, it was nice to think that they'd have their union blessed.

Where or how meant nothing to him.

But women? They planned weddings. Big and small.

"We're not getting another minister," Jane said. "And we're not getting married here."

"But we're not leaving here, you know. Especially not us 'Feds,'" Logan reminded them.

Sloan was glad to see that Logan was amused rather than offended. Most of the time when they worked with locals, all went well. Sloan knew that because once upon a time he'd been the local the Krewe of Hunters—with Logan at the helm—had worked with. That had been the beginning for him. Now, he'd been with the Krewe for some time and he loved where he was, though he didn't particularly like murder and mayhem. But he'd known as a young man he'd been meant to fight for the rights of victims, whether living or dead. And working with the Krewe was the best way he knew how to accomplish that role.

Jane punched Logan in the arm.

The two had known each other for years. Logan had been a Texas Ranger. Sloan had spent time working in Texas, too, but Jane had been a civilian forensic artist who'd worked with Logan's group many times before any of them had ever heard of the Krewe of Hunters. They sometimes seemed like a brother and sister act.

"No matter what Detective Forester said, we all know damned well we're not leaving. Not until we know what happened to our minister," Jane said.

"It was an accident, don't you know?" Kelsey said. "That, or the ghost did it."

"We've yet to come across a malevolent ghost," Logan reminded Kelsey.

"And I don't believe for one minute that a ghost did anything," Kelsey said. She looked at Jane. "Have you seen any of the ghosts that haunt the place?"

Jane shook her head. "I didn't see any signs of anyone haunting the castle when I was here before, nor have I seen any yet. How about you?"

Kelsey shook her head. "But you and Sloan arrived much earlier. I thought that maybe while you were out in the garden, or over by the old graveyard, you might have seen someone."

"We're forgetting one thing," Logan said.

"What's that?" Jane asked.

"We're suspicious people by nature. We're called in to solve unexplained deaths, attacks, and other events. And this might have been accidental," Logan said. "Maybe Reverend MacDonald just wasn't paying attention. Don't forget, we never suspect anything but what is real and solid until we've given up on real and solid."

"Then again," Sloan pointed out, "if we're not suspicious, I don't think anyone else will be. Because it *appears* to be real and solid that our minister tripped and broke his neck tumbling down the stairs." He stroked Jane's dark hair and looked into her luminous eyes. "You met the Reverend MacDonald in the village, right?"

She nodded. "When I came here and saw the castle on the hill, I thought it was just perfect. I had gone into a coffee shop and the clerk there told me that it was open for tours. After I spoke to Mrs. Avery and discovered we could get this date, I went back down to the village and inquired about someone at the library. I met with Reverend MacDonald in the same coffee shop and he was delighted. He couldn't marry us on a Sunday because of his church services, but a Saturday would be marvelous. And I told him I'd have a room for him here, so that he'd be ready for the services."

"What else do you know about him?" Sloan asked her.

"Nothing, except that he's from the area. A bachelor. He loves when his youth groups have cookie sales. And the parents he works with are wonderful and love to work at creating carnivals to support the church."

"Doesn't sound like a man anyone would want to hurt," Logan said.

"No," Kelsey agreed.

"He looks great on the surface," Sloan murmured. He caught Logan's eye and he knew. What had happened might have been a tragic accident. But, they wouldn't just accept that as fact. They'd dig and see what might lie hidden beneath appearances.

"Okay, then," Kelsey said. "I'm up and off."

"Off where?" Jane asked her.

"To the local library. I'll see what I can dig up about this place," Kelsey said. "And then I'll head to the church and speak with people and find out what I can about our good Reverend MacDonald."

"Then I'm... not really off," Jane said. "I'm going to talk to Scully Adair. Bad things have happened here before. We need to find out more about the bride who died."

"I'll head into the village, too," Logan said. "And see what I can dig up by way of gossip there regarding both the reverend and the castle folk. I think I saw Mr. Emil Roth head out. It would be good to have a chat with him. The castle's hereditary owner should definitely know what there is to know about the castle."

"We'll meet back upstairs in a couple of hours?" Jane asked. "In the bridal suite? It's the biggest and gives us the most room to work."

"We might as well make use of the size," Sloan agreed dryly.

They wouldn't be laughing tonight, sipping champagne, eating strawberries and enjoying a totally carefree time as their first night of being husband and wife.

"You know, maybe you two are not going to become legally wed here," Kelsey pointed out, a smile in her eyes, "but there's no reason to make a perfectly good room go to waste."

"Don't worry," Sloan told her, smiling and meeting Jane's eyes. "We don't intend for you two to stay long."

"A man just died," Jane murmured.

"In our line of work, someone has frequently just died," Logan said softly. "And that really shows us just how important it is to *live*."

Jane smiled and nodded. "We have champagne and fruit and chocolate. And we're willing to share. We'll meet in the suite in about two hours. And we will know the truth."

Sloan looked at Jane as they all nodded. She was so beautiful. Calmer where Kelsey could be animated, serene often in a way that seemed to make the world stand still and be all right for him. She could be passionate and filled with vehemence when she chose and courageous at all times—even when she was afraid.

God, he loved her.

* * * *

Scully Adair's place was the reception desk in front of the doors that led to Mrs. Avery's medieval and elegant office on the ground floor of the castle. Mrs. Avery, Jane thought, was going to be a tough nut to crack. She was all business and no nonsense. But, of course, if she heard Jane talking with Scully, she'd probably butt right in. So Jane waited, standing by the office door. Soon enough, Scully came out, her pretty features furrowed in a frown, her movements indicating that she was disturbed and restless. Her fingers fluttered as she closed the office door. There was a twitch in her cheek.

"Hey," Jane said softly.

She was glad that Scully didn't scream in surprise. Instead, her slender fingers flitted to her face. Her hand rested at her throat.

"Um, hey," she said. "I'm so, so sorry. I mean, what a wedding day, huh?"

"I'm not worried about my wedding," Jane said. "Sloan and I will marry somewhere soon enough. But were you going for lunch or a cup of coffee?"

Scully nodded with wide eyes. "Coffee, with a stiff shot."

"May I go with you?" Jane asked.

"Sure. I guess."

Jane fell into step with her as they walked along a corridor to the far end of the ground floor. There, an archway led into a cavernous kitchen. Pots and pans hung from rafters. A giant fireplace and hearth filled one end. Other than that, the place was state of the art with giant refrigerators and freezers, a range top surrounded by granite, a work table, and other modern appliances. There was also a large table in a breakfast nook. Old paned windows looked out over the cliff top where flowers and shrubs grew in beautiful profusion.

Chef Bo Gerard, a man who greatly resembled Chef Boyardee, and his two young assistants, Harry Taubolt—dark-haired and lean, a handsome young man in his mid-twenties—and Devon Richard, blond, a little heavier, a little older, and bearing the marks of teenage acne— were already there. They all looked morose. Each had a mug in front of him as if they were all imbibing in coffee, but a large bottle of Jameson's sat in the middle of the table between them. The three looked up from their cups and smiled grimly at seeing Scully, then leapt to their feet when they saw Jane.

"Miss, guests aren't really allowed back here," Chef Gerard said.

"Oh, leave her be. What, does she look stupid? They're going to look up everything about this place," Scully said. She walked past the table, heading toward the granite counter and a coffee pot. "Miss Everett, coffee? You can lace it or not as you choose. The guys already have the booze on the table. Me? My minister dead on my wedding day? I'd be drinking."

Jane smiled. "Coffee, yes, lovely, thank you."

She accepted a cup from Scully, who sat and poured herself a liberal amount of Jameson's from the bottle on the table.

Not about to let an uncomfortable silence begin, Jane dove right in. "Scully, you said that we shouldn't have been allowed to plan a wedding here. Why? What happened before."

"Scully!" Chef said.

Scully stared at him and then looked at Jane. "You know the legend, of course. I was so startled and so scared when I saw the poor Reverend MacDonald. I looked at *her* picture. I mean, seriously, who knows? Maybe she can push people down the stairs."

"Scully, you're an idiot," Harry Taubolt said, shaking his dark head. "You see ghosts everywhere."

"There are ghosts," Devon Richard said, staring into his cup. He looked at Jane then as if she had somehow willed him to do so. "There are ghosts. They can move things."

Chef let out an impatient sound. Harry snorted.

"You forget where you put things or what you've done, that's what happens," Chef said.

"No," Devon said, shaking his head firmly. "When I come out to the Great Hall and find a napkin on the floor, I know I didn't put it there. When I've preset a plate with garnish, then the garnish is on the counter top, I know I didn't put it there." He turned to stare at Harry. "And you know it happens. You just have to deny it, or you'd be scared."

"You think that Elizabeth Roth is the ghost?" Jane asked.

"No," Scully said.

"Yes!" Chef snapped firmly.

"An old ghost," Harry said softly. "Elizabeth was due to marry John McCawley just before the start of the Civil War. McCawley was from the South. He wasn't in the military, he hadn't made any declarations about secession, but the family wasn't happy about the marriage. I say one of them did McCawley in when he was out in the woods. Hunting accident? Hell, no one believes that. Nathaniel Roth, Elizabeth's brother, was out in the woods at the same time. He must have shot McCawley. And Elizabeth couldn't bear it or the fact that her family would be party to such a thing. She killed herself—that we know. And she hates the family. She couldn't be married here, so she won't let anyone else be married here. She pushed your minister down the stairs."

"She looked beautiful and gentle, not like a vengeful murderess," Jane said. She turned quickly to Scully. "Who do you think is haunting the place?"

"Scully," Chef said.

But Scully laughed. "Jane is an FBI agent. You think she can't find out?" Scully told Jane, "Mrs. Avery decided three years ago that she'd allow a man and woman from Georgia to be married here. Cally Thorpe was going to marry Fred Grigsby. Cally fell down the stairs, too. Detective Forester didn't mention that fact because he was working somewhere else when it happened. He'll know now, but, anyway, what the hell? That was ruled an accident, too."

"So," Jane said carefully, "you think that Cally was pushed?"

"How many people really just fall down the stairs?" Scully demanded and shivered. "I think I have to quit. I mean, I love this place, but we were alright before Mrs. Avery booked another wedding. What is the matter with that woman?"

"How many of the people working here today were working here when Cally Thorpe died?" Jane asked.

They looked around the table at one another.

"Let's see," Chef began. "Harry, you had just started. Devon, you'd been here a month or so. Mrs. Avery, of course, and Mr. Green has been here since he was a kid working with his dad on the property. Me, of course. I've been here eight years."

"What about the maids?" Jane asked.

"Just Phoebe. The other two girls started in the last few years," Scully said. "I've been here for five... oh, God! I was the one who found Cally. Her eyes were open, too. She was just staring toward the ceiling. No. It wasn't the ceiling. It was the painting." She leaned forward, focusing on Jane. "She was staring at the painting of Elizabeth Roth, right there, right where it hung on the wall."

"Maybe it's true," Devon said quietly. "Maybe we're all okay as long as no one gets married here. Maybe Elizabeth has remained all these years—and she'll kill someone before she allows a wedding to take place in this house!"

Chapter Three

Sloan had feared he might have some trouble with Emil Roth. After all, he was liable for what had happened, being the castle's owner. Even if lawyers could argue that the man wasn't responsible for another's accident on a safe stairway, he was liable in his own mind.

That had to hurt.

Sloan had seen him head out the front with the police when they'd left, and he hadn't seen him since, so he decided to take a walk outside first and see if he was down by the gates or perhaps just sitting on one of the benches in the gardens. While the castle was on a cliff and surrounded on three sides by bracken and flowers, beautifully wild, the front offered sculptures and rock gardens and trails through flowers and bushes and even a manicured hedge menagerie. Mr. Green apparently worked hard and certainly earned his keep. But Sloan couldn't find Emil Roth outside. He tapped on the caretaker's door and Mr. Green opened it to him, looking at him suspiciously.

"Yeah? You got a problem here? You gotta bring it up with management," Green said.

"No, sir. No problem. It's beautiful. I've never seen such a perfectly manicured lawn. Yet you keep the wild and windswept and exotic look around the place, too," Sloan said. "I was just looking for Mr. Roth."

"He ain't out here," Green said. He was an older, grizzled man, lean yet strong, his skin weathered and permanently tanned from years in the sun.

"Then, thank you. And, sincerely, my compliments. You keep this up all alone?"

"Two kids come to mow and hedge sometimes, but… yeah, I do most of it," Green said.

Sloan thought he might have seen a blush rise to the man's cheeks.

"I've been doing this since I was a kid, over fifty years now. The old Emil—this Emil's father—hell, everyone was named Emil in the darned family—just opened the place to the public about forty years ago. My dad was still in charge and he taught me. People like greenery. It's a concrete world, you know? Some people come just to see the grounds."

"I can imagine. Hey, so how has it been for you? What do you think? I mean, the castle goes way back, but even in the United States, it has a spooky history. The obligatory ghost," Sloan said.

Green narrowed his eyes. "Sure. All old places have ghosts."

"You've seen something," Sloan said.

"Naw."

"I can tell!"

"Sane people scoff at ghosts, you know."

"Only sane people who haven't seen them yet," Sloan said.

"Have you seen a ghost?"

"One or two, I'm pretty damned sure," Sloan said. "You gotta be careful—because people don't think you're sane once you mention the unusual."

Green nodded in complete, conspiratorial agreement. He lowered his voice, despite the fact that they were alone with no one remotely near them.

"There are ghosts around here. A couple of them. There's—" He hesitated, as if still not sure, but Sloan stayed silent, watching him, waiting. "—a man in boots and breeches and a black shirt who watches me sometimes. He tends to stay behind the trees, down toward what's left of the forest to the rear of the property. And as far as Elizabeth Roth goes, I've seen her. I've seen her often, from the upstairs window. Her room—Elizabeth's room—it's the bridal suite now. I guess you're staying in it."

Sloan nodded. "That's us. I'll watch out for Elizabeth," he said. "Tell me, has anything ever indicated to you that the ghosts could be— mean? Vindictive?"

Green shook his head. "Naw, in fact... hell, one day I slipped on some wet grass and went tumbling down. It was summer and I blacked out. When I woke up, all dizzy and parched, a water bottle came rolling down to me. Now sure, bottles can roll. But I think John McCawley was there. He rolled that bottle to me. I took a drink, got myself up, and all was well. There's nothing mean about the ghosts in this place."

"You were here when another accident took place, right?"

Again, Green nodded. "Poor thing. That girl broke her neck on the stairs, same as the minister today. We checked the banister. The carpeting on the stairs is checked constantly to see that it's not ripped. The stairs aren't particularly steep or winding. Go figure. Bad things happen."

Sloan thanked Green and headed back toward the house. The foyer and Great Hall were empty. He heard voices coming from the kitchen but headed toward the stairs. At the top, he could see one of the maids.

Phoebe Martin.

She seemed to still be in shock and was stroking a polish rag over the same piece of banister over and over.

Sloan walked up the stairs. "You doing okay?" he asked.

"It's just so sad. How about you?"

"We're all right. Did you know Reverend MacDonald?"

"No, I'm bad, I guess. I haven't gone to church in years. And I was raised Catholic. I wouldn't have known Reverend MacDonald anyway. He was at the really small parish just outside town, and he was an Episcopalian, I believe."

"You never saw him around town?"

Phoebe shook her head. "No, I guess we didn't shop at the same places. And, I admit, I'm pretty into clubbing. Not many ministers go clubbing, I guess."

"Ah, well. I was hoping to talk to Mr. Roth."

Phoebe's eyes widened. "Can you believe it? He was here when this happened, and he wasn't supposed to be."

"Since he is here, I was hoping to talk with him."

"That's his suite, there, at the end of the hall." She lowered her voice. "That was always the room that was kept for the master of the house. And there has been a Roth here since the castle was brought to the United States." She hesitated. "You know, don't you, that the bridal suite was once Elizabeth Roth's room when she was alive?"

"I've been told."

Phoebe looked at him with wide, worried eyes. "You need to be careful. Especially careful now."

"I don't believe Elizabeth would want to hurt Jane or me."

"She hurt the Reverend MacDonald," Phoebe said. "I truly believe it."

"Phoebe, sadly, accidents do happen."

"They happen more often with ghosts," she insisted.

"What does Mr. Roth believe about the place, or do you know?" Sloan asked.

"He doesn't believe in ghosts. Which is good—I guess. But then, he's not here a lot. Too quiet for Mr. Roth. He likes Boston and New York and travel in general. I guess if I had his money, I'd travel, too."

"Everyone can travel some," Sloan told her.

"Sure," Phoebe said. "But, still... be careful, please."

"We'll do that. I promise," Sloan told her. "And perhaps, if you're worried, you might not want to work on the banister."

"Oh. *Oh!*" Phoebe said. "Right!" Gripping the banister tightly, she started down the stairs.

Sloan smiled, thanked her, and headed down the hall. He knocked at the double French doors that led to the suite. Emil Roth answered so quickly that he wondered if he'd been waiting for a summons.

"What can I do for you?" Roth asked.

Sloan studied the man. He was young to have such financial power, Sloan thought. Late-twenties, tops. And he seemed to enjoy the look of a Renaissance poet. His haircut would make him perfect for a Shakespearean play. But his gaze was steady as he looked at Sloan.

"Since you're here, I was hoping you'd give me a tour of the castle and a tour of your family history," Sloan said.

Roth stared at him. He was a man with a medium build and light eyes that added to what was almost a fragile-poet look.

"Sometimes, family history sucks, you know?" he said. "I'm sorry about your wedding. I mean, really sorry that a man is dead. By all accounts a good and jovial man. And I'm sorry that my family history is full of asses. But I don't think that it means anything. A man fell. That's it. He died. So tragic."

"I agree. But, we're not getting married today and we're still here. And history fascinates me," Sloan told him.

Roth grinned at that. "You're a Fed involved with a special unit that investigates when deaths that are rumored to be associated with something paranormal happen. I'm young, rich, and not particularly responsible, but I'm not stupid either."

Sloan laughed. "I wouldn't begin to suggest that you're stupid. I believe that, tragically, Reverend MacDonald fell. But I am fascinated with this place. Jane didn't really check out much of the history here. She fell in love with the castle. She wanted a small and intimate wedding more or less on the spur of the moment. And sure, under the circumstances, I'd love to know more about the 'ghosts' that supposedly reside here."

Roth grimaced. "The maids have been talking again."

"Everyone talks. Ghost stories are fun."

"So I hear. Mrs. Avery thinks that they create the mystique of the castle. I personally think that my ancestor's desire to bring a castle to the United States is interesting enough. But, we do keep up a lot of the maintenance with our bed and breakfast income, parties, and tours. So, I let her go on about the brilliance of a good ghost story. But, what the hell? I'll give you a tour."

"That's great. I really appreciate it," Sloan told him.

"What about your fiancée? Maybe she'd like to come, too?" Roth suggested.

"Maybe she would. I'm not sure where she is… I'll try her cell," Sloan said.

Jane was number one on his speed dial and, in a matter of seconds, she answered. He cheerfully explained where he was and asked what she was doing. She said that she'd be right there.

As they waited, Roth asked Sloan, "How do you like your room? No ghostly disturbances, right?"

"Not a one," Sloan told him.

"You should see people around here when they come for the ghost tours," Roth said. "They all have their cameras out like eager puppies. They catch dust specs that become 'orbs.' Sad. But, then again, we're featured in a lot of books and again, I guess my dear Mrs. Avery is right."

"I understand she's a distant relative," Sloan said. "Pardon me for overstepping, but it doesn't sound as if you like her much."

Roth grinned. "I'm that transparent? Sad. No, I don't like her. Her grandmother was my grandfather's sister. I guess we're second cousins or something like that. But, no, I don't like her. She's self-righteous and knows everything. I understand keeping the place up and keeping it maintained, but she's turned it into a theme attraction. I'm really proud of it as a family home. But... anyway, in my father's will he asked that I keep her employed through her lifetime—as long as she wishes. So, there you go. She's no spring chicken, but she's a pretty healthy sixty-plus. I have a few years to go."

Sloan heard footsteps in the hall and saw Jane coming.

They always managed a real balance when working, as did the others. Those in the Krewe of Hunters units tended to pair up—maybe there was just something special that they all shared and that created a special attraction. Jane had belonged to the Krewe before he had. He'd met her when she'd come to Lily, Arizona, his home, where he'd returned when his grandfather had suffered from cancer. She'd been both amazing and annoying to him from first sight. He'd been attracted to her from the start, falling in love with her smile, her eyes, her mind. In his life, he'd never been with anyone like her. She seemed aware of everything about him, faults and flaws and "talents," and she loved him. They hadn't been in a hurry to get married, but they'd both wanted it.

She met his eyes with the same open gaze she always did.

He walked to meet her, slipping his arm around her shoulder. "I'm really pleased. It's not a good day, certainly, but Emil Roth has offered us a real tour. History, and all else."

"That's kind of you, Mr. Roth," Jane said.

"But you saw the castle before, right? You took the ghost tour, didn't you?" Roth asked her.

"I took the tour. So I know about Elizabeth Roth and her beloved, John McCawley. He was killed in a hunting accident the day before the wedding, and then Elizabeth killed herself."

"Come on then. I do give the best tour," Roth said. "And call me Emil, please."

"Then we're Sloan and Jane," Sloan said.

Emil smiled and nodded. "Let's start in the Great Hall and go from there."

He seemed happy. Sloan looked at Jane. He took her hand and she smiled and shrugged and they followed Emil Roth. At the Great Hall, he extended his hands, as if displaying the massive room with its décor of swords and coats of arms and standing men in armor.

"Castle Cadawil was built in 1280 and the Duke of Cadawil held it all of two years, until the death of Llywelyn the Last in 1282 and the conquest of Edward I from the Principality of Wales. That's why, to this day, the heir apparent to the British crown is called the Prince of Wales. Anyway, the castle wasn't a major holding. It was on a bluff with nothing around it that anyone really wanted to hold for any reason. So, through the centuries, it had been abandoned, half-restored, abandoned again. In the early 1800s, my self-made millionaire ancestor saw it there and determined that he could move a castle to New England. And he did so. Of course, when it came over, it was little but design and stone. Antiques were purchased and through the years, Tiffany windows added. My family apparently loved their castle. But then, as you know, tragedy struck before the wedding of Elizabeth Roth and John McCawley."

"What do you think about that?" Jane asked him. "Did the family love and welcome McCawley, or did someone hate him?"

"Enough to kill him?" Roth asked.

"He died in a hunting accident. Other men in the family were out there, too, right?" Jane asked.

"Yes, they were. And it's an interesting question. There are no letters or family records that reflect anyone's feelings on the matter and the two men involved would have been my great, great, great, grandfather, Emil Roth, and my great, great, grandfather, another Emil Roth. I don't like to think that my ancestors would have killed a man they didn't want marrying into the family."

"What happened?" Sloan asked. "McCawley was shot?"

"With an arrow, they were deer hunting," Roth said. "But, you see, they weren't the only ones out there. A number of wedding guests were there. You two wanted a small wedding. The wedding of Elizabeth Roth was the social event of the season."

"Of course," Jane said.

"No one saw anything? No one knew who missed a deer and killed a man?" Sloan asked.

"If so, no one admitted anything. He was found by Elizabeth's father who, of course, immediately rushed him back to the castle and called for a surgeon. But it was too late. Elizabeth came running down the stairs and—"

Roth paused in his speaking, looking troubled.

"And?"

"The story goes that John McCawley died at the foot of the stairs. The men carrying him paused there because Elizabeth was rushing down. When she reached him, he looked into her eyes, closed his own, and died."

"How sad," Jane murmured.

"And then, of course, that night, Elizabeth took an overdose of laudanum and died in the early hours of the following morning, when the wedding should have taken place."

He led them out of the hall.

"If you look at the arches, you can see that the foyer was originally a last defense before the actual castle. There would have been a keep, of course, in Wales, and a wall surrounding it. We have the lawn in front and the wild growth to the rear, except for where the grass is mown just out the back. Following along to the right of the castle, after the entry, you reach the offices and such and going all the way back, you get to the kitchen. Heading upstairs, are the rooms. Mine, of course, was always the master's suite. Where you're sleeping—and though they weren't actually married here, many a bride and groom have slept there—was Elizabeth's room. There are four more bedrooms. Your friends are in one. Reverend MacDonald was in another, and there are two more guest rooms. The attic holds five rooms. Phoebe lives in one and the other two maids come in just for the day or special occasions. Chef has an apartment over the old stables, and Mr. Green has an apartment on the property, too."

"Mrs. Avery doesn't live here?" Jane asked.

"Yes, she's on the property. You passed her place coming in. The old guard house at the foot of the cliff. But her assistant, Scully, lives in the village as do the other cooks."

He looked at Jane curiously.

She asked him, "Is there a big black spot on my face that no one is mentioning to me?"

Emil Roth laughed. "I beg your pardon. Forgive me. It's just that when I look at you and your face, tilted at a certain angle, you look so much like her."

"Her?" Jane asked.

"Elizabeth," Emil said. "Come look at the painting again."

Sloan wasn't sure why the idea disturbed him but he followed as they headed to look at the painting on the wall. Elizabeth Roth was depicted with her hair piled high atop her head, burnished auburn tendrils trailing around her face. Her eyes appeared hazel at first but when Sloan came closer, he realized they'd been painted a true amber.

Just like Jane's.

There was something in the angle of the features. It was true. Jane bore a resemblance to the woman who'd lived more than a century before her birth.

"Do you have roots up here? Maybe you're a long lost cousin," Emil teased.

Jane shook her head. "My family members were in Texas back when people were exclaiming 'Remember the Alamo!' I've no relatives in this region. It's just a fluke."

"But an interesting one," Roth said. "So, what would you like to see next?"

"Where is Elizabeth buried?" Sloan asked. "And, for that matter, her fiancé, John McCawley."

"I understand he never actually became family so he has no painting in the castle," Jane said. "But surely they buried the poor fellow."

"Absolutely. Out to the rear, at the rise to the highest cliff. They're both in the chapel."

"I think I'd like to pay them tribute," Jane said.

"If you wish," Roth said. Smiling, he turned to lead the way out of the castle. "Although, I will warn you."

"What's that?" Sloan asked.

"On a day like today, with a fog settling over the graves, people have been known to see ghosts wandering about."

Sloan looked at Jane. "That's okay. We'll take our chances."

Chapter Four

The old chapel had been brought over to the States from Wales, Roth explained as they left via the rear, out through the kitchen's delivery doors.

Jane was curious that he had chosen to leave by this route. If she remembered right, there were other exits, more elegantly designed, leading to the wilds of the rear and the cliffs that overlooked the sea.

Chef and his two cooks were no longer sitting at the table imbibing in coffee and Jameson's, she noted as they went through. They were all busy at some kind of prep work. She assumed that the employees ate dinner at the castle as well since they didn't need that much prep for four guests and the master of the house, who they hadn't expected to be there anyway.

Chef Bo looked up from his work at a saucepan and acknowledged Roth and stared broodingly at the others as they went through.

His two assistants just watched.

"There's another way out as well. The two arches at the end of the Great Hall lead to smaller halls that bypass this area," Roth explained. "And there's a servants stairway back there, too. I just thought it would be fun to see what was going on in the kitchen."

He was almost like a child who knew that he was in charge, and was yet surprised by it and curious as to his effect on others.

"Smells divine!" he called as they passed.

Three "thank yous" followed his words.

There was a large doorway under a sheltered porte-cochère when they stepped outside. Most likely, parking for large delivery trucks. They walked around one of the walls and were in the back. An open-air patio, set on stone, offered amazing views of the Atlantic Ocean. A light fog swirled in a breeze and seemed in magical motion, barely there. A fireplace, stocked with dry logs, remained ready for those who came out to enjoy the view when it was cool, and Jane imagined they might hold barbecues out there too. Bracken grew around the patio with wild flowers in beautiful colors. Other than the patio and the chairs, if one stood on the cliff and looked out or up at the rise of the castle walls, they might have been in a distant land and in a different time.

But Jane looked to her right.

At the base of a little cliff that rose to another wild and jagged height, was the chapel. It was surrounded by a low stone wall. Within the wall were numerous graves and plots. The chapel had been built in the Norman style with great rising A-line arches and a medieval design. Two giant gargoyles sat over the double wooden doors that led inside.

"Sometimes," Roth said, "I do feel just a bit like a medieval lord. Pity it's far too small and dangerous here for a joust."

"It's really lovely," Jane said.

"Yes, and I'm a lucky man," Roth said. "Primogeniture and all. The oldest son gets everything. Of course, in my case, I was the only child. If I do have children, I'll change things, that's for sure."

Somewhat surprised, Jane looked at Sloan.

Was that for real? If so, he seemed like a pretty decent guy.

She smiled.

There was that wonderful part of their relationship that seemed like an added boon. The ability to look at one another and know that they shared a thought.

"Shall we head toward the chapel?" Roth asked.

He stood a bit down on a slant from them. He wasn't really that small a man, probably about six feet even. But Sloan seemed to tower over him. Jane was five-nine and in flats, but with his Renaissance-poet look, Roth somehow seemed delicate and fragile.

"Thanks. We'd love to see it," Sloan said.

They followed him to the stone wall. There was a gate in the center and a path that led to the chapel. The gate wasn't locked. It swung in easily at Roth's touch and they followed him. He kept on the stone path and headed directly to the chapel where the door was also unlocked.

"You're not worried about break-ins of any kind?" Sloan asked him.

"Maybe I should be. I guess people do destroy things sometimes just for fun. But Mr. Green is always at his place. He hears anything that goes on. He only looks old. Trust me, he's deceptively spry. Caught me by the ears a few times when I was a kid. Guests here are welcome to use the chapel and the only way up here is by the road, so I guess it was just never kept locked. Progress, though. Maybe I'll have to in the future. It's really kind of a cool place. You'll see. Simple and nice."

It was indeed. Tiffany windows displayed the fourteen Stations of the Cross along the side walls, each with its own recessed altar. The high arches were clean and simple and there were five small pews set before the main altar. A large marble cross rose behind the altar.

"Actually, there's a time capsule in here," Roth told him. "Emil, who brought the castle over, is under the main altar with his wife. Their children are scattered along the sides. Sometimes, of course, the daughters moved away, but there are a good fifty people buried or entombed just in the chapel. But you want our own Roth family Romeo and Juliet. Over there—first altar. Come on."

His footsteps made a strange sound as he hurried along the stone floor. Sloan and Jane followed. There were six altar niches along each side of the structure. Someone had obviously been a stickler for symmetry. The first, closest to the main altar, had a window that depicted Judas's betrayal of Christ. The altar beneath it was adorned with a large silver cross. On exact angles from the prayer bench below the altar were two marble sarcophagi or tombs. One was etched simply with a name. John McCawley. The other bore just a first name. Elizabeth. Beneath her name was a tribute. *Daughter; the rose of our lives, plucked far too swift, and we left in life, adrift. In Spring she lived, in Spring she remains. There 'til our own sweet release, 'til this life on earth for all shall cease. Beloved child, we'll meet again, where sorrows end and souls remain.*

"It sounds as if she was deeply mourned," Jane said.

"They say that her father was never the same. He lived as if he'd welcome death every day."

"It's amazing he didn't fall apart completely and lose everything.

But, then, of course, she had a brother. Your great-great-great—however many greats—grandfather," Sloan said.

Emil laughed. "It was my great, great, great grandfather. And he apparently had a wonderful friend as an overseer who'd studied at Harvard. He kept the place going. So this is it. What else can I show you? I mean, you're guests. You're free to wander as you choose. And, of course, this was horribly tragic, but you were supposed to be married today. We'll do anything we can. If you want—"

"We're just fine," Jane said quickly. "Will you be joining us at dinner?"

Roth seemed pleased, as if she were giving him an invitation rather than asking a question.

"I'd be delighted. Much better than eating alone," he said.

"Chef seems busy. Don't others eat here as well?" Jane asked.

"They do. But when I'm here, I just wind up eating in my room," he told him. "And, actually, I have some e-mails to answer. Anything else, just knock on my door."

"We'll wander here for a minute, if it's all right," Sloan told him.

"My house is your house," Roth told them with a grin.

He left them.

When he was gone, Jane looked at Sloan and asked, "Anything?"

"Quiet as—a tomb. No pun intended, of course."

She grimaced at him and headed to the grave of Elizabeth Roth. She set her hand on the tomb, trying to feel something of the young woman who had lived such a short and tragic life. But all she felt was cold stone.

Sloan watched her.

She shrugged. "Nothing. But I can't help but feel that somehow, what's happened now, with Cally Thorpe and Reverend MacDonald, has something to do with the past."

"You really think it's possible that a ghost pushed them both down the stairs?" Sloan asked her, frowning.

"It's not something that we've ever seen. So, no, I don't. But I can't shake the feeling that it's all related."

"Why?" Sloan asked.

She smiled. "I guess that's what we have to figure out."

"Let's walk to the room," Sloan said. "Maybe Kelsey and Logan are back and have come up with something." He reached out and took her hand. "I love you."

She nodded. "I'm not worried about our lives. I'm just sorry that Marty MacDonald is dead."

"If we can stop something from happening in the future, at least he won't have died in vain."

"Let's head up," she said.

* * * *

"There's no dirt to be found on the Reverend MacDonald," Kelsey announced. "His church is being draped in mourning, his deacon has sent for an emergency cover priest to take care of Sunday services. There are no allegations of his ever being flirtatious, too close to the children, or involved in any kind of scandal. But we have more reason to think it was just an accident."

"Oh?" Sloan said.

He was always amazed by the Krewe's ability to find whatever was needed to make their work go smoothly.

The bridal suite—Elizabeth Roth's room—actually consisted of a drawing room or outer area, the bedroom itself, two large dressing rooms, and these days, a small kitchenette area. Kelsey had managed to get hold of a work board. With erasable markers, she'd already started lists of what they knew and what they had learned. Staring at lists sometimes showed them what went with some other piece of information in another column. They were gathered in the drawing room, Sloan and Jane curled on the loveseat together, Kelsey at her board, and Logan thoughtful as he straddled a chair and looked at the board.

"Why should we be more prone to think that it was an accident?" Sloan asked.

"I spoke with the reverend's deacon. He's been battling a heart condition for a long time. It's possible he suffered a minor heart attack and fell," Kelsey said.

"Maybe the M.E. will be able to tell us more from the autopsy. Anything from your end, Logan?" Sloan asked.

"The reverend was well liked. No hint of improprieties or anything along that line," Logan said. "People were sad. But many of his friends did think he was a walking time bomb. Apparently, a lot of people knew about his condition. And he liked pastries. A woman in the bakery told me that she'd designed a whole line of sugar-free desserts to help him keep his weight down."

"Okay. No one out to get the reverend." Kelsey wrote on the board.

"Both Elizabeth and John McCawley are entombed in the chapel," Jane volunteered. "Along with the rest of the family."

"The caretaker, Mr. Green, sees the ghosts all the time," Sloan said.

"But I don't believe a ghost is doing this," Jane said flatly. "From what I've heard, both Elizabeth and John McCawley were good people—deeply in love. I do, however, have a suspicion that John's death wasn't accidental."

They were all silent.

Kelsey frowned and looked at Sloan.

Sloan spoke to Jane at last. "I don't know if we'll ever have an answer to that. Even if we were to meet their ghosts, they might not have known themselves. What we need to figure out is if someone is killing people here now, in the present, and stop them from killing anyone else."

"Of course," Jane said. She rose, stretched, and walked over to the board. "Personally, I find our young host to be interesting."

"You think that Emil Roth pushed the reverend down the stairs?" Kelsey asked.

"No, and I'm not sure why not. Except that he doesn't seem to be into a lot of family rot. He doesn't see himself as some kind of a lord of the castle. He's young and rich and spoiled, and I think he knows it. I'm not even sure that he likes the castle. He definitely doesn't like Mrs. Avery. He has to keep her here, though. It was part of his father's will. She's a distant relative."

"Ah, the plot thickens," Logan said dryly. "But why would she kill people?"

"To keep the ghost legend going? Maybe she wants some of the television ghost hunters to come in here. Great publicity for the place," Jane suggested.

"Logan," Sloan said, "let's call the home office and get someone there checking into financials for this place. As far as I can tell, the Roth family has more than Emil could spend in a lifetime, even if he tried wasting every cent of it."

"There's no reason for the man to have killed a minister," Kelsey said.

"Or anyone, really," Sloan noted. "But, we'll get a financial check done on the family and make sure. So, anyone get any dirt on the people living here?"

"Not yet. Observation may help," Sloan said. "We'll be dining with the master of the house, and I believe dinner is at six."

"Ah, yes, the wedding feast." Jane murmured.

"We can still—" Sloan began.

"No, we can't!" Jane said quickly. "The wedding feast will be fine, without the wedding."

"Okay, so, just take note here. We have a list of everyone in the house or on the grounds at the time of Reverend MacDonald's death. We've decided that the reverend had no outside enemies. We don't believe Emil Roth is involved, but we'll keep looking. According to what we learned about Reverend MacDonald, it really seems likely that it was a tragic accident," Kelsey said.

"And that would be better than the alternative," Logan said.

Jane rose and walked over to a table where a bottle of champagne sat in a silver bowl of ice with crystal flutes around it. She didn't make a move to open the champagne. She spun around. "I say we go down for a cocktail hour and keep talking with whoever comes near us."

"Okay," Sloan said, rising again.

"Sure," Kelsey agreed.

"Who knows? Too bad there isn't a butler here," Logan said.

"There should have been a butler," Jane said.

"Because the butler often did it?" Kelsey asked.

Jane smiled. "No, it's a castle. There should be a butler. But—" Her voice trailed as she looked at Kelsey's board. "I wish that I believed that Reverend MacDonald just fell. But I don't."

"A hunch?" Kelsey asked her seriously.

They tended to pay attention to gut feelings. But, of course, everyone was wondering if Jane wasn't influenced by the circumstances here at the castle.

"We'll get images of everyone in the house and send them to the main office," Sloan said. "They can find out things about the past by just running searches, and it will be much easier for them to do that than us."

She smiled. "Yes, please. And maybe we can take a walk right before dinner and see if we can chat with any of the locals."

"The locals?" Kelsey murmured.

"Local ghosts," Jane said. "Who knows just what they might know?"

Chapter Five

"How is everyone doing?" Emil Roth asked as they entered the Great Hall.

He was there before them and held a crystal decanter of something dark in his hand. He waved it about as they entered. Jane thought he might have been there imbibing for some time.

"Brandy," he said, "anyone want to join me?"

"Club soda with lime?" Sloan asked him.

"Wise man," Roth noted. "Since people seem to trip down stairs around here. It's best to keep a clean and sober mind. I, however, will just crawl up the stairs. It's hard to trip when you crawl."

He set down the decanter and poured a soda for Sloan, but as he handed the glass over he was looking at Jane. He shuddered, then smiled. "I'm sorry. So sorry! Really. It's just you do bear a strange resemblance to Elizabeth Roth."

"Resemblances can be strange, of course," Jane said. "But sometimes it just depends on what angle an artist gave to a rendering."

"You know a lot about art?" he asked her.

"Jane is a wonderful artist," Kelsey said.

"I'm a forensic artist," Jane said.

He shuddered again. "You draw or paint dead people?"

"Sometimes. But, sometimes, I paint the living. When they're missing, if they have amnesia, if we need to get their images out to the public for a reason."

He gave a slightly sloppy smile. "So you could sketch me?"

"Certainly," she told him.

"Ah, yes. You could, but would you?" he asked.

"If you wish," she said.

"How rude of me. A tragic day. It should have been your wedding. And here I am, asking you to sketch me."

"I don't mind at all," Jane said.

"I'll run up and get your sketch pad," Sloan offered.

Emil lifted his glass to Sloan. "Don't run, not on those stairs."

"I'll be careful," Sloan promised.

"Do you need an easel? Is there something else I can get you? Draw what you really see, too, okay? I don't need to be flattered and I'd like a true image."

Logan pulled out a chair at the table for Jane as he told Emil, "Jane has a unique talent for catching expressions and what makes a person an individual. I'm sure what you'll get is honest."

Jane laughed softly. "I won't try to be unflattering."

Emil drew out the chair across from her. "Am I good here? Do you need more light?"

"I'm fine. As soon as Sloan brings down the pad, we'll be set to go," she promised.

"Please," Emil told Logan and Kelsey, "help yourselves to drinks. I believe Chef will send someone in with hors d'oeuvres soon."

"Thank you," Kelsey told him. "Jane?"

"Diet cola, thanks," Jane said.

"Ah, nothing more exciting?" Emil asked her.

"We're just not feeling all that festive, I guess," Jane said.

Sloan arrived with her sketch pad and a box of pencils. She smiled and thanked him.

"Ready when you are," Emil told her.

"I've already begun," she said.

"You're not drawing."

"But I am studying your face," she said softly.

"Ah," he said. "Should I pose? Lean in? Rest my chin on a fist?"

"No," she told him, picking up a pencil.

She began to sketch. To her amazement, she thought that it was one of her best, and quickly so. She changed pencils frequently, finding light and shadows. She caught his youth, something of a lost empathy in his eyes, and a world weariness he might not have expected. She also caught a bit of the handsome young Renaissance man. Or, perhaps, a rich kid adrift because he could probably be more than what the world seemed to expect of him. When she finished, she hesitated, looking at him.

"May I?" he asked.

"Certainly," she told him.

He took the drawing and studied it for a long time. "Could I possibly have this?"

"Of course," Jane told him.

"May I snap a phone pic of it?" Logan asked him. "It's really excellent. I'd love to have it, too."

"Yes, definitely," Kelsey said.

Mrs. Avery came walking into the room, her lips pursed. She seemed unhappy that Emil appeared to be enjoying his guests. Perhaps she was just unhappy that he was there at all.

"Will you have hors d'oeuvres soon?" she asked politely.

"Yes, we will, Denise. But, first, come here. You must see this!"

"Really, Emil—" Mrs. Avery began.

"Oh, come, come, Denny! Come over here and see this. You must sit, too, if Miss Everett is willing. I'm quite astounded by the likeness she created of me." Emil said.

"I have business—" Mrs. Avery began.

"Yes, yes, you do. You work for me. Sit for a spell. Jane, will you?" Emil asked.

"If you wish."

"Will this take long?" Mrs. Avery asked.

"Five minutes," Sloan said.

Jane thought there was something firm in his voice. He used a tone she knew, though it wasn't often directed at her anymore. People complied with that tone.

Mrs. Avery sat.

She began to sketch and caught the woman's high cheekbones and thin lips. Because it seemed that the sketch was coming out a little too harsh, she set a tiny stray curl upon the forehead and down the face. The sketch caught the true dignity of the woman, but softened her as well. Jane was surprised to see Denise Avery's face as she studied the drawing.

She looked up at Jane with a smile. "That's really nice. Thank you."

"And she'll let you keep it, Denny," Emil said. "After Logan snaps a pic, that is."

"I would love to keep it. Thank you," she said.

Before she could rise, Chef stuck his nose and then his body into the Great Hall. "May I begin with the service?"

"Oh, not until Miss Everett does a sketch," Mrs. Avery said. "Come, sit!"

Jane looked at Sloan.

He grinned at her with pleasure. Logan, she knew, would get a snapshot on his camera of every shot. That night, he'd get every drawing, along with names, to their base. Then they'd know if everyone was who and what they claimed to be.

Before they were done, she'd sketched everyone working at the castle except for the two maids who only came in from nine to five—Sonia Anderson and Lila Adkins. Before she finished with everyone, she asked Chef to bring in the hors d'oeuvres. And as he and his assistants, Harry Taubolt and Devon Richard, served the food, Sloan began speaking with them. By the time she was done with her last sketch for the night—that of Scully Adair—it was agreed that they would all—guests, owner, and employees—eat together that night in the Great Hall.

"It's nice to be together," Scully told Jane, sitting beside her.

The food was all on the table and they passed things around.

It had all gone surprisingly well.

"Considering the fact that a man died here just hours ago," Devon Richard said.

"An accident," Harry said. "It's awkward, isn't it? I mean, none of us really new the reverend, so we can't mourn him as if we lost a friend. And yet, he died here, and we're having dinner."

"People still have to eat," Mrs. Avery said.

"Yes, I know. And work and breathe and go on. It's just that I feel we should be mourning," Avery said.

"And things shouldn't go on as if they were so normal," Phoebe Martin said. Then she laughed uneasily. "Of course, this isn't normal. I've never dined in the Great Hall before."

"This is our way of mourning," Emil Roth said, and they were all quiet for a minute.

"We should say something," Chef announced. "I mean, it doesn't feel right. It just doesn't."

Sloan stood. He'd wound up across the table from Jane. "Shall we join hands."

They rose and did as he suggested. Sloan said a little prayer for Reverend MacDonald ending with, "May he rest in peace, a good man. He'll reside with the angels, certainly."

"Thank you," Emil said when he sat.

"The hall is quite something. But, I can see why you like to eat in your room, Mr. Roth, when you're here alone," Mr. Green said. Even he had been called in for a sketch and dinner. "Of course, I do remember the days when the family was alive and cousins came from many different places, old aunts and uncles, too. Then, the place was alive with laughter, kids running here and there."

A silence followed his words.

"The castle is still a happy place," Mrs. Avery snapped. "You should hear the people when they come here. They love to laugh and to shiver! And our overnight guests are always delighted. Why, we have some of the best ratings to be found on the Internet."

"I wasn't implying that it wasn't happy," Mr. Green said. He looked quickly at Emil Roth. "I certainly meant no disrespect."

"None taken, my man," Roth said. "I say, pass the wine, will you, Phoebe? And do fill your glass first."

Phoebe looked at him, plucked up the wine, looked at him again, then poured herself a large glass.

Emil smiled at her and waited patiently.

Jane made a mental note that one of them would definitely make sure he got up the stairs okay that night. But as the wine flowed, the conversation became more casual. And when Chef and Harry headed to the kitchen to return with the dessert, Jane slipped away, determined to step outside for a few minutes. She headed out to the front. There were dangerous cliffs in the rear of the property, and she didn't intend to become a victim of the castle herself. She walked down toward the caretakers cottage where Mr. Green lived, then kept going, toward the guard house and Mrs. Avery's home.

She turned and looked back at the castle and saw the windows to her own room. They'd left the lights on. She stared upward for several seconds before her breath caught.

Someone in the room.

At one of the windows.

Watching her.

As she watched them.

* * * *

Jane was a special agent, the same as he was. She'd passed the academy and was in law enforcement. But she was still the woman he loved, the woman he was supposed to have married that day. So when Sloan realized Jane was out of the Great Hall, he followed. He didn't know why he felt such a sense of anxiety, but he did. He saw her, far down the path to the castle, as soon as he exited and came down the few stone steps at the entrance.

She was just standing on the path, looking back.

He hurried to her. She smiled as he came to her and pointed up at the castle.

"Someone is there," she said.

"Someone?" he asked.

"Were they all in the Great Hall?" she asked.

"When I left, yes."

"Then I believe Elizabeth does haunt our room," she said.

Sloan looked up. There was nothing there then.

She smiled. "No, I'm not losing it. Someone was there. Now, they're not."

"I believe you," he said.

"You know, I'm really not losing it in any way," she said, turning to him so that he slipped his arms around her. She smoothed back a lock of his hair. "I don't care where or when we marry one another. It doesn't matter. And it doesn't matter that we weren't married today. It does matter that a man died. A good man."

He smiled and nodded. "I know that."

Impulsively, he went down on a knee and took her hand. He kissed it both dramatically and tenderly and looked up to meet her eyes.

"I love you with the depth and breadth of my heart and soul. In my heart, you've already been my wife, my love, my soul mate, my life mate.

Not to mention one hell of an agent. And artist, of course."

She laughed, drawing him to his feet and giving him a strong buff on the arm. "That started off so beautifully!"

"Hey, you are an amazing artist. And agent. You want to be an agent tonight, right?"

"I do," she told him. "It's just that speech, it could have stayed romantic."

"Want me to try again?"

"No!" She laughed. "I say we get back up there and make sure that Emil Roth makes it to his room."

"And then we'll make it to ours," he said.

"And then we'll make it to ours," she agreed.

Hand in hand, they made it back to the house. In the Great Hall, Mrs. Avery was saying that she needed to get some sleep. Chef told her that breakfast came early, and Phoebe Martin was headed upstairs, but when she saw Jane and Sloan come in, she stopped.

"Thank you so much, Jane, for the sketch. It's wonderful. And thank you both for somehow making a nice evening out of a horrible day. Good night. And don't forget, if you need anything—anything at all—we're happy to oblige."

"Thank you, Phoebe," Jane told her.

She scampered on toward the stairway. Jane followed her. As she did so, she heard Sloan and Logan talking to Emil Roth, convincing him that they'd see him to his room. It was time to sleep. The men and Kelsey were looking to see that Emil was safe. Jane followed Phoebe up the stairs, and then on up to the third floor.

Phoebe turned to look at her when she reached her door.

"Thank you," she said.

"You're welcome."

"You're worried about all of us."

"There was a lot of wine flowing down there at the dinner table."

But Phoebe looked at her with wide eyes.

"You don't believe that the reverend's death was an accident, do you?" she asked.

"Actually, we found out that he had a heart condition. That might have caused him to stumble. But we'll know more when the M.E. makes his report," Jane said.

But Phoebe still watched her. "That won't make any difference to you, will it? You think that he was killed."

Jane said, "The police seem to believe it was an accident."

"Do you think we're all in danger?"

"No," Jane said.

That wasn't a lie. Whoever the killer was, they were part of the castle crew. And the killer certainly wasn't in danger.

Phoebe shook her head. "Thank you for tonight."

"Of course," Jane said.

She left Phoebe to descend the stairs to the second level.

Careful as she did so.

* * * *

Within another ten minutes, everyone was where they should be or on their way to their own homes. Sloan watched as Jane came down from the attic level, her hand firmly on the handrail of the far less elegant steps that led from the second floor to the attic. She joined him, Logan, and Kelsey on the second floor landing by their rooms.

"One of us will be up through the night. I'm taking first shift and Kelsey will be second. You two deserve to get some sleep or whatever tonight."

"We're fine," Sloan assured him.

"We know that," Kelsey said, grinning. "We just want you to know that we're on the awake duty, or guard duty, or whatever you want to call it."

Sloan started to protest but Jane caught his arm. "Just tell them thank you, Sloan."

"Thank you," Sloan said.

Jane dragged him into the room.

"I'm, uh, up for whatever you're in the mood for," he said.

But she walked away from him, leaving him in the entry and heading into the bedroom. She stood there for a while and then walked back out.

"She's not here," she said.

"No?"

She shook her head with disappointment. "I thought that she would be. I thought that tonight we'd see her."

Sloan walked to her and took her gently into his arms. "Maybe she knows that we're here. Maybe she knows why we came. And maybe she's as good and sweet as history paints her. What she really wants is happiness for others."

She'd felt warm in his arms. Warm, soft and plaint, trusting, so much a part of him that their heartbeats seemed the same. But then she stiffened and pulled away from him. He realized that she was looking out one of the windows. The drapes hadn't been pulled closed. She walked to it and he followed closely behind her.

And he saw what she saw.

There was a man standing in the moonlight. He was by the caretaker's cottage, looking up. He seemed to be in breeches and a blousy poet's shirt. His hair was long, his thighs encased in boots.

"John McCawley," Jane whispered.

Sloan had to agree.

The figure in the moonlight faded.

Jane turned into Sloan's arms. "The past has something to do with this. I know it."

"We should get some sleep," he told her.

She nodded and headed into the bedroom. It was supposed to have been their wedding night. But he knew her. She was upset. The minister she'd brought to the castle had died here.

"I love you," she said.

"I know," he told her.

"I'll be in bed," she said. "Just give me a few minutes."

He let her go and walked over to the board Kelsey had set up that day, studying what she had written. *Who had something to gain from the death of a minister?*

He went over the names.

Mrs. Avery, he thought. The distant relative. The woman who had allowed Jane to book the castle for the wedding.

He walked into the bedroom. Jane hadn't even disrobed. She was lying on her side, her eyes closed, sound asleep. He laid down beside her and drew her into his arms. He held her as his mind whirled until he managed to sleep himself.

And then—

He woke.

He didn't know why. It was almost as if someone had shaken him awake.

But there was no one there.

Curious, he rose and walked back out to the foyer, then opened the door to the hall. Logan was opening the door to his room at the same time. Sloan looked down the other way. Someone was approaching Emil Roth's room in the darkness.

"Hey!" Sloan shouted.

The figure paused and turned to him. He could make out little of the person in the darkness. Whoever it was had bundled up in black pants, a black hoodie, and what even seemed to be a black cape of some kind. In the pale glow of the castle's night-lights, something gleamed.

A knife?

"Stop," Sloan demanded.

He stepped from his room, listening in the back of his mind for his door to close, for the lock to catch. He wasn't leaving Jane alone without a locked door. For a few seconds the figure stared at him and he stared back.

"Stop!" Sloan ordered again.

The figure began to run down the stairs at a breakneck speed.

Sloan raced after the person, Logan at his heels.

Chapter Six

Jane awoke to the sound of Sloan's voice, disturbed, aware she needed to be up. But she felt a soft touch on her cheek. Not the touch of a lover, rather the brush of gentle fingers that a mother, a sister, or a caring friend might give. For a moment she lay still, her Glock on the bedside table. If there was someone there, no matter how lightly they touched her—

She opened her eyes.

And saw Elizabeth Roth.

The ghost looked at her with sorrow and grave concern. And then, when she realized that Jane was awake, she vanished.

"No!" Jane said. "Please, help us. Don't go!"

But there were more shouts in the hallway and the apparition disappeared in a matter of seconds, fading from Jane's sight. Jane bolted up, grabbed her gun, and headed into the hall.

It was empty.

She cautiously moved out of the bridal suite. She backed her way to the door to Kelsey and Logan's suite and ducked her head in. Neither was there. Almost running, she made her way to Emil Roth's suite. The outer door was open. Taking every precaution, she pushed the door inward and made her way into the room. Like the bridal suite, it had an outer foyer area with a grouping of chairs and a wet bar. Roth family plaques adorned the walls along with prints of medieval paintings. She made her way through to the bedroom, pushed the door open, and quickly flicked on the light, hoping to first blind anyone who might have attacked Emil in the night, or who might be lingering in the room.

To her astonishment, Emil Roth was there.

And he wasn't alone.

She was awkwardly greeted by the sight of flesh. Way more of Emil Roth's pale body than she had ever wanted to see and a pair of massive, gleaming breasts. Way too much of a skinny derrière. Emil's flesh, a woman's flesh—sweaty, writhing flesh—writhing until she turned the light on and they both stopped moving like deer suddenly blinded by headlights.

The woman screamed.

Emil Roth roared. "What the hell?"

Jane instantly turned the light off. "Sorry—sorry! Your door to the hallway was open. I was afraid that someone was hurting you."

She heard the tinkle of the woman's laughter. And then, in the darkness, she realized she knew who the woman was.

Scully Adair.

"I wasn't hurting anyone, I swear!" Scully said. "But, please, don't say anything! Please, don't say anything to Mrs. Avery. I'll wind up fired—"

Scully started to rise.

Jane lifted a hand to her. "I won't say a word, I swear it. Please don't get up on my account. I won't tell Mrs. Avery a thing."

"Hey, now, I own the place," Emil said.

"Whatever!" Jane told them. "I will not say a word. It's between you all. Forgive me. Sorry, I'm out of here. Pretend I was never here. Just do what you were doing, I mean, um, you just might want to lock your door."

She flew back out of the room, shaking, slamming the door in her wake. The locks were automatic, she reminded herself. They'd been warned about that—step outside and it would catch behind you. For a moment, she leaned against the closed door. Visions stuck in her head that she prayed she could quickly clear.

She gave herself a mental shake.

If Emil Roth was fine, what was going on? Where the hell was Sloan? Where were Kelsey and Logan? She hurried to the stairway and gripped the banister tightly, looking behind and around her as she started down the stairs to the castle's foyer. Still, she saw no one. The giant double front doors to the castle were ajar. She walked outside. A moon rode high, the air was still, and a low fog lay gentle on the ground. There was a night-light coming from Mr. Green's cottage and a slightly lower light emitted from the guardhouse where Mrs. Avery was supposed to be sleeping. She wasn't sure why, but she walked the distance around the grounds, on alert, ever ready to be surprised by someone lurking in the night or watching and waiting. But no one accosted her. Instead, she felt as if she was being beckoned toward the chapel. She wasn't afraid of the dead. The dead had helped her many times. She made her way through the gate at the low stone wall that surrounded the chapel. She was afraid of the living. They were dangerous, in her mind.

But no one jumped up or slunk around from a gravestone or a tomb.

She reached the chapel door and pushed it inward. Someone was sitting in a pew, looking at the altar.

He rose.

She looked at John McCawley, tragically killed in a hunting accident the eve of his wedding.

He looked at her a long moment. "You see me? You see me clearly?"

"I do," she told him.

He seemed incredulous, then he smiled, and she saw that he had been a truly handsome young man with a grace about him. "Forgive me. I see people pointing into the woods and saying that they see me when I'm standing next to them. And the ghost hunters! Lord save us all. A twig snaps and they scream, 'What was that, oh my God!'"

"There are several of us here who see the—" She paused. She wasn't sure why, but saying "dead" seemed very rude. "Who see those who have gone before us."

"Really? Amazing and wonderful. I heard one of the maids whispering about it today. You do look like my love, like my Elizabeth. Are you a descendant?"

"I'm really not. I'm sorry," she told him.

"Ah, well, no matter." He studied her anxiously. "If you see Elizabeth—I know she's here. I see her at the window. But you—you with this gift of yours, if you see her, tell her that I love her. I wait for her. I'll never leave her. I love her in death as I loved her in life."

"Why don't you tell her yourself?" Jane asked.

He shook his head. "It's as if I can't breach the castle. I try to enter. I don't know why. The family arranged the wedding, but they didn't want us together. There were a number of us out that day—Emil Roth, father and son, among them. I watched the blood flow from me, but I never knew who'd done the deed. And yet, I prayed that my love would go on—that Elizabeth would rally and find happiness. She loved me, but she wasn't weak. She should have lived a long life and she should have found happiness. But she did not. I'll never leave her now. I will watch her at the window for eternity."

"I'll tell her," Jane said. "But there is a way—there is always a way. We'll figure it out, and you two may tell each other everything you wish to say."

As she spoke, she heard her name cried out loudly and with anguish.

Sloan!

"Here!" she cried. "I'm in the chapel."

A moment later, the door burst in and Sloan rushed to her, sweeping her into his arms. He was oblivious to the ghost, oblivious to everything but her.

He shook as he held her.

"Hey," she said. "I'm fine. Where have you been? Where are Kelsey and Logan?"

"Right behind me. There was someone about to break into Emil Roth's room. We all chased whoever it was down the stairs and out into the yard, but they disappeared as if into thin air," Sloan said with disgust. "I went back to the room and then I banged on Roth's door and—Roth is sleeping with his help."

"I know," Jane said.

Logan came striding in, followed by Kelsey. "There you are," Kelsey said, pushing Sloan aside to give Jane a hug. "We were worried sick."

Jane told them, "Hey! You guys left me."

"We were chasing a mysterious figure," Logan explained.

"The door locked, right, when I left?" Sloan asked, worried.

She nodded. "I just came out looking for you." She frowned.

"Hey—now, we're all out here and Emil Roth is back in his room."

They turned as if they were one and went racing back to the castle. They weren't careful then as they raced up the stairs.

At the door to Emil Roth's suite, they suddenly paused. "Whatever he's doing, we have to interrupt him. We're trying to keep him alive," Sloan said.

Logan nodded and banged on the door. Emil Roth, dressed in a silk robe, opened the door. Seeing them, he groaned. "You all again."

"Mr. Roth, someone was sneaking toward your door in the middle of the night. I believe they meant to cause you some harm," Sloan told them.

"It was me," said a squeaky, apologetic voice. Scully Adair, clad in an oversized shirt, her hair still in disarray, walked slowly out of the bedroom. She gave them a little wave. "Sorry. I'm so sorry."

Jane shook her head—trying to dispel unwanted images that rose before her mind's eye. "You don't need to apologize. You're both adults."

"But, Scully, it wasn't you," Sloan said. "It was someone wearing black, evidently sneaking around, who was headed toward Emil's door. We chased them, and whoever it was disappeared right outside the front door."

"Why would anyone want to hurt me? To most of the world, I'm worthless," Emil said dryly.

"You're not worthless!" Scully said passionately.

"You seem to be a fine enough young man, sincerely," Jane told him.

"But, beyond that, you are worth a fortune," Kelsey reminded him.

Emil Roth shook his head. "If I die, the only living heir—or heiress—is Denise Avery. But she doesn't just get everything. There are all kinds of trusts. The castle will be left to posterity. It will go to the village and be run by a trust and a group of directors."

"But she'd still make out all right," Logan said.

Emil waved a hand in the air. "She'd get a few million."

"Oh, Emil!" Jane said. "People have died for far less than a few million."

"But—Denise," Emil said.

Jane turned to Sloan. "Where was she when you all went running after the figure into the night?"

"We woke up Mr. Green and Mrs. Avery," Logan said.

"But both took their time answering their doors," Sloan said.

"Which, of course, is more than possible when you're sound asleep," Kelsey said.

"This can't be—real," Emil said.

"We didn't imagine the figure we chased away," Sloan said flatly.

"So what do I do?" Emil asked.

"You sit tight," Logan said firmly. "We're waiting on some answers from our home office, and the M.E.'s report. We'll have that info in the morning. For tonight, sit tight. One of us will stay in the hall through the next few hours. When the sun comes up, you'll be with one of us through the day until we get to the bottom of this."

"Really?" Scully asked. "I mean, the police said that it was an accident when the reverend fell. And someone was running around the halls? It could have been the ghost."

"It wasn't a ghost," Sloan said flatly. "It was flesh and blood that tried to get to you tonight, Emil. Dressed in black, sneaking around. And a man died here less than twenty-four hours ago. Let's be smart about this."

Emil nodded. "Yes. Thank you."

"Let's do what we can with the rest of the night," Logan said. "I'll take the hall first." He glanced at his watch. "Each of us takes an hour and a half. That gives everyone a few hours of sleep before morning. Kelsey, you relieve me. Sloan and Jane, you'll be up last."

"I meant to go home," Scully murmured.

"You can't now," Kelsey said flatly.

"But I'll be in the same clothing and Mrs. Avery—"

"I do own the place," Emil said again.

"You're a little shorter than Kelsey, but about the same size," Sloan said. "We'll get you some clothing. For tonight, sit tight."

They left Emil Roth and Scully Adair and adjourned to the hall.

"You know, we're forgetting people," Jane pointed out. "Chef lives over the old stables. I'm not sure where that is. And Phoebe Martin is up in the attic."

"The stables are down the hill and to the right of the gatehouse," Sloan said. "And the attic, you walked Phoebe up there tonight, right?"

"Doesn't mean she stayed there," Jane pointed out.

"But what would Phoebe or Chef have to gain from hurting Emil

Roth?" Kelsey asked.

"The only one to benefit would be Denise Avery," Sloan said.

"But she was there, down at the gatehouse, when you banged on her door, right?" Jane asked.

"Oh, yes, spitting fire, warning us that she had the right to throw us out," Logan said.

"Let's get through the night," Sloan said. "And hope we get something to go on in the morning."

Logan turned to Kelsey. "Get some sleep. I'll wake you in a bit. And you two," he said to Jane and Sloan. "Go on in and—whatever. You have three hours."

Sloan slipped his hand to the base of Jane's spine and urged her toward their door. They entered and he waited for the click. He cupped her head between his hands and kissed her tenderly, the feel of his fingers feathering against the softness of her flesh an arousing touch. He had a talent for the right move at the right time. He could walk into a room and cast his head in one direction and she would just see that he was there and want him. He could be a joker. He could walk naked from a shower and tease and play and tell her that the offer was evident.

But, right now, he wasn't sure what was on her mind. He could always make her long for him.

"She's been here."

"What?" he asked her.

And she told him about waking up to the feel of something on her cheek, of Elizabeth being there and looking at her worriedly. She told him about John McCawley waiting in the church, forever watching the windows for his love.

"Why can't he come in the house?" Sloan asked her.

"Maybe he was never really invited inside—invited to be a part of the family," Jane suggested.

"Did you ask him about any of this?" Sloan asked.

"I didn't really have time. You screamed for me and he disappeared."

"We'll talk about this with the others tomorrow," he said. "And until then—" He paused, his fingers tracing a pattern down her cheek, his eyes focused on hers. "Until then, we'll get some sleep."

She smiled. "When this is over, let's go to an island. A resort. Maybe one of those all-inclusive ones. One where we have our own little hut on the beach."

"No ghosts," he said.

"No ghosts."

"Or Mrs. Avery."

"You think she's guilty?"

"She has the only motive," Sloan said. "Can you think of another?"

At the moment, she couldn't.

She kissed his lips with a promise for the future.

"Go to sleep," he told her. "I can't sleep anyway, right now. I'll take both our turns watching the hall. I'll be back in once it's full light. Logan will be up by then."

She headed into the bedroom, exhausted. She knew Sloan. He'd be pacing in the foyer area of their room for a while, thinking.

But she fell quickly asleep.

She awoke.

And felt Sloan's warmth beside her. She loved that she lay with him at night and woke with him in the morning. She even loved that they could disagree, even argue, that life with him was comfortable—and yet, she could see him, breathe his scent, watch him walk from the shower and want him as if they'd never made love before.

She rolled over to tell him that she loved him.

But never spoke the words.

A shrill scream pierced the castle's quiet.

Chapter Seven

"I guess that Mrs. Avery wasn't responsible," Sloan said.

The scene was a repetition of the previous morning. Only now, it was Denise Avery who lay at the foot of the stairs, her neck broken.

Sloan looked at Logan, who'd been on guard duty. "What happened?"

"She was never on the second level to descend to the first," Logan said, looking at them.

This time, it had been Scully Adair—dressed in one of Kelsey's tailored work suits—who'd made the discovery when she walked down the stairs. Her scream had alerted the castle. Now, everyone was there, including Mr. Green.

Chef and Harry and Devon rushed in from the hall to the kitchen. Phoebe Martin had come running from the Great Hall and the two day maids, Sonia Anderson and Lila Adkins, hurried from the office. It was chaos, everyone asking each other if they'd seen Mrs. Avery.

"Whoa!" Sloan shouted. "Stop. All of you!"

They went silent.

Phoebe stared at Sloan with fear. Scully Adair seemed to be in shock. Harry and Devon just looked sick.

Chef shook his head. "I knew I should have taken that job out at the really haunted hotel in Colorado."

Mr. Green just stood there, hat in hand, shaking his head. "Sorrowful end. The reverend? He was a good man. Mrs. Avery? Not so much. Still, a sorrowful end."

"We're going to have to call the police," Jane said.

"Already dialing," Logan told them.

"Let's leave her as she lies for the M.E.," Sloan said. "We'll head into the Great Hall and wait for the police."

They obeyed like sheep. Chef, Harry, and Devon drifted to one side of the table—team kitchen. Phoebe Martin, Sonia, and Lila to the other side. Emil Roth—appearing to be in total shock—walked to his place at the end.

Scully looked at the room uncertainly. At last, she walked to the wall and sank down against it and seemed to curl into herself.

"Did anyone see her this morning?" Logan asked.

"I did," Mr. Green volunteered. "I saw her walking up to the castle from the guard house."

"Did you speak with her?"

"No," he said. Then, he added, "I only speak with her when I have to."

"We saw her—the three of us," Chef told them.

"Yeah," Harry said. "She came in telling us that if we were all going to get so chummy with the guests, Chef needed to plan cheaper meals."

"Nice," Scully muttered.

"Did you see her?" Jane asked the maids.

The three of them shook their heads.

"Not until she was there. At the foot of the stairs. But, I knew. The minute I heard Scully screaming, I knew," Phoebe said. She stared at Jane. "It's the ghost. She's angry. Elizabeth is angry. You tried to get married here when she couldn't. I think she's trying to kill you!"

Sloan cleared his throat. "I really don't think that Jane and the reverend and Mrs. Avery resemble one another in any way. Nor do I think that a ghost is killing people."

"So she just tripped?" Harry asked hopefully.

"Personally, I don't think so," Jane said matter-of-factly.

"But the reverend just fell yesterday!" Harry protested.

"And she fell today," Kelsey said.

"So, if she didn't just fall—" Harry began.

"Someone pushed her," Devon finished.

"And who would want to kill that old battle-ax?" Chef demanded sarcastically.

The police didn't knock, they burst right in. Detective Forester immediately looked at the FBI agents. "Four of you are still here—and another person is dead? What now?"

Everyone began to speak at once again.

Sloan assumed that Detective Forester was decent at his job. But he probably didn't deal with situations like this often. And Detective Flick, at his heels, merely followed the path that his boss took.

"Hey!" Sloan shouted. "Tone it down. Let the detective get his questions out in an orderly fashion."

They all went silent like errant school children.

"The ghost did it!" Phoebe said again. "The ghost did not want people getting married here. Maybe Elizabeth Roth didn't even want to hurt the reverend. He was just there and she had to stop the wedding. And so, to stop killing other people, she had to kill Mrs. Avery, who kept letting people try to get married here."

Forester stared at her as if she'd completely lost her mind.

"Who saw what happened?" Forester demanded.

"No one saw anything," Sloan said. "My co-workers and I were on the second floor. Scully Adair came down the stairs and found her."

"No one else was around?" Forester demanded of Scully.

Scully shook her head.

"Where were the rest of you?" Forester asked.

Mr. Green told him he'd never entered the house. Chef and cook said that they'd been in the kitchen, but that she had been in to see them just moments earlier.

"We had just gotten here," Lila said.

"We rode in together," Sonia said.

"I was still up in my room," Phoebe said.

"So she just fell?" Forester said, bewildered. "Someone has to know something." He spun on Mr. Green. "Who can vouch for you?"

Green just looked shocked. "I'm always outside."

"And you?" he demanded of Phoebe.

She stared back at him in horror. "Miss Everett walked me to my room last night. Damn you! Why will no one listen to me? The ghost did it."

"I want this place shut down to the public immediately," Forester told Emil Roth. "And no one leaves."

He made the announcement as if that were the answer to the dilemma.

"I don't really have anywhere else to go," Mr. Green muttered.

They heard activity at the door. The medical examiner had arrived. Forester told the group to stay in the Great Hall. Sloan ignored the order, getting a nod from Logan, and followed out on the heels of the detective.

The medical examiner shook his head as he stared at the corpse. "I'll get her temperature for time of death—"

"We know the damned time of death," Forester snapped. "Can't you tell if she was pushed or not?"

"When I have time for an autopsy," the man snapped back.

"Doctor," Sloan asked. "Did you discover anything yesterday that might have caused the reverend to fall? I heard he had a bad heart."

The medical examiner looked at him and nodded. "He was a walking time bomb. There was damage to his heart. Whether that caused his fall or not, I don't know. But he didn't suffer a heart attack before he came crashing down the stairs. And Mrs. Avery, I think she was in decent health. She certainly appeared to be."

Sloan said, "But she didn't fall from the top of the stairs. We were out in the hallway on that landing and we didn't see her." He actually hadn't been on the landing himself. Logan had been there. But, to Sloan's knowledge, Logan never missed anything.

"She fell from midway up?" Forester asked.

"She had to have. She was never on the second floor landing," Sloan said.

"It's a broken neck for sure," the medical examiner said. "If you want to know more, I'll be able to tell you in a few hours. She'll be an immediate priority at the morgue."

Forester thanked him. The medical examiner looked at Sloan and nodded. He had the feeling that he'd be getting any information just as quickly as Forester.

"What do you have to say?" Forester asked, looking at Sloan.

"I don't know what is happening any more than you do," Sloan said. "But three people breaking their necks on a stairway in a matter of years—two of them within two days? I don't see that as accidents, nor as coincidences. Something is going on here."

"You are saying that these people have been murdered?" Forester asked.

"I'd say it's likely."

"And what do you say we do to find out what is happening?"

Sloan was surprised. Forester's anger was all bluster. He was bewildered. There were no knives involved, no guns, no gang wars, and no obvious motive for killing. A husband hadn't gotten too angry with a wife. A mistress hadn't suddenly turned on a man who'd promised to leave his wife and marry her.

And yet, people were dead.

"Detective, we've been researching everyone here. We expect some reports this morning. But, questioning the people here could prove helpful."

Forester nodded. "I'll do it. Whatever you find out, you'll tell me, right?"

"Of course. This is your jurisdiction. We just happen to be here. We're happy to help. But I need to get together with my team."

Forester nodded and seemed better equipped to take control. "I'll see the employees one by one in the Great Hall. You and your team may return to your rooms. I'll send the cooks and the maids to the kitchen and start with Mrs. Avery's assistant."

Forester walked ahead of Sloan to return to the Great Hall. When they were there, he announced his intentions. "Chef, you and your helpers stay together. Miss Martin, Miss Anderson, Miss Adkins, you will stay together, too. You're welcome to wait your turn in the kitchen. Mr. Roth, we'll have to speak with you, but you're welcome to return to your room until Detective Flick comes to bring you down. Please understand, no one is being accused of anything but we must ascertain what happened here. Therefore, I need to speak with all of you, one by one. Mr. Green, you may return to your apartment. Just be ready to speak to us when we call you."

For a moment, everyone was dead still. Then, Chef rose. "Coffee sounds damned good. And breakfast. Detectives? Should I plan for you, too?"

Sloan was surprised when Forester looked at him—as if for approval.

"Chef, it's kind of you to look out for everyone," Sloan said.

He motioned to Logan, Kelsey, and Jane. As the others shuffled out, except for Scully Adair, who looked like a caged mouse, he and the Krewe members made their way to the stairs and up to the bridal suite.

"It wasn't Mrs. Avery after all," Logan said dryly, stating the obvious.

"Whatever motive could there be?" Kelsey asked.

"Motives for murder," Jane mused. "Greed? That seems to be out. Revenge? Who would have a motive for revenge against the reverend and Mrs. Avery?"

"Jealousy," Logan put in.

"Love," Jane said.

They all looked at her.

"Unrequited love?" she said.

"But who loved whom and wasn't loved in return?" Kelsey asked.

"Let's see what they've gotten us from the home office," Logan suggested.

He sat at Sloan's laptop, found his mail, and ran through everything that had been returned. "I sent them copies of Jane's sketches from last night along with names and everything else, and so far no one has a criminal record. Mr. Green has been here all his life. Our host, Emil, had some trouble with drinking and being rowdy in college, but that doesn't suggest he'd become homicidal. The maids? Lila Adkins is taking college courses by night. She hasn't even had a parking ticket. Sonia Anderson is halfway through a community college now. She wants to be a nurse. Phoebe Martin took the job here years ago when she was divorced. She took it because she could live at the castle, according to the records. Chef? He had offers all over the place but Emil Roth really liked him—they met at a restaurant in Boston—and offered him a husky salary. The two cooks? Devon Richard has applied to the police academy—with good scores. He'll probably be hired on when they have a position. And Harry Taubolt plans on staying to study with Chef. He wants a food career." He looked up at the others again. "Are we certain that Lila and Sonia left the castle last night?"

"Their cars were gone," Sloan said.

"I think we can rule them out. But how do we narrow down the others?" Kelsey asked.

"We're looking at Emil Roth, Scully Adair, Chef, Harry Taubolt, Devon Richard, Phoebe Martin, and Mr. Green," Logan said.

"Except that we know Emil Roth and Scully Adair were in Emil's room when whoever we saw on the stairs was sneaking around the house last night," Sloan said.

"So Chef, Harry, Devon, Phoebe, or Mr. Green," Jane said.

"And Mr. Green was in the caretaker's cottage when we went there. But he had time to slip in. The main thing is that whoever had been in the house just disappeared, as if into thin air. We need to find out where he or she got in and out of the house," Sloan said.

"We could start a search—" Kelsey said.

"Or just ask," Sloan suggested.

"Emil Roth," Jane said.

* * * *

Jane wasn't sure why but she felt the need to be in the room alone. Not that Logan, Sloan, and Kelsey weren't as good as she was when it came to communicating with the dead, but, in her experience, the dead sometimes chose who they would and wouldn't communicate with.

This time, she was certain, it was her.

Kelsey went down to the kitchen to talk to the cooks and maids. Sloan and Logan went down the hall to speak with Emil Roth about the architecture of the castle.

She sat quietly in the bedroom and said, "Elizabeth, I know that you're here. Please, speak with me. Tell me if you've seen anything, if you know anything that might help us."

The air didn't stir, and yet she felt that someone had heard her.

"I saw John McCawley last night," she said. "He wanted me to tell you that he loves you. That he'll never leave you. He watches you at the window. But you know that. That's why you go to the window. So that you can see him."

Slowly, Elizabeth appeared before her and walked to where Jane sat on the bed.

"I didn't kill myself," she said. "They said that I took the laudanum on purpose. My poor father believed that I did it myself. But, I did not."

That wasn't what Jane had expected to hear. "I'm so sorry. But who would have given you the overdose?"

"It was in the tea, I think," she said. "I believe it was my father's maid. She knew that father had no faith in John. Father was so mistaken. I hated his money. John hated his money. Everyone believes that if you have money, that's all that anyone wants. But I loved John. Maybe she believed that if John and I were both gone, and with mother gone, just my brother left... but she underestimated my father. He had loved my mother. There was no affair between them. And still, I'm certain that she tried her best. She had her brother kill John in the woods and make it look as if he'd been killed by my brother or my father! And then, of course, it was easy for her to make it look as if I were a suicide."

"What was the maid's name?" Jane asked her.

"Molly," Elizabeth said.

"What became of her?"

"My father fired her. She became uppity and thought she ruled the place. But he took care of her. He fired her and banned her from the property."

"And what did she do?" Jane asked.

"She left the house, cursing us all!"

"Did you know Molly's last name?" Jane asked.

Elizabeth shook her head.

Jane jumped up. "I have to get into your family's records."

"They're in the office. There's a display case there with the records from the 19th century."

"Thank you," Jane told her.

"How can that help?" Elizabeth asked her. "Our deaths were so long ago."

"I'm not sure, at the moment," Jane said.

She left Elizabeth and the room.

Greed was just one motive for murder.

But unrequited love and revenge were two others.

Chapter Eight

"There are no secret entrances to the castle," Emil Roth told them. "But, of course, don't forget, there are two back entrances."

"But they can only be reached by the back, right?" Sloan asked.

Emil nodded.

Sloan looked at Logan. Their disappearing figure of the night before could have circled around the castle and come in through one of the back entrances. But what then?

"And there are servants' stairs that go up to the second landing and the attic," Emil said.

"Of course," Sloan said, irritated that he'd forgotten that in old places like this there was bound to be a second set of stairs.

Okay, one mystery solved.

"What are you thinking?" Emil asked Sloan.

"I'm thinking that someone has really been planning on attacking you and is getting rid of others in the hopes of ruining your life."

Emil looked at Logan. "Do you agree with that?"

"That's where we need your help," he said.

"I swear to you, I'm not the best human being in the world, but I'm not the worst. I haven't hurt anyone in a vicious business deal. I support equal rights. I'm decent," he said. "Not to mention, the only people here are my employees and you people."

"Is there any reason, say, Mr. Green, would harbor you any resentment?" Sloan asked.

"Not that I know of. He's happy, I'm happy. He tells me what he should do, and I tell him to go ahead and do it."

"What about the maids?"

"I overpay them. They have it easy."

"And Scully?" Sloan asked. She'd been with him—in bed—but that could have been part of a ploy. Perhaps two people working together.

"Scully," he said. "I love her."

Sloan and Logan looked at one another.

"Does she have an ex-boyfriend?" Logan asked.

True, they were both grasping at straws.

"Not that I know about. We started seeing each other about three months ago. Honestly, that's why I slipped back here and didn't go to Africa. We needed more time together. We wanted to be sure, really sure that we wanted to be together forever. And we are sure."

"Why was she so worried about what Mrs. Avery would think?" Sloan asked.

"Because, if we weren't really certain she wanted to keep her job. You know, everyone would have thought that she was after my money. She was so afraid of that. She has a degree in hospitality, so she could work anywhere. She's been offered good jobs by the major chains. But she wanted to stay here. Her mom and dad are here. Her dad isn't well. But to think she wanted my money? That was just stupid!"

There was a tap on the door and Sloan opened it.

Detective Flick was standing there. "Detective Forester would like to speak with Mr. Roth now."

"Of course," Emil said.

He followed Flick out. Sloan and Logan came too, but Flick motioned for them to hold back.

"Detective Forester asked that you head to the morgue. The medical examiner called. He has something. We want you to go so we can keep the questioning here going."

Sloan looked at Logan, who lowered his head to hide a grin. More probable, the medical examiner had specifically asked that the two of them come.

"We'll head right there," Sloan said.

"If you'll be good enough to tell us where it is," Logan said.

Flick gave them directions, then hurried ahead to make sure Emil Roth made it down the stairs okay. Sloan strode quickly down the hall to tell Jane where they were going. But she wasn't in the bridal suite. He called her cell and she answered promptly.

"I'm in the office, looking at records."

"What are you thinking?"

"It's vague at the moment, but revenge is looking good."

"Who's taking revenge on whom?" he asked.

She laughed. "I don't know yet. But as soon as I do, I'll call you."

He hung up and he and Logan headed to the morgue. The village was quaint and small, but the morgue was state of the art. The reverend's body had already been claimed. Mrs. Avery remained. She looked small and thin lying on the morgue table.

"Here is what I want you to see," the medical examiner said.

They looked at the shaved head which revealed a dark bruising.

"I don't know about the reverend, but Mrs. Avery didn't take an accidental fall. She was struck on the head. And then she was pushed down the landing and the murderer was quite lucky. She broke her neck on the way down. Gentlemen, this is no accidental death. I'm classifying it a homicide!"

* * * *

Jane learned that Elizabeth's "Molly" was Margaret Clarendon. She'd been employed by Emil Roth from the time he'd moved into the castle until three months after the deaths of John McCawley and Elizabeth Roth. She'd died, unmarried, according to the records, sixth months after her dismissal, when she'd careened off a cliff. Whether she'd thrown herself off or fallen, there was no record. But her death had been labeled accidental. Had Margaret Clarendon thrown herself off the cliff? Remorseful for what she had done? Or bitter, because with all her machinations she'd failed to win the lord of the castle? No way to tell from the records. So Jane left the office and headed up the stairs again to the second level. As she climbed, she remembered to grip the handrail.

Halfway up, she ran into Scully Adair.

"Do you know anything?" Scully asked her anxiously.

"No, Scully, I'm so sorry. I wish I did."

"They questioned me forever. They think I'm a murderer!"

"Not necessarily, Scully. They have to question everyone like that," Jane assured her.

"They still have Emil in there," Scully said.

"He'll be fine," Jane said.

"I just wish he'd come out. They're talking to everyone so long."

"They're being thorough, listening for something someone might not even realize is a clue to what is going on."

"I'm going to get some coffee and something to eat. Do you want to come?" Scully asked her.

"I'll be there in a minute. I have something to check on," Jane said. "I promise, I'll be right along."

Scully nodded, then gripped the banister tightly as she went on down the stairs.

When Jane reached the bridal suite, she was alone. Elizabeth was nowhere to be seen and Jane didn't sense her presence. She went straight to her computer and video-phoned Angela at the home offices of the Krewe in Virginia.

Angela was with the first Krewe of Hunters. She'd earned her stripes in New Orleans. She was now married to Jackson Crow, the field director for all Krewe agents. While Jackson managed most of their commitments, there was still their overall head, Adam Harrison, who'd first recognized those out there with special intuition—that ability to talk to the dead. He was an incredibly kind man with a talent for finding and recruiting the right people for his Krewe.

Angela came online. She was a beautiful blonde who looked like she should have starred in a noir movie.

"Anything?" she asked Jane.

"So much!"

Jane told her about the morning's events, then said, "I need you to do a search on a woman named Margaret Clarendon, who lived here in the mid-1800s. Find out anything you can about her—before and after she worked for the Roth family."

"What are you thinking?"

"Elizabeth Roth believes that she was murdered, and that her fiancé was murdered, too. She thinks she was killed by this maid."

"And that will help you now?" Angela asked.

"I think so," Jane said. "There's no one to benefit from Emil

Roth's death or from him being ruined. There has to be another motive."

"And you think Margaret Clarendon, despite the fact that she might have been a murderess, felt that ill was done to her?"

"We've seen it before. Sometimes there's a descendant out there who feels that they have to right a family wrong," Jane said.

"But remember that sometimes people just act on greed, jealousy, or revenge. Modern day psychos or self-centered asses," Angela reminded her.

"I'll watch from all sides," Jane promised her.

She said good-bye and they cut the connection. Jane drummed her fingers on the table for a minute, and then hopped up again. She was going to have to wait for results, but she couldn't sit idly by.

Time to try to pay a visit to John McCawley again.

* * * *

"Here's what I can't figure. If Mrs. Avery was hit on the head, she had to have been hit on the head with something. Where is that something she was hit with?" Sloan asked.

"Whoever hit her took it with them," Logan said.

Sloan was the one driving as they headed back to the castle. He saw a coffee shop and switched on his blinker, ready to pull into the lot.

"We're stopping for coffee," Logan said.

Sloan grinned. "I thought we'd try for a little more gossip."

"Sounds good to me. And coffee, too," Logan told him.

They went in and were noticed right away by the hostess, who stood at the cash register. A number of patrons were sitting around at the various faux-leather booths. They were definitely the outsiders, probably known as the people who were the guests at the castle. Where bad things happened.

"Sit anywhere?" Sloan said, smiling at the cashier.

"Wherever," she said.

He and Logan claimed a booth. A waitress came over, offered them menus, and took their orders for coffee. She scampered away, then returned quickly. She looked as if she was both anxious and afraid to talk to them.

She flushed as she poured the coffee and caught Sloan's eyes. "I'm sorry. I mean, it's a small village. You're guests at the castle, right?"

"Yes, we are. Sad business there, though," Sloan said.

"My God, yes! The poor reverend. Everyone loved him, you know. And now they say that Mrs. Avery has fallen down the stairs and broken her neck, too!"

Her nametag identified her as Genie.

"Yes, Mrs. Avery died," Sloan said.

"The poor woman," Logan agreed.

The cashier, apparently, couldn't stand being out of the know. She headed over to the table with a bowl of coffee creamers.

"Poor woman, my foot," she said. "Denise Avery thought she was better than anyone in town. She really thought Emil would run himself into the ground with drugs, or his stupid bungee jumping, or parachuting or whatever. He fooled her."

Sloan and Logan glanced at one another and up at the cashier. Her tag noted her name as Mary.

"Oh, I know!" she said. "I must sound horrible. But she came in here all the time and was rude."

"I applied to work at the castle," Genie said. "She looked at me as if I were flypaper. I didn't stand a chance. I wasn't pretty enough."

"You're quite pretty!" Sloan told her.

Which was true.

"Oh, no! Mrs. Avery wanted really pretty girls to work there. Even as maids. I mean, who cares what your maid looks like if she does a good job?"

"Hmmph!" Mary said. "That woman wanted to tease Emil. She wanted to get him going with whoever she brought in. And then remind him, of course, that he had a position in life, even if he wasn't fulfilling it. She just wanted to mess with that man."

"She's gone now," Genie reminded her.

Mary crossed herself. "It's not good to speak ill of the dead."

"But truth is truth," Genie said. "The reverend? He was a good man."

"Bad heart, though," Mary said.

"Oh, dear!" Genie said. "We are terrible. What would you like to eat?"

"What's fast?" Sloan asked.

"The special. Stew," Genie said.

"We'll take it," Logan told her.

"Sounds delicious," Sloan said.

It was actually terrible, or maybe it just seemed terrible because they'd been eating Chef's food. But it was fast and filling and they were out of there in no time. Sloan wasn't sure what they'd gained, but they'd gained something.

"Mrs. Avery was quite a manipulator," Sloan said.

"She was so determined to seduce Emil Roth with the maids, but he went and fell in love with Scully Adair," Logan mused.

Sloan looked at him. "Do we know what happened before he fell in love with Scully Adair?"

"It would be interesting to find out," Logan said.

* * * *

Jane was amazed at how quickly the day ended and darkness fell. It seemed that they'd just awoken with Mrs. Avery at the foot of the stairs. Then the police had come and begun their investigation. She had spoken with Angela, Kelsey had hob-knobbed with the kitchen staff and maids, and Logan and Sloan had headed to the autopsy. The hours had flown by, and as she came down the stairs, she could hear Detective Forester in the Great Hall. He'd certainly taken a long time with every single person who'd been in the house. She listened a second and realized from the slow answers he was receiving that Forester was now questioning Mr. Green. She thought about stopping by the kitchen, but decided to head on to the chapel.

She needed to talk with John McCawley.

She headed out again, just as she had the night before. There was no moonlight yet, the autumn sun fading, a brooding darkness hanging over the cliffs brought on by an overcast sky. She'd exited by the front to avoid running into anyone at the rear. She walked around the castle, from the manicured front to the wild and atmospheric rear, and hurried to the chapel.

John McCawley was waiting in front of the altar, staring up at it.

"Did you see her?" he asked, turning. "Did you see my Elizabeth?"

"I did," she told him. "And I told her and, of course, you know that she loves you. She thinks she was murdered. She didn't kill herself."

"What?" he asked.

"She believes that there was a maid at the house—Margaret or Molly—who wanted her father's attention. And that Molly believed that she could start by ridding the world of the two of you. And Molly had a brother—"

"David," John told her. "He was always coming to the stables, asking for any extra work."

"She believes that David shot you and that Molly poisoned her."

"Can you prove it?"

"Probably not after all these years," Jane said. "But you know. The two of you know. Maybe that's enough."

His face darkened and he began to frown. Jane thought that she had said something that disturbed him. But then she realized that he was looking behind her.

She spun around.

And saw a figure dressed in black.

She started to draw her Glock, but before she could something came hurtling at her. Ghosts didn't have much strength—thus the tales of rattling chains and squeaking floors and chairs that rocked themselves. But they did have something. And Jane was sure that John McCawley had used all of his strength to cast himself before her. She dove behind one of the pews, drew her gun, and fired. The solid *thunk* she heard confirmed that her bullet had found the wood of a pew.

She rolled and took aim again.

But there was no one there.

The wraith in black was gone, and so was John McCawley.

She rose. Her phone was ringing.

Angela.

She answered, watching the door to the chapel.

"I found out more about your Margaret Clarendon," Angela told her. "She does have a descendant working at the castle now."

Chapter Nine

Detective Flick was waiting for Sloan and Logan when they entered the castle. He immediately directed them to Detective Forester, who had set up in the Great Hall. They sat and told him what they'd discovered at the M.E.'s office.

"We're going to need a search warrant," Forester said. "We need to find whatever object carries Denise Avery's blood."

"You don't need a warrant."

Emil Roth stood at the arched entry to the Great Hall.

"I own the property. I give you my permission to search every room. I believe there's a legality about guests in rooms, but I believe my guests will give you permission, too. Am I correct, gentlemen?"

"Of course," Logan said.

"Then I'll call in some backup," Forester said, "and we'll get to it tonight."

"I think that's an excellent idea," Logan said.

"Where are Kelsey and Jane?" Sloan asked.

"Kitchen, I believe," Forester told them.

Logan and Sloan headed out of the Great Hall to the kitchen. Kelsey was sitting there with Chef and Harry and Devon.

"Something to eat?" Chef asked.

"No, thanks. We had some horrible food in town," Logan told

him.

Chef grinned. "I do have the reputation for being the best around."

"I'd not argue it," Logan assured him.

"Why would you stop in town when you're staying here?" Chef asked. "And how were you out when the rest of us are prisoners here? Oh, yeah, I forgot. You're Feds."

Logan slid into a seat at the kitchen table. "We went to hear gossip."

Sloan remained standing. He still didn't know where Jane was. "We heard a lot of interesting gossip. Apparently, not many people liked Mrs. Avery. In fact, they seemed to think that she was trying to make everything in the world go wrong for Emil Roth."

Chef shrugged. "She treated him like he was a kid. When he hired me, not long after his dad died, they had a huge fight. I overheard them. She told him that he didn't have the know-how to run anything and that he shouldn't make decisions without her. I'm surprised he didn't kill her. He was the heir, but she acted like she owned everything."

"But he didn't kill her, did he?" Sloan asked.

"Emil?" Harry asked. "He's a decent guy. He's like a regular guy, but with money. He'd be normal as hell if people like Mrs. Avery didn't keep telling him that he had responsibilities as if he were Spiderman or something."

"Where's Jane?" Sloan asked them.

Kelsey, who'd been sitting at the table, frowned. "I'll go see."

"Wait. I'll just try her phone," Sloan said.

He dialed Jane's number and listened as they continued to talk.

"The people in town even seemed to think that Avery hired only attractive maids to try and get Emil involved with them," Logan said.

"Was that her plan?" Harry asked.

"I never had it figured as an actual plan," Devon said. "Go figure. That dried up old prune of a biddy setting Emil up for sex!"

"Did it work?" Logan asked

"At first, maybe. A few girls wound up being fired for various infractions. Oh, never for flirting with or co-habiting or whatever you want to call it," Chef said. "They'd be fired for failing in their duty, for disturbing a guest, things like that."

Logan heard an unspoken *but*. "What?"

"That all ended a few months ago," Devon said.

"Just spit it out, they know everything," Harry said. "They're Feds, remember? Emil is crazy about Scully Adair. And Scully is crazy about him. I don't know how they were managing to hide it from Mrs. Avery. All the rest of us knew."

"But, he did see people before that?"

"Yeah, sure. He's young, good-looking, rich. Who wouldn't have seen him?" Harry asked.

Jane's phone was ringing and ringing with no answer. Sloan ended the call and looked at Logan and Kelsey.

"Now we go and find Jane," he said. "She's not answering, and I'm pretty sure I know who we're looking for. Kelsey, go get the detectives. Logan, will you search the house? I'm heading out to the chapel."

"What can we do?" Chef asked.

"Stay put," Sloan told him.

* * * *

Jane cautiously stepped out of the church. The overcast sky seemed to have fallen closer to the ground, a dense fog rising to meet it. The graveyard, benign by day, now seemed to hold dozens of places to hide. Winged angels cast shadows over crooked stones. Trees grew at a slant and gargoyles loomed over tombs, warding off all evil. Standing in the doorway for the chapel, she was in clear view.

"You know I have a gun and I do know how to use it," she said, addressing the graveyard. "You might as well come out. I'm sure that you want me to think that Scully Adair is doing all this. After all, you know that Scully is a descendant of Margaret Clarendon. And you must have heard that there were a few references to the fact that Margaret was suspected of having helped Elizabeth along to her death. But, you know what? I don't think that Scully herself knows that she has any relationship to the castle. Margaret's child with Emil Roth went up for adoption. We only found out the truth because we have access to all kinds of records. Phoebe, you were good. I mean that scream you let out when you *found* Reverend MacDonald was really something. And the shock in your eyes? Amazing. So, you had an affair with Emil Roth. You thought you were the one. And I don't believe that you did kill Cally Thorpe. That was really just a tragic accident. But if people started dying at every wedding, that would give the castle a real reputation. But that wasn't enough. You figured you'd get rid of Mrs. Avery. Make it really ghostly. You hated her, because she sucked you in. She fed you the story about Scully and her being a descendant of Margaret. You thought you'd replay history, except this time you'd win!"

Jane barely ducked in time as a piece of broken plaster wing off a cherub came flying her way. By the time she was up again, her quarry had moved. Slinking low, she ran from one tomb to the next.

"Phoebe, my Krewe will have figured it out by now, too. Killing me will get you nowhere. Nor is there anywhere for you to go. You'll be arrested, and you'll face murder charges. If you give yourself up right now, I can try to help you."

Jane had moved away from the chapel a fair distance. Phoebe was leading her to the rear, a place where the graves began to ride down the slopes off the cliffs. She raised her head, trying to see in the near darkness. She thought she heard something—coming from behind her.

She was certain that Phoebe was before her!

Something thumped into the gravestone she'd ducked beneath.

An arrow.

She heard laughter from the fog-riddled graveyard before her, eerie in the strange dying light and the cool air.

"No one gets married here! They don't marry here. They *die* here!" Phoebe called to her.

Jane thought she heard a snapping sound on the ground, coming closer. She rolled quickly and slunk on the ground, staying low. She was armed and she could aim. But she couldn't make out a damned thing to shoot at.

"Brides die!" Phoebe cried, laughing.

The sound was both ahead and behind Jane.

In fact, it seemed to come from all around.

* * * *

Sloan was quickly on his feet, racing to the back of the house. At the rear exit from the kitchen, he thought that he felt someone behind him.

He turned.

And she was there. Elizabeth Roth.

She stared at him with a drawn face and worried eyes.

"I'll find her!" he promised.

"The fog has fallen," Elizabeth said.

"I'll find her!" he said. "Come with me?"

"I can't leave the house."

"Try."

She shook her head.

He couldn't wait.

He bolted out of the castle and was instantly astounded by the pea soup of New England fog he found himself within. He could still see the spire of the chapel, so he headed toward it. He made his way through the gate, down the path, and threw the chapel door open.

Jane wasn't there.

But he heard something.

Laughter.

Eerie in the strange fog. It seemed to come from the left, and then from the right.

"Jane!" he shouted. "Jane!"

He heard her reply.

And as he did, he realized that shouting had been a mistake. She was might be risking her life to shout out a warning to him.

"It's Phoebe and someone else, Sloan! Someone else with a bow and arrow, hunting us down," Jane shouted back to him.

He dropped to the ground just as something whizzed by his head. He tried to calculate the source of the arrow that had come his way. But whoever was shooting with a bow and arrow was now halfway around the church.

The laughter had come from the far rear.

On his hands and knees, he crawled around the graveyard.

* * * *

Jane tried to determine where she was, but with the distance they'd come she thought she might be in the back of the chapel, near the cliffs.

"I'm going to get you!" Phoebe said, her voice startlingly near.

She couldn't see anything. So how could Phoebe?

She didn't reply.

Then Phoebe began to chant. *"Good girls die, the bitches lie, the brides go straight to decay. This time round, the good girl dies and the bitch's lies will let her win the day!"*

"How do you see this as winning?" Jane cried out. "Emil is seriously in love with Scully. He'll marry her and you'll go to jail."

"Not true. Scully is right here with me. And if you don't show yourself now, she's going over the cliff!" Phoebe cried.

"I don't believe you. Scully was in the castle."

"She's here now. Wanna hear her scream?"

Jane heard a muffled cry.

Scully.

She winced, bracing against a gravestone.

"If you don't come out, she goes over the cliff right now!"

Sloan was out there, too, she thought. He had to be.

She'd be all right.

Or would she?

* * * *

Sloan kept silent and crept along the earth.

Another arrow flew past. That one, he was sure, had been sent blindly. He crept for what seemed like a lifetime but, looking at his watch, he saw that two minutes had passed. Another arrow flew by. This time he saw the arch and pattern.

He crept in the right direction.

Slow and silent.

At last he found himself behind the archer.

He waited and watched, forcing himself to be patient.

When the archer went to string another arrow, he pounced.

And together, they started rolling downhill.

* * * *

Jane realized there was nothing to do but stand. Her Glock was tucked into the back of her jeans.

"I'm here," she cried.

"Come out where I can see you!" Phoebe demanded.

"Where is that?"

"Come closer to my voice."

She did as told and tripped once over a broken stone, but then she saw images appear before her. Phoebe had somehow taken Scully hostage. She stood with Scully, close to the edge of the cliff, and held a knife to her throat.

"Drop the gun," Phoebe said.

"Let Scully go first," she said.

"Drop the gun, or she goes over."

"You're going to die or go to prison," Jane said.

Phoebe shook her head. "You'll be dead. And the whole thing will look like the crazy Krewe of Hunters unit—the *ghost unit*—went off the deep end and killed everybody. Then Emil will come back to me. He's young and sweet and pliable. He'll love me again."

"You were never anything but an affair to him, Phoebe. He loved Scully from the start."

"Put the gun down. She's already bleeding," Phoebe warned.

Should she pretend to do as instructed, then shoot? She could aim for Phoebe's head, but if either woman moved—

Someone lightly touched her.

And she heard a whisper that seemed part of the fog.

"Your love is behind you. Duck down. I'll do what I can."

Jane reached for her gun, dropped to the ground, and told Phoebe, "She's coming for you."

"Who?"

"The ghost of Elizabeth Roth. She's disgusted with what you're doing, trying to use the past to make a mockery of the present. She's there. At your side. Can't you feel her? She's touching you now."

"You're full of—" Phoebe began and broke off.

Elizabeth Roth was there, standing next to Phoebe, touching her hair.

Jane flew to her feet, sprinted forward, and caught Phoebe and Scully together, bringing them all down.

They landed hard, but Scully was free.

"Get up and run!" Jane ordered.

Thankfully, Scully had the sense to obey.

Phoebe still held her knife. She jumped to her feet in a fury, knife raised, ready to leap to where Jane had fallen.

But a shot rang out.

Phoebe paused midair. Then her body was propelled backward, disappearing into the fog. Jane heard her scream until a distant thud, flesh impacting rock, silenced everything.

An unearthly quiet returned.

Then shouts everywhere.

Logan and Kelsey. Forester and Flick. Chef and Harry and Devon and Lila and Sonia. All coming from the castle. Someone walked out of the fog toward her, gun in hand. Impossibly tall and broad and wonderful and always there for her. Her partner, in life, in work, and in breathing. Sloan didn't speak as he drew her to her feet and into his arms.

He just held her.

And their hearts beat together.

* * * *

"But, Mr. Green?"

It was Emil who seemed the most shocked. He'd trusted the man, thought he'd had a champion in him.

It was nearly morning again.

And, as the survivors gathered in the Great Hall while Forester's crew worked to find the bodies down the cliff, Sloan knew they were all grateful to know that there wouldn't be another one at the foot of the stairs that morning.

"Why Mr. Green?" Emil repeated.

"I think he just became involved with Phoebe. When you stopped seeing her, she started planning her revenge. I think she was trying to find a way to make her past part of yours. Instead, she discovered that Scully is a distant relative," Jane said.

"And," Sloan explained, "once she'd come up with her plan, she knew she needed help. And poor Mr. Green, alone and lonely. He was no match for Phoebe. He did what she told him. I believe she had him convinced that she had to do what was right for you and if so, she'd be with him forever and ever."

"But she wanted me," Emil said, confused.

"She didn't tell Green that part. She took care of the killing herself. But she needed him to help when it came to getting rid of you and Scully."

"As if she'd have ever gotten away with it," Logan muttered angrily. "The Krewe of Hunters doesn't lose. We come on harder and harder until a case is solved."

"We'll never really know what was on Green's mind, will we?" Kelsey asked.

Sloan lowered his head and shook it.

When he'd tackled Green, he'd subdued him and tied his hands. He'd never suspected, though, that the bound man would pitch himself over the cliff. But that's exactly what had happened once Green realized Phoebe was gone. He looked up. Logan was watching him, knowing what he was feeling.

"We try to save the victims first and always," he said.

"You saved Scully for me," Emil said.

Sloan decided not to tell him that Jane had saved Scully. He'd saved his own love and his own life with a well-placed shot.

"What will happen now?" Jane asked. "With this place?"

"I think I'll close it," Emil said. "Funny, I always dreamed I'd be married here one day. I'm not huge on tradition, but my parents were married here."

"I think you should be married here," Jane told him. "Prove to the world that the castle isn't evil. Only people can be evil. Make the castle a place of joy."

"She's right," Scully said.

"We get to be bridesmaids!" Lila said.

"Oh, yes! Except, of course, we get to be in on picking the dresses," Sonia added.

"You'll need a best man," Chef told Emil.

"And ushers," Harry said.

Detective Forester stood. "I'll at least expect an invitation. And one for Flick, too, of course."

"You got it," Emil promised. He looked at Jane. "But, you did plan to have your wedding here, you know?"

"But we're not the lord and lady of the castle," Jane said.

"I think we'll be headed for an island in the Caribbean," Sloan told him.

"You'll always be welcome here," Emil told them. "And anywhere I have holdings. And, I know that with Scully at my side, I'll make good. And we'll do good things. I swear it!"

"I believe you will," Sloan assured him.

"Flick and I will be leaving now," Forester said.

"I'll walk you out," Sloan offered.

Jane stood as he did. He smiled at her. They were both still muddy and grass-stained. They might not be married at the castle, but he did intend to make good use of the elaborate shower in the bridal suite as soon as he could.

They walked to the door and out onto the front lawn.

Emil was going to need a new caretaker, too.

But, as they waved good-bye to the detectives, Sloan was certain he'd never seen the place more beautiful.

Elizabeth Roth had realized that she could leave the castle. She stood with her beloved John down at the gates, oblivious to all else. She and John didn't notice the car that drove by them. They were engaged in a long kiss. And as the car passed, the sun rose high above them, crimson rays of extraordinary light raining down, more like twilight than dawn.

Sloan lifted a hand to shield his eyes, blinking against the glare.

When the light shifted, they were gone.

"Do you think—?" Jane asked.

"I don't know. But I do know they're together."

"Like we'll always be," she said.

"Shower," he said. "And then—"

"We'll fool around?"

"Isn't that how all of this started?"

That it was, she thought.

"Then, off to the Caribbean," he said. "Some place warm, with lots of blue water and sunshine. And we'll fool around for a lifetime."

She lifted her dirt-smudged face to his.

And he kissed the most beautiful lips he'd ever seen.

When Irish Eyes Are Haunting

Dedication

Dedicated with love to my cousin, Patrick DeVuono, who grew up with me in the family where leprechauns were real and the wonderful tales our elders told could leave us in awe—and give us the chills!

In memory of my Mom, born in Dublin, the most intelligent and wonderful woman I ever knew. When she couldn't give us a real answer, she would smile and say, "Let's look it up!"

And for Granny, who was about 4'11"—and could convince us that indeed, the banshees would be getting us in the outhouse if we didn't behave—even when we didn't have an outhouse.

For Aunt Amy and Katie (and Sam! Who made marrying an Italian a good thing!)

For all my mom's family, the wonderful Irish Americans.

And, for Ireland, of course. I'm an American and I love my country.

But, I also enjoy every second of being in Ireland, and loving the land that bred so many people I adored so very much.

Chapter One

"Ah, you can hear it in the wind, you can, the mournful cry of the banshee!" Gary Duffy—known as Gary the Ghost—exclaimed with wide eyes, his tone low, husky and haunting along with the sound of the crackling fire. "It's a cry so mournful and so deep, you can feel it down into your bones. Indeed. Some say she's the spirit of a woman long gone who's lost everyone dear in her life; some say she is one of the fairy folk. Some believe she is a death ghost, and come not to do ill, but to ease the way of the dying, those leaving this world to enter the next. However she is known, her cry is a warning that 'tis time for a man to put his affairs in order, and kiss his loved ones good-bye, before taking that final journey that is the fate of all men. And women," he added, looking around at his audience. "Ah, and believe me! At Castle Karney, she's moaned and cried many a time, many a time!"

Yes! Just recently, Devin Lyle thought.

Very recently.

Gary spoke well; he was an excellent storyteller, more of a performer than a guide. He had a light and beautiful brogue that seemed to enhance his words as well and an ability to speak with a deep tone that carried, yet still seemed to be something of a whisper.

All in the tour group were enthralled as they watched him—even the youngest children in the group were silent.

But then, beyond Gary's talents, the night—offering a nearly full moon and a strange, shimmering silver fog—lent itself to storytelling and ghostly yarns. As did the lovely and haunting location where Gary spun his tales.

The group sat around a campfire that burned in an ancient pit outside the great walls of Castle Karney, halfway between those walls and St. Patrick's of the Village—the equally ancient church of Karney, said to have been built soon after the death of Ireland's patron saint. A massive graveyard surrounded the church; the Celtic crosses, angels, cherubs, and more, seemed to glow softly in a surreal shade of pearl beneath the moon. That great orb itself was stunning, granting light and yet shrouded in the mist that shimmered over the graveyard, the castle walls, and down to embrace the fire itself—and Gary the Ghost—in surreal and hypnotic beauty.

Gary's tour was thorough.

They'd already visited the castle courtyard, the cliffs, the church, and the graveyard, learning history and legends along the way.

The fire pit they now gathered around had been used often in the centuries that came before—many an attacking lord or general had based his army here, just outside the walls. They had cooked here, burned tar here for assaults, and stood in the light and warmth of the blaze to stare at the castle walls and dream of breeching them.

The walls were over ten feet thick. An intrepid Karney—alive at the time of William the Conqueror—had seen to it that the family holding was shored up with brick and stone.

"The night is still now," Gary said, his voice low and rich. "But listen if you will when the wind races across the Irish Sea. And you'll hear the echo of her wail, on special nights, aye, the heart-wrenching cry of the banshee!"

Gary—Devin knew from her cousin, Kelly—was now the full-time historian, curator, and tour director at Castle Karney. She'd learned a lot from him, but, naturally, she'd known a lot already from family lore. Kelly Karney was her cousin and Devin had been to Castle Karney once before.

The Karney family had held title to the property since the time of St. Patrick. Despite bloodshed and wars, and multiple invasions first by Vikings and then British monarchs, they'd held tenaciously to the property. So tenaciously that fifteen years ago—to afford the massive property along with repairs and taxes—they had turned it into a fashionable bed and breakfast, touted far and wide on tourist sites as a true experience as well as a vacation.

Gary, with his wonderful ability to weave a tale, was part of the allure—as if staying in a castle with foundations and a great hall begun in the early part of the fifth century was not enough!

But Gary had gained fame in international guidebooks. While the Karney family had employed him first for the guests of the B&B, they'd always opened the tours to visitors who came to the village and stayed anywhere there—or just stopped by for the tour.

"Indeed! Here, where the great cliffs protected the lords of Karney from any assault by the Irish Sea, where the great walls stood tall against the slings, rams, arrows, and even canon of the enemy, the banshees wail is known to be heard. Throughout the years, 'twas heard each night before the death of the master of the house. Sometimes, they say, she cried to help an elderly lord make his way to the great castle in the sky. Yet she may cry for all, and has cast her mournful wail into the air for many a Karney, master or no. Saddest still, was the wailing of the banshee the night before the English knight, Sir Barry Martin, burst in to kidnap the Lady Brianna. He made his way through their primitive sewer lines of the day, thinking the castle would fall if he but held her, for she was a rare beauty and beloved of Declan, master of Karney castle. Sir Martin made his way to the master's chambers, where he took the lady of the house, but Declan came upon him. Holding the Lady Brianna before Declan, Sir Martin slew her with his knife. In turn, Lord Declan rushed Sir Martin, and died himself upon the same knife—but not until he'd skewered Sir Martin through with his sword! It was a sad travesty of love and desire, for it was said Sir Martin coveted the Lady Brianna for himself, even as he swore to his men it was a way to breech the castle walls. While that left just a wee babe as heir, the castle stood, for Declan's mighty steward saw to it that the men fought on, rallying in their master's name. Aye, and when you hear the wind blow in now—like the high, crying wail of the banshee—they say you can see Brianna and her beloved. Karney's most famous ghosts are said to haunt the main tower. Through the years, they've been seen, Brianna and her Declan—separately, so they say, ever trying to reach one another and still stopped by the evil spirit of Sir Barry Martin!"

There was a gasp in the crowd. A pretty young woman turned to the young man at her side. "Oh! We're staying at Karney Castle!" she said. "And the main hall is just so hauntingly—haunted!"

"Ahha!" Gary said, smiling. "Hauntingly haunted! Aye, that it is!"

"We're staying there, too!" said an older woman.

"Ah, well, then, a number of you are lucky enough to be staying at the castle," Gary said. "Ten rooms and suites she lets out a night! Be sure to listen—and keep good watch. Maybe you'll see or hear a ghost—there are many more, of course. It's been a hard and vicious history, you know. Of course, you need not worry if ya be afraid of ghosts—while the main tower is most known to be haunted, Brianna tends to roam the halls of the second floor, and that's where only the family stays."

Devin felt a hand on her shoulder and heard a gentle whisper at her ear. "You, my love. Have you seen Brianna?"

It was Rocky—Craig Rockwell, the love of her life, seated by her side, their knees touching. And it was the kind of whisper that made her feel a sweet warmth sear through her, teasing her senses.

Rocky was her husband of three days.

But though she smiled, she didn't let the sensual tease streak as far as it might. Oddly enough, his question was serious; partially because they were staying in the old master's suite, since they were family, through marriage—Rocky, through her. Devin, because her mother's sister April had long ago married Seamus Karney, youngest brother of the Karney family.

His question was also partially serious because they were who they were themselves—and what they did for a living, rather strange work, really, because it was the kind that could never be left behind.

She and Rocky had been together since a bizarre series of murders in Salem. Devin owned a cottage there, inherited from a beloved great aunt. Rocky had grown up in nearby Marblehead and had—technically—been part of the case since he'd been in high school. As an adult, he'd also been part of the FBI—and then part of an elite unit within the FBI, the Krewe of Hunters.

Devin had been—and still was—a creator of children's books. But, she'd found herself part of the case as well, nearly a victim.

Somehow, in the midst of it all, they'd grown closer and closer— despite a somewhat hostile beginning. As they'd found their own lives in danger, they'd discovered that their natural physical attraction began to grow—and then they found they desperately loved one another and were, in many ways, a perfect match. Not perfect—nothing was perfect. But she loved Rocky and knew that he loved her with an equal passion and devotion.

That was, she thought, *as perfect as life could ever get.*

And, she'd discovered, she was a "just about as perfect as you were going to get" candidate for being a part of the Krewe as well. That had meant nearly half a year—pretty grueling for her, really—in the FBI Academy, but she'd come through and now she was very grateful.

Rocky had never told her what she should or shouldn't do. The choice had been hers, but she believed he was pleased with her position—it allowed them to work together, which was important since they traveled so much on cases. While the agency allowed marriages and relationships among employees, they usually had to be in different units. Not so with the Krewe. In the Krewe, relationships between agents aided in their pursuits.

While Devin had never known she'd wanted to be in law enforcement before the events in Salem, she felt now that she could never go back. She belonged in the Krewe because she did have a special talent—one shared by all those in the unit.

When they *chose* to be seen, she—like the others—had the ability to see the dead.

And speak with them.

It wasn't a talent she'd had since she'd been a child. It was one she had discovered when bodies had started piling up after she returned to live in Salem. The victim of a long ago persecution had found her, seeking help for those being murdered in the present in an age-old act of vengeance.

She still wrote her books, gaining ideas from her work. And being with the Krewe made her feel that she was using herself in the best way possible—helping those in need. She'd never wanted the world to be evil. And the world wasn't evil—just some people in it.

She did have to admit that her life had never seemed so complete. But, of course, that was mainly because she woke up each morning with Rocky at her side. And she knew that no matter how many years went by, she would love waking to his dark green eyes on her, even when his auburn hair grayed—or disappeared entirely. She loved Rocky— everything about him. He was one of the least self-conscious people she had ever met. He towered over her five-nine by a good six inches and was naturally lean but powerfully built, and yet totally oblivious to his appearance. Of course, he took his work very seriously and that meant time in a gym several days every week. Now, of course, she had to take to the gym every week herself.

Rocky was just much better at the discipline.

Better at every discipline, she thought dryly.

And also so compassionate, despite all that he'd seen in the world. When her cousin had called her nervously, begging her to come to Ireland, Rocky had been quick to tell Devin that yes, naturally, Adam Harrison and Jackson Crow—the founder and Director Special Agent of their unit, respectively—would give them leave to do so. And it had all worked out well, really, because they'd toyed with the idea of a wedding—neither wanted anything traditional, large, or extravagant—and they'd made some tentative plans, thinking they'd take time after and head for a destination like Bermuda.

They chose not to put off the wedding; in fact, they pushed it up a bit. And instead of Bermuda or the Caribbean, they headed to Ireland.

A working honeymoon might not be ideal. Still, they'd been living together for six months before they married, so it wasn't really what some saw as a traditional honeymoon anyway. And, St. Patrick's Day was March 17th, just three days away from their landing on the Emerald Isle that noon. Her cousin, Kelly Karney, had promised amazing festivities, despite the recent death of Kelly's uncle, Collum Karney—the real reason they had come.

A heart attack, plain and simple.

Then why was Collum discovered after the screeching, terrible howl of the banshee with the look of horror upon his face described by Brendan?

"They say," Gary the Ghost intoned, his voice rich and carrying across the fire, and yet low and husky as well, "that Castle Karney carries within her very stone the heart and blood of a people, the cries of their battles, the lament of those lost, indeed, the cry of dead and dying…and the banshee come to greet them. Ah, yes, she's proven herself secure. 'Castle Karney in Karney hands shall lie, 'til the moon goes dark by night and the banshee wails her last lament!' So said the brave Declan Karney, just as the steel of his enemy's blade struck his flesh!"

Devin turned to look up at the castle walls.

Castle Karney.

Covered in time, rugged as the cliffs she hugged, and… Even as

Devin looked at the great walls, it seemed that a shadow fell over them to embrace them, embrace Karney. A chill settled over her as she looked into the night, blinking. The shadow as dark and forbidding as the...

As the grave.

As Gary said, as old as time, and the caress of the banshee herself.

Chapter Two

"Devin?"

The grip of cold that had settled over Devin immediately broke; she felt Rocky's warmth and turned back to him.

"Hey, my love, forget me already?" Rocky asked softly. "Any ghosts yet?" His eyes, as darkly green as a forest in the campfire light, held concern.

"No," she whispered back and forced a smile. "But, of course, I have heard the story about Brianna and Declan before."

"No self-respecting castle would be complete without a tragic love story," Rocky said softly. "You're worried. It may all be fancy. Collum, from what I understand, was a very big man who loved red meat and ale and might well have been a prime candidate for a heart attack," he said gently.

She nodded, squeezing his hand. "We'll find out, won't we?"

She meant her words to be a statement. There was a question in them instead.

Rocky pulled her back against him. "We'll find the truth," he said with assurance. "And we'll see that Kelly is fine."

She nodded.

Tragically, Kelly's mother—Devin's Aunt April—had been killed in a car crash when Kelly had been ten and Devin just nine, but Seamus and Kelly and Devin's family had maintained a close and caring relationship, despite her death, and despite the fact that Seamus wasn't actually Devin's mother's brother but her brother-in-law.

Devin and Kelly had both been way too young to understand the difference in how a person was an aunt or an uncle—they just were.

Devin had always adored her uncle Seamus and even when she'd been older and known the difference, he'd been just as good as any blood relation as far as she was concerned. Seamus kept their young lives filled with wonderful tales at all times, many of them, naturally, about Castle Karney.

Devin's family had joined Seamus and Kelly once, when the girls had been young teens. Devin had met the two older Karney brothers, Collum and Brendan, at that time.

Collum, the oldest, had inherited the castle. He and Brendan had lived and worked there together—neither having married—and both discovered that in modern times, castles demanded a lot of love and elbow grease.

But neither Collum nor Brendan had procreated—which left Seamus Karney and then Kelly Karney to inherit the estate, a complicated state of affairs, or it might have been had Ireland not made many changes in the past decades and if Seamus had not seen to it that his daughter had carried dual citizenship from the time she was born.

Kelly had loved her Uncle Collum dearly—just as she loved her Uncle Brendan.

Devin loved Kelly and Seamus—and that was why they were there.

Brendan had called Seamus and asked that he and Kelly come to Ireland after the death of Collum.

He didn't like the way that Collum had died.

Not that anybody liked it when someone died, but Collum had died strangely, to say the least—in Brendan's opinion.

In a way, that seemed to make Gary's stories especially chilling.

They'd heard the banshee wailing at midnight, or so Brendan had told Seamus and Kelly.

And the following day, Collum had been found in the old master's chambers, sitting in one of the antique, high-backed, crimson chairs—eyes open in what was surely horror—just staring at the hearth.

A heart attack, the doctor had said. No nonsense, a heart attack.

And it might have been.

But Brendan hadn't thought it was right, not one bit. So Seamus and

Kelly had come. What they'd found when they'd arrived and all they'd been told had been enough to set the wheels in motion that had brought she and Rocky to where they were right now.

"We have to find the truth," Devin said, her voice low but passionate. "Kelly and Seamus are very precious to me. Of course, so far, we've not had much chance to see or speak with the living—much less, um, anyone else. All we've done is drop off our bags. We haven't even seen Kelly and Seamus yet. Just Brendan."

Kelly and her father had been down in the village when they'd arrived, at a dinner with a marketing friend who arranged for the creation and delivery of their special "Karney Castle" soaps and shampoo and conditioner, and all the little amenities that hotel guests liked to take with them.

After arriving in Dublin, going through customs, getting their rental car and making their way to Karney, Devin and Rocky had arrived at the castle just in time to be warmly greeted by Brendan, drop their bags, and head for Gary's Ghosties and Goblins night tour—at Brendan's insistence.

Devin had been there before, but Rocky was new to this wondrous part of the Emerald Isle, and the tour was a great way for him to get an intro, so Brendan told them. And Devin had been a "wee" little thing at the time she had been there.

Devin was pretty sure she'd been thirteen or fourteen when the family had come, and she'd been five-five or five-six by then, but to Brendan—a great bear of a man at about six-four—she supposed that was "wee."

Brendan had seen to it that she and Rocky had a chance for a quick look at the old master's suite where they'd be staying, time to freshen up and make sure they wouldn't mind where Kelly had wanted them to stay, and then head out.

Their room in the central tower was called the old master's suite because there was a new master's suite—created in the Victorian era with all the niceties that came with the more modern day. Collum—now dead and buried—had lived in the old suite; Brendan was in the new suite. Kelly and her father, Seamus, had rooms in the main tower as well, which was always reserved for family.

Only there wasn't much family anymore.

Tavish Karney—Kelly's grandfather—had been one of two boys;

Tavish's brother, Brian, twenty years his junior, had gone on to procreate late in life, leaving Kelly with two Irish second cousins, Aidan and Michael, close to her own age. When the cousins came to stay—they were due in late the next day, always there to celebrate St. Patrick's Day at the family castle—they were also housed in the main tower.

As Brendan had sadly told them, the family was down to himself, Seamus, Kelly, Aidan, and Michael. Not many left of a once great and mighty family. Family needed to be keepers of a great and historic castle. Of course, Ancient City Tourism was forever trying to buy them out, put a nightclub in the old castle, and shake everything up.

Brendan—as Collum before him—meant to keep Karney Castle in the Karney family. Devin knew that Seamus and Kelly felt just as passionately that their heritage must be preserved. Castle Karney deserved the best and while its place on the historic register might save it from destruction, it just might not be enough to keep it from becoming a gimmicky attraction.

"You're right; we've just arrived," Rocky told Devin softly, his words bringing her back from her thoughts. They were both seated cross-legged on the soft, rich green grass of the lawn area that surrounded the pit and the grating. Rocky took her hands, his eyes on Gary across the rising yellow flames of the fire between them. "And," he added, lowering his voice still further, "this is an excellent way for me to begin, to understand the lay of the land, so to speak." He hugged her more tightly to him, as if he was aware of the chill she'd felt earlier when looking up at the walls.

He was aware, of course. He was Rocky, intuitive—and much better at this than she, much more experienced.

"So then tonight," Gary announced, "eh, you've learned about the Tuatha Dé Danann, the great race of Irish supernatural kings and queens, gods and goddesses, if you will, those of the distant past, revered 'til the coming of Christianity! Ye've learned of Dearg-Due—an Irish female vampire known long before Bram Stoker—an Irishman, I might add—created Dracula. We've talked about our Irish headless horseman—the Dullahan. Many more, and of course, those well-known, our leprechauns and our banshees! I'm now Gary the Ghost, signing off, wishing you sweet dreams—and reminding you, of course, that gratuities are not at all necessary, but deeply appreciated."

"There's a man worthy of gratuities," Rocky said, coming to his feet and reaching down a hand to help Devin up to hers. He pulled her into his arms. "Love it here. So far, it's a great honeymoon," he told her, green eyes dancing.

"I'll make it up to you," Devin promised.

Rocky laughed. "I mean it—I love it. Who gets to stay in the haunted master's suite of a family-owned castle? Sit beneath a crystal moon and hear old-fashioned storytelling in such atmospheric conditions? Then again, who gets to bathe in a great old claw-foot tub like the one up in our room? Okay, maybe they have those other places, but it's pretty cool looking, don't you think?"

Devin grinned. "Definitely. Yes, we'll put that on the evening's agenda."

Rocky might have been about to say something a bit risqué, but Gary Duffy finished speaking with some of his other customers and came to shake hands with Rocky and smile at Devin.

"So?" he asked, sounding a bit anxious, looking from Rocky to Devin. "I hear you're the American cousin."

"I'm Kelly Karney's cousin, yes," Devin said.

"Lovely to meet you. Or meet you again. I think I saw you once before—when we would have both been kids," Gary said.

"Possibly—I was here once as a teenager," Devin said.

"And how do my tales match up with family lore?" Gary asked.

"Wonderfully," Devin assured him.

"The night was great," Rocky told him. "You're really entertaining. Certainly one of the best guides I've ever seen."

"Ah, now coming from an American, that is a great compliment," Gary said. He was an engaging man of medium build, in his late twenties, with a thatch of red hair, freckles, and a contagious grin. "I hear you're staying in Collum's old suite—the old master's suite."

"It's where my cousin has asked us to stay, yes," Devin said.

"I guess you're not the scared type then," Gary said. "No, you're not. To be honest, I looked you up. Krewe of Hunters, eh? You're FBI. I am a bit confused. Collum died of a heart attack. And the FBI has no jurisdiction here."

"Kelly is my cousin; we're here to be with her," Devin explained quickly.

"Ah, yes, of course," Gary said. "We're all hurting from the loss of Collum. St. Paddy's Day won't be the same without him, but—tradition. Time marches on and cares little for any one man, eh? Well, I'm curious, I must say. Some call you people the 'ghost unit.' Are you a ghost unit? Does the American government really believe in such a thing?"

"That question from a man who goes by the moniker 'Gary the Ghost,'" Rocky said lightly.

"I make my living telling such tales," Gary said. "And real history, too, of course—stranger and sadder than most ghost stories. But, alas! The world enjoys a good scare and luckily for me, Irish folk are full of fancy. I apologize again—I didn't mean to be rude. But...I am a historian and a curious type. Like I said, when Kelly told me that you were coming and that you were with the law in America, I looked you up."

"When we're working," Rocky said, "we investigate cases that have something unusual about them—something unexplained. We find the explanations. But, I assure you, I've never heard of a case of a ghost murdering a man as of yet."

"So, you've heard the suggestion that a ghost might have murdered old Collum?" Gary asked.

"Everyone seems to be edgy—with lots of talk about the banshee," Rocky told him.

"That's the rumor," Gary said. He shrugged. "Forgive me. I try to take Mondays and Tuesdays off, but I'm here seven days a week sometimes. I grew up beneath the great castle on the hill—loving it. The family is like my own and naturally, I know what's going on most the time. Sadly, Collum was like a bull—and his habits were not at all healthy. Dr. Kirkland said heart attack, and it's not much of a mystery. But, if you will. Come—let's head to the Karney Castle Pub. I'll buy you a beer. You can entertain me a bit with a few or your tales."

Rocky glanced at Devin. She realized that they'd both been looking forward to getting into the massive old bathtub—but they'd also planned on waiting to see Kelly and Seamus. It didn't seem at all a bad idea to spend the time waiting with the man who supposedly knew the history of the castle better than any other.

"We'll be doing the buying," Rocky said, "after such a night of entertainment. In fact, we'd love to buy you dinner, if it's available at this hour."

Gary grinned. "Tour ends at nine; dinner goes 'til ten. I'd be deciding on fish and chips or shepherd's pie as we walk!"

They did so. Some of the other members of Gary's tour group, those staying at the castle, walked in groups ahead of them. The massive gates at the great wall were open—permanently, now that hostile invaders were no longer expected—and led into a vast courtyard where vendors had been setting up for the coming festival days; their carts and stations were now dark, many covered in tarps.

The central tower—stonework built circa 1000 over original earthwork foundations founded around the year 300—stood before them with the north wing—built circa 1200—to the left and the south wing—built circa 1400—to the right. The Castle Pub was in the right wing with the floors above it containing a museum on the second floor, and storage and household items on the third floor and in the attic. The guest rooms were all in the north left wing. The main hall of the oldest part of the castle, the central tower, offered check-in, and a lobby area while still maintaining historical truth. The coat of arms of the Karney family held prominence over a great hearth that stretched twenty feet. The crest was surrounded by mounted weapons from swords and shields to dirks, staffs, and more. Two mannequins in full armor—one from the eleventh century and one from the sixteenth—stood guard at either side of the hearth. There was no counter—check-in was done at a seventh-century desk that sat discretely just inside the double doors to the main hall.

They entered through the main door. A note on the desk advised guests to "Ring if ye must; bear in mind 'tis late! Pub that-a way!"

They followed the sign to the pub.

It was charming, with lots of carved hardwood, many of the images at the six small booths those of creatures and beings from Irish myth and legend. A long bar offered ten different beers on tap and a sign on the bar offered the pub's limited menu of bangers and mash, shepherd's pie, fish and chips, vegetarian salad, and vegan salad.

There was an especially atmospheric little cover of benches in the pub, right where the old family chapel—now deconsecrated—had once been; the Karney family had worshipped at St. Patrick's of the Village for centuries now. Double wood doors—always open—led to the little section and beautiful stained glass windows that looked out. A small altar had once stood before those windows; now they offered a tinted and fantastic view of the courtyard. A small door near the great stained glass window was roped off; Devin knew that it led down into the castle's catacombs, basement—and one time dungeon.

Once a year, the Karney family had a cleaning company head down to sweep out the spider webs and then they would allow tour groups down. The liability for doing it more than once a year was just too high.

Above ground, however, the tiny old chapel area was charming.

They chose a table there.

A friendly waitress with a white peasant blouse, ankle-length skirt, and wreath around her head came their way after tending to a group ahead of them. A lone, busy bartender stood behind the long bar pouring a number of beers at once, worthy of a reality show.

Devin noticed that little had changed since she had been to Castle Karney when she'd been about thirteen.

"Ah, Gary! So ye've tricked some new friends into dinner again!" the waitress said.

"Indeed, but these are special friends, Siobhan!" Gary said.

"Oh?" Siobhan asked, smiling, and waiting.

"I'm Kelly Karney's cousin, Devin Lyle," Devin said. "Nice to meet you, Siobhan. And this is my husband, Craig Rockwell."

"Ah, very American, you keeping your name, eh?" Siobhan asked, grinning. "I'm Siobhan McFarley. A pleasure to meet you both!" She frowned. "Sorry about the latest troubles in the family, eh?"

"You mean Collum's death?" Devin asked.

"Aye, that I do," Siobhan said, and shivered visibly. "Scary, now, weren't it? I heard it, you know, the banshee's cry the night before. You heard it, too, right, Gary?"

"Ah, now, luv, that's nonsense!" Gary said. "I heard nothing—but then, I was away from the castle that night. Finished me tour and headed on home, down in the village. I heard nothing."

"We'd just cleaned up here—closes at ten, but we're known to cheat a bit on the side of the patron, you know, so it's closer to eleven when we close the door," Siobhan said. "At twelve—it was twelve exactly—I heard the sound of her wailing away! I tell you, the goose bumps rose all over me. Creepiest sound I ever did hear."

"Wolves," Gary said. "They cry from the forest sometimes, you know." He looked at Rocky and Devin. "Beyond the road here, and away from the sea, there's a great forest. You must have passed it on your way."

"We did, indeed," Rocky said. "But, if the wolves were howling that night, wouldn't you have heard them in the village as well?"

"Not if you're sleeping, which I must have been," Gary said. He looked at Siobhan with a teasing eye. "Some of us work around here."

"Aye, and that would be me!" Siobhan protested. "Not running my mouth as if I'd kissed the Blarney Stone like a lover! Hauling pints here and there and what have you for hours on end!"

"Teasing, me luv, but I must have been asleep," Gary said. "Two weeks ago tonight; Collum has been in his grave but ten days now."

"Glad I am that you're here for Kelly, for she's a sweetheart, if ever there was one," Siobhan told Devin. "Anyway, now, some of your last tour is here, Gary, and it's just me and Allen at the bar, so what will you have?"

Devin and Rocky decided to try different local beers; she ordered the shepherd's pie and he ordered the bangers and mash. Gary decided on the fish and chips.

"Just give the cook the order, Siobhan, I'll bring them to meet Allen at the bar and get the beers," Gary said.

"Thank you!" Siobhan said, relieved. She hurried on.

Gary rose and Devin and Rocky did the same. "Allen Fitzhugh!" Gary said, approaching the bar.

The young man looked up briefly—he was pouring a Guinness with care, taking the time warranted of the rich, dark Irish beer.

He smiled at them, a man with slightly unruly amber-colored hair with amber eyes to match. His shirtsleeves were rolled up as he worked. He was of medium height and build, attractive with his quick, curious, and welcoming grin.

"Kelly's cousin, Devin Lyle, and her husband, Rocky Rockwell."

Allen paused long enough to wipe his hand on a broad green apron before shaking hands across the hardwood bar.

"Rocky Rockwell?" Allen asked.

"Craig Rockwell. If your last name is Rockwell, you just become Rocky, I guess," Rocky said.

"Good to have you," he said. "American pragmatism will be welcome!" he said. He added more somberly, "An American cousin for our Kelly will be good, too."

"We're delighted to be here," Devin said.

"It was strange, the night old Collum died," Allen said, still surveying them solemnly. "I've never heard anything like that wail—the banshee's wail. Never. I'd heard that expression about the hair standing up on the back of the neck—never had it happen before that night!"

"It must have been very eerie," Devin said.

"Banshee, banshee, banshee," Gary said, shaking his head. "We've come up so our American cousins could meet you—and to help our Siobhan. So, sir, if you don't mind?"

"What's your pleasure?" Allen asked him.

Gary rolled off their beer orders and Allen, with a delightful brogue as well, described each in a manner to equal that of the best wine steward or sommelier to be found.

They thanked him and returned to the table.

Gary leaned toward them across the booth. "Everyone here is unnerved. Doc Kirkland says it's just the way a man looks when he's died of a heart attack. But—as you realize from the tales I weave—we are a fanciful people. The housekeeping staff, pub staff—all are certain now that the banshee wailed and that the death ghost came and met old Collum face to face. And thus he died—staring out in horror, as if he'd seen some beastie. Collum was a good man; they need to honor him and let him rest in peace."

As he spoke, Devin looked toward the door.

Kelly was back.

Her cousin was a beautiful young woman with rich, flowing, red hair, and fine, delicate features. She was tiny—a mere five-two. A slight spattering of freckles across her nose added to something of her gamine-like appeal. She and Devin didn't look much like cousins—Devin stood over Kelly a solid seven inches, her hair was nearly black to Kelly's true red, and her eyes were blue while Kelly's were a lovely, gold-studded hazel.

"Devin!" she cried with delight, finding her seated in the booth. She rushed over, speaking as she did so. "I'm so sorry, but our business here is with friends, and meetings and all can go to all hours. I never thought that we'd be so late! But Uncle Brendan said he'd sent you out on the tour."

Devin was out of the booth to hug her before she reached the table.

"We're fine—just fine," Devin said.

Kelly glanced affectionately at Gary with a quick smile. "I figured you'd be entertained, but I was sure we'd be back before it ended."

Devin thought that she felt her cousin trembling, despite her words and manner.

Rocky slid from the booth to meet Kelly, and Gary rose as well.

"I hope you were good!" Kelly teased Gary.

"Luv, I did my best!" Gary told her.

"We have been in excellent hands—Brendan was completely welcoming and Gary is a great guide," Devin said quickly. "And, of course, Kelly, this is Rocky—or Craig Rockwell, my husband."

"Wonderful to meet you, wonderful, and thank you—thank you so much for coming!" Kelly said.

"Of course. It's beautiful and quite historic, and Gary is full of fascinating information," Rocky assured her. "Join us, can you? Or should we be joining you, Kelly, and saying hello to your father?"

"Yes! Should I say hello to Uncle Seamus?" Devin asked.

"He's headed on to bed," Kelly told her. She smiled. "He thought you two would be in bed already for the night—you are newlyweds. But, I knew you'd wait up to see me," she added, smiling at first and then growing a little anxious. "Are you all right? Are you sure you're all right—in that suite? Collum did die there," she added softly.

"Kelly, I'm sure many people have died there through the centuries," Rocky said pleasantly. "We'll be okay. From everything I've heard, Collum was a fine man, and I'm honored to be staying in his chambers."

"Of course—they're ghost hunters!" Gary said cheerfully. "So you want them in that room specifically, don't you?"

Kelly flushed a bright red color. "I don't...I mean...I wish I did know the truth. There's so much rumor going around."

"Kelly," Gary said softly. Watching him, Devin thought that the man really cared about her cousin. "It's rumor—just rumor. People have to talk when someone like Collum dies. It's sad—because he was a great guy. But, there's no conspiracy, no curse, no reason other than that his heart had taken a beating."

"I know, I know," Kelly said. "Still." She gave herself a physical shake and smiled brightly. "So, here's hoping you like St. Patrick's Day. Did you know that the Americans were the ones who really turned it from a solemn holy day into a big celebration? Here, there was always a procession. A church procession. And music, and wailing, and all that. But, now, we have the dancers from the church, Ren fest vendors, parades, and all. It will be great."

Kelly greeted Siobhan when the waitress came with their food, ordered a beer, and talked as they ate. When it was time to go, she insisted it was all on the house—or the castle, as it was—but Rocky insisted on paying. After all, they'd invited Gary to dinner.

Gary bid them good-bye and headed out to the car park in the courtyard, leaving Kelly standing with Devin and Rocky in the great hall.

"I'm so scared!" she admitted.

"Kelly, why?" Devin asked. "Rocky and I haven't had much time yet to ask any questions, see the M.E., or look around, but it truly sounds as if your uncle died of natural causes. Gary certainly seems to think so."

"There's just something, something different," Kelly said. "All I can say is I feel it, Devin."

"What do you feel?" Rocky asked her.

Kelly looked from Rocky to Devin.

"Something menacing...something dark and terrible and evil. Like the prophecy," she said.

"What prophecy?" Rocky demanded.

"You're kidding!" Devin said.

"What prophecy?" Rocky repeated.

Devin sighed and explained. "Castle Karney in Karney hands shall lie, 'til the moon goes dark by night and the banshee wails her last lament," she quoted.

"And what is that from?" Rocky demanded. "It's what Gary the Ghost quoted during the tour, right?"

"Declan Karney," Devin said, still looking at her cousin with sympathy. "He supposedly said those words before impaling himself on Sir Barry Martin's sword after his wife, Brianna, was slain. Kelly! He meant that he'd die—which he did—before letting any man take Karney Castle from the Karney family. There's nothing about the family dying out in that prophecy. He meant it as a battle cry—a cry of revenge, a promise that he'd kill his enemy—which he also did."

"I'm just glad that you're here," Kelly said. She studied Devin anxiously. "I know you have had trouble...but you're the strong cousin and you're..." she paused to look at Rocky, "...you're tough! And something is going on here. I know it. I've—I've seen..."

"Seen what?" Devin prodded her.

"The black shadows," Kelly said.

"What?" Devin asked. Her voice came out sharp. Too sharp.

But, Kelly hadn't noticed.

"Strange black shadows. They seem to watch us from corners when the light is dim, as if they're waiting for the right moment, ready to encompass us...devour us. I think that they're the death ghosts. The banshees!" she said, her eyes solemnly on Devin's. "You'll see. Wait, watch, and listen. Death is here," she whispered. And then she added, "Oh, Devin! I believe that death itself now resides here! You'll know—you'll know when you hear the banshee wail!"

Chapter Three

Rocky lay awake in the massive bed in the old master's room.

The mattress was new, brand new. Apparently, Kelly had tried her best with just a few days in which to work to make the room fresh and new without compromising the integrity of the history to be found within it. The bed itself was circa 1400 with four massive carved posters, a headboard with the family crest deeply etched into it, and tapestry for the canopy and drapes. A hearth—not as long as that to be found in the great hall downstairs but a good seven feet or so—was on the opposite wall while a standing mirror, wardrobes, and a hardwood table and chair set on the rug before the hearth completed the room. It was intriguing to lie on the bed and wonder about the battle plans made at the table, the compromises wrangled out, and the regular day-to-day business of running such an estate.

The chairs at the table were large and antique—upholstered in red velvet. Collum Karney had died in one, Rocky knew. There were four of them—two at the table, two drawn up on either side of the hearth. He believed that Collum had been sitting in the chair at the left of the hearth, perhaps watching a fire burn as it swept away the continual chill of such a castle. Even in the midst of summer, Devin had told him, the rain could come strong and hard and the wind, picking up off the coast, could blow fiercely.

Fires were welcome.

One burned gently now. He speculated on the chair and the hearth for a moment, wondering about Collum and what might have come into the room to scare such a strong and stalwart giant of a man.

Naturally, he'd fully inspected the master's chambers. There was a door to the nursery, now set up as a dressing room. Another door led to a library which had a door to the hallway as well. He hadn't found any tunnels or chambers from which someone hidden might have jumped out. As yet.

Of course, someone could have entered freely from the hallway. There were massive bolts on the doors, but that didn't mean that Collum had bolted the door to the hallway on the night he had died. Since a housekeeper had found him in the morning, he apparently had not bolted his door.

When they first arrived, he'd stood silently in the center of the room and waited, listening, *feeling*.

But, he'd sensed no presence of the dead.

Devin, doing the same, had shaken her head. Then she'd smiled. "It's never that easy, is it? Can't just say, 'Hey! Collum, what happened to you?'"

"Maybe—but looks like we'll have to ask questions to get answers," Rocky had told her.

She'd grinned. "Well at least it's nice to be alone. Really alone!"

"For now, yes," he'd said softly, grinning as well.

And then she'd been in his arms.

It was their honeymoon.

There was the tub as well. The wonderful claw-foot tub just behind the dividing wall in the bath where plumbing had finally been added in the 1950s. Thankfully, they had built and "plumbed" around the original, with its elegant racks and the big iron grates for heating water. They were no longer needed to heat the water, but they remained—charming with their tie to the medieval past.

Yes, it had been wonderful...

And it was still *wonderful* to lie beside his wife. *Wife*. He loved the word, and loved it because he could use it now—and because Devin was his wife. He remembered the first time he had seen her, standing in the center of the road at night, raven's hair flying around her head and beautiful face, as if she were a mystical goddess sent down to rule the earth. Of course, the circumstances hadn't been that good—she'd just found a dead girl. And in getting to know Devin—in falling in love with her—he'd nearly lost her. The case had been one, however, that had extended over years, plagued him and haunted him since he'd been in high school. But they'd found the truth, *survived the truth*—and set the past to rest. Afterward, Devin had decided that she didn't want to sit on the sidelines, that she had everything that it took to join in their ranks—and she'd done so.

They hadn't wanted a big wedding. Just their closest associates—Krewe members—and their families up from the warm climes where they'd retired. Devin's folks believed she was just visiting Ireland to support Kelly—and that it was a lovely honeymoon option. That was best.

And almost true.

Up on an elbow, he studied Devin. Her back was to him—long and sleek and provocative. The covers came just below her hip at an angle and it was almost as if he were looking at an artist's rendering of a stunning woman in an elegant repose. She was sleeping soundly. He really shouldn't wake her. It was nearing midnight.

They'd already had an incredible time playing in the massive claw-foot tub. He could close his eyes and smile and picture her sitting across from him in a swell of bubbles, laughing as they used their toes to investigate and stroke one another, until she'd come into his arms and they'd slid and laughed and made love in the heat and the bubbles and the steam rising around them.

But now, the clock hadn't quite struck midnight yet.

Still, cruel to wake her…

Maybe he'd just touch. With a feather-light touch, he drew his fingertip down the sleek and sensual line of her back and spine, just to the place where the sheet hid the rise of her hip. Once…and twice…

And then she turned to him with her brilliant blue eyes, a smile curving her lips, and he knew that she had only been drowsing and that she'd felt his first touch and was laughing inside until she'd decided on mercy.

She rolled into his arms, burying her head against his chest and delivering kisses against his flesh. He was instantly aroused, aware that his every muscle seemed to twitch, that she could awake a fire in him instantly, and that she could tear at his heart with a whisper or a word. He felt her move low against him, felt her hair fall upon him like caresses in silk and his arms wrapped around her as he groaned and then pulled her up to him, meeting her mouth with his own with desire and hunger and love. He meant to play, to tease, to worship the pure beauty of her form, and yet the fire burned so quickly that she smiled as she straddled and set atop him, until they rolled again, entwined, and lay side by side, then rolled again, moving, writhing, making love, laughing breathlessly at awkward positions, their laughter fading as urgency prevailed until they climaxed almost simultaneously and fell beside one another—panting for breath.

Then she curled into his arms again. She whispered that she loved him, more than she had ever imagined possible. He returned the words.

"I love you more than life itself," he vowed.

For a moment, she stared down at him and the solemnity of his words seemed to encase them as if they were one.

"I love your eyes," he told her.

"My eyes?" she asked.

"Oh, yes."

"I was thinking of other things I love about you right now," she said, laughing. And then she abruptly jerked.

Somewhere in the castle, a clock was striking midnight. The sound seemed to reverberate through the stones in the walls.

"Amazing the Karney family has survived so long!" Rocky said, laughing. "How the hell did they ever sleep?"

Devin started to smile again, but then froze.

He did, too.

Along with the sound of the great clock striking midnight, there was another sound.

It was like a cry on the wind, a wolf's howl, a screaming lament. It was as if the wind roared and the sea churned and all came together in a mighty crescendo.

It was a sound unlike anything Rocky had ever heard before, and looking up at his wife, like a fantastic character of fantasy herself, blue eyes diamond bright and wide, black hair a fan about her pale flesh, Devin spoke softly.

"The banshee," she said.

Chapter Four

Breakfast was in the pub. It was part of the "bed and breakfast" aspect of the castle. The "pub" didn't turn into a "pub" until 11:30 a.m. It was then when it opened not just to those staying at the castle, but to visitors staying at other B&Bs or hotels or guest houses in the village.

Some of those staying at the castle hadn't heard the clock or the strange wailing sound that had seemed to shake the very stone. Some had, and most of them stopped by the booth where Devin ate with Rocky, Kelly, Seamus, and Brendan. Some were regulars for St. Paddy's at Karney and had known Collum. They offered their sympathy to the family.

And then asked about the wailing sound that had shaken the castle at midnight.

"Ethereal—not of this earth!" and elderly man said.

Devin saw a stricken look in Kelly's eyes and answered quickly. "Ah, well, we heard it, so it was real and of this earth!" she said lightly.

"It's the sound of the wind when it strikes against the cliffs below on certain nights," Seamus explained.

"Hmph!" one woman told them. "It certainly gives credence to those tales told by Gary the Ghost!"

"Wicked cool!" said their teenaged daughter. And the two smiled and chatted and they walked on to their own table.

"' Wicked cool?'" Brendan asked.

"Aye, brother!" Seamus said, nodding. "They must be from New England. It's an expression used there. Ask me niece, Devin there!" he said, lifting his coffee cup to her. "She's a wicked lovely creature, she is!"

"That's kind, Uncle Seamus. Thank you," Devin said.

"Wicked cool," Brendan repeated. "Wicked lovely. I like it!"

"But do you believe it?" Rocky asked him quietly.

"That Devin is a wicked lovely creature? Indeed, I do!" Brendan said lightly.

"Thank you, again Brendan, but that's not what he means," Devin said, smiling gently.

Brendan was still and thoughtful for a minute and then he looked at Rocky. "I don't know," he said quietly. "The sound came the night before the morning the housekeeper found Collum dead."

Kelly reached out a hand to cover her uncle's.

"It is the wind tearing against the cliffs, Uncle. I know it," Kelly said. She didn't believe it at all, Devin knew. She just wanted her father and her uncle to believe that she wasn't unnerved or frightened.

"Either that," Rocky said, "or someone's mechanical idea of a prank."

"Mechanical?" Seamus asked.

Seamus, like Brendan—and as Collum had been—was a big man, broad-shouldered, tall, and with a full head of snow-white hair. They had been built ruggedly, Seamus had told Devin once, because rugged was their heritage. Maybe because they hadn't come from the city, but they'd all been born at Castle Karney, a place as wild as the jagged cliffs that led to the tempest of the Irish Sea.

They'd come from a long line of warriors, he'd once told her proudly—except that now, of course, he prayed for nothing but peace around him, in Ireland, and about the whole of the world.

"I've been thinking about the sound all night," Rocky told them. "I got up and took a look around the tower—it really might be some kind of mechanism."

"Looking around the tower," Brendan said. "So that's what you were doing after you and Devin came to my room and you left Devin there to guard me through the night 'til you returned!"

"I just kept you company," Devin said.

"And nothing happened, thank the good Lord!" Seamus said, crossing himself.

"And had the banshee been real…" Devin murmured.

"Bizarre that the sound came directly at midnight. Nature isn't good at planning noises at a precise time. Anyway—it remains to be seen," Rocky said.

Brendan looked at Rocky and nodded sagely. "Ye're here to investigate, and that's a fact. Honeymoon, my arse!" he added, looking reproachfully at Seamus.

"Ach, now, brother. 'Twas Kelly who called on the two of them now," Seamus protested.

"It is our honeymoon. Really," Devin told him. "But, of course, it's true. What we do is investigate."

"There's nothing like meeting the family," Rocky said politely, causing them all to laugh.

"Ah, yes, meet the family!" Brendan said.

"I mean it; it's wonderful to be here," Rocky said.

"You're a good niece!" Seamus told Devin. "And you," he added, nodding to Rocky, "you seem to be a fine man for my niece."

"Thank you," Rocky said.

"Investigate with my sincere blessing!" Brendan said. "I knew my brother well. I never saw such a look on his face. Something odd is definitely afoot, and not even Gary the Ghost really believes in the tales he tells. We love them all, we do. We love our ghosts—and our pixies and leprechauns and so on. But…something is afoot." He offered them a grim smile. "*Wickedly* afoot! Collum, just in ground not quite a full two weeks, visitors a-flooding the place, and the festival on the way. We've got to know. It would be a hard enough thing, losing m'brother, as it were. But, to wonder like this…'tis painful."

"I'm so, so sorry, Brendan!" Devin said.

She noticed the way he looked over at Kelly—as if seeing her there pained him as well.

And then she realized that he was worried about her.

"You and Kelly and Uncle Seamus are going to be fine," Devin said, determined.

He quickly glanced her way, looked down and nodded.

"Uncle Brendan tried to get me to go home," Kelly said. "He called us for the funeral and to come—and since, he's tried to make me go back to the States."

"I shouldn't have had you here," Brendan told Kelly and Seamus.

"Collum was my brother, too, Brendan," Seamus said. "Just because I'm an American now, doesn't mean he wasn't my brother. Or," he added softly, "that I'm not still Irish or that Kelly escapes that, either."

"Kelly escapes that?" Rocky said, looking perplexed. "I've some Irish in my background—and I love it," he said.

Devin shook her head. "You're talking about the prophecy—which does not say that something will happen to every Karney. Stop it. We'll find out if something is or isn't going on. If it is, I don't believe it's the banshee. Is there anyone who held a grudge against Collum or the family?"

"Something is going on," Kelly said flatly, looking hard at Devin. "You heard the banshee wail."

"We heard something," Rocky said firmly. "A banshee? That's questionable."

"You don't have any belief in our myths, legends, and ways?" Brendan asked.

"Oh, I do. I just don't believe that what we heard was a banshee," Rocky said.

"You found something?" Seamus asked him.

Rocky shook his head. "No, but I didn't go banging on anyone's doors and I can't say that I know the castle well enough to really explore."

"We can fix that!" Kelly said excitedly. "I mean, sounds bizarre, but it is our castle—you can go wherever you choose!"

"Thank you. I'd like to make a few calls this morning, and then I'd very much enjoy a private tour by one of the masters—or the mistress—of the castle," Rocky said.

"What will you do first?" Seamus asked, looking at Rocky. Devin lowered her head, not offended that Rocky would be their go-to man—and not her. Her mother had always told her that Ireland was now racing toward a world beyond discrimination with all haste, but when her mom had been young, there had been separate rooms in most pubs for women.

Sexual discrimination died hard in many a place—even in the States, she knew. But, in the Republic of Ireland, divorce had only been legal since 1997, which, of course, wasn't really discriminate on either side—just hell for people who discovered they simply couldn't live together. Old ways died hard, especially in a small village like Karney.

"We're going to see your doctor and coroner," Rocky said. "And talk to him about Collum's death."

Brendan sniffed. "He acts all big shot—he's a country doctor, and that's a fact—I don't care about all his high-falutin' medical degrees. He's a doctor, a fair one, but it's just that we're small here, and so, he's the coroner, too."

"But, he has a solid medical degree, right?" Rocky asked.

"He has medical degrees," Brendan said. "Went to school in Dublin—and over at Oxford. And we have a sheriff and a deputy sheriff, too, but, seems to me, they all want the obvious and that's it."

"Brendan, I know you've been asked, but tell me what happened the day before Collum died, and then when you discovered his body," Devin said.

"Ah, the day before," Brendan murmured, drumming his fingers on the table. "We'd been to the church—you know our church has a relic, a bit of bone, said to have belonged to Saint Patrick himself?" he asked, distracted by the idea and smiling.

"That's—great," Devin said, not sure how to respond.

He nodded. "And, as you know, I think, for years and years—centuries even—St. Patrick's Day was mainly a holy day here. Parades and celebrations and all have become part of the festivities in later years. So, of course, we're traditional here. Early in the day, at least. There's a fine parade in the village with Father Flannery carrying the cross and a host of his altar boys walking along, the choir singing in their place and all. We'd been to see the good Father due to all that, plotting the parade course and all. And we have a big show out here—just outside the walls, where the old fire pit is—with dancers and singers from St. Patrick's of the Village. He's a fine fellow, Father Flannery, he is. Anyway, so we met with him. Came back, reviewed the list of vendors who we've given space to within the walls for the fest—it will start tomorrow and go through St. Paddy's—and then I went to pay bills and Collum spent time arguing with the Internet people. We ate dinner together at the pub. Collum went up to his room and I stayed down here talking with some guest, filling in some historical gaps, that kind of thing. Didn't see him again until I saw him—dead. The housekeeper was in his room, screaming her head off. I came running and saw what she saw. Called the emergency number and they alerted the sheriff and Dr. Kirkland. They told me to try to resuscitate—and I would have tried, God help me, he was my brother—but he was dead. Stone cold dead."

"You couldn't have revived him," Rocky said.

"No," Brendan said softly, looking into space. He shrugged. "The central tower was alive with activity, official cars coming and going—and the hearse, coming and going." His eyes fell directly on Rocky's again. "I just want the truth—and justice for Collum. And…safety. Safety for Castle Karney." He hesitated again. "For my brother and myself, and most importantly, for Kelly. If there's something out there, 'tis better to know. And…"

"And?" Devin prompted.

"If it was the banshee, and it was me she wailed for last midnight, then see to it that you get yourselves and Seamus and Kelly out of here as quick as possible," Brendan told him.

Rocky nodded, meeting Brendan's eyes. "There's one thing I need for you to do today," he told them firmly, looking from Kelly to Brendan to Seamus, who all sat across the booth from them.

"What's that?" Kelly asked.

"Stay together—go nowhere alone. Be in the public eye, if possible. Can you promise to do that for me?" Rocky asked.

"As you wish," Brendan said.

He looked then, Devin thought, like a lord of the castle of old. Strong, judicial, fair.

And yet…

Convinced of his own power as well.

"Seriously, Brendan, you three stay together. Do not be alone," Devin told him.

"Of course, lass. As you say," Brendan told her. "And what then? Will the two of you be staying with an old man in his chambers night after night?"

"If that's what it takes," Rocky said firmly.

"On your honeymoon?" Brendan asked.

Rocky laughed.

He and Devin looked at one another.

"If that's what it takes," they said in unison.

Chapter Five

The village was charming.

There was one main road edged by buildings in soft shades of beige and taupe with thatched roofs. Most were entered directly from the road—called Karney Lane. There were winding streets that wove at odd angles off into lightly rolling land beyond and those, too, were filled with homes and businesses. They stretched out into the distance until the houses and buildings became further and further apart and rich, green farmland where sheep and cattle grazed was reached.

The church and the village hall were at the center of Karney Lane, and Dr. Kirkland's office was just two buildings down from the church.

The receptionist who met them at the front was a thin-lipped, lean, and dour woman; she wanted to know their business and was disgruntled that they didn't have an appointment.

Devin was about to get angry; Rocky brought out the charm.

She finally said that she'd check with Dr. Kirkland, but she wanted them to know, he was weary of hearing that a banshee had killed Collum Karney.

Devin had been expecting a man in his fifties, perhaps, white-haired and typical of a charming country village. After meeting his receptionist, she thought he might be an old soldier—as rigid and grumpy as his receptionist.

She was mistaken.

Dr. Kirkland was a good-looking man in his thirties or early forties—polite and mystified, but happy to give them a few minutes of his time.

"American reason here, I hope!" he said.

"We hope it's reason," Rocky said. "But, of course, we're here with the question you've surely answered a dozen times. Are you certain that it was a heart attack? You performed an autopsy?"

"Ach!" Kirkland said, shaking his head with weary impatience. "Everyone wants to make something of nothing. Am I certain? Collum Karney died of a heart attack, plain and simple. I'd been telling him to watch the red meat and start more moving about for years. His poor arteries! They were as clogged as could be."

"I heard he died with a look of horror on his face," Devin told Kirkland.

Kirkland waved a hand in the air. "All the talk about ghosts and banshees a-wailing! Good lord, 'tis charming we have our legends and history." He paused for a moment to grin at her. "And a history that pretty much so—as you Americans might say—sucks with invasions and battling, but, 'tis nonsense that he was frightened to death by a vengeful ghost! Why would a ghost seek vengeance on old Collum—a descendant?"

"Yes, why would one?" Rocky said. "But, did you perform an autopsy?"

Kirkland stiffened at that. "I did not cut into the man. I'd been treating him for years, warning him for years. I know a heart attack when I see one."

"Heart attacks can be brought on," Rocky said.

"You mean that sound? Wolves or the wind," Kirkland said, disgusted. "And you think a man like Collum Karney would be frightened by the sound? You dinna know the man. He was a giant of a fellow—with clogged arteries!"

We're going to get nothing from him, Devin thought. And they didn't have the authority to demand an autopsy.

Brendan Karney, however, did.

Rocky smiled pleasantly and thanked Kirkland for his time.

"A pleasure, and welcome to the village. Everyone comes to Dublin—it's nice you've come further," Kirkland said. "We do get a fair amount of visitors now, because of the castle. We'd have more—if the Karney family allowed for a themed nightclub or something of the like. I'm afraid they're a wee bit too filled with Karney pride—nothing that might mar their great history. It is wonderful history in a land invaded one time too many. Ah, forgive me, one of you is a relative, right?"

Devin explained her family connection and Kirkland told them, "How fine! Well, as I was saying, we're on the map now—what with the castle being a select destination these years. But, still, the castle, she has only ten rooms for let, and it's the tourist eager to learn history who comes rather than the tourist longing for a few nights at the Temple Bar pub section in Dublin. Spicing it up to current times might help, don't you think?"

He didn't really want an answer—he seemed to assume that since they were Americans, they naturally agreed.

"We do get the tourist eager to see a ghostie or two. Naturally, all is booked now," he added. "Everyone is Irish on St. Patrick's Day, eh? Used to be, we were more solemn here—honoring a saint in a religious manner. But, we've taken note from our American cousins and we're all festive these days—does a lot for tourist dollars."

"Aw, well, Dr. Kirkland, the estimate is that thirty-five million Americans are mainly of Irish descent—and that worldwide, it's eighty million. That's a lot of people who really are Irish in a way," Devin told him.

"Yes, you're right. Everyone is Irish on St. Patrick's Day," Kirkland said.

"Do you know of anyone who would have wished ill for Collum Karney?" Devin asked.

"Wished ill?" Kirkland said.

"Wanted him dead," Rocky said flatly.

"Why would anyone? He was a fine fellow—beloved by employees and visitors. Many came back year after year—not just for the castle, but because Collum and Brendan made sure that each stay was like coming home," Kirkland said.

"I imagine the castle is worth a small fortune," Rocky said.

"The property, the castle…yes. But after Collum there would be Brendan to inherit—and after Brendan, Seamus, then Kelly. Then there are still two cousins!" Kirkland said.

"That would be a lot of heart attacks," Devin murmured.

"And if they all died, the property would go to the Irish Republic," Kirkland told them. "There's no reason for any living soul to have killed the man," he finished and then added quickly, "If you don't mind, we're a small village, but I am the only doctor 'til one reaches the outskirts of

Dublin."

"Of course, of course, and thank you," Rocky told him.

"What do you think?" Devin asked Rocky after they bid Dr. Kirkland—and his sour receptionist—good-bye.

"I think there should have been an autopsy," Rocky said.

"But, do you think that Collum was frightened to death?"

"Not by any howling of the wind or banshee wail," Rocky said. "But—we both heard that noise last night. It did rip right through the castle. And I do believe that Brendan might have died last night—except that we disrupted the killer's plan by heading to his room."

"But how—or by who?" Devin asked. "And since there are more people to inherit and the property would just go to the state, why would anyone kill him?"

"Maybe someone is more eager to sell than Brendan?"

"Not Seamus—not Kelly!" Devin said with certainty.

"If we want certainty, we need an autopsy," Rocky said.

"We'll have to ask Brendan and Seamus and Kelly," Devin murmured. "And—wow. Digging up a loved one. Of course, we'll have to have county authority."

"It can be done. I wouldn't want the autopsy here. Not unless we get Kat in," Rocky said thoughtfully.

He was referring to Special Agent Kat Sokolov, Krewe member and medical examiner. Devin wasn't sure where Kat was assigned now, if she was in the Virginia Krewe offices or out on a case. But the idea appealed to her. Kat's significant other was Will Chan—one time magician, photographer, and computer genius—now a Krewe member, too.

"Tricky," Devin noted. "We're going to have to convince someone to dig up a dead man a reputable doctor signed off on as far as the death certificate—and convince him that we should have an American FBI doctor in to make sure it was all done right."

"Life, my love, is tricky!" he reminded her. He paused in the street, staring down at her, and she suddenly wished that they had come for nothing more than their honeymoon. The Village of Karney was charming and beautiful. She could easily see forgetting what they did— and doing nothing but taking hikes up the cliffs, shopping in the quaint stores, enjoying a romantic meal or two in one of the small and intimate restaurants—and, of course, spending hours in the canopied master bed or giant claw-foot tub.

"Do you want to visit the sheriff?" Devin asked.

He smiled.

Devin's mind was on business.

"I don't think we're going to get any more from him than we got from the good doctor, Kirkland," he told her. "I want to explore the castle. That wasn't a banshee. Someone there is playing games—games that intend to leave one victor and a field of dead. And," he added, "we will need to speak with Brendan and see about an autopsy for Collum."

She nodded, looking unhappy. Although Devin had only met Brendan once before, she certainly cared about him—because she loved Uncle Seamus and Kelly. And she wasn't happy about making circumstances worse for them.

Then again, they were there because Brendan was no fool, and while legend and so-called prophecies might play at the back of his mind, he suspected something very real rather than imaginary.

"Let's go on to the castle then," she said.

They started along the road, coming to the church and the rolling graveyard.

St. Patrick's of the Village wasn't grand in the way that great cathedrals were—it was still beautiful and an attraction in itself. Rocky had listened to Gary the Ghost's history lesson on the church and read a number of the plaques on the old stone walls as well. There had been a church on this location since the fifth century; the church had been built atop an old Druid field—as natural to the inhabitants of the time as combining a few of their holidays and turning a few of their gods and goddesses into "saints." The original wooden structure had burned. So had a second. The third structure—built of stone—had survived since the ninth century with medieval restoration and additions.

The whole of it sat over catacombs that stretched far and wide beneath the village and held remains from those who had died since the first structure had been built. The graveyard itself was so old that many of the remaining graves from the first centuries after St. Patrick were noted by curious stones—their messages and memories to the living worn down by time and the elements.

But the graveyard was also filled with medieval art and architecture. Celtic crosses rose above tombs and stood almost starkly on patches of overgrown grass as well—the individual names and memorials to those they guarded also lost to the trial and error of time. It was both a beautiful and forlorn place, for no matter how the church and graveyard might be loved and tended by those entrusted with their care, time and the elements wore on.

"Do you know Father Flannery?" Rocky asked Devin.

"I met him, of course," Devin said. "Years ago. I doubt that he'd remember me."

"Let's see if he's about," Rocky suggested.

"If you wish."

A low stone wall—easily walked over—surrounded the church and some of the graveyard. Some of the wall was long broken or worn down, and still, it seemed that the little wooden gate created some kind of crossing—from the everyday world into that of something higher.

Just to reach the double wooden doors of the church they passed a number of tombs, gravestones, and great obelisks and Celtic crosses. Parishioners of the village were still buried here—the modern concept of a distant cemetery had never come to Karney.

Devin, a few feet ahead of Rocky, tried one of the large doors. It gave easily in her hands and they stepped into the old church. Devin backed to a side, allowing him to enter, and they both took a moment to let their eyes adjust.

He'd researched the church already. While the first might have been a creation of the Dark Ages, the present structure seemed to have Norman overtones, and while small, it had the appearance of a greater Gothic structure.

Simple wooden pews filled the church. Most of those in Karney, Devin had told him, were still Catholic and came to church regularly. It wasn't just church—it was where the villagers gathered and enjoyed one another's company.

There were lovely old side altars—many with tombs of a revered knight, perhaps, or even more modern warrior—one who might have died in the pursuit of independence for the Republic of Ireland.

The main altar was very simple, marble in structure, and while he knew there were secular colors for each season, St. Patrick's was now decked out in green. Beautiful tapestries with scenes of the days of Ireland's patron saint covered the massive windows and the altar itself—even the runner that led from the front door to the altar.

His eyes had barely adjusted when he saw a figure walking toward them. At first, in the shade of the church, he appeared to be some kind of a wraith, a fantastic creature of myth and legend bearing down upon them. Rocky quickly realized that he was a man in the long dark robes of a priest.

"Hello, welcome to St. Patrick's!" Father Flannery said in greeting, a soft, pleasant brogue causing a roll to his words.

"Father Flannery," Devin said. "I'm not sure if you remember me, but I'm Kelly Karney's cousin from America."

"Indeed, lass, aye, of course!" the priest said. He was a man in his mid-forties, Rocky thought, lean and tall, with sparkling blue eyes and sandy hair. His smile seemed sincere—as did his expression as his smile faded and he said, "I'm so sorry you've come at troubled times for the family, but, glad indeed that you're here for them at such a time." He turned to Rocky. "And, you, sir, are Mr. Craig Rockwell, husband to our Devin."

"I am," Rocky said.

"Truly, we're so pleased that you're both here," Father Flannery said.

"It's a loving family," Devin said. "I'm glad to be here."

"What do you think, Father Flannery?" Rocky asked. "There's talk of banshees coming for all the Karney family."

"I'm a priest, young man. What do you think I think?" Flannery asked him, shaking his head. "I'm from County Cork and believe me, we have our tales there as well. We've created some of the world's finest writers and storytellers—all because it's nearly impossible here to grow up without learning about the Little People and our races of giants and, of course—our banshees."

"So—"

"I think poor Collum was taken at the time our great Father above decreed, and that's the way of life," Father Flannery said.

"A heart attack—plain and simple?" Rocky said dryly.

Father Flannery sighed. "Brendan is just not convinced his brother died of natural causes. They were friends as well as brothers. Imagine a family where those not first in line for an inheritance don't seem to give a whit—and just help out? Brendan can't deal with the loss, and I've done my best to counsel him. That's a reason many of us are so glad that you're here—some American reason into the mix!"

"Well, thank you," Rocky told him.

"Have you visited your uncle's grave?" Flannery asked Devin.

She glanced at Rocky before answering. *Collum hadn't really been her uncle.*

"No, I haven't," Devin said.

"Come, I'll take you out," Flannery told them.

They left the church by a rear door, heading along a stone path into the vast field of tombs and gravestones.

There were modern markers in bronze and granite, ancient stone cairns, mausoleums and vaults. Rocky realized that Devin did know where they were going and that they were headed through the maze of memorials of the dead toward the far, westward edge and a vault built into a rise of rolling land.

A chain of keys dangled from a belt at his robe and he opened the massive iron gate to allow them entry into the vault.

Rocky wasn't sure what he was expecting—perhaps shrouded corpses decaying upon dust-laden shelves.

But that wasn't the case. Fine marble covered all the graves. There were two large sarcophagi in the center of the tomb. Rocky quickly saw that they belonged to the Karney couple of myth and legend, Brianna and her beloved husband Declan, he who had throne himself at the enemy Sir Barry Martin in order to see that he died as his wife had.

"Collum is here," Father Flannery said quietly, pointing to the side of the vault.

Cement covered the grave; a tombstone bearing his name had not yet been installed. But flowers strew the floor on the ground there and filled many vases set there as well. As he watched, Devin made the sign of the cross and lowered her head as if saying a little prayer for her uncle.

Devin had grown up Catholic—but she'd also spent a great deal of time with her beloved Wiccan aunt in Salem. She was a spiritual person, a believer—they all were, more or less, in the Krewe. But he knew that she believed in one true tenet, and that was the fact that in her mind, all good men and women believed in decency and kindness and that religion didn't matter. Yet, here, of course, she honored her uncle as he should have traditionally been honored.

He lowered his own head. Father Flannery softly murmured a prayer.

Something caused Rocky to look up—to look over at his wife.

Her head was no longer bowed in prayer. She was staring wide-eyed and frowning at the back of the vault. She stood frozen and straight, and he was certain that she saw something there.

Something that did not belong.

He strained to see through the shadows.

"Ah, and as the sayin' goes, Collum," Father Flannery murmured, "'may ye have been in Heaven a half hour afore the Devil ever knew ye were dead!' I know that to be true, for you were a fine man, my friend!"

"Sorry, I am a man of God. But I am from County Cork," Flannery added, perhaps believing that Rocky's curious expression was for him.

Devin spun around. "Of course. He was a very fine man," she said.

She turned and walked out of the vault.

Rocky stared into the darkness at the far reaches of the large family tomb. But all he saw was darkness. He followed his wife into the light of the day.

Chapter Six

They were heading out of the cemetery and up the great slope that led to the castle walls, with Father Flannery far behind them, when Rocky asked Devin, "What happened back there."

"Rocky, I don't know!" Devin told him, her beautiful blue eyes meeting his with concern. "There was something there—some kind of a presence."

"A ghost?" he asked. "Perhaps Collum?"

She shook her head. "No, it wasn't like any ghost I've met before," she said. "It was different; it was dark...like a shadow." She hesitated a bit awkwardly. It was strange. They weren't just both Krewe. They were husband and wife. They usually said whatever they were thinking—no matter how absurd it might sound to someone else.

"I felt it—or saw it—before. Last night. It seemed to settle over the castle. Just a—a darkness. Like massive raven's wings, or...a huge shadow," she finished, shrugging and looking at him a bit lamely.

"Darkness—like some kind of evil?" he asked. He hoped there was no skepticism in his voice. He knew what it was like when people doubted your judgment—or your sanity.

She smiled. "No, not evil. Just—something different. And I almost felt as if the darkness..."

"What?" he asked.

"Wanted to touch me," she said softly.

A strange ripple of fear went through him. "You're not a Karney," he said gruffly. "But if you even begin to think that you might be in danger—"

"Hey!" she protested. "I'm trained, experienced, and tough," she reminded him. "I became part of the Krewe. But, it's not like that. I mean, you said it yourself last night—we've never known a ghost to kill anyone. Ghosts linger to help the living or find justice or...in some instances, because they feel like they are an integral part of history. I didn't feel that. Just...something different."

"Well, stay close, kiddo, okay?" he asked, his tone still a bit too husky. Sometimes, he wasn't easy. A man's natural instinct was to protect the ones he loved—to protect his wife.

He knew that he sometimes had to remember that yes, she had gone through all the courses. She was a government agent. She was trained, and she—just as he had—had chosen her own course in life. He didn't have the right to try to lock her in a closet until danger was gone.

The instinct still remained.

"I'm going to have to get back in there," she said flatly.

"We're going to have to get back in there," he said firmly. "Is Father Flannery the only one with keys? Wouldn't the family have keys to their own vault as well?"

"Yes, of course," Devin said. "We can get them from Brendan."

They heard music as they approached the castle walls. The loud wail of Irish bagpipes seemed to cover the whole of the cliffside.

"They've started with the celebrations," Devin said. "Five days of them here with St. Patrick's being right in the middle. The vendors we saw getting started when we left are set up now and there's Irish step dancing competitions and in the afternoon, there will be contests for sheepherding dogs out by the pit." She glanced at him with a dry shrug. "I hope you like the sound of pipes."

"Not sure I could take it all day every day, but here...they certainly sound fitting," he assured her.

By the time they reached the gates, they were amidst dozens of people coming and going.

Once they were inside, it was as if they'd stepped through a mystical door and entered another world.

The great walls were lined with portable kiosks. Vendors sold leather goods, plaids, flutes, and even bagpipes, clothing, jewelry, costuming, food, soft drinks, and of course, whiskey and beer. A bandstand was set against the westward most section of the wall. One band took the place of another; their lead singer announced that they were the Rowdy Pipers, and as Rocky and Devin paused to listen, they burst into a rock song—with bagpipes.

"Fantastic!" Rocky said, smiling.

"They are darned good," Devin agreed. She pointed to an area near the bandstand where there were about twenty young girls in plaid skirts, white shirts, knee high socks, and black shoes. "I believe those are the St. Patrick of the Village dancers. They're probably pretty amazing."

"I imagine," Rocky agreed, looking through the crowds of people.

They all seemed happy. And polite. They waved and smiled, apparently glad to welcome friends and travelers alike.

"I don't see Kelly, Seamus, or Brendan," he told Devin.

She frowned, looking around as well. People were milling at the various vendor booths or kiosks.

"I don't see them either. I know that Kelly's second cousins are due in sometime today; they might be at the castle waiting for them—or settling them in. A Karney announces the dancers and thanks the church—and St. Patrick himself, of course," she murmured. "Oh, there they are! And they're with Kelly's cousins Aidan and Michael. Well, Seamus and Kelly are there. I don't see Brendan."

Devin waved a high hand to her cousin who looked up and smiled, returning the wave. She said something to her father and cousins and they all turned and made their way toward Devin and Rocky.

"Hey!" Kelly called, a little breathless as she reached them first. "Rocky, these are my cousins—second cousins, whatever. Wait, my dad's cousins, I think—Michael and Aidan Karney. Guys, you might remember Devin, and this is her husband, Craig Rockwell, known as Rocky."

There were greetings all the way around, Devin hugging the two new arrivals. They were both tall redheads, slim, with freckles, and easy smiles. Rocky estimated that the men were in their mid-to-late thirties, maybe fifteen years younger than Seamus and ten years older than Kelly.

"Nice that you're here," Michael said. He seemed to be the older of the two—his hair was a little darker, his voice a little deeper.

"We never miss St. Paddy's at the homestead," Aidan told him. "And I've my band along this time. Lads are staying down in the village—hopefully, you'll enjoying hearing us play."

"If they've fortitude!" Michael teased.

"Eh!" Aidan said.

"Teasin'!" Michael assured them. "Actually, Aidan's group is great. He forgot to mention there's a lady with the band. Lovely voice she has. She gives the band the last bit of excellence that they needed to head over the top."

"She and the lads are staying in the village," Michael explained. "The castle was sold out. My own family castle. Ah, well, I asked Collum and Brendan last minute and ye can't oust a paying guest like that. They're fine, though. Put them at Molly Maguire's bed and breakfast. They'll be up for a wee bit of a drink tonight."

Seamus was staring toward the doors to the castle's central tower. A frown furrowed his white brows.

He looked over at Rocky.

"He was right behind us, just leaving another of his notes on the desk to check into the pub if anything was needed or amiss," he said.

"Brendan?" Rocky asked.

"Right behind us! Right behind us!" Seamus said. He started to run toward the castle.

Rocky ran faster.

He burst through the giant wooden doors to the great hall.

And he froze.

Brendan was there.

On the ground.

Chapter Seven

Kelly let out a terrifying scream.

Devin ran right into her cousin's back, pushing her forward, and she caught Kelly by the shoulders, moving her so that she could see.

She strangled back a scream herself.

There was something that seemed frighteningly medieval and oddly poetic about the way Brendan Karney lay. His massive back and shoulders were flat on the floor of the great hall, his eyes wide open, staring upward at the wall where the great crest of his family held prominence dead center over the massive stone hearth and the crest surrounded by medieval shield and crossed swords.

Where now a few were missing.

He'd gone down with such a sword in his hand, taken from that wall—but it had never drawn blood. One of the fine fifteenth century dirks that had belonged in its proper place at the side of the crest had not drawn blood either—it lay near the left hand of the dead man, as if he had wielded the sword in one hand and the dirk in another to battle an enemy—and unseen demon, so it appeared.

Because Brendan Karney had not been wounded in any way that met the eye—he was just there, staring, eyes wide open with horror, at whatever man or beast he had meant to battle.

"Call the emergency number," Rocky said.

He was already on his knees by the dead man.

"Dammit!" Rocky roared. "Emergency!"

Kelly collected herself, shaking as she pulled out her cell phone. But her voice was clear and distinct when she asked for help.

Rocky had already begun work over Brendan, practicing cardio pulmonary resuscitation.

Brendan had appeared to be dead!

But, he wasn't.

Devin hurried over to come to her knees by Rocky's side, grateful that training worked and that she quickly kicked into response mode rather than shock. She let Rocky continue counting and using the "hands only" practice for an unconscious heart attack victim. He sat back, letting her take over, then used his own careful force again.

As she worked on her knees, she felt a strange sensation sweeping over her.

The same eerie feeling of cold that had touched her in the Karney family tomb.

She dared to look around. And she thought that, lurking in the shadows beneath the stone staircase that led to the floor above the great hall, there was something.

A shadow in the shadows. A great raven's wing. Something…

Dark.

Darker than dark.

She didn't dare look; Rocky had realized that even lying prone, eyes wide open, Brendan might still be alive. And while it didn't look good, they just might be able to save him.

Even if the banshee had wailed. Even if she waited, lurking in the shadows.

Devin gave herself a serious mental shake and continued listening to Rocky.

Apparently, emergency med techs were on hand at the festivities; what had seemed like a lifetime was most probably only the passing of a minute or two before men were rushing in, ready to take over.

Kelly would ride in the ambulance; Seamus would follow. Rocky didn't think that the man was in any condition to drive, but Devin insisted that she was—she would bring Seamus to the hospital.

Rocky didn't want her to go and him to stay—but one of them needed to go and one of them needed to stay, and that's the way it was.

Someone had to find out what was happening, what was causing the "banshee" wail at night and what demon—real or imagined—had come to put Brendan Karney into such a state.

"I'll call you as soon as I know anything," Devin promised Rocky.

She smiled, looking at him. She loved him so much. She could see the fight he was waging within himself, hating to be away from her at all.

But they'd come to find the truth.

Kelly was her cousin while Rocky was the most experienced agent. They were right doing what was needed right where they were.

As Devin headed out of the car park in the castle courtyard, she could see that villagers and tourists who had been milling around were speaking to one another in hushed whispers, gathering together for support as they watched the ambulance leave.

The pipes were silent.

A few of the vendors were already closing down.

Devin gave them no more mind, concentrating her attention on her driving.

She didn't exactly know where they were going, and she didn't think that Seamus was going to be much help with directions.

* * * *

The sheriff, a man named Bryan Murphy, arrived as the ambulance departed. Rocky was left with the cousins to tell him what had happened.

Murphy was a tall, broad-shouldered man, clean-shaven, and probably in his late fifties. He seemed a capable man, weary perhaps, but determined to learn what he could about what had happened.

"Brendan was fine," Michael said solemnly. He and Aidan and Rocky stood with the sheriff in the great hall—right before the hearth, beneath the family crest and the weapons—and by the sword and dirk that still lay on the stone floor.

"My brother and I arrived at the village just about an hour or so ago," he continued. "We checked some friends in down at another B and B, and brought our things up to our rooms in the central tower."

"Brendan was fine, just fine—all jovial and happy that we were here," Aidan said.

"Didn't look sick in the least," Michael agreed.

"He didn't look sick at all," Rocky offered. "He was fine this morning. When we found him, he looked terrified."

"Can't see how this happened," Michael said, his expression definitely confused. "We were all coming out to the courtyard. Brendan was going to announce the dancers, in honor of St. Paddy and the church and all. He was right behind us—and we wandered on down and it wasn't until we saw the Americans—my pardon," he said quickly, looking at Rocky, "it wasn't until we saw Devin and Rocky." He seemed awkward all of a sudden. "Bryan Murphy, Craig or Rocky Rockwell," he introduced. "Or did we do that. Forgive me. Brendan was...*is* a brilliant man."

"Aye, and so soon after Collum," Aidan said.

"Another heart attack?" Sheriff Murphy murmured.

"Not just a heart attack," Rocky said flatly. "Who pulls weapons off a wall when they're in the midst of a heart attack?" he asked. "Brendan was defending himself from some threat."

Aidan and Michael looked at one another and Rocky could almost hear their thoughts.

Aye, the banshee!

Sheriff Murphy looked at Rocky. "I understand you're some kind of FBI man in the States, Mr. Rockwell. You may think we're quaint and outdated here, but our forensic work is done in Dublin County with some of the finest and most qualified doctors and technicians in the world. I know you feel that we're lacking—after all, Brendan and Seamus called you and your wife over here. But, as you've all told me, Brendan was alone just a matter of minutes. Seamus, Kelly, Michael, and Aidan had just been with him. There was no threat. There's been no break-in; no one in the courtyard saw any kind of a disturbance. Just as Collum Karney was alone in his room, Brendan was alone here. They were both big men, living hard. They believed themselves to be powerful, strong like the warrior lords of old who ruled here. If you can find anything suspect, I'd be more than grateful to hear about it."

Rocky looked at Murphy. "Sheriff, I have no doubt that you're extremely capable and I'm sure in many ways you and your people surpass our expertise. I can't help but find it odd that one man dies of a heart attack and his brother is found unconscious and nearly dead barely two weeks later—surrounded by weapons as if he were defending himself."

"You don't know the village," Aidan said softly.

"He means you don't know how superstitious we are," Michael told Rocky.

"You mean about the banshee wailing last night at midnight?" Sheriff Murphy asked. "Oh, indeed, I heard about it early this morning. The sound was heard clear down the slope. Yes, we are a superstitious people. Whether a legend is true or not is not really the point, though, is it?"

"You mean you think that both Collum and Brendan believed it—and had heart attacks?" Rocky asked.

"Possibly," Sheriff Murphy said. "We'll have to pray that Brendan comes out of this—and if he does, perhaps he'll tell us just what he battled. As it stands now, I've nothing to investigate. There's no sign of forced entry anywhere, there's no witnesses—*there's no harm can be seen that was done to either Collum or Brendan.*" He turned to Rocky again. "Young man, seems you're a fine enough fellow yourself. If you find anything I can go on, I shall be delighted to throw myself and all my forces against it." He turned to Michael. "What will we announce to the people? We have to get something out on the radio—Father Flannery must say something at mass. 'Tis a hard thing. The castle has always been the center of our celebration, and St. Patrick's Day is a saint's day and holy to us. Day after tomorrow. Do we allow our five days of festival to go on?"

Michael and Aidan looked at one another. It appeared, Rocky thought, that the brothers didn't want the responsibility of making a decision.

"Would be Seamus needs to answer that question now, Sheriff," Michael said.

"Seamus is at the hospital with his brother," Sheriff Murphy said. "As is Kelly. This decision lies with the two of you."

Rocky was startled when they turned to look at him.

"There's tradition," Michael said.

"And bad taste, too," Aidan added.

"It was one thing with Collum dead and buried," Michael said.

"But now Brendan! Aye, and both of them, fine men," Aidan said.

"And traditionalists," Michael said. "Rocky, what would you do?"

"I say carry on," Rocky told them. "Brendan isn't dead. Not that we know. And Brendan would want the celebration of the saint carried on."

Michael nodded and turned to the sheriff. "We carry on," he said.

"And you're satisfied, Mr. Rockwell?" Sheriff Murphy asked.

"Until I have something to give you, sir, as you've said," Rocky told him.

Michael walked with Murphy to the door. Aidan stood awkwardly by Rocky. He looked at him. "You think that something is going on here, don't you? I suppose you think we're all a bit daft, thinking that there be leprechauns and banshees and all. They're just legends. Stories we've been told for years. Like Dracula and all that." He grimaced. "Another great tale written by an Irishman," he added sheepishly.

"I don't think you're daft at all," Rocky said. Aidan apparently wasn't aware that he belonged to—what even old friends in the agency referred to as—the ghost squad.

"But," he added, smiling. "I've yet to find a ghost or supernatural creature who could commit murder—or even attempted murder. I think that something is going on. And I do intend to find out what it is. Aidan, if you or Michael need me, I'll be up in the old master's chambers."

He left Michael and headed upstairs to the room he shared with Devin.

The room in which Collum—and many a Karney before him—had died.

Chapter Eight

Devin spent a tense hour in the waiting room with Seamus and Kelly.

The three of them knew that they were hanging on by a thread and every second now mattered for Brendan Karney.

He teetered on the edge of death.

Devin didn't tell Kelly that she'd believed that Brendan was dead when she'd seen him on his back in the great hall. She wanted to think that they might have saved him now. She knew the odds were against him.

For the hour, she sometimes paced. She sometimes hugged Kelly or Seamus. She sometimes watched them hug one another—wishing there was something that she could do.

And then, miraculously, after they waited that tense hour, a doctor came out to talk to them.

Brendan Karney wasn't out of the woods.

But he was stable.

He was unconscious—yes, a coma. But, for now, that was best.

Seamus and Kelly asked if they could just sit with him. The doctor said that they could.

And so, after the waiting, Devin decided that she'd just give him a kiss on the forehead and then leave him to his brother and his niece and head back. When one of them wanted to come home, someone in the family would come for them.

She called Rocky and reported the situation. He told her how pleased he was that it seemed Brendan had a chance. He was, he told her, exploring the master's chambers—and then he'd go beyond. She was to take her time and return to the castle when she was ready.

By the time she was nearly back—and in front of St. Patrick's of the Village—she knew that she wanted to stop at the graveyard.

She parked just on the side of the church. The sun was waning and it would soon be dark, but there was still enough crimson and purple light for her to make her way through the tombstones and crosses, Victorian funerary art, mausoleums and sarcophagi to the Karney vault.

She was irritated that she'd forgotten to ask for a key and wondered what she'd accomplish by standing just outside the gate.

But even as she approached it, she heard something on the air. Something that made her stand still, the hair at her nape rising.

It was a cry, mournful and terrible. Soft—but something like that of a wolf that cried to the moon above.

It was…eerie.

And not like the sound she'd heard the night before.

She was frightened, yet she continued to the vault.

And she knew that the cry came from within.

She stood at the gates to the vault and forced herself to try to peer within. She gripped the iron bars to steady herself, but the gates pushed inward and she stumbled into the vault.

She felt it again.

The darkness. The strange darkness that was like raven's wings, a shadow, yet there, palpable…

"Who is here?" she asked, hoping for her best special agent voice, praying that the fear that gripped her and the thunder of her heart couldn't be sensed.

Perhaps it was the ghost of a Karney—long gone, or perhaps, more recently so.

She was startled to hear a soft, female voice, rich with an old country brogue, beautiful and lilting.

"You see me?" came a whisper.

No, she didn't see anything.

"Talk to me, please. You're in distress. Tell me how I can help you," Devin said.

And then she saw.

A woman emerged like a shadow from the far reaches of the vault. She walked toward Devin as if she did have flowing black wings that moved her.

When Devin could see her at last, she inhaled sharply; her breath caught.

The being before her was stunningly beautiful, tall and lean, and her hair was one with the black cape about her and the long black gown that fell to the floor. Her face was fine, like that of a porcelain doll. She was pale as the snow, with red lips and deep, dark, haunting eyes.

"Let me help you," Devin whispered. "Who are you?"

"Deirdre," the image said.

"What can I do?"

The woman lifted a hand, as if reaching out to her.

"I don't know," she said at last. "I don't understand. I have been with the Karney family through time and now...now, something is happening. I'm not scheduled to be here, and yet I am drawn again and again and...there is evil afoot, as it was in the time of Declan."

"Declan? Declan Karney? His wife was murdered by Barry Martin and all died in the chamber that day."

"Death—as it is not supposed to be!" Deirdre said.

"You're...a family member?"

"Aye, in a sense."

"You're..."

"I come in darkness, but to bring those I embrace to sweet light. I am the gentle change from mortal coil to what lies beyond," Deirdre said.

"You're a—banshee?" Devin asked. Her knees were going to give. She grasped for the iron bars of the gate, definitely not wanting to fall.

Pathetic! She had known the dead before—why not a banshee?

The woman smiled slightly as Devin said the words. "I am Deirdre, called to help man, and my family is the Karney family. I am saddened, deeply saddened, lass, for 'tis not me making the horrible sound ye've heard with the wind at night. And I am called when 'tis not the proper time, and I know not what to do."

"Collum Karney did not die a natural death," Devin said flatly.

"He was not yet to be taken; still, I was summoned, and too late, for he floundered in fear and I wept for him, I tried to embrace him and ease away his anguish and...he is now at peace," she ended. "Then yet again, I am swept from the wind and the sea to the castle...I was there, there with you today, for it seemed that Brendan would join his good brother."

"But he's alive; he's stable," Devin said.

"Still, I know the need to hover—to stay," Deirdre said.

"He remains in danger—or others are in danger?" Devin asked.

"I don't know; I greet the dead. What men do before they are called, I cannot see. Sometimes, we are called when a battle rages. We see the fight. But now...I don't know what is going on."

"Did Collum Karney tell you anything?"

"Only that the Devil sent Barry Martin back to finish off the Karney clan," Deirdre said.

"Barry Martin! A ghost returned to slay Collum?" she asked.

"I know only what he said," Deirdre told her. She lowered her head, a picture of strange beauty. "A fine man, and taken too soon." She looked up. "Someone comes," she said softly.

Devin turned quickly. Someone was coming. She heard hurried footsteps coming close to the vault and saw a figure in the long, dark robes of the Church.

Father Flannery.

He seemed to be frowning, worried.

Concerned that she was there?

She looked back; she could no longer see Deirdre. She wasn't sure if she'd disappeared into the shadows, or if she was just—gone.

"Devin, lass, is that you?" Father Flannery called.

For a moment, Devin felt uneasy. She was halfway in the shadows. *In the vault.*

The way he was moving forward, he could push her, all the way in—to the back, the far reaches of the vault and whatever might lie in the shadows.

And then she chastised herself.

Father Flannery was the village priest.

Right! It wasn't as if men hadn't used religion to hide evil deeds before in history!

"Are you all right, Devin?" he called to her.

He stopped just outside the vault. He peered in almost hesitantly.

He meant her no harm.

Devin felt like a fool. Worse. She'd had evil thoughts about a man of the cloth.

"I'm fine, Father Flannery."

She stepped out into what remained of the light. The crimsons, pale streaks of gold, and mauves were leaving the heavens. Darkness would come in earnest soon.

"What are you doing there, child?" he asked, now perplexed himself.

"I'm not at all sure," she told him. "I left the hospital and just—I felt drawn to stop. Perhaps to say a prayer. You've heard, I assume, that Brendan was rushed to the hospital this afternoon?"

"Yes, of course, sorry business, and I am sorry, so sorry!" Father Flannery said. "That's why I worried so much. This is strange. Poor Collum—and now Brendan. I saw you here, and I must confess, and our good Father above himself knows why, but...I feared for you."

"I'm not a Karney," she said.

He frowned, looking at her. "No, of course not. I don't know. You're at the castle...you are, in a way, family. But—you think that the family is in danger, the way that you spoke as you did?"

"Yes, Father, I do," she said.

He shook his head. "There's no reason, lass. None with a wee lick of sense. Too many heirs."

"Not so many. Collum, Brendan, Seamus—Kelly. And then Michael and Aidan," she said.

"And the Republic of Ireland," he reminded her.

"I think that what's happened is too much to take as coincidence," Devin said.

"Ah, lass, don't go round saying that now!" he warned her.

"You think that would put me in danger? So you think that someone is causing these attacks, too—and not a banshee!" Devin said.

He seemed distressed. "One—poor Collum—a heart attack. Two? Aye, girl, I question what should not happen. Thing is now, dear lass, it's growing late. And graveyards at night...well, they're dark, for one. You need to be getting on back to the castle. Among the living," he added softly.

"As you say, Father, as you say."

"Let me walk with you to the road."

He did so, bringing her back to where she had parked her car to the western side of St. Patrick's of the Village.

"Are you ever afraid of the graveyard, Father?" she asked him.

"No," he told her. "I am at peace with the Father above. If he were to say it was my time, then I would pray that He'd welcome me with open arms."

"Father, I believe that I'm at peace and that I'd be welcomed, too. But that doesn't mean that I'd particularly like to go right now," Devin told him. She studied him.

Was he unafraid because he knew something?

And knew that he wouldn't be touched?

She tried to dismiss the thought. She'd already aggravated herself once by being suspicious of a priest.

She'd grown up knowing that the world was filled with beliefs. She tried to respect all of them. But she knew, too, that ideals and beliefs were one thing—that while tenets and beliefs might be filled with good things, they were also upheld by men. And men, as the world knew, were easy prey to temptation.

"Do you know anything, Father?" she asked him bluntly.

He paused, staring at her.

"I only know that the wind blows hard out of the north at times, that this is a wild coastline, and that...that men can be pure evil. I believe that there is a cry that may well be the tears of a banshee. And I know that there are shadows in time and life and that shadows often harbor evil. That's what I know. I pray for all at the castle. I pray that if there is a truth, you will find it," he told her.

She believed him.

"Thank you, Father," she said.

She stepped into the driver's seat and headed the rest of the way toward the castle, looking up at the sky.

St. Patrick's Day was coming.

A day for feast and celebration.

She swore she would not let it be a day when the banshee was called upon to work.

Deirdre.

A fitting name...

Devin didn't wonder if she had imagined the woman in the shadows. She wasn't afraid. She was grateful.

There was, indeed, a banshee.

And, just the same, she was certain there was someone out there playing at the banshee's business.

Chapter Nine

It wasn't at all a closed-door mystery, Rocky thought dryly.

There would have been plenty of ways for someone to slip in and surprise Collum Karney in the master's chambers.

There were two doors that led to the hall. Easy enough.

Of course, the upstairs of the central tower chamber of the castle was now filled with guests.

He and Devin had the old master's chambers.

Brendan slept in the "new" master's chambers.

Seamus, Kelly, Michael, and Aidan all had rooms there.

But, other than Brendan, none of them had been in residence when Collum Karney had died.

He was certain that Kelly and Seamus hadn't been there, at any rate. They'd still been in the United States.

He couldn't, of course, be certain that Michael or Aidan hadn't slipped up from Dublin, where they lived. It wasn't much of a drive at all. One of them—or both—could have hopped in a car and easily driven up.

Yet, neither of the two had been in the house when Brendan had been shocked into a heart attack and coma that day. They'd been with Seamus and Kelly.

Had they rigged something that might have appeared to have been a monster of some kind, come for Brendan?

He'd been one of the first back into the great hall of the castle. He'd seen nothing.

His attention had been drawn to the man dying on the floor!

But, still, there had been no sign of rigging of any kind.

Yes, he'd left Michael and Aidan downstairs when he'd come up to the master's chambers. But, he'd popped his head down often enough and the two hadn't even been there; they'd been in the pub, he'd discovered, heading there himself in his attempt at exploration.

So what was the plan here? He wondered. Seriously? Kill every heir to Karney Castle? To what end?

The castle reverted to the Irish Republic when the family died out.

There was, of course, the possibility that Collum Karney had died from a simple heart attack.

But two simple heart attacks did not happen so closely—especially when one of the men who had suffered a heart attack had been found with medieval weapons nearly in his grasp.

At this point, he decided that they needed help from the Krewe. Not wanting the walls to have ears, he headed out beyond the walls of Karney to a point near the fire pit where they'd heard Gary's stories the night before. Once there, he put a call through to Jackson Crow.

Adam Harrison—who sometimes seemed like a supernatural creature himself—ageless, dignified, and, sometimes, possessing amazing abilities to cross state, agency, and hopefully even international lines—was the founder of the Krewe of Hunters. Jackson Crow—an agent from the start and Adam's first choice to run the units as a supervising special agent—was their practical leader.

He called Jackson and told him everything that had gone on in chronological order, taking the time to describe those around the castle to the best of his ability. Jackson listened in silence so long that Rocky hoped he hadn't lost the connection.

But then Jackson spoke. "I can send Will Chan and Kat Sokolov," he said. "And I'll speak with Adam. God knows, he has some amazing abilities. He may be best friends with the president of the Irish Republic—if not, I'm sure he knows lawmakers and law enforcement over there somewhere!"

"We have no real authority here," Rocky reminded him.

"Well, not so true since 9/11," Jackson said. "We have agents who deal now with combined forces all over the world. Trust me—we'll pull something off."

Rocky did trust him. He apologized. "We'd handle this completely ourselves, of course. It's a family matter, but…I can't do an autopsy. And

I think someone is creating a banshee with a sound system, and that's Will's expertise. So, thank you."

"Hey, what's a good special unit for?" Jackson asked him lightly. "And, really, Rocky, hell, do you two know how to enjoy a honeymoon or what?"

"Yeah, yeah, funny, thanks!" Rocky said. "Also, I'm going to shoot you an e-mail—can we have some personal information checked out on our key suspects?"

"You have key suspects?"

"At the least, I have key players. I'm trying to find out if there was a possibility that one of Tavish Karney's nephews might have been in the area the night that Collum died. After Brendan, Seamus, and Kelly, those two are the next to inherit."

"We'll be on it," Jackson promised.

Rocky thanked him again and said good-bye.

Hitting the "end" button on his phone, he looked up toward the castle. It was truly magnificent—rich in history, the accomplishments of man, the terror of time—a monument to resistance and persistence.

It suddenly occurred to him that the castle itself was the key to the games being played—and the key to discovering the truth. The very history of the place played into what seemed to be happening.

He headed back through the courtyard to the castle. While the area seemed more subdued than it had been earlier, there were still people milling about. There was no entertainment on the stage; a sound system was playing softly—the melodious voices of Irish tenors singing traditional songs fell lightly on the air.

He hurried past the activity. On an impulse, he headed through the main tower to the pub.

It was busy—very busy, and even as he entered and heard the hum of conversation, he could pick out snatches of what was being said.

"Thank the Good Lord above that Brendan lives!" someone said.

"Aye, but did you hear? Seems he was battling the Devil!" said another.

"···found with weapons!"

"Medieval weapons!"

"And the banshee! Aye, the banshee wailed something fierce the night before!"

"Just like with old Collum!"

Conversations ceased as Rocky neared the bar. The men standing about nodded his way in a friendly manner, but still eyed him as if he were a bit of an oddity. It seemed everyone knew that he was the man married to Kelly Karney's American cousin.

It was certainly a small village.

"Evening," he said.

Allen came over, his smile a bit grim. He leaned toward him around the taps. "Any word? Brendan is hanging in still?"

"The word right now is good," Rocky told him. "He's stable."

"Has he said what happened?" Allen asked.

"He's still unconscious, and apparently his doctors believe that's best for the moment," Rocky said.

"Thank God. Two Karney men in two weeks! Two too many! So, Rocky, what can I give you?"

"Guinness, please. You pour so well, I'm not sure I'll be able to enjoy it in the States again."

"Americans keep trying to cool down a beer that should be room temperature," Allen said, shaking his head with sympathy for a people so misguided.

Rocky accepted his beer and leaned against the bar, listening to the snatches of conversation he could gather once again.

His attention was drawn to the alcove—the old chapel—where they'd been seated the night before.

Siobhan was there, waiting on a large table of men and women who seemed to be laughing and celebrating one minute—and then raising their glasses to one another soberly the next. He realized that they were trying to enjoy their St. Patrick's celebration—while looking to honor and pray for the master of the castle the next.

But it wasn't the guests at the table who intrigued him at that moment.

It was Siobhan.

She was laughing and taking an order…

And then jumping—and turning.

She paused, staring at the side of the room. He saw that there was a door there. It was closed—locked, Rocky presumed.

There was a red velvet cord across the door and a sign that read "No admittance."

"You doing okay?" Allen asked him.

"Fine, thanks," Rocky said. "Allen, that door leads down to the old crypts?"

"Aye, crypts and the old dungeon."

"Interesting down there," Allen continued. "You know it's locked off most of the year—liability insurance! Bet the old lords of the castle dinna think about liability insurance! Anyway, Gary can give you a great tour, if you've a mind for it, and I'm sure you being family and all, it won't be a problem."

"Thanks, I'll see about that," Rocky told him.

"Another beer?"

"No, thanks. I'm fine for now," Rocky said.

He set his glass and some money on the bar and headed out.

He intended to see the crypts.

But he intended to do so alone.

* * * *

Devin returned to Castle Karney—anxious to find Rocky.

But while she found Michael and Aidan—getting a bit toasted, almost truly *crying* into their beer—in the pub, the two couldn't tell her where Rocky was.

Siobhan—who seemed unnerved—told her that she'd seen Rocky, but it had been a while ago.

Allen said that he'd ordered a Guinness, stayed a spell, and then moved on.

He wasn't in the master's chambers.

Feeling like an idiot, she pulled out her cell and called him.

He didn't answer.

She mulled the idea of staying in the master's chambers and just waiting, but she was too anxious.

She headed out of the tower to the courtyard.

Night had come, and the moon was out. She wasn't sure if it was full or almost full, or even when the full moon was supposed to be. That night, however, it was so beautifully high in the heavens that it cast down a brilliantly luminescent glow.

People still milled in the courtyard; despite what had gone on that day—or perhaps because of it—people lingered. The vendors—especially the food and drink vendors—were busy.

People apparently knew who she was. They stopped to ask her about Brendan. She assured them that on last report, he was doing well.

She walked out to the great walls and saw that a large group was gathered around the fire pit.

Gravitating in that direction, she saw that Gary the Ghost was giving a night tour.

That night, he was talking about St. Patrick. She heard his rich voice as he dramatically spoke to the crowd.

"Our patron saint was a slave. Aye, not born on Irish land a'tall, but a slave brought here. Irish pirates kidnapped the lad when he was about sixteen and brought him to these shores. That was, say, right around the year 432 A.D. He worked the land—on cliffs such as these. Close your eyes and imagine if you will.

Shaggy cows and bleating sheep munching upon rich grasses on the slopes of Slemish mountain. It was there they said that he came, the slave who would become known as Ireland's greatest saint came—to find sustenance. Even as a lad and a young man, aye, he came to the cliffs and the rugged sea, finding peace and richness in the elements and the strength and will to survive. After six years, he escaped and returned to Great Britain. But voices urged him back to Ireland as a missionary; he brought the word of God and forever changed the face of this land, for few came to embrace the Mother Church as Eire. Patrick refused to take bribes from kings; he went on trial for refusing to bow before those on earth. But he prevailed. Some say he rid Ireland of snakes—some say, I will admit, that Ireland never had snakes!"

Those words drew laughter from the crowd.

"Ah, but we're full of legend, right? St. Patrick did live and die, though we don't know the exact dates. They don't matter. He was a man who defied power and his own fear to create a better place, and we honor him every year with his feast day, March 17th. Here, we've but two days to go. At Karney, we're a bit different; two days before his feast day, the day of—and two days after. We remember him as the Irish we have become, with love, with dance, with music. This year, the night of his feast day, even the heavens will honor him. They're predicting a solar eclipse! If you're staying, you'll have a fantastic sight as the moon rises and the night comes."

Applause welcomed his words.

Devin smiled and walked on, heading around the cliffs.

She could still hear Gary, telling more tales. She could turn back and see the fire blazing at the pit.

There were people there, everywhere, coming and going from the castle walls.

But as she headed up to the peak by the walls, where the cliffs held high over the sea and the wind blew beneath that light of the moon, she felt that she was alone.

And she felt that she needed to be alone.

She looked out to the water. The wind moved around her. It wasn't a storm wind, she thought, but the wind that always blew here, stronger than most, flattening the long grasses that grew along the cliff top and creating mounds of whitecaps out on the Irish Sea. Far westward was Scotland, to the south, the civilization of Dublin and the charm of Temple Bar, the history of the great living city, and a day-to-day lifestyle as busy as that of any major metropolis.

But here, here at Castle Karney, it was different.

They were caught in a pure taste of the past, of a different, medieval time, when stone was the true king, defending the inhabitants from the rams and arrows of all who came to assault the fortress.

Castle Karney had never been taken.

Not by the enemies who had come to seize her.

She could only fall from within.

By belief in an ancient evil.

That belief played upon by evil indeed—the evil of a man or woman with an agenda of their own.

Devin stood very still. The sounds of Gary's tales and the music from the castle walls seemed distant. She felt as if she were removed from the real world—as she needed to be.

She waited. And then she turned.

She knew that Deirdre would be there.

And she was. She stood a short distance away, her black hair flowing long and free with the sea-swept wind, her long gown cascading around her in that wind as well. She looked both sad and proud; she waited patiently, as if she'd known Devin was contemplating on the beauty, the sadness, and the history of Karney.

While knowing that she would come.

"I feel it," Deirdre said. "And it's wrong. You must stop it."

"Can you help me?"

"The sound that comes at night; the wail. It is not me." For a moment, Deirdre wore an expression that Devin might have seen on any perplexed young woman.

"How they believe that to be a banshee's cry, I know not!" Deirdre said.

"We will find the cause of the cry," Devin said.

"And hurry!" Deirdre urged her.

"Of course," Devin said.

"No, you must really be quick. There's but two days before St. Patrick's feast. And that's when the moon will be black by night."

As Devin watched, Deirdre seemed to disappear, becoming one with the night and the wind.

And she realized what her words meant. They were part of the prophecy.

Devin whispered aloud.

"Castle Karney in Karney hands shall lie, 'til the moon goes dark by night and the banshee wails her last lament."

Chapter Ten

Devin hurried back to the castle.

This time, she found Rocky in the master's chamber. She stared at him as she entered, completely taken by surprise. Rocky was in the big claw-foot tub.

Maybe she shouldn't have been surprised; it was supposed to be their honeymoon and he did love the tub.

But...

"Hey!" she said.

"Hey," he told her. He gave her a come-hither grin. "Join me."

She just stared at him for a moment. Normally, the invitation would start something unbelievably sweet and sensual rising within her.

And not that it didn't...

Soap suds sluiced down the bronzed expanse of his chest. His hair was damp. He looked ruggedly handsome.

And clean, of course.

"Rocky, Brendan was nearly murdered today."

"Yes. And I believe I'm on my way to solving the problem."

"What?"

"I took a little excursion on my own."

"Oh?"

"This place is incredibly historic, you know. They still have original torture implements down in the dungeon. Apparently, the inhabitants of Karney were not known for being blood thirsty, and they did make many compromises—claiming to be for the Church of England when necessary. But, they were also careful—watching out for spies among their own after the Battle of the Boyne!"

Devin shook her head. "Rocky, I love you so much. And I'm into history, too. But—"

He held the edge of the tub, turning to look at her very seriously. "Devin, you know that I believe that someone is doing this through machinery. And now I'm even more convinced that I'm right. I saw Siobhan tonight. She kept looking at the door in the old chapel that's now part of the pub. It leads to the crypts—and there's a door that leads downward from the great hall—closed and 'locked' with one of those velvet ropes over it. There's also a dumbwaiter in the dressing room next to us. Someone could have easily come here—brought something up here—the night that Collum died. I managed to crawl into the dumbwaiter—or whatever the medieval lords would have called it—down to the great hall. From there, I slipped past the velvet rope and the supposedly locked door down a flight of stone stairs to the crypt—torture chamber first, crypt when you head to the south away from the great hall and beneath the pub. There's dust in most of it—and areas swept clean. A bunch of dirt and spider webs, too, thus the bath," he added dryly. "I've also been in touch with Jackson Crow back in the main office; they're going to do searches on Michael and Aidan and find out if they might have slipped over here for a few hours on the night Collum died."

Devin stared at him for a moment in wonder and smiled slowly. She dropped her bag on the floor and quickly doffed her jacket, kicked off her shoes, and drew her sweater over her head.

Rocky looked at her with questioning brows arched high.

"You're so good," she told him.

"Ah, lass!" he said, nicely mimicking the accent they'd been hearing since their arrival. "Ya' have some faith in me, y'do!"

She stripped down all the way and crawled into the tub with him. It was a big tub, though still a little awkward. She managed, however, to finagle herself around so that she lay halfway atop him and could set her hands on his shoulders and meet his eyes before she kissed him, a kiss as long and wet and steamy as the water around them.

"You do have faith," he whispered, his eyes bright as they met hers after.

"Indeed," she said, laughing herself. She lay nearly atop him and clearly felt the rise of his erection against her thighs.

He drew her closer, pressing the length of their bodies tight.

"Faith well-warranted!" he vowed.

It was tricky—not an easy accomplishment, but they laughed as she maneuvered herself to completely straddle him, and there, in the great old tub, in the midst of soap bubbles, steam, and the delicious wetness, they made love.

Devin collapsed against him and he held her tight, then after a moment said, "My lord, I would suffer any torture for a repeat, but my knees are all but broken!"

She laughed and finagled her length off of him and out of the tub, grinning as her push against him pressed his knees harder against the tub.

"Sorry! So sorry!" she said.

"Ach! I'll show you sorry!" he promised.

In a minute, he was up and out, too. She shrieked softly as he reached for her, still soaking wet. She made a beeline for the bed where he met her, and they crashed atop, surrounded by covers and pillows and the down comforter. There it was easy to make love again, kissing the dampness from one another's bodies, sleek and slippery and still burning with the heat both of the water and that which came from within.

Finally, they lay spent and exhausted in one another's arms, entangled in the sheets and the bedding.

After a while, Rocky said, "I wonder if there are ghosts that haunt these chambers; so many have died here. It would be natural."

"I actually don't believe there are any," Devin said.

"Oh? Why?" he asked, coming upon an elbow to stare at her.

"The banshee sees that they are able to move on."

"The banshee?"

"I met her this evening."

"What?" He nearly pounced upon her, rising above her, arms on either side of her shoulders as he stared down at her intently.

Devin smiled and said softly. "I met the banshee. She's the shadow that we see and feel. Very lovely, really. Her name is Deirdre. But, she's very upset. She's insulted for one—banshees do not sound like that awful noise we heard!"

Rocky moved, sitting up, looking around the room. "Is she—here?"

"No. She would never intrude. She's gracious and polite. Honestly! Do you think that I would have jumped into the tub as I did if she were?"

"No, no, of course not," Rocky murmured. "Can I meet her?"

"I suppose—but she's not different from the ghosts or spirits we've encountered before. I don't have a cell number for her!" Devin said.

He gave her an impatient glance. "Has she seen anything? Does she know anything?"

Devin nodded gravely. "She was able to get a bit from Collum, but only a bit. She was late on the scene; he wasn't supposed to die. He said something to her about Sir Barry Martin—he who murdered Brianna and died with Declan Karney—coming back for him as a devil or demon from hell. Rocky, someone has to be doing this—but who?"

"When we find out exactly what's going on," Rocky said, "we'll know who is doing it!"

Devin started suddenly, aware that the ringer on her phone was going off in the jeans she had shed so quickly.

She leapt out of bed and hurried back to the tub area, grabbing up her jeans and finding her phone.

"Hello?" she said quickly.

"Devin?"

"Yes. Kelly?"

"Yes, it's me."

"Oh, no. Has something happened? Brendan is…"

"Holding his own; still unconscious. But," Kelly said quickly, "Devin, I'm scared. My dad went down for some coffee and I was alone here. I think someone was in the hall—someone watching me. It didn't feel right. I don't know how to explain it. But—I'm afraid. My dad came back. But, I'm just out in the hall now. I don't want to leave him alone here. Even for a minute."

"I'll come right back, Kelly," Devin promised.

Rocky was already up and dressing; he'd heard her conversation.

"We can't both leave the castle," she said. "Michael and Aidan are here. And they may be guilty or—they may be vulnerable as victims."

He shook his head. "We won't both leave. I'm walking you down to the car; you'll go and stay with Kelly and Seamus until morning. I'll have you spelled then. I'll keep guard here."

"How will you have me spelled?"

"I believe that Will Chan and Kat Sokolov will arrive in Dublin early in the morning. They'll have been on a night owl flight."

Devin nodded slowly. "All right. That seems best. What about the sheriff? Don't you trust him?"

"I trust us," he said simply.

A few moments later, she was in the car.

By then, the courtyard was quiet; the vendor's stalls were covered for the night.

The music had gone silent.

The moon rose high over the night.

"Rocky!" Devin said.

"What's that?"

"There's going to be an eclipse. A solar eclipse of the moon. On St. Patrick's Day night, it will be dark!"

"And?" he asked.

"The prophecy!" she said. "Remember? 'Castle Karney in Karney hands shall lie, 'til the moon goes dark by night and the banshee wails her last lament.'"

His lip went grim and tight for a moment. "So that's it, then," he said softly. "Someone is playing not just on the banshee legend, but on history and the prophecy as well. All right. The moon may go dark—but we'll see to it that the banshee has no cause to wail at all."

Chapter Eleven

The night was quiet.

Rocky sat up in one of the great chairs by the hearth, allowing himself to doze now and then.

He was armed.

He'd chosen a small knife from the weapons above the hearth in the great hall. It was unfortunate that they had come as tourists—without their weapons.

But this killer wasn't walking around with a gun. A gun would be too obvious. This killer was trying to murder his victims in ways that made it appear that natural causes or fear itself had done them in.

So far, the killer had attempted to kill older men who had lived their lives steeped in legend.

They hadn't gone after an able-bodied American trained in arms and self-defense.

He jarred upright to the least crackle of the fire. He slipped out to the hall now and then, and even back downstairs. He checked to see that the pub was locked up tight for the night.

There was no movement. The castle guests were in their own wing, most probably sleeping.

As were Aidan and Michael. Rocky would have heard them had they left their rooms.

He checked in with Devin at the hospital every so often.

She was fine. Brendan was fine.

At seven a.m., he received the call he expected; Will Chan and Kat Sokolov had arrived. They had landed in Dublin; they would be there within a few hours.

Rocky was grateful that they were on their way. Kat was a tiny, very pretty blonde—the last person one would expect to be an excellent medical examiner. Will Chan was intriguing—his background was Trinidadian and Chinese and a mix of American-Northern European. He'd been in magic, in theater, in film—and computers. If anyone could figure out a computer or machine engineered haunting, it was Will.

Together, they were a handsome, engaging—and deadly competent couple.

Rocky was cheerful as he rose and headed down to the pub.

Michael and Aidan were there and hailed him when he came in, urging him to join them.

"Where is the missus?" Aidan asked him.

"She spent the night at the hospital with Kelly," Rocky explained.

"Ah, of course," Michael said. "He's doing well? Brendan is doing well?"

"Stable and holding," Rocky assured them. "How about you two? You sleep well? Any interruptions?"

"The banshee?" Michael asked solemnly.

"Don't make him think we're daft," Aidan said. "No, but, I admit—I didn't sleep well. It's unnerving. First Collum. Then, Brendan. And that wailing people talked about. I slept with my door bolted, I'll tell you that."

"I considered going back to Dublin," Michael admitted.

"You can't. We're always here for St. Paddy's Day," Aidan said.

"Aye, but, people aren't usually dropping like flies around the feast day," Michael said. He looked hard at Rocky. "Do you think we're in danger?"

"I think that something is going on. And I will find out what," Rocky said.

"We're all right—we're all right as long as Seamus and Kelly are all right," Aidan said.

"And you think something is going to happen to Seamus next?" his brother asked, appalled.

"They're next," Aidan said softly.

"Have you been back up here lately—as in around when Collum died?" Rocky asked.

"Aye—we came for the funeral," Michael said sadly. "Collum's funeral."

The two sounded sincere.

But, it was difficult to be sure.

"I meant before that," Rocky said.

"Are you suggesting something?" Aidan demanded.

Rocky shook his head. "No. I'm wondering if you saw or heard anything peculiar."

"I hadn't been here in months," Michael said.

"Nor I," Aidan said flatly.

"Well, thank you. We will get to the bottom of it all," he assured them with a smile.

He rose and left them.

Upstairs in his room, he checked his e-mail. He had received information from the home office. He went through everything that they'd been able to pull on Michael and Aidan Karney, Siobhan McFarley, Dr. Kirkland, Sheriff Murphy, Allen Fitzhugh, and Gary Duffy.

Sheriff Murphy had a wonderful record. He'd been a police officer in Dublin with dozens of commendations before coming home to Karney to take on the role of sheriff.

Dr. Kirkland had once had a run-in with the law; charges had been dropped. He'd been soliciting a prostitute. That didn't make him a killer. But, it was interesting.

There were no police records of any kind on the others.

But, there was an interesting notation.

Aidan Karney had made a charge in the village—at the local pharmacy.

He had done so on the day before Collum Karney had died.

* * * *

Devin jumped up with a cry of delight when she saw the tiny blonde visitor enter Brendan Karney's hospital room.

In doing so, she woke Seamus and Kelly, who had been dozing in other chairs.

"Kat!" she said.

"Hey! A trip to Ireland, a bit unexpectedly," Kat said, greeting Devin with a hug. Devin quickly turned to introduce her to Brendan and Kelly.

"She's another of your team?" Seamus asked, perplexed, most probably because Kat didn't look ferocious in the least.

"Trust me, she's hell at a shooting range," Devin said, laughing. "And she can fathom any secret from the dead," she added.

Kat nodded, looking at Seamus. "Sir, we need your signature. We've set the wheels in motion. I can perform an autopsy tomorrow, with your permission."

"Tomorrow? Oh, no. Nothing happens like that on St. Patrick's Day!" Seamus said.

"It does when the right people are involved," Kat said softly. "And I think, with the information we've been given, that it's imperative we have your brother out of the ground as quickly as possible."

Seamus looked at his daughter and nodded.

"Anything you need," he told her.

"For now," Kat said, "I'm here to spell you, Devin. Will is with Rocky at the castle. They're expecting you back."

"Great," Devin said. She looked at her Uncle Seamus and Kelly. "Do either of you want to come with me?" she asked.

Kelly shook her head, looking at her father.

"We'd like to see him gain consciousness," Kelly said.

"Of course." Devin smiled and glanced toward Kat. "You'll be safe," she promised.

"Trust me—deadly things come in small packages," Kat promised them.

"Of course. We'll be fine—we'd have been fine on our own," Seamus said sternly, looking at his daughter.

"There's nothing like safety in numbers," Devin said cheerfully. "All right then—I'll be in touch!"

She left the hospital and headed back toward the castle.

As she came upon the church, she paused again. She wasn't sure why; she didn't intend to linger.

She felt the urge to go back to the Karney family vault.

She parked and headed into the graveyard. A bit of a distance from the vault, she paused.

It was like many such a vault in old Irish cemeteries and graveyards where the rocky terrain led to hillocks and cliffs and caverns. It was built right into the side of a rock-covered rise.

She stared at it a moment, but couldn't put her finger on the reason why the placement seemed so curious.

With a shrug, she moved toward it.

She saw that Father Flannery had apparently seen to it that the gate was now locked. But, holding the lock, she saw that it hadn't snapped. She twisted it to the open angle and walked in.

She felt nothing; saw no shadows. But she moved inward.

As she went deeper into the vault, marble slabs no longer covered the shelves that held the dead. A few wooden covers, Victorian era, perhaps, were decaying. Further back, there were shrouded mummies.

She stopped when she reached them; there was no light back there.

For a moment, despite the smell of the earth and decay, she paused, listening—trying to feel for any presence.

But there was nothing and she turned back.

Before she stepped back out of the vault, she paused. Someone was walking across the graveyard, head down, footsteps hurried.

It wasn't Father Flannery.

She ducked back inside, still watching.

It was Aidan Karney. He kept coming.

Devin shrank back into the vault, heading behind the tombs of Declan and Brianna and sinking low.

Aidan came into the vault. He stood there, letting his eyes adjust.

Aidan had been smart enough to come with a flashlight. He played it over the tomb.

Devin stayed low.

Aidan let out a sound of impatience and disgust.

He turned around and left the vault.

Devin waited. And waited.

She realized that he would have seen her rental car.

But, when she carefully emerged at last, he was nowhere to be seen.

She hurried back to the car and drove on to the castle.

When she arrived, activities around the courtyard were already in full swing. She saw that Father Flannery was on the stage by the western wall, surrounded by musicians. He announced that they were praying for Brendan Karney, who was holding his own. Then he announced the St. Patrick's of the Village band and singers and stepped aside, leading the audience in applause.

The band and singers began a beautiful version of Danny Boy.

She continued on into the castle.

No one was in the great hall and Devin walked up to the master's chambers. She found a note from Rocky telling her to head on down to the crypt via the tower stairs and follow the instructions on the note.

She knew the crypt and the dungeons, of course. She'd been awed and amazed when she'd come as a teenager.

The foundations of the castle were vast. They held a scent that wasn't exactly bad, and wasn't exactly rot. But the sea roiled near the castle and deep in the ground, everything smelled verdantly of the earth.

The main room, beneath the great hall, had once had cells where prisoners were held.

A few of the barred cells remained.

There was also a display of torture instruments used throughout the centuries. There were thumbscrews, brands, pinchers, an Iron Maiden, a rack, and all manner of chains and shackles.

There were creepy, bad mannequins on the rack, in the Iron Maiden, and held to the wall by chains.

There were, however, electric lights and when they were turned on—as they were now—the mannequins simply displayed a lack of talent in their creation.

And yet Devin felt oddly as if they were watching her.

"Stop it!" she told one, shaking her head as she walked by.

"Rocky? Will?" she called.

For a moment, she thought that no one was going to answer her.

"This way!"

Rocky's voice urged her toward the crypts. She walked in that direction.

Here, there were no mannequins.

There were coffins—and there were the mummies of the very ancient still aligned on their eternal beds of wood and stone.

There were only a few lights strung overhead; they weaved with heavy movement from above casting weird shadows over the bones and shrouds of the long, long dead of Karney Castle.

But Rocky was there, hurrying out to greet her with something like enthusiasm.

"We've found places where the dust has definitely been disturbed. Someone has been down here with some kind of a device. Also, it looks like they were dragging something heavy, or something with a train of fabric. But, it all disappears into the crypt and we can't figure out if they were perhaps coming and going through the pub—or what?"

Will Chan came walking out behind Rocky.

"Hey, newlywed," he teased, coming forward to greet her with a hug.

"Hey, thanks for coming," she told him.

"Not a problem," he told her. "Here's the thing so far. I believe—as Rocky suggested—that the sound that filled the castle came from here. You could create an amazing wail that reverberated through the stone with a simple amplifier. As far as actually appearing in the master's chambers, easy enough as well. The dumbwaiter rises and falls from just above. Someone has definitely been on the stairs. The problem we're having is determining where the someone is coming from or going to, as they must have had a way out of here for them and all that they used."

"They might have just walked out of the great hall," Devin said.

"But, at that time of night? Do they lock the great hall itself?"

"They do. When the pub closes, everything is supposedly locked," Devin said.

"Would that suggest a pub employee?" Will asked.

"Maybe. But, why? No pub employee stands to gain if the Karney family goes down," Devin said.

"Maybe they're full of information anyway," Will said.

"Are you suggesting a late lunch?" Rocky asked him.

"Not a bad idea."

"What about Aidan Karney?" Devin asked.

"Aidan," Rocky said. He glanced at Will and asked her, "Why?"

"He came into the vault," Devin said.

Rocky stared at her hard. "I stopped again on my way back from the hospital."

"You shouldn't be doing that alone," Rocky said firmly.

"You really shouldn't be," Will agreed.

"Aidan never saw me," she said.

"What did he do there?" Rocky asked.

"Turned on a flashlight, made a noise, and left. Why?" she asked.

"Because he's a liar," Rocky told her. "He claimed he hadn't been here in ages before he came for Collum's funeral. He used his charge card in the village the day before Collum died."

"So, we have a real suspect," Will said. "What we need to do is keep a sharp eye on him."

"Watch," Rocky agreed. "Pretend we know even less than we do—and watch. If the killer is going by that prophecy thing, he's going to be in a hurry. We may well catch him in the act."

Rocky's phone rang. He tried to answer it; the signal couldn't penetrate the depth of the castle and the call went dead.

"We'll head up," he said.

The great hall was still empty when they emerged.

The call had come from Kat.

Rocky quickly called her back. Will and Devin watched him as he spoke. He hung up and told them, "No time for lunch. Whoever it is that Adam Harrison knows in Ireland wields some real power. Will, if you don't mind, I'll have you go to the hospital and keep watch over Brendan. Devin, you and I need to head to the graveyard; the sheriff and graveyard employees will meet us there along with county officials. Kat can start on her autopsy tonight. Collum Karney is about to leave the vault."

Chapter Twelve

It was sad to be at a funeral; to watch a coffin lowered into the ground or set into a shelf in a mausoleum or vault.

Sad to see flowers cast upon a coffin.

Somehow, it was just as sad to see the proceedings when Collum's coffin was removed.

The sound of the marble being split from the shelf seemed grating. Watching the men heave the coffin out and onto the stretcher was just as disturbing. Devin realized that she was associated with the family and that made it worse.

It was very solemn.

Father Flannery was there, saying prayers. Other than his words, the whole day seemed silent.

Many of those who would have been celebrating the day before St. Patrick's Day had gathered at a distance to watch as well. Whispers and rumors were running rampant, Devin was certain.

In the midst of it, Dr. Kirkland arrived, striding across the graveyard, avoiding Celtic crosses and stepping heedlessly on gravestones.

"What is the meaning of this? Why wasn't I consulted?" he demanded.

Sheriff Murphy stepped forward. "Sorry, Kirkland. Orders came down from the county; an autopsy is happening."

"What? You're going to find proof that a banshee killed the man?" Kirkland demanded. He saw Rocky and Devin standing near and turned his wrath on them. "Who do you think you are? How dare you come here assuming your methods and means are superior and that we're all a pack of superstitious idiots? This will not be the last of this, not by a long shot, no indeed!"

He stormed off. Rocky and Devin looked at one another.

"Another suspect?" Rocky asked softly.

"Why?" Devin asked.

"The million dollar question," Rocky murmured. "Come on; the coffin is in the ambulance. We'll follow it to the county morgue—into Kat's hands."

They did. Kat greeted them there and assured them that Will was watching over Brendan, Seamus, and Kelly.

It had grown late. With the body safely in her hands and Kat and the county examiner ready to work, the two of them left, returning to the castle.

They were exhausted and famished and headed to the pub. Allen was behind the bar; Siobhan was working the floor. She seemed not irritable, but distracted that night.

"All this going on—it gives the body a chill, that's a fact!" she told them. "And, of course, with St. Patrick's tomorrow, it's like a zoo here, people squawking for this and that and not a wee bit of manners among them!"

"We'll get our drinks from Allen," Rocky assured her.

"Aye, and thank you on that!" Siobhan said.

Rocky and Devin went to the bar. Allen was harried as well; he still managed to pour a perfect pair of pints for them.

"If you need help, I can hop back there with you," Rocky offered.

Allen gave him a grin. "I may call on you. We're really moving. Believe it or not, several of the vendors ran out of beer. That's—that's sacrilege in Ireland!"

"Call me if you need me," Rocky told him.

"Ah, but you're a lawman," Allen said.

"I had lots of jobs before I became one," Rocky assured him.

Allen grinned. Rocky and Devin returned to their table.

Devin had purposely chosen a booth in the old chapel section.

"We were right beneath here today," she told Rocky. She leaned closer to him. "There has to be a hiding spot we don't know. Either it is someone who belongs at the castle and has a room here—like Allen—or it's someone who knows where to put things out of sight. And not in the crypt, as one might think."

"I believe that whatever is being used actually leaves the castle walls," Rocky said. "But, how? That's the question!"

"I'm sure we can find an answer," Devin told him. "So many vendors have come and gone—maybe they're using a vendor?"

Their food came and they ate. Rocky had just taken his last bite when Siobhan stopped by the table. "Allen says that if you're certain you don't mind, he'd love some help behind the bar," she said.

"All right, then," Rocky said, rising. He looked at Devin.

She smiled. "I'm fine. I'll be thinking—and watching." And she would be. She'd noted that Michael and Aidan had just come into the bar. Aidan seemed distracted. Michael was calm and collected.

Rocky went behind the bar. Devin pulled out her phone and pretended to give it her attention.

She watched Aidan. He seemed dejected. But, as she watched him, she felt that she was drawn to watch Siobhan again. Every time the waitress came into the chapel area, she seemed distracted.

"What bothers you here?" Devin asked her, catching her when she would have hurried by.

Siobhan crossed herself. "We're over the dead!" she told her.

She didn't get a chance to say more. She dropped the heavy glass beer mug she had been carrying as sound suddenly ripped through the castle.

The great clock was beginning to chime the midnight hour.

And along with it had come another sound.

The banshee's wail. The same sound they had heard just a night ago.

Rocky looked her way. He leapt over the bar and went racing out of the pub toward the center tower.

Devin jumped to her feet, as well, to follow him.

Yet, even as she reached the great hall, she saw that Michael was following Rocky—and Aidan was following him.

But Aidan suddenly stopped and headed out the main doors.

Devin stood for just a moment's indecision.

Then, she followed Aidan.

* * * *

Rocky swore, ruing the fact that they'd actually managed to get Collum to autopsy that day.

Kat would have still been with Seamus and Kelly, and Will would have been with him.

But, as he tore past the velvet chain, jerked open the door and ran down the steps, he realized that the sound was already gone.

When he flicked on the light and reached the dungeon, it was empty.

There was something there, though. Someone had been there. Someone had just been there! He could sense it—feel it!

There was a noise behind him and he spun around. Devin?

No.

It was Michael Karney.

Karney looked at him impatiently and started on through to the crypts.

"Dammit!" he swore.

He turned in the shadows there and looked at Rocky. "Someone comes here. I know they come here."

To Rocky's surprise, Michael suddenly turned, pushing at the shroud and bones of a long dead ancestor. "There's got to be something—some way that they're escaping. And whoever it is, they'll get to Brendan, Seamus—then Kelly, and then me!"

Rocky set his hands on the man's shoulders. "They didn't go that way—and you're now covered in bone dust. That way is foundation wall—it has to be something else. Some other way. The other steps are here—the steps down to the crypt from the old chapel."

"We would have seen them—the pub was full," Michael said irritably.

"Then we have to take it slowly, carefully, and methodically," Rocky said. He sighed.

There had to be something somewhere. A tunnel—and escape. But where?

"Start on this side," he told Michael wearily. "Look low because whatever it is, it leads beneath the courtyard."

The two of them began to look. It was tedious. They were both white with dust, sweating profusely despite the damp cold of the crypt.

Michael paused. "We need Aidan—he can help. He's in as much trouble here as we are."

And Devin? Where was Devin?

Rocky was surprised by the depth of the fear that gripped him. He pushed past Michael, finding the stairs to the pub directly above the crypt.

They were narrow, winding. The door above didn't give. Locked.

But, no. He was certain it wasn't going to be locked as it should have been.

He hefted his shoulder against the door and it opened.

He spilled out into the lights of the pub like a ghost risen from above.

His arrival was met by dozens of screams.

He ignored them, looking around the pub, then looking for Siobhan and Allen. He didn't see Siobhan.

Allen was behind the bar, trying to calm people and still pour his perfect pints.

Rocky raced over to him. "Allen, where is Devin? Where did she go?"

"She raced after you," he said.

"And Aidan—where's my brother?" Michael asked.

Allen dead paused for a minute. "Are you crazy—they raced out after you! After that, I don't know. Look at this place—does it appear that I could be watching people!"

They all froze after his words. A different cry suddenly filled the night.

It was lilting; it was high. It was mournful and truly beautiful.

The real banshee!

Rocky turned and gripped Michael by the shoulders. "Come on—come on, now! We're finding where that escape is, and we're finding it now!"

"But they didn't come with us…how do we know…?" Michael stuttered.

"We don't know where it lets out," Rocky said. "We do know that it leads from the crypts. Let's go—now! And we'll find it—don't you see, someone's life depends upon it now!"

* * * *

Aidan could stride quickly when he chose.

The courtyard was quiet; no one was about.

Aidan didn't seem to notice—he was on a mission.

Which meant that Devin was on a mission, too.

She was quickly running to keep up with him, running into the night. They passed the storytelling area by the pit and headed down toward the road to the village. She realized—huffing and puffing somewhat despite the fact that she was in pretty good shape—that they were heading to the center of the village.

To St. Patrick's of the Village.

And the graveyard that surrounded it.

She gave up trying to hide the fact that she was following him. He had absolutely no interest in looking back.

The wind rose; it seemed to be pushing her forward. The air was damp and cool. The moon rose high over them, as if guiding them along. It shimmered over the massive Celtic crosses and small headstones and footstones, mausoleums and vault.

Aidan hopped the little stone fence.

Devin did the same, hurrying after him.

He made straight for the Karney family tomb. When he reached it, he pulled open the gate.

Still not locked!

She followed, slowing her gait. Aidan disappeared into the vault. She waited a second, catching her breath, and then she crept to the entry. She could see him deep in the vault.

Once again, he'd thought to bring a flashlight.

She crept in, pausing by the tombs of Brianna and Declan Karney, watching the light. He was heading deep into the back—deep into the hillock that covered the family vault.

She began to follow, moving along carefully. She left behind any semblance of the modern world, entering the tunnel where the sides were lined with shelves of the dead, ghostly in their decaying shrouds. Some shrouds were gone; one skull was turned toward her. The jaw had fallen off. The skull seemed to scream out a warning.

She kept going.

Aidan paused ahead; she feared that he was going to turn.

Wincing, Devin threw herself onto one of the shelves—by the looks of the gown, she was next to the bones of a deceased lady of the manor. The dust covered her; the bones seemed to rattle in anger at the disturbance. She nearly sneezed.

She caught herself, barely daring to breathe.

Aidan went on.

She crawled out of her hiding space and went after him, coming closer and closer behind him.

He paused suddenly and spun around. She didn't move quickly enough; she froze in the glare of his light.

Aidan screamed. His flashlight fell.

"Jesus and the saints preserve us!" Aidan muttered, falling on his knees. "No, lady, I beg of you, I'm not even next in line!" he pleaded.

Stunned, Devin gathered herself together and headed for him. She picked up the flashlight. He was on his knees, still muttering prayers, crossing himself.

"Aidan! It's me—Devin!" she said.

He went still and then looked up carefully, looking at her with only one eye open—as if that would help if she were a demon.

"Oh, my God!" he breathed. "You look like death itself!"

"I had a run-in with some bones," she told him. "Aidan, what are you doing here?"

"I'm finding the bastard—or the banshee!" he told her.

"In here?"

He let out a soft sigh.

"Aye, in here! I think that there's a tunnel—leads all the way back to the castle crypts. I was reading a history about the Battle of the Boyne. Men escaped this way after the battle. A priest helped them burrow through the back of the graveyard. I figured that the tunnel still had to exist. It was after the Battle of the Boyne, you know, that the Catholic populous was displaced—lest they bargained like the lords of Karney! But before their bargaining went on, they helped dozens escape to America."

"Have you been all the way through here?"

"I wanted to—I came today. But I couldn't make myself do it. Then we heard the sound again tonight at midnight and I wasn't going to be a patsy—let them kill the others and come for me!"

"Ah!" Devin said softly. "Well, then, shouldn't we go on?"

She was answered—but not by Aidan.

A voice rang out from the darkness beyond.

"You need go no further. Alas, my friends, you found what you're seeking. Fools. Aidan, it was never going to get to you. Or Michael. You should have left well enough alone—you should have stayed in Dublin. And Devin! Sweet American beauty! Ghost-catcher agent! I'm so sorry.

Alas, you had to come. Ah, well. You do love history. Now you can be part of it."

A shot rang out.

Aidan screamed, but not because the shot hit him; it slammed into the rock at his knees, frightfully close.

Devin slammed the flashlight out and grabbed Aidan, wrenching him to his feet.

Another shot ran out and then another.

She ran some distance and then paused, making use of the dead again. She shoved Aidan into one of the shelves, thrusting the bones aside. She felt him shivering, urged him to silence. She fell to the ground as well, sliding into the lowest shelf. Her fingers curled around something.

A thighbone.

It was going to have to do.

She lay still, barely daring to breathe. She waited.

The killer spoke as he walked toward them.

The killer.

The storyteller.

The historian.

Gary the Ghost.

"Come out, come out!" he called. "Don't you see, it's only just and fair! I'm the one who knows Karney, knows the castle and the history. And I love Kelly, you see. I've loved her since she was just a child. Now, I'm not at all sure, family tales being family tales, but word is that my great-grandmother had an affair and a child was born, my grandmother. The affair, naturally, was with a Karney. So, you see, I should be in line for the title and the castle as well. All I had to do was get rid of the old men—all seeped in the legends, thank the lord! Collum, such an easy mark. I substituted his digitalis with placebo pills, let out a fierce cry through a cheap, lousy speaker—and voila! All right, well, I do have a wee bit of the theater in me—I dressed up. Ach, so easy! Do it all and just leave nicely without a fuss through the tunnels. Because I know the place. Because it should be mine. And, of course, Kelly—lovely Kelly. She'd have been heartbroken, turning to me for comfort. There you have it. All right and just and...I will find you. I will find you!"

And he would. He was right by them.

He might go straight past them. Just a few more steps...

Aidan sneezed.

And Devin knew that Gary would shoot him without a thought—right where he lay, already in a crypt.

She took her thighbone and planning a careful strategy—she slammed it as hard as she could in the direction of his legs.

He let out a howl of pain and fell to his knees. The gun he held went flying. But he saw her.

In the dim light, he saw her. And his fingers wound around her throat.

She found another weapon…a rib?

Slashing as hard as she could, she turned it on him.

And then, she heard a sound. Footsteps—footsteps racing hard down the path. She saw around Gary, saw enough to realize that something huge and white and filled with vengeance and wraith was bearing down on them.

Rocky.

He ripped Gary from her, throwing him so hard against the opposite wall of shelving for the dead that bones clanked and fell.

Devin rolled from her slab and stumbled up, feeling along the floor for the gun. Her fingers fell upon it.

Just as a foot fell upon her hand.

She looked up.

Siobhan was there.

The woman kicked her hard then, in the face, and sent her rolling.

Rocky had hold of Gary—the storyteller was no match for the honed agent.

"Let him go," Siobhan said. She triggered on a small light; the vault was illuminated. Devin could see the living and the shadows and the dead.

They were twisted, some covered, some not. Some down to bone. A few in tattered clothing still.

They heard Siobhan click the trigger of the gun.

"Let Gary go—now."

Rocky did so. They all stared at one another.

"What in God's name do you have to do with this?" Devin asked.

"What?" Siobhan seemed confused by the question. "Don't be stupid. I'll rule the castle—rather than work my buns off at it!"

"No, how could you? Gary means to marry Kelly," Devin said.

"Don't be ridiculous," Siobhan said. "I've helped him along. I've been up at the pub, slipping down to him what he needed, telling him when it was safe, when it was not. Gary—tell them. It's me you'll be marrying when they're all gone."

"Of course," Gary said.

"He's lying," Rocky said. "You're a fool. He's lying! You can tell."

"He wouldn't have lied to me when he intended to kill me," Devin said flatly.

Siobhan pointed the gun at Gary.

"You've played me, man?"

"No!" Gary protested.

Devin felt a cold wind and then a shadow.

"She's coming!" she said suddenly.

Siobhan turned the gun on her.

"Who's coming?" she demanded.

"The sheriff is on his way and a host of county police and other agents," Rocky said. Devin knew he was trying to force her to turn the gun on him.

"And the banshee," Devin said.

"Don't be daft, lass, I was the banshee!" Gary said.

"You were the fake banshee, but there's a real banshee for the Karney family. She's not evil—she helps with the transition," Devin said. "And I feel her; she's coming. She's behind you—coming this way. Can't you feel her?"

Gary turned to look back into the darkness.

"There is something, someone, something!" Gary cried. He turned back to Siobhan. "Shoot, shoot, shoot now! Shoot it!" he screamed.

Siobhan took aim. Her hand was starting to tremble.

"Woman, you're an idiot!" Gary raged, turning to come for her.

But, just as he did, Siobhan managed to fire. She caught Gary dead center in the chest.

The explosion seemed to rattle the bones...

Of the living and the dead.

Gary went down. He stared at Siobhan in disbelief and fell to his knees.

"No!" Siobhan screamed.

Devin saw the darkness coming behind Gary.

Deirdre was there. Her arms went around Gary as he fell the rest of the way to the earth.

"Ah, lad, too greedy, too cruel, and now, you must answer to your

Maker," Deirdre said.

In her beautiful black mourning, she was on her knees, holding Gary. She looked over at Devin. "I knew one of them was leaving this earth tonight; I did not know which—ah, sadly, aye—he is of Karney blood!" she said.

And then, it seemed she was gone.

Rocky instantly rushed Siobhan, wrenching the gun from her. There were more footsteps pounding toward them.

Michael reached them first. "My brother, my brother!" he shouted.

Devin managed to point to the slab where Aidan lay—silent and still.

Michael fell to his knees by the slab. "Oh, Aidan!"

Before he could burst fully into tears, Devin touched his shoulders. "Michael, he's fine. He just passed out. He'll be all right."

Sheriff Murphy and more men were coming.

Devin looked over at Rocky.

He was as covered in tomb dust as she was. She didn't care. She went into his arms.

He held her there, and then he took her hand, and they walked out into the graveyard and the night.

There might be a darkness come St. Patrick's Day night, but the Karney family would be alive in good number and for the moment, the moon cast down a magnificent light.

"Idiot, I was terrified that I'd lost you!" Rocky said, shaking.

"I'm pretty dangerous with a thighbone," she told him.

"You went off alone. You can't do that. Not because you're my wife or a woman, but because we all know to call for backup," he told her.

"I thought it was Aidan. I was afraid I was going to lose him."

"I was afraid I was going to lose you!"

"But you didn't and…I'm sorry. I truly have no excuse. But, we found the truth. We're both here and…did you see her, Rocky? Did you see her—the banshee?"

"I did," he told her. "She was beautiful." He smiled. "And I could use a cold one. I don't think Allen is too busy anymore. I think we cleared the place out, coming up from the crypt and looking like this. But, if he is, I can pour my own. Sheriff Murphy isn't a bad fellow at all. He has this handled. Shall we?"

Hand in hand, looking as if they were ghosts risen from their graves, they left the graveyard behind.

They didn't mind the walk.

The moonlight was upon them, like a gentle beacon.

And while they might appear to be part of the realm of the dead, they were alive.

Very much alive.

Epilogue

Nothing stopped St. Patrick's Day in Ireland.

And so it was that the church service came first, and then the church parade, with Father Flannery bearing the relic said to contain a fragment of the saint's bone. Then there was music and dancing and a fine flow of spirits and delicious food.

Devin and Rocky found themselves part of the "fool's" parade that followed, carried in chairs of honor by costumed performers playing the giants of Ireland's legends.

Kat—who had discovered that Collum's body bore no trace of the medication he should have been taking—was pleased to be there simply on vacation.

Will was thrilled to have downtime with the woman he loved.

Brendan had come to during the night—Kelly had told Devin that it was exactly at midnight, when the clock at the castle would have chimed.

When Gary Duffy had set off his "banshee" wail—and made his demon-banshee surprise appearance, wielding a great sword. Brendan would have battled him, he swore fiercely, if his mind hadn't played tricks. If he hadn't...fallen to the false banshee. The thing had come at him waving an old battle-ax; he'd gone for his own weapons, felt the wind of the banshees battle ax—swirled and fallen and hit his head, felt a seizure in his chest...

And seen stars.

If they hadn't come, he was certain, his brother's killer would not have counted on another heart attack; he would have done Brendan in with the battle-ax. They'd arrived back in just the nick of time.

Brendan was allowed to leave the hospital for an hour of the festivities—time to hear the cheers of love he received from the crowd gathered for St. Patrick's Day.

And from his family, of course.

He was whisked back, and Kelly, begging their forgiveness, went back with him and her father.

Michael and Aidan played hosts. Aidan explained that his credit card had been stolen in Dublin. Gary had most probably gotten it—and used it quickly to cast suspicion on him when the time was right.

"If he meant for them to die and then he wanted to marry Kelly, he was going to need a scapegoat," Aidan said.

Devin agreed.

Siobhan wasn't talking. She had lawyered up.

It was suggested, though, that she was going to use insanity. All she'd done since she'd been arrested was mutter about the banshee that had come for Gary.

Somehow, the day was everything it should have been. Proud, just, and filled with love for Ireland. That night, many people gathered outside the castle walls by the cliff.

Devin stood, smiling, feeling the wind in her hair.

Castle Karney was magnificent.

She could hear Aidan—he was telling visitors about the castle.

It was impossible to attack by sea. The rocks below where they stood were as treacherous and lethal as bullets. The castle itself sat up on a high tor at the edge of the water—landside, attackers could be seen from the parapets before they so much as neared the stone bastion of the outer walls.

Indentations marred those walls—indentations from dozens of guns and arrows and cannons. But the walls were more than ten feet thick and the time of medieval war had come to an end before even the most deadly of cannon balls had managed to do real damage. The castle had never surrendered; the Karney family had, upon occasion, negotiated. Due to the canny bargaining on the part of the lords of the castle, it remained a great structure, a living museum, and a testament to history.

She was all that and more, Devin thought.

She was where a family held together, through war, through trial, through whatever came.

She was where a family really loved one another.

Rocky's arms came around her.

"It's still our honeymoon, you know. Do you long for a white sand beach and warm seas?" he asked.

"I thought we'd stay right here—maybe take a few side trips. But, I know of this particular place where I've had a tremendous amount of fun. I think you have, too. Wondrous fun."

She turned into his arms, came on her toes, met his eyes, and then whispered in his ear. "It's a tub. A big old claw-foot tub!"

"I'm feeling the need for a bath, I must say," he told her huskily.

Devin smiled. The eclipse was coming.

But, she knew, everything in her world was light.

They were who they were. Hard times would come again.

But for now…

There was that glorious old tub.

"Lead the way, my love," she said.

And he did.

All Hallows Eve

Prologue

Come to me. Please, come to me.

The words seemed real to Elyssa Adair, like a whisper in her mind, as she looked up at the old mansion.

The Mayberry Mortuary was decked out in a fantastic Halloween décor, customary each year starting October 1. It sat high on a jagged bluff near the waterfront in Salem, Massachusetts. Just driving toward it, at night, was like being in a horror movie. Dense trees lined the paved drive and it was surrounded by a graveyard. The old Colonial building, when captured beneath the moonlight, seemed to rise from the earth in true Gothic splendor.

She shivered and looked around at her friends, wondering if the words had been spoken by one of them. Vickie Thornton and Barry Tyler sat in the backseat, laughing with one another and making scary faces. Nate Fox was driving, his dark eyes intent on the road.

No one in the car had spoken to her.

She gave herself a silent mental shake. She could have sworn she'd actually heard a whisper. Clear as day. *Come to me.* Strangely, she wasn't afraid. She loved the artistry of Halloween—the fun of it—and few places in the world embraced the day like Salem.

This was home and she loved Salem, despite the sad history of witch trials and executions. A lot of that was steeped in lure and myth, but the local Peabody Essex museum and other historic venues seemed to go out of their way to remind visitors of the horror that came from petty jealousy and irrational fear.

"Boo," Nate said, leaning toward her.

She jumped with a start.

She'd been deeply involved in her thoughts and the view of the old mansion. Nate, Vickie, and Barry all giggled at her surprise.

"Do you have to do that," she murmured.

He frowned, his eyes back on the road. "Elyssa, we've done this every year since we were kids. So are you really scared now?"

"Of course not," she said, and tried to smile.

She loved Nate. They were both just eighteen, but they'd been seeing one another since their freshman year. She was young, as everyone kept reminding her, but she knew that she would love him all of her life. Despite them being opposites. She was a bookworm, born and raised in the East, red hair and green eyes. He was from South Dakota, a Western boy, whose mom had been from nearby Marblehead but whose dad had been a half Lakota Sioux. He was tall and dark with fabulous cheekbones and a keen sense of ethics and justice. He was their high school's quarterback, and she was debate team captain.

"Don't be silly," she said. "Last year, I played a zombie, remember?"

And what a role. She'd arose from the embalming table and attacked one of her classmates who'd played the mortician, terrifying the audience.

Nate grinned. "That you did. And what a lovely zombie you were."

Please.

She heard the single word and realized no one in the car had spoken it. Instead, it had vocalized only in her mind. Incredibly, she managed not to react. Instead, she pointed out the windshield and said, "Looks like someone has decided to toilet-paper the gates."

White streamers decorated the old wrought iron, which seemed original. Time had taken its toll on both the gates and the stone wall that had once surrounded the property. She'd never minded that such an historic property was transformed each year into one of the best haunted houses in New England. And despite the decorations, the house remained open daily until 3:00 P.M. for tours. It had been built soon after Roger Conant—the founder of Salem—moved to the area, around 1626, starting out as a one-room building. Nearly four hundred years of additions had blossomed it into a spacious mansion, the last editions coming way back in the Victorian era. In the early 1800s it had been consecrated as a Catholic church, deconsecrated by the 1830s when a new church had been built closer to town. Some said the site had then been used for satanic worship, taken over by a coven of black magic witches, but she'd never found any real support for those rumors. During the Civil War it served as a mortuary—drastically needed as the torn bodies of Union soldiers returned home. That continued until the 1950s when the VA made it a hospital for a decade. Finally, the Salem Society for Paranormal Studies bought the property. Along with historical tours, it offered tarot card and palm readings and ESP testing of anyone willing to pay the fee. The society had repaired and restored the old place, eventually garnering an historic designation, ensuring its continued preservation.

In the 1970s, Laurie Cabot came and created a place for dozens of modern-day Wiccans, and the area soon become a mecca for everyone and everything occult. Overall, though, the society people were barely noticed, except by fundamentalists who just didn't like anything period. Actually, the Wiccans had brought a great deal of commerce to town, and that was something to be appreciated.

Please, please, come. I need you.

Elyssa didn't move, not even a blink. Now she knew. Those words were only in her head. Maybe she needed sleep. Definitely, she shouldn't drink any more of the cheap wine Nate's brother found at the convenience store.

Last night's overindulgence had been plenty enough.

They drove through the gates and past the graves. Like every other New England cemetery, this one came with elaborate funerary art and plenty of stone symbolism. One angel in particular had always been her favorite. She occupied a pedestal near the drive, commissioned for a Lieutenant Colonel Robert Walker in 1863, there to guard his grave, on one knee, head bowed, weeping, her great wings at rest behind her back.

They drove by and the angel seemed to look up—straight at

Elyssa. Again, she heard the words in her head.

Please, help me. Find me.

"Look at the people," Vickie said.

The lines to get inside the haunted house stretched down the main walk to the porch, then around the corner of the house. The mansion was huge—seven thousand square feet over three stories, with a basement and an attic. Creepy windows filled the gables and projected inside dormers from the slate roof, like glowing eyes in the night.

"It's three days before Halloween. What were we expecting?" Nate asked. "This place is popular. But it looks like there are vendors walking by with hot chocolate. We'll have fun in line."

"Elyssa, can't you get us into the VIP line?" Barry asked. "Don't you still have friends here? Didn't they ask you back to work inside the haunted house this year?"

She nodded. "I just couldn't make it happen, not with getting the whole college thing going for next year. But, I'll see what I can do. John Bradbury still manages the place. He's a good guy to work for."

"Don't you know Micah Aldridge too?" Vickie asked. "Isn't he one of the main guys in the paranormal society?"

"He's never around at night. He and that weird, skinny lady from Savannah—Jeannette Mackey—have their noses up in the air at this kind of thing. They think they're a little above all this fun."

They parked far away, almost in the graveyard, and walked back to the line.

"Work your magic," Vickie told her.

Elyssa headed toward the makeshift desk and plywood shelter in the front where Naomi Hardy was working ticket sales. She was surprised to see that she'd been wrong. Micah Aldridge was there, helping with the sales.

Elyssa smiled at Naomi, then leaned down to talk to Micah. "I thought you hated this silliness."

He was a good-looking man who worked his dark hair and lean, bronzed features to add an aura of mystery to his appearance. His usual attire was some kind of a hat and long coat, reminiscent of a vampire, regardless of the season, and tonight was no exception.

"I don't hate what pays the bills," he told her, adding a smile. "Wish you would have worked this year. It's always great to see you."

"I just couldn't, not with college coming up." She drew in a breath. "Micah, I have some friends with me, and we're happy to buy tickets, but we can't afford VIP entrance and the line—"

Her words trailed off and she grimaced.

"Say no more, little one," he said.

To her surprise, he didn't let her pay. Instead, he set a BE BACK IN A MINUTE sign before his seat. He then whispered to Naomi Hardy, a pretty young woman of about twenty-five, who was selling the tickets to each person in line. Naomi was John Bradbury's assistant. She knew Naomi took a room in Salem for the month of October, but lived down in Boston.

Naomi smiled and nodded an understanding, then said, "Enjoy."

Micah led them up to the porch to wait for the next group to enter. She thanked him profusely, but he brought a finger up to his lips, signaling for quiet.

"Not even time for hot chocolate," Vickie noted, smiling.

"We'll get some after," Nate said.

In the mansion foyer they were greeted by a hunchback Igor-like actor who told them a tale about black masses in the house, mad scientists, and more. They then began the walk-through, starting with the dining room where skeletons had gathered together for a feast. One was a live actor who rose to scare each group as they entered. Next came the kitchen—where a cook was busy chopping up human bodies for a stew and offering the visitors a bloody heart.

Staged gore had never bothered Elyssa. She didn't mind the mad experiments in one of the bedrooms, or the Satanists sacrificing a young woman in the tarot card room. She didn't even mind the demented baby or the usual scare-factor pranks typical for haunted houses.

In an upstairs bedroom, they came to the mad scientist's lair where an actor was busy dissecting a woman on the bed, vials, wires, tubes, and beeping machines all around him. The woman—despite the fake gore—looked familiar.

Then she realized.

It was Jeannette Mackey.

Elyssa smiled and kept quiet, but when the rest of her group had filed out, she paused and hurried to the bed.

"What are you doing here?" she asked.

Jeannette grinned at her and replied with her sweet accent. "Darlin', when you can't beat'em, you've got to join'em."

Elyssa laughed, found Jeannette's hand, and squeezed it. "You and Micah working the show and Naomi Hardy on the ticket booth. Did they not get enough kid volunteers this year?"

"Gotta get back to work," Jeannette said. "New group is coming in. But, no, we're doing this just because we love the place."

Elyssa grinned and hurried out.

The other bedrooms on the second floor offered a Satanist mass, a headless tarot card reader, and two displays of movie monsters with ice picks, electric saws, and more scary weapons.

Then it was time to head down—way down.

Elyssa had always been oddly uneasy in the basement. That's where the embalming had once been done, and it hadn't changed much since the days when the house had served as an actual mortuary. The trestle tables were still there. The nooks and crannies where shelves with instruments had been kept remained too. Hoses above stone beds still hung, where real blood and guts had been washed away, the bodies readied for embalming. There was something sad and eerie about the place.

Vickie screamed and gasped delightedly. Barry kept an arm around her—except when he was jumping himself. There were motion-activated creatures in the arched nooks along the way. One, some kind of an alien creature, took Nate by surprise and he leapt back, causing them all to laugh.

But Elyssa's attention had been drawn to another of the basement nooks, a figure of a hanging man. She'd seen the group before them walk right by it—no blood, no gore, no actor to jump at them. To locals the image was nothing new. It could be seen throughout Salem, representative of men like George Burroughs or John Proctor, who'd also been convicted of witchcraft and hanged, like the women, during the craze.

Her head began to pound.

And she was drawn toward the image.

Yes, thank you. Come. Please, help me stop this.

She stared through the darkness and her first thought was how life-like the image was. But, of course, the man had been hanged. He was dead. No life existed. She could see every little hair on his head. He was dressed in Puritan garb, as if a victim of the witch trials. The nook had been painted to look as if it were outside at the hanging tree. He might have been about thirty-five or so in life, with dark hair and weathered features. And the smell. Rank. Like urine and rot. The area had really been done up to haunt all of the senses.

She moved closer.

Yes, yes. Help. Please, oh, yes, please.

The voice whispering in her mind grew louder.

One more step.

And then she knew.

The figure was real. Not an actor there to scare those who came so giddily through the house. And she knew him. He ran this place. He'd even given her a job here at the house last year.

John Bradbury.

Hanging, dead.

She screamed, which only evoked laughter at first. But she kept screaming and pointing. Her friends tried to calm her. Nate tried to show her that it was just part of the scare fest. A prop.

But he suddenly realized that it was much more.

White-faced and grim, he shouted, "That's a real body. He's dead."

The night seemed to drag on forever with the police, bright lights and horrified actors wanting to go home, Mayberry Mortuary haunted house closed down. Eventually, there was hot chocolate as they sat in the mortuary café, answering questions for cop after cop.

But, that wasn't the worse part.

That came when Elyssa finally made it home in the wee hours, lying in her bed, drifting in and out of sleep.

She felt her mattress depress and when she opened her eyes, John Bradbury was there.

Thank you. But you have to know. They're going to kill again, unless you stop them.

Chapter One

"There?" Sam Hall asked.

"Oh, yes. Yes. Touch me there. Right there," Jenna Duffy moaned in return.

"Right here? I can touch and touch and—"

"Ohhhh yes. That's it."

Jenna rolled over and looked up at him, eyes soft, smile beautiful. He'd been straddled over her spine carefully balancing his weight as he worked his magic. Now he towered over her front.

"I think," she said, reaching up to stroke his cheek, her eyes filled with wonder, "that you missed your calling. The hell with the law. The hell with the FBI. You could have been an amazing masseuse. My shoulders feel so much better."

"You shouldn't spend so many hours reading without taking a break and walking around."

Jenna nodded. "I don't know how Angela does it. She has such an eye for the cases and requests, when we're really needed. I've read them over and over."

She was referring to Special Agent Angela Hawkins, case facilitator for the Krewe of Hunters at their main offices—and wife of Jackson Crow, their acting field director. Both he and Jenna loved their work. When they weren't in the field, he maintained his bar licensing in several states by working Krewe legal matters. Jenna assisted Angela in reading between the lines, determining where the team was most needed. The requests for Krewe help were growing in number; and while new agents came on all the time, it was still a race to keep up.

"We have tomorrow," he said. "Then vacation."

"Sun, sea, and tanning oils for exotic massages," Jenna said, laughing.

He stared down into her eyes—greener than the richest forest—and marveled at the way he loved her. Her hair, a deep and blazing red, spread out across the pillows in waves. It seemed incredible that this remarkable, beautiful, sensual woman could feel the same for him. That they could lie together so naturally, that laughter could combine with passion, and that they could live and work together.

And still be closer each year.

He smiled and kissed her.

Her fingers ran down his spine with a teasing caress, finding his midriff, then venturing lower.

"What are you thinking about?" she asked.

He groaned softly.

"Pardon?"

"Sex. Here, now," he said. "The perfect place. In bed—both of us on it."

She frowned.

"And you weren't?"

She smiled and caressed him in one of her most erotic and sensual ways. "There?" she whispered teasingly.

"Oh, yes. Right there."

"I can touch and touch and touch."

He kissed her lips, then her collarbone and her breast, moving lower. He loved her so much, truly loved her, and every time they made love, it seemed sweeter and sweeter. Her skin was satin, her hair the fall of silk, and her movements—

Those were the best.

They slept after, entangled in one another's arms, and he thought about heading to Atlantis and how he'd planned to ask her then if they shouldn't begin to think about a wedding in the near future.

What a beautiful night.

But in the morning everything changed.

With the phone call.

* * * *

A wickedly big and warty witch atop a broomstick rode above a sign that advertised "Best Halloween Ball Bash in the Nor'East."

New England. Halloween.

Nothing went better together.

And the holiday decorations would just increase as they neared Salem, Massachusetts, the days ticking off closer and closer to the hallowed day. Costume shops abounded, as if they'd sprouted from seeds of alien pods tossed down by a space ship. But people everywhere liked to party.

Unfortunately, this was not going to be a vacation in the Bahamas. Sadly, Sam thought about the tickets he and Jenna had changed and the rooms in the fantasy casino they'd canceled. He didn't mind. If Jenna needed to do something else, that was fine. As long as he was with her.

And he was.

"So," he said, frowning slightly as he glanced over at Jenna before looking back at the road. "Talk to me. We're here to see a relative but, somehow, I never met her when you and I first got together, back with the murders at Lexington House. And, a relative I also haven't met since."

Then again, they hadn't been back to Salem that many times over the past few years. Jenna's parents lived in Boston—when they weren't visiting friends and family in Ireland—so they'd only made it that far when they popped up for a weekend. Her uncle, Jamie O'Neill, her next-favorite relative, often came down to Boston when they were there.

Jenna didn't look at him. She was gnawing her lower lip, staring out the window. She'd grown more and more withdrawn since they'd left Boston's Logan Airport and started driving up US 1 toward Salem. He wasn't sure if she had even heard him.

Salem.

His home.

And while Jenna had come from Ireland as a child and grown up in Boston, her ties with Salem were deep. Her Uncle Jamie lived here, and she'd spent a tremendous amount of time, while growing up, with him. Salem was where he'd fallen in love with Jenna. And when they'd left, he'd assumed he'd open a law practice in northern Virginia.

Instead, he'd found himself in the FBI academy.

And then part of the Krewe.

Thing was, though, until the call came, he'd never expected to be heading here. And he'd never expected that she'd close down. Jenna was an experienced agent. She dealt with a lot of bad things. She had a tremendous compassion for others and a stern work ethic. She'd been almost silent as they'd ridden to work, explaining only that they were going to have to change things up. No vacation right now. She'd gotten a call from an Elyssa Adair, someone he'd never heard her mention before. She was sorry, so sorry, about the trip, and she wanted to wait until they saw Jackson before explaining why this was so important. As soon as they'd arrived at work, he'd arranged for them both to speak with Jackson Crow at the Krewe of Hunters special unit headquarters.

He wasn't surprised that Jenna had so quickly been given permission for the two of them to travel to Salem. Krewe cases were often accepted on instinct, or because there was a particular reason a Krewe member should be involved. He was surprised, though, by Jenna, who was usually open and frank and outgoing, especially with him. They'd been together nearly five years. He'd changed his entire life to work with her and, of course, to deal with the fact that the dead seemed to like to speak with him.

And he loved her.

With all of his heart, with everything in him.

He knew that she felt the same way about him, which made it so strange that she'd seemed to shut him out, even while asking that he accompany her and assist on the case. At the moment, however, there wasn't a case. Not one that they'd been invited to join in on at least. A man was dead. He'd been associated with the old Mayberry Mortuary Halloween Horrors. Police were suggesting that he might have killed himself over financial matters. There was an ongoing local investigation. But, so far, the death was being considered a possible-suicide.

That much, he knew.

The minute Jenna had begun to talk about a cousin he'd never met, Elyssa Adair, and the fact that Elyssa had discovered the dead man in the haunted horror attraction, he'd probed for background.

John Bradbury, born in Salem, schooled in Boston, had returned to Salem to operate the mortuary under the business umbrella Hauntings and Hallucinations, Inc. The company was doing fine. However, the year before, Bradbury had gone through a tough divorce, and, apparently, due to past substance abuse problems, had lost all but supervised visitation rights with his three children. His ex-wife—while crying on a newscast—had told the world that it had been John's mental instability that had led to his self-medicating with drugs and alcohol and their subsequent divorce.

This was still New England, and while Sam held his own devotion to his home sector, he was aware that some of the old Puritanical values still hid in the hearts and minds of many. Mental weakness was kept to one's self. Everyone was shocked that the man killed himself, considering how calm he'd appeared to his employees and how happy he'd been when managing the mortuary in its guise as a haunted house. It would be easy to accept the death as an apparent suicide. Bad things happened around Halloween. Holidays seemed an impetus for those dealing with severe depression.

They were passing through Peabody—an old stomping ground for anyone who'd grown up in the area. Beautiful old Colonial and Victorian homes, big and small, grand and not so grand, were decked out in ghostly fashion, all the more eerie as night began to fall. Scarecrows, skeletons, ghosts, ghouls, black cats, and more abounded.

But the best was yet to come.

Salem prided itself on being Halloween central.

Jenna finally turned his way and said, "She's a little scholar. Elyssa was in Europe when we were here last. She earned six months study abroad before she was even a freshman. She's a great kid, a second cousin once removed or however you come about that. My dad's cousin's daughter's daughter. She's all grown up now, a senior and just turned eighteen. She's never seen a dead body—much less a hanged dead body."

Except in museums, probably. Many of Salem's attractions had scenes of life's finales, men and women convicted and executed after their so-called witch trials.

"I can imagine how bad it was," he said.

"She was nearly hysterical on the phone, and, of course, her folks are upset that she called me. They seem to think she's having a bad reaction to what happened. But I told her mom not to worry, that I was happy to come and see Uncle Jamie and that we had some vacation time coming anyway." She paused and looked at him apologetically. "I said I was happy to help her in any way that I can. The thing is—"

Her voice trailed.

He waited.

He knew her dilemma, listening intently when she'd explained the situation to Jackson Crow. Elyssa believed that a dead man had called her for help. Then that same dead man had appeared to her later to thank her for finding him, fading away with a warning that a killer had to be caught before more people died. Elyssa's parents would want Jenna to assure the young girl that what was happening in her mind was because of the horror she'd seen, not because a dead man could really speak to her.

"It's going to be hard," Jenna said. "I can't tell her that she's imagining things if, in fact, she's not. And if this man was really murdered, someone has to discover the truth about his death."

He reached across the car and squeezed her hand. "You'll do what's right. You always do."

She nodded and squeezed back.

They really hadn't talked about this much at all. Instead, they'd left the office, packed, and hopped onto the first plane. Angela had seen to it that a rental car was waiting for them. Normally, she would have seen to it that they had a hotel room too.

But, not in Salem.

Sam still owned a house here. His parents' home, where he'd grown up. Once, he'd wanted to sell the house and say good-bye to Salem. But Jenna and her Uncle Jamie had changed that. He'd learned something about his childhood home because of them, because of all of the bad that had happened.

Three things.

People made bad things happen.

Places weren't evil.

And when the dead remained, it was for a reason, usually to make sure that the living finally got it right.

He entered Salem and drove down Walnut Street, heading into the historic district. People, off to early holiday parties, filled the sidewalks in costume. Around this time of the year it was difficult to tell the practicing Wiccans from all the amateurs.

"How cute," Jenna murmured, noting a group of children, all in costumes themed to *The Wizard of Oz*.

They stood at a stop sign, and Sam took a minute to look at the group and smile. He was about to move through the intersection when he suddenly slammed on the brakes. A costumed pedestrian had rushed into the street and thrown himself on the hood of the car, grinning eerily at them. He stayed for a beat while Sam felt his temper flaring. The person in the costume stared at him through the windshield, donning a red latex mask. It seemed the entire body was red beneath a black cape, the eyes blood-streaked yellow. The person suddenly pushed off the car, cackling with laughter.

"Ass," Sam yelled.

"Total dick," Jenna said.

"Vampire, demon?"

"Boo-hag," Jenna said.

He didn't know about a boo-hag. "What's that?"

"I guess it's a regional thing, from the Gullah people. They're from regions of Africa, mainly brought to this country as slaves. They got together and formed a group hundreds of years ago. They have a language, kind of like a Haitian *patois* joined with English, and all kinds of cultural stuff. And of course now, with time passing, the mix is African, Creole, and so on. They're known to have lived in the low country of South Carolina, down to north Florida at one time."

"And what do these boo-hags do?"

"To the Gullah, there is a soul and a spirit. The soul goes to Heaven, assuming the person was good, the spirit watches over the family. Unless it's a bad spirit. Then, it becomes a boo-hag. Like a spiritual vampire."

"A spiritual vampire?" Sam asked.

She turned to him, grave and knowing, a slight smile in her eyes. "When you slept eight hours and woke exhausted, that might have been a boo-hag. They suck energy out of the living. Usually, they leave their victims alive so they can feast off of them again. If a victim struggles, that's when you find that person dead in the morning."

"And how do you fight a boo-hag?" Sam asked.

"You need to leave a broom by your bed. Boo-hags are easily distracted. They'll start counting the bristles and forget they came to suck your energy. To rid yourself of a boo-hag, though, you have to find their skin while they're out of it, and fill it with salt. That will make them insane with agony when they put it back on."

"Guess we need to sleep with salt and brooms," he said. "Easy enough to find at Halloween. How the hell do you know about all this? This is Salem, Mass, not the Deep South."

"You had to have known my mum's mother. She taught me all about the banshees and leprechauns. She loved legends. And she also had a dear friend from the low country who lived in Charleston."

"Wish I could have known her," Sam said. He was suddenly glad of the obnoxious drunk who'd thrown himself on the car. Jenna had finally become Jenna.

"Those eyes," she said, with a shiver. "Spooky."

"Contacts, most likely."

"Good ones, too. But there are a lot of great costumes at Halloween. You know that."

He did. "And no costume parties, huh?"

She grinned. "No costume parties. But you'd make a great John Proctor. He was supposed to have been a big, tall, strong dude."

"Before he was hanged," he said.

She grimaced at that.

They were nearly in the historic section.

He turned to her sheepishly. "I forgot to ask. My house? Or is Uncle Jamie expecting us?" Sam asked.

She turned to him, more relaxed than she'd been. "Uncle Jamie is expecting us."

"Okay, just so I know where I'm going."

She nodded, and he noticed a darkness settle over her again. There was something so pained about her eyes, and yet there was so much appreciation in them he felt a tug at his heart. He remembered meeting her when Malachi Smith had been accused of the brutal murders at Lexington House, and how strong and determined she'd been. Between her and Jamie, he'd found himself representing the young man pro bono. Even in the height of danger and true horror there, she'd never looked like this.

But this time her family was involved.

"I'm here," he said. "Jamie is here. And you're the best damned agent I know. Things will work out fine."

"Thanks," she said.

He drove to Jamie O'Neill's eighteenth century house, not much different from his parents'. Jamie kept the place in excellent shape. He was an exceptionally good man who'd almost gone into the priesthood. Instead, he'd studied psychiatry and donated an awful lot of pro bono work, always helping the underdog. Sam had known Jamie before he'd returned on the day of the Lexington House murders. He'd even met Jenna, though all he remembered of that day was being called upon by his parents to supervise a group of rowdy teenage girls.

Today, Jamie's house seemed strange as he eased onto the old stone drive in front. Like a dark cloud had settled over it. But the afternoon was waning. Massachusetts's autumns brought night quickly. Still, it seemed to Sam that clouds sat over the house and nowhere else. Jenna's family was certain that the property was haunted, but by nice ghosts they claimed. Ghosts that went about their business and left the living to their own. He was curious about Elyssa Adair and her family. Apparently, they didn't possess Jenna's mom's and dad's ability to shrug off anything that might be paranormal.

The door opened and he saw Jamie O'Neill step out on the porch. He wore a sweater and jeans, but cast a grave look about him that Sam could not remember seeing often. He lifted a hand in greeting, as Jenna ran up the walk to hug him. Sam opened the trunk of the rental car and grabbed their bags.

A young woman burst from the house behind Jamie. She had red hair, similar to Jenna's. Tall, lean, pretty, upset, yet relieved.

"Jenna. Thank you for coming."

Sam knew that the young lady had to be Elyssa Adair.

"That was never in doubt," Jenna said, engulfed in a tight and enthusiastic hug.

Sam moved forward, setting the bags down as Jenna disentangled herself and turned to make the introductions. "Elyssa, this is Special Agent Sam Hall. We work together and we're together, too."

"Uncle Jamie told me all about that," Elyssa said.

The younger woman stared at him with beautiful eyes that weren't quite as rich a green as Jenna's. Then she threw her arms around him and hugged him.

Withdrawing at last, she said, "I knew you would come, too."

He was puzzled. "Can I ask how?"

"The ghost told me. John Bradbury specifically said you were coming, and that was before Uncle Jamie ever mentioned you. He said he knew you when he was alive."

Chapter Two

"Come in," Uncle Jamie said after greeting Jenna and Sam.

Jenna looked at her uncle anxiously, wondering why she had such a bad feeling about what was going on. Elyssa had calmed and smiled at Jenna.

"Are you all right?" Jenna asked, hands on her young cousin's shoulders. She hadn't seen Elyssa for years, although they kept up on Facebook. Their lack of a visit hadn't been on purpose, just the way life had fallen into place.

"I'm fine," Elyssa said. "Now that you're here."

There was that unshakeable faith Elyssa seemed to have in her. Which was a lot to live up to.

"Let's talk," she said to both Elyssa and her uncle.

For a man who accepted just about anything on earth and maintained his faith with the loyalty of an angel, Uncle Jamie could be very matter-of-fact. "We need to, before Susan gets back."

"Susan?" Sam asked, following Jenna across the porch to the front door.

"Elyssa's mother," Jamie said.

A minute later Uncle Jamie had served them all coffee and they sat around the dining room table. Jenna felt Sam's hand on hers and met the strong gravity in his eyes.

"I'm here," he said softly.

She nodded, a thank you in the squeeze she returned on his hand.

"From the beginning," she told Elyssa. "Tell me everything."

Elyssa glanced nervously at Uncle Jamie, took a breath and began.

"Mom says I'm crazy. Dad is looking into 'trauma doctors.' I'm pretty sure he means shrinks." She paused. "Uncle Jamie came to the house. Mom thinks he's almost a priest—and he was almost—so she let me come here and she even said it was okay to talk to you because you're with the FBI. She thinks you'll make me understand the difference between a suicide and a murder. And Uncle Jamie has been the best person in the world for me because he doesn't think that I'm crazy. He seems to believe in...whatever it is."

Jenna thought about how much she really loved her uncle. He told her once that he believed deeply in his faith, so he had to accept that there was life after death. And who was he to declare that departed souls might not linger, trying to help others.

"What makes the police think it was suicide?" Sam asked.

Elyssa flushed uncomfortably. "There was a kicked over stool found near where he was hanging, right in the niche."

Sam shrugged. "Could have been planted."

"Why don't you tell us what happened exactly, from beginning to end?" Jenna said.

"We're open to hearing everything you have to say," Sam added.

Elyssa looked at Sam and nodded. She seemed to have taken an instant liking to him. Unlike Jenna, who'd admired Sam's stature and reputation from the beginning, but had not been all that enamored. It had been Uncle Jamie who'd known that Sam would come around to their way of thinking, and their determination to find the truth about the Lexington House murders. And then she'd been lucky. Sam had fallen in love with her, while she was falling hard for him. And now she couldn't imagine her life without him. It didn't hurt that he really was a gorgeous man, rugged, tall, smooth and dignified, with a rock hard jaw and a steely determination when he made up his mind to get something done.

Elyssa launched into her story. She'd just been out for a night of fun and heard a strange voice in her head, which she ignored. She'd tried to connect with John Bradbury when they'd reached the mortuary, but he'd not been around.

Then she found him.

Hanging dead.

The haunted attraction had been closed down and she'd answered questions over and over again. Back home, her mom had actually made her tea with whiskey in it so that she could sleep. But then she'd opened her eyes and John Bradbury had been sitting at the foot of her bed, telling her that he was grateful, but that she had to stop what was happening or other people would die.

"He didn't by any chance tell you what was happening, did he?" Sam asked.

"He doesn't really know. He was working downstairs in the embalming room when someone slipped a noose around his neck. He heard people talking, two people, he thinks. Then someone said something about the witch trials and wacky cults. Another voice said something about that person needing to shut up. And then the person who'd spoken first said what the hell did it matter? Bradbury would be dead. Who cares."

"The witch *trials?*" Jenna asked, adding, "Not Wiccans today?"

Elyssa nodded. "The witch trials, that's what he said. Someone was talking about the witch trials and cults. But, what they said exactly, I don't know." She looked hopeful. "Maybe now that you're here, John will come and talk to you instead of me. I can't remember all that he said. I'm not sure he knows exactly what he heard."

"We'll look into whatever new groups are in town," Sam said. "And, of course check out the older covens and groups too. Most of the Wiccans in town are good and peaceful people. They practice their faith like any religion."

"Good people come in all faiths," Uncle Jamie said. "Elyssa knows that."

"I mean, that's the thing. I couldn't figure out why he appeared to me. I'm in my last year of high school," Elyssa said. "I have midterms coming up. I'm not the police or even an investigator. Early this morning he came back. He wasn't a creepy ghost or anything. He didn't pop into the shower on me or anything like that. He appeared right when I'd finished dressing. Mom said I shouldn't go to school today. When I first woke up—that's when I called you, Jenna—I was still feeling freaked out. Then you said that you'd come and I was so relieved. I was finally hungry and was going to go out to get some breakfast when he appeared at my bedroom door. He thanked me again and said that you and Sam could help."

Sam smiled at her. "He came back and talked to you in your room and you didn't scream or pass out? Pretty brave kid."

Elyssa smiled. "Maybe I'm like you."

"Maybe you are—and it's really not so bad," Jenna told her.

"Should we have known this man?" Sam asked.

"He was from Salem," Jenna told him. "Five to ten years older than you. Do you remember his name from anything?"

Sam reflected for a moment and then shook his head. "I'm not really sure."

"He knew you, or about you," Elyssa said, staring at them both expectantly.

"We should start with the covens and cultists," Jenna noted. "Though that could be a long list. Seems like new things sprout up here every Halloween."

"I'll get Angela working on it back at headquarters," Sam said. "I'd like to get into the autopsy. I'll call Jackson, see if Adam Harrison has any sway up here."

"Adam has sway everywhere," Jenna assured him.

Adam Harrison, the dignified philanthropist who'd finally organized his little army of psychic researchers into an FBI unit, did seem to have sway everywhere. He was a good man, one who'd made a great deal of money and managed to keep his principles. His son, dead in a car accident in high school, had been one of those special people with an unusual ability. Eventually, Adam had learned that his son was not the only one.

"Excuse me," Sam told them. "I'm going to make some calls. You know Devin Lyle and Craig Rockwell are from this area, too. We might need some help covering the ground."

"Good idea," Jenna said. In all the rush she'd forgotten that her co-agents were also from Salem. Then again, Elyssa's hysterical call that morning had made her forget everything. "Hopefully, they're not already on assignment."

"We'll see," Sam said, and headed out to the living room where he could call privately.

Uncle Jamie glanced at his watch. "Susan is due back soon. What are we going to say to her? I can't encourage a child to lie to her parents, but Susan and Matt will see her locked away in an institution."

"I'm not a child," Elyssa reminded them. "Come June, I'll be both a high school grad and over eighteen."

"And that means you'll stop loving and caring for your parents?"

Jamie asked.

"Of course not. But Uncle Jamie, they think I'm crazy."

"It's going to be fine," Jenna said. "Your mom knows that you called me, right?"

Elyssa nodded. "I seem to have the gift. My mom doesn't, so she'll never understand."

"Some people never do," Jenna said. "But that doesn't mean she doesn't love you. So what we're going to do is this. You'll say you can't help but be concerned and worried. And I'll say that Sam and I have come because we've realized just how long it's been since we've been back here, so why not check out this situation for you. How's that?"

She looked at Jamie and Elyssa.

"Omission in itself can be a lie," her uncle said. "But, okay, it's not a lie."

The admission came just in time, as the doorbell rang. They could hear the door open and Sam's deep voice as he introduced himself to Susan and Matt Adair, Elyssa's parents.

"Jenna," Susan Adair said, hurrying across the room with a huge hug. "Have you had a chance to speak with Elyssa? You've explained that, while it's sad and tragic, poor Mr. Bradbury took his own life. All I think about are his children. This will be so hard for them."

"Not to worry," Jenna said. "We've assured Elyssa that we'll look into it all and that she needs to worry about school and midterms."

Sam laid his hands on Jenna's shoulders. "It never hurts to be thorough. That's what the bureau is all about. But Jenna is right. Elyssa doesn't have to worry or be concerned about a thing."

"See," Susan said, turning to her daughter triumphantly. "That's all good."

Matt Adair had been hovering by the door, watching the reunion. He was fit—an athletic man, coaching football at the local high school. They were quite the odd couple. Susan, Irish-looking with carrot red hair and amber eyes, a ball of fire and energy. Matt, except for when he was on the football field, a model of quiet and calm.

He greeted Jenna with a hug, then said, "I never like to say there's nothing to worry about."

Elyssa let out a sigh. "He's worried because I was babbling, and he's afraid my peers are going to make fun of me. That's the least of my worries. Honestly, Dad. My feet are on the ground, and I've never been swayed by peer pressure."

And, to the best of Jenna's knowledge, she hadn't been. Elyssa was bright and happy. She made friends because she was honestly interested in others and enjoyed meeting people. Between them, Susan and Matt had raised her right. A daughter open to new experiences, but comfortable in her own.

"It's always smart to be cautious," Uncle Jamie murmured. "Now, how about some food. I've taken the liberty of ordering out. Italian. And I think the delivery person just drove up."

"I'll head out and get it," Sam offered.

"And I'll give you a hand," Matt said.

"Wait," Susan said. "Why does anyone need to be cautious? This was a suicide. Right? Our daughter found the poor man and that's that."

But no one answered her.

Jenna hurried to help Uncle Jamie with plates and Elyssa found silverware and glasses. The delivery order included lasagna, salad, and breadsticks and the next few minutes were spent passing food around.

"What's new in town?" Sam asked, when everyone was satisfied with a plate filled to their liking.

"They keep building ugly new structures," Matt said.

"It used to be so quaint here. But commercialism is ruining the place," Susan added, shaking her head.

"But a lot of the old shops are still around, right?"

"Oh, yes, and more." Susan said. "New England seems to be moving into an age of diversity. We now have a large Asian population."

"And Hispanic," Matt said.

"Russian, too. Mostly Eastern Europeans," Uncle Jamie said. "We have a new family from Estonia at my church these days, and a number of Polish."

Susan shrugged and smiled. "And islanders. South Americans and Southerners."

Jenna had to laugh. The way Susan spoke, it seemed that Southerners were the most foreign of anyone who'd moved to Salem. "The world moves all over these days. People go different places for work, to study, and some just to live."

"I actually love all of the different languages, the people and accents," Susan said. "But I have to say, if this weren't my home, I don't know if I would have moved here."

Jenna was curious. "Why?"

"Snow," Elyssa said. "Mom hates the snow."

"I don't hate the snow. I hate shoveling snow. And chipping the windows covered with ice."

"Oh, mom, you love Salem. We couldn't pry you out of here with a fire poker."

Elyssa seemed exceptionally happy. As if what had been so horrible was not half so bad anymore.

"Tell me about the new shops in town," Jenna said, glancing at Sam. No better way to learn the lay of the land than ask the locals.

"There's a great place called Down River on Essex Street," Matt said. "I love it. All kinds of books, new and used, and wonderful art and artifacts."

"It's owned by one of the silly Southerners who moved north to shovel snow," Susan said. "Pass the garlic bread, will you please?"

"And there's a restaurant and shop that opened near there," Matt told them. "Indian, from across the ocean. Great food. Beautiful saris and shirts."

"Too much curry, that's the way I see the food," Susan said.

"What about the old places?"

"Most of them are still around. And, of course, there are a number of covens. I think we also have people practicing Santeria or voodoo or something like that." Susan shook her head. "Evil spells." And her hand with the fork shivered halfway to her mouth.

"Most people," Uncle Jamie said, "whether they're practicing Santeria or voodoo or if they're Baptists or Catholics or Episcopalians, are good people. Today's Wiccans tend to be lovely, not wanting to hurt anyone."

"You really do see the good in everyone," Susan said.

"Most religions are good. What men and women do with that sometimes is the problem. I just don't go assuming they're out to do evil."

"I hope not," Matt said. "Halloween seems to bring out all of the kooks. Especially in Salem. And we did have that terrible incident with those murders just a year or two back."

"We know about that," Sam said. "We had colleagues involved with the investigation."

"We're going to hope that everyone behaves for Halloween," Susan said sternly. "And plan on all good things, right, Elyssa?"

The young girl nodded. "I'm going to the school dance, then a party at Nate's house. I'm going to be an angel. Not costume-wise. I'm going as Poison Ivy. But I'll be an angel."

When it was time for the Adair family to leave, Elyssa caught Jenna by the door and gave her a tight hug once again. "Thank you so much for coming. You've made me feel sane again."

Jenna smiled and watched the family go.

As the car drove down the street, Sam turned to Uncle Jamie. "Okay, so what's really going on around here?"

Jamie stared at him. "What do you mean?"

"I know you're in on everything happening. Santeria, voodoo. What else is there that we need to know about?"

The older man sighed and shrugged. "We do have two voodoo priestesses in town. They read tarot cards and do palm reading. But that's not new for Salem, as you know. A few neighbors have complained about chickens. I assume they're being used in their services."

"And the Wiccans? Have you heard of anything troubling there?"

"They're like any group, squabbling now and then."

"Were any of the groups upset about the things going on at the mortuary?" Sam asked.

"Now that I think of it, there was a town meeting. Quite honestly, it was all the usual. A woman complaining that having the mortuary be a theme park attraction for Halloween made fun of witchcraft. She objected to the image of everyone who practiced the Wiccan religion being portrayed as a broom-riding, warty old woman. Someone else was complaining that the haunted house took away from the historic value of the town. Another guy gave a great oratory about the freedom of being in America. Be Wiccan, a Buddhist, whatever, and accept all else. Some clapped for him, some said freedom came with responsibility and respect. But cooler heads prevailed. It's Halloween and every self-respecting town has to have a great haunted attraction. Besides, Salem makes a lot of money at Halloween."

"Think you can make us a list of names of people who seemed to be heading toward the fanatical stage on their speeches?" Sam asked.

"Absolutely."

"You talked to Jackson?" Jenna asked Sam.

He nodded. "Devin Lyle and Craig Rockwell are going to come straight here from a situation in San Diego. They'll be here by tomorrow night, or the next morning at the latest."

"That's Halloween," Jenna said.

"I'm off," Sam said, smiling at the other two. "Care to join me?"

"And where are you going, and what do you think you can discover at this time of night?" Uncle Jamie asked.

"Angela and the home office are online, seeing what they can find out. Thankfully, everyone has a blog or is on Facebook these days. They like to bitch, so we may find something out through their posts. So where else does one get the skinny on what's happening? The best local bar in the center of the action. Except, what would that be now? Hard to say. So I'll just hop from one bar to another and see what's there."

Chapter Three

"There," Jenna said, motioning with her head.

"Where, what?" Sam asked.

They'd entered a relatively new place on Essex Street called The Sorcerer's Brew. Nicely adorned with lots of carved wood and old kegs and trunks for tables and seats. The menu was full of old standards like clam chowder, scrod, fish, meat and chicken, many done up blackened, with cilantro or sriracha sauce. The signature cocktail was also called The Sorcerer's Brew, and they had taps for twenty different beers on draft.

Definitely a tourist stop.

The Peabody Essex museum was just down the street along with a number of the historic houses open to the public. Ghost tours left from the front of nearby shops and a number of store windows offered haunted mazes, 3-D haunted experiences, and slightly twisted versions of the ghosts of Salem, all which utilized various scenes of the condemned coming back to life to curse those who'd accused them. Like most new places that sprang up, the locals checked in now and then. Especially at Halloween, when they were working late and craved a quick bite, a drink, or a cup of tea after work.

Sam followed Jenna's pointed finger and saw a pair of young women seated in a carved wooden booth toward the windows at the front of the restaurant. He followed her as she moved through the crowd.

"Who are they?" he asked.

"Old friends," she told him, and then she grinned. "Actually, you know them. You chaperoned all of us one day years ago."

And he remembered. Part of the teenage wild gang.

"Stephanie," Jenna said. "Audra."

The two women turned, then both sprang to their feet. There was a lot of gushing and hugs. Sam stood by and waited, then he was introduced. Stephanie had long dark hair and was dressed in black jeans and a black sweater. Audra too had long hair, dressed in a black-tailored shirt and long skirt. Stephanie still looked like a girl with big brown eyes and a gamine-like face. Audra cast a more sophisticated appearance.

"My God," Stephanie said, giving him a hug. "I'd heard you two were together now. I didn't get to see either of you when you were here on that awful Lexington House case. But, oh, a big-time lawyer, eh? Do you remember us? Audra and I were the other kids you had to watch that day. We tormented you, didn't we? But we all had these massive crushes on you. It's great to see you. Are you moving back?"

"Of course, I remember both of you," Sam said, lying. Actually, he didn't remember either of them, only Jenna. "It's great to see you. And no, we're not moving back. We're just here to visit."

"Sit down, join us, can you?" Audra asked.

Sam took a seat on the wooden bench next to Stephanie. Jenna slid beside Audra.

"We know why you're here," Audra said.

"We do?" Stephanie said. "I actually don't. What's going on?"

Audra drew an elegantly polished purple nail along the sweat on her beer mug. "The death at the mortuary. Elyssa Adair found the body."

"That's true," Sam said.

Jenna looked at him, shrugged, and went with his direction. "She was upset and called me. So that's why we're here."

"The whole thing is a little strange, isn't it?" Sam said.

Audra agreed with a shrug. "If that's what I did for a living, manage haunted houses, and I decided to do it all in, I would think that doing something like that would be a great final statement to the world."

Stephanie gasped. "You don't think he committed suicide, do you?"

"We don't really know anything at all," Sam said. "We're just here with the family."

"Did you two get married?" Stephanie asked.

"Not yet," Sam said. "But it's coming. What do you two know about the mortuary and the haunted house? Anything odd going on there?"

"You mean besides a man found hanged to death?" Audra asked.

"Yeah. Besides that."

Stephanie shrugged and said, "The paranormal people aren't happy about renting to the haunted house people. They're above all that, you know. And the haunted house people just think that the paranormal people are crazy. Micah is kind of a self-important jerk and Jeannette Mackey thinks that she's a serious psychic and that all the Wiccan palm and tarot readers in town are idiots. But when it comes to keeping the mortuary going, they force themselves to get along. Oh, my God. You don't think Micah murdered him, do you?"

"We don't know what to think," Sam said.

"But you've come home to solve this murder, haven't you?" Stephanie asked. "This is your home, Sam, right?"

He nodded. "Absolutely."

Jenna looked at Audra. "Are you in a coven?"

"I practice Wicca, but no, I'm not in a coven. I like practicing the tenets on my own. A lot of people don't really practice, they just join covens and then charge for tarot and palm readings and whatever else. Then they charge to be mentors. I don't like the charging part of it, so I practice on my own."

"Oh, come on, there are good covens in the area," Stephanie said.

"Some," Audra agreed. "But only a few."

"So do Wiccans argue with each other?" Sam asked.

"The only argument I know about is between Gloria Day and Tandy Whitehall," Audra said. "Old school versus new school, and all about money. Gloria runs the Silver Moon Festival throughout October. Tandy is much younger and has started doing some really wickedly wild parties. They're always vying for the most publicity. Everyone else is divided. Some support the new, others the old. But mainly they just bitch about each other privately."

"Then there's that idiot who went to court to support the drunk who killed a guy in the crosswalk. Said he was a warlock and that he was going to hex everyone," Stephanie said.

"Male witches aren't warlocks. They're witches, right?" Sam said, frowning.

"They are," Audra agreed, flicking a hand in the air. "At least, in my circles they are. But there are zillions of diverse ways to be a Wiccan or practice the Old Religion. There's Shamanic, Celtic, Gardnerian, and more, not to mention paganism, Pantheists, and Druids. What we all have in common is a love and respect for nature. Most of the holidays are about the same, speaking of which, Halloween is Samhain to us.

"Anything else going on?" Sam asked.

"I need another beer if we're going to play twenty questions," Stephanie said. "And you two haven't had anything to drink yet. What's happened to the service around here?"

"I'll take care of it," Sam said. "I guess they're swamped. What are you all drinking?"

"Local brew. Black Witches Ale. Give it a try," Stephanie said.

"Okay, four mugs of Black Witches Ale coming up."

Sam walked over to the bar and waited his turn, observing those who were there, some in street clothes, others in partial costume. Those were the ones who worked at the historical or Halloween venues, glad to be out of Puritan or creature garb for the night.

"Every place in Salem," an older man next to him said, and sighed. He shook his head, then glanced at Sam apologetically, as if realizing he'd spoken aloud. "Sorry—commercialism! Good for Salem, hard on those who live here!"

"It is almost Halloween," Sam said.

"Can't wait until it's over."

Sam offered his hand and introduced himself. "I'm from here; home for a visit with some family of a friend."

They shook hands.

"The place has changed. I remember when Laurie Cabot started up with the first witch shop. You would have been young."

"I remember," Sam said.

"Nowadays, we got everything. This morning, damn if there

wasn't a chicken head out on the embankment by my place."

Sam asked him where he lived, which was just a few blocks down from where they were, not far from the Elizabeth Montgomery *Bewitched* statue.

"We have Creole neighbors. Don't know what they're practicing, but come on, chicken heads?" The man sighed again. "My wife does say that Mrs. DuPont makes a heck of a chicken pot pie, though. Chicken heads and suicides. I'm telling you, the real stuff going on here now is worse than Halloween. Good for the economy, but crazy for regular folks."

"You're referring to John Bradbury's death?" Sam asked.

"I am. Sad thing. Nice guy. He'd come in here now and then. I'm a realtor and have some late nights. Anyway, Bradbury was always excited about bringing his artistic craft home to Salem. That's what he called it. He loved the old mortuary up there. He told me he wished he could buy it and, if ever he could, he'd turn it into a permanent attraction. Put more history in it, that kind of a thing. He loved the history of Halloween and how the Christian church managed to combine with the pagan ways."

The harried bartender came to them and Sam let the older man place his order first, then asked for the beers. The man thanked him and told Sam he'd be seeing him and moved on. As Sam collected the four steins of Black Witches Ale, he heard a couple at the bar arguing.

"Don't do it," the man warned.

"She's a bitch, and I'm going to take her down," the woman said defiantly.

"You're being ridiculous. There are enough people here to make everyone successful and happy. And, besides, that has nothing to do with practicing what we believe."

"It has to do with pride and with that nasty little bitch Gloria Day trying to take over from everyone else."

"Stop talking," the man said. "Someone will hear you."

"Maybe someone out there is practicing black magic. Not a Wiccan religion, but pure Satanism. Bradbury talked against her, and look where he is."

"It was a suicide," the man said.

"Maybe. Maybe not."

Sam pretended to get thrown against the man's arm. When the

fellow turned to look at him, he quickly apologized. "Sorry. It's so busy in here."

"It's okay," the man said.

"I don't remember it being this crazy. I'm from here, but…wow. Sam Hall, by the way. Nice to meet you, since I nearly sloshed beer on you."

The man frowned. "Sam Hall. You're that big-time attorney. Sorry, I'm David Cromwell and this is my wife, Lydia."

"Nice to meet you both," Sam said and decided not to tell them that he wasn't really practicing law anymore. "By the way, what should I do on Halloween? I hear there are all kinds of things going on and since I haven't been home in ages, I wouldn't mind some advice."

"Tandy Whitehall's Moonlight Madness," Lydia said. "Tandy has been here forever and she's the real deal. She gets fabulous bands and, if you get a reading at the party, it'll be a good one. It's just lovely."

David Cromwell had lowered his head and was gritting his teeth. Bingo. Sam knew that he had hit the core of their argument. Lydia was a huge Tandy Whitehall fan. In the morning, he'd find out how vicious and divisive that fight might be. John Bradbury was dead, and he'd apparently been vocal against the usurper as well.

"Thanks so much," Sam said.

He headed back to the table with the beers. Stephanie and Audra were bringing Jenna up to date on what was going on with their families. They all paused to thank him as he returned.

"Slow waiter," Jenna teased, looking at him.

He sensed she was ready to go, as he'd caught her glance at him while he talked to the Cromwells at the bar. A few minutes later, Jenna yawned and said that they needed to get some sleep.

"And who knows? Uncle Jamie might still have a curfew going for me."

Audra said, "If you think we can help you in any way, please, don't hesitate to let us know."

"Thanks," Sam said.

"Don't look now," Audra said, "but that's Jeannette Mackey. See the athletic looking woman who just went up to the bar? She's Micah Aldridge's VP or whatever for the paranormal part of the mortuary."

"Really?" Sam muttered.

"I know her," Audra said. "She's older than we are by several years, but I know I've met her a few times. She was on the news a lot, even in Boston. Interviewed on her views on the past and the present and parapsychology."

"I remember when she first started talking about creating a 'true home for the power of the mind,'" Sam said.

He saw the bartender greet her and hand her a large glass of whiskey. "We should pay our respects on the way out."

"Definitely," Jenna said.

They bid her friends goodnight. Sam slipped an arm around Jenna and together they headed for the attractive woman swilling down the drink that had been poured for her.

"Miss Mackey," Sam said.

The woman spun around and stared at Sam, a little wild-eyed, then said, "Samuel Hall, attorney, right?"

"Correct. And this is Jenna Duffy. I believe you two have met somewhere along the line, too."

"Jenna, yes, how are you? You and Elyssa are cousins, right?"

"You have a good memory. We came up to support the family. I understand you and John Bradbury worked together. We just stopped by to say how sorry we are."

"Thank you. I had tremendous respect for John. It was an incredibly important job he had. His company was growing bigger and bigger and his ideas and management were brilliant. I can't tell you how much money the haunted house aspect makes, and what wonderful funds we received because of it. Survival, really. Oh, not that I like a haunted house. But, hey, it was so important I'd play a part in all the schlock when necessary." She looked at the empty glass in her hand. "We're all in shock. Of course, Micah is taking it in stride. I guess he is the stronger one, between us."

"If there's anything we can do, please let us know," Jenna said.

"Of course. And if you need me for anything." Her voice trailed. "A suicide. John. I still can't believe it."

"Actually, we're not sure we do believe it," Sam said.

"What?" Jeannette asked, sounding stunned.

"We'll be looking into it," Jenna assured her.

"Of course, you will, of course. As sad as it is, oh, my God. You think that someone would have harmed him?" Jeannette asked.

"Do you know of any enemies he might have had?" Jenna asked.

"John? None. He was polite and courteous to everyone. He had a bit of a problem with Gloria Day, but that's a long story. Even so, he was still decent to her. She just didn't like playing off Tandy Whitehall's thunder." She lowered her voice. "And the Wiccans, you never know what they're up to." She let out a soft sigh. "Excuse me, will you? I'm going to go home and try to get some sleep."

"Us, too," Sam said. "I just want you to know that we're sorry."

She thanked them, turned, and hurried out.

"What do you think?" Sam asked Jenna.

"I think we have a lot to look into."

The streets were still crazed with activity. It was nearing midnight and there were parties galore around town. Children and adults alike seemed to enjoy dressing up for the season. They turned the corner to cut down by Burying Point and the memorial to those who'd been condemned to hang along with Giles Corey, "pressed" to death. They passed a few late night ghost tours, the guides dressed in Puritan garb.

Many people believed Salem to be one of the most haunted cities in the world. Easy to understand why. There were those who'd been condemned to death, along with those who died imprisoned, or others who went mad from fear or from what was done to them. A rich history permeated, one that needed to be remembered. Fear could cause normally decent people to do terrible things. Or, even worse, to practice the sin of silence, too afraid to speak out against injustice.

Jenna stopped by the memorial with its stone benches, each dedicated to one of the victims.

"John Proctor spoke out, and he died for it," she said. "I always think about that. He threatened Mercy Warren, his servant girl, with a beating if she didn't stop with the fits, and it worked once."

"You believe all of this has something to do with the witchcraft trials and the modern Wiccans?" Sam asked.

She shrugged. "The case that Devin and Rocky worked up here had to do with someone who'd been murdered before she could be tried. And, according to Elyssa, John Bradbury's ghost mentioned something about witches."

"I actually heard a woman back in the bar mention to her husband that John Bradbury had supported Tandy Whitehall against Gloria Day."

"May mean nothing."

"But could be everything. Another guy told me about finding chicken heads by his house. His neighbors, the DuPont family, practice Santeria or a religion that considers chickens to make good sacrificial offerings."

"Maybe they just like fresh meat at dinner?"

"At least we've got the feel for Halloween in Salem," he told her, slipping an arm around her shoulders as they continued to walk. "I want in on the autopsy. It'll take place tomorrow. Adam Harrison is going to work with the governor, who will call the mayor. I also want to get to the Mayberry Mortuary. It was closed once the body was found. The police and forensic people probably haven't finished with it just yet."

"If they suspect just a suicide," Jenna murmured.

"I don't know what they suspect. The lead detective on the case is a guy named Gary Martin. I don't know the man. I hope it's someone Devin or Rocky might know."

Jenna shook her head. "I don't know the name either."

"I should be able to meet with Martin in the morning and get into the autopsy."

"I'll head to the Mayberry Mortuary," Jenna said.

They came to the cemetery and Sam stopped. He could see the old tombstones with their death's heads, cherubs, angels, and other decorations, opaque and haunting in the moonlight. The main gates were locked at this time of night and it was, of course, illegal for anyone to enter. He thought for a moment he saw movement by one of the gnarled old trees.

"What is it?" Jenna asked.

He shook his head. "Nothing. Let's get back and get some sleep. It's been a long day."

She agreed.

The crowds had thinned, a few groups here and there, less as they left the cemetery and some of the major attractions behind and headed down the street that led to Uncle Jamie's house.

As they turned a corner, Jenna said, "There's another one, or the same guy on a costume bender. Another boo-hag."

She was right. Across the street, a group in costume was walking toward the wharf, heading back to one of the new hotels near the water. And there was someone in the same costume that had jumped onto their car.

A boo-hag.

Sam had been born and raised in Salem and he'd never even heard of a boo-hag before. Now he'd seen two in as many days.

The group was walking with their backs toward Sam and Jenna. Suddenly, the man in the boo-hag costume turned, stared their way for a moment, then headed off.

"That was eerie," Jenna said. "Movie monsters and most creatures seem almost ho-hum around here, but that costume gets to you."

"A boo-hag," Sam said. "Definitely creepy."

He didn't mention that there was something more. The way the eyes seemed to focus on them, the way they seemed to burn, even at a distance, as if they were formed of fiery red-gold, burning like the flames of hell.

Chapter Four

Sam knew that they often dealt with terrible things. That was the occupation he and Jenna had both chosen. Partly because of their "gifts," and partly because they wanted to make a difference. But this situation seemed more personal. He'd intended to give Jenna all the space she needed. But alone, in the darkness of their room at Uncle Jamie's, she turned to him with a sweet and urgent passion. The warmth of her naked body next to his, flesh against flesh, and the fever that seemed to burn in her became electric. No words, just her moving against him, touching, a feather-light caress at first, then a passionate love, both tender and urgent. He held her afterward, naked and slaked against him, and he thought that they both would sleep well.

Home was wonderful.

But home was also a place where nightmares could be rekindled.

He didn't want her facing any demons in her mind. But that night Sam was the one to dream. He saw something coming toward them out of a strange and misty darkness. Red, with shimmering golden eyes that seemed to burn with evil.

Then he realized that the thing wasn't coming at him.

He wasn't next to Jenna anymore. She was some distance away, sleeping, laid out on the bed, eyes closed, a half smile on her face.

And the thing was going for her.

He tried to run, to block the horrible menace from reaching the woman he loved. No matter how hard he tried, he was slowed down by the thick red mist.

The thing was now on Jenna, leaning over her, stiffening, inhaling, as if prepared to suck the life from her. The red mist became thicker and thicker. He realized he was fighting, straining, trying so hard to reach her. But it was no longer red mist that held him back. Instead, the barrier had become a sea of blood.

He woke with a start.

Morning.

His phone ringing.

An aura of fear stayed with him and he fought it; reaching for the phone and checking on Jenna, who was just beginning to rouse.

Jackson was calling. The right people had talked to the right people, and the FBI had been officially asked into the investigation. While suicide in the death of John Bradbury was a valid theory, the media had gone wild over the whole situation. Whispers of foul play ran rampant. He thanked Jackson for the assist and hung up.

"That's perfect," Jenna said, when he explained the call.

"I have to get to the autopsy," he told her.

"And I'll head to the mortuary."

"Maybe you should come with me," he said, recalling some of the dream.

"Don't be silly. We need to move fast on this. There are so many people we're going to have to interview, so much we have to find out. We have to divide the load. I know the mortuary, but we need to know the layout, how someone might have gotten in. That can only come from a visit."

She was right and he knew it.

He still didn't want to be away from her.

"Devin and Rocky will be here—"

"We can't wait on them," she said, frowning then smiling. "Sam, I'm a good agent. I was an agent before you were an agent, remember? I'll be careful. I promise."

He hesitated. "I had a nightmare," he said.

"You did?"

"A boo-hag was after you."

She smiled. "Sam, boo-hags aren't real."

"The one in the street was real. So we have to watch out."

"I swear, I'll be careful."

"Maybe—"

"Sam, I'm good at what I do. And when you're back from the autopsy, we'll meet up and go together from there."

He rose.

She was already up, heading to the shower. He started to follow her. She laughed, paused, and told him, "No time for that. I'll be right out. We need to move this morning."

"So you think you're that irresistible?" he asked her.

She grinned. "In a shower, you're irresistible."

And she closed the door on him.

"Nice lip service," he told her through the door.

"Lip service is later," she said.

He grinned at that, stared at the closed door for a minute, and then gathered his clothing for the day. He couldn't be unreasonable. He'd had a nightmare. Part of coming home, perhaps. And yet, in their world, nightmares could be real or, at a minimum, whispers of threats to come.

* * * *

"Hauntings and Hallucinations rents the space from us for the event," Micah Aldridge told Jenna.

It was just nine in the morning but she'd arrived at the Mayberry Mortuary to meet with Micah. Sam had headed for the autopsy and his meeting with Gary Martin. Adam Harrison had performed his usual magic. The FBI wasn't taking *lead* on the investigation—the situation didn't warrant it yet—but they were to be given access to information and leave to investigate. She hadn't met Martin and hoped that he didn't intend to dismiss the death as a suicide with no possibility of foul play. Things were always easier when everyone cooperated with everyone else. Most of the time it worked that way. But every once in a while they hit a local law enforcement officer who was more proprietorial, not wanting federal interference.

"I have to admit," Micah said. "I kind of loathed the idea of having something so schlocky here when we are trying to do real research. But bills have to be paid and we make enough from the Halloween rental to carry us through the year."

She nodded. "Makes sense."

She studied the beautiful old building. By daylight, the skeletons, spiders webs, and jack-o-lanterns all appeared to be just nicely arranged paper and props, nothing more. By night, with special lighting, the place appeared eerie, especially the cemetery surrounding it. When it wasn't Halloween season, the place still cast a certain melancholy about it, a poignancy that perhaps reflected the shadows of lives gone by.

"You've been here before, haven't you?" Micah asked.

"I took an historic tour when I was about fifteen," Jenna said. "It's been a while. But I would like to take a look inside."

They entered through the foyer. Double doors led into a massive living room and to the ornate stairway that led up to the second floor. The living room was filled with creatures, spider webs, a giant tarantula, and other oddities. On one wall a painting had flesh when first looked at, but turned skeletal from a different angle. A grand piano, complete with a skeleton player, sat by the windows to the porch. By night, the interior lights would show him in an eerie symphony.

"They do a good job," Jenna said. "Where are the stairs down to the basement?"

"John made it all possible," a female voice said.

She turned to see a young woman entering from the foyer. Attractive, with a wealth of long dark hair and a pretty face, but her eyes welled with tears as she approached.

"I'm Naomi Hardy."

"Jenna Duffy."

"Naomi and John Bradbury worked hand in hand," Micah said. "His death has been hard on her."

Concern filled Micah's voice.

"John was a true visionary," Naomi said. "He went to shows across the country, always looking for the newest innovations in creepy, chilling, *fun* scares. But he insisted we keep some real history too, to go along with all the whacko legend and scary movie stuff. He was so good. Head of the artistic branch, and every year at Halloween, he managed this place himself. I still can't believe he's gone."

"I am truly sorry for your loss," she said.

"Jenna is with the FBI."

"You're here over a suicide?"

"Elyssa Adair, who found the body, is my cousin," Jenna said.

"I'm really here to help her through this."

The explanation seemed to satisfy Naomi.

"John had the best job in the world. But then he'd had such a horrible divorce. His wife should have been shot. He'd had some drug problems as a kid and she dragged every bit of that into court, destroying his reputation. He had a hard time getting over it. All his success, and he could barely see his own children."

Which made the ex a definite suspect.

"Is the wife still around?" Jenna asked.

"No. That was the first thing the police asked. But she was nowhere near here. Home with the kids and she hadn't seen John since their last court date, months ago. She went on TV. Blamed his past, his drug problems, everything on him."

Tears welled in Naomi's eyes, which she brushed aside before asking, "What are you doing here at the mortuary?"

"Tying up the loose ends."

Naomi shrugged, as if uninterested. "If you'll excuse me, we're reopening tonight and now it's all on me. Micah, I'll be down at the ticket booth if you need me. Jenna, a pleasure to meet you, even under these circumstances."

She and Micah walked upstairs. Without darkness and actors, all of the haunting paraphernalia seemed worn and sad. Micah pointed out what was usually the tarot card reading and séance room. Another bedroom was used for psychic testing. She was interested in the entire layout, but really wanted to get to the basement to see if she could sense or feel anything. Elyssa wasn't lying. John Bradbury had appeared to her. But it would be helpful if that ghost would speak with her or Sam.

"Is there only one entrance to the basement?" she asked.

Micah nodded. "From the house, yes. The stairs are in the back of the kitchen. There's also an entrance from the back driveway that slopes down to a door. I guess it made for easy deliveries when the place was used as a funeral home."

Micah seemed fine about going down to the basement, but then again, he'd been alone here when she arrived. If the place was haunted in any way, Micah certainly didn't care.

She followed him to the ground floor landing and around the grand staircase to a door and more stairs that led down.

"It's a mess," Micah told her. "The police moved just about everything. Naomi will be taking over as manager and she'll see to it that everything is in order before tonight."

"Reopening already?" Jenna asked.

He shrugged. "I'm truly sorry. I liked John. He was a great guy. But life goes on and we have to pay the bills."

"Yes, I guess so," she murmured.

"The stairs are fairly narrow," Micah said. "In the old days, the dead came in through the back entry, and the coffins went back out that same way. Hauntings and Hallucinations carries some major liability insurance and we have strict rules about how many people can come through at one time. We're not the responsible party here, just the lessor, but we don't want anything bad to happen to anyone. Well, dead is bad, but the poor guy did himself in. You know, I saw John every day for the last couple of months and I had no idea he was so depressed."

Jenna didn't reply or correct him. Better to stay silent.

They'd reached the basement. The long stone embalming tables remained, each piled high with Halloween decorations. The police had indeed made a mess.

Micah pointed. "In the nooks and cubicle areas we have motion-activated creatures and characters. You can see the giant alien there, the werewolf over here, the vampire and mummy. That crazed killer over there scares the bejesus out of most visitors. Over there is where it happened."

She studied the cubicle, empty except for a giant iron hook that had long been attached to the ceiling above. The rope by which John Bradbury had hung had been removed, but the black lighting set up by the haunted house company remained. She thought that the basement, with its stone foundation pillars, wooden beams, and strewn paraphernalia seemed not eerie, but sad. The soft lighting made if look almost as if surrounded by a red mist. She walked over to where Bradbury had died.

"What were these crevices for?" she asked.

"I really don't know." He paused. "Poor John."

She stood still and wished Micah wasn't with her. Some alone time might be beneficial here.

"The exit from the basement is over this way," Micah said. "We have visitors leave the house via the basement and walk back up the path to the parking lot when they've finished the tour."

He walked toward the back door.

Jenna hovered a moment, waiting, standing still, trying to imagine what had gone on when Bradbury had died.

"Jenna?" Micah called to her.

"Coming," she said.

She waited another few beats, then turned to join him at the exit. And it hit her.

A movement in the air, a change in the temperature, the sense that they were not alone. She felt a brush against her cheek, and heard a whispered voice in the red mist aura.

I did not die by my own hand.

* * * *

The autopsy happened down in Boston where the Office of the Chief Medical Examiner was located. Sam was pleased to discover that the medical officer on duty was Dr. Laura Foster, a woman he'd worked with several times when he practiced law in Boston. She was bright, determined, and good at her job. There was even a Salem connection. Laura was the descendant of a woman accused of witchcraft during the craze. Her ancestor wasn't hanged. Instead, she died of the horrible conditions in the jail where she was held.

Detective Gary Martin was there too. He was pushing fifty, with short-cropped steel-gray hair. When he'd shaken hands with Sam, Martin had expressed surprise that the FBI had interest in an apparent suicide, but seemed to accept Sam's explanation that they were involved only because of family.

"If there's one thing I've learned," Martin said. "It's that you can never be sure of anything. With John Bradbury, it certainly appears he killed himself."

"It could have been made to look like suicide," Sam said.

Martin appeared skeptical. "Like I say. Anything's possible. Maybe the autopsy will tell us something we don't know."

They stood off to the side while Laura Foster went through the preliminaries, then made a Y incision in the chest and dictated her notes. Death appeared to have come from a broken neck. Otherwise,

John Bradbury had been a healthy, forty-five-year-old man, with a strong heart and clear lungs. The last meal remained in the stomach. Clam chowder, white fish, greens. Everything was recorded.

When she stopped speaking, Martin asked, "Suicide?"

"Could be," Laura said. "But, I doubt it."

Sam was listening carefully.

"I'm not a forensics expert," she said, "or a detective. The rope was taken and bagged as evidence yesterday. I saw it. From the way it was tied and the way he hanged, I can't see how he could have slipped it around his own neck. Also, these abrasions here, on the side of the neck. They suggest he was dragged while the rope was in place, choking him." She pointed at the body. "Marks here suggest he was digging at the rope before he died. This man was fighting and kicking. That's what broke his neck. He died fast, much quicker than simple strangulation."

"If he killed himself," Martin said, "he might have been fighting to the end. Perhaps regrets?"

Laura shook her head. "I can't say definitively death was by his own hand."

"So you're calling it a murder?" Martin asked.

Sam remained stoic, practicing something he learned a long time ago as a trial lawyer. Never let them know what you're thinking.

"I can't call this a suicide," Laura said.

"Just great," Martin said.

So much for an open and shut investigation.

"I'm sorry," Laura said. "I'll be doing more testing, but I suggest you start investigating this as a murder."

"Can you give us a time of death?" Sam asked.

"No more than sixteen or seventeen hours. So I'm saying between the hours of two and four, yesterday afternoon."

Martin left the room.

"He didn't want a murder," Laura said to him.

"No one ever does. Thank you for being stubborn."

"I'm not being stubborn, Sam. You know me. I call it the way I see it." She hesitated, nodding to her assistant, who was waiting to sew up the corpse. "It's just science—and justice, right?"

"Absolutely."

He stepped closer to the body. Sometimes, though not often, the dead could be reached by simple touch. But John Bradbury's spirit was not with them in the room.

He thanked Laura again.

"I hate it when people use Salem," she said. "When they do something like this, stringing a man up as if he was one of the victims from the old witch craze. It's mocking at its worst. Ignore Mr. I-Want-A-Suicide out there and catch this killer."

"Martin's not a bad guy. He was just going with what appeared to be obvious. The word was out that John Bradbury had been having a bad time lately. An excellent candidate for suicide. But we owe it to him to find the truth."

She nodded. "Glad you're on this, Sam."

He left the room. Martin had already stripped off the paper mask he'd worn inside. Sam did the same.

"Who the hell murders a guy like that?" Martin asked. "And how did you know?"

"I didn't," Sam said. "We're involved only because of Jenna's cousin, Elyssa."

Martin shook his head. "I guess that's your story and you're sticking to it. You Feds gripe my tail. You just come and go as you please, sticking your noses into what should be a local matter."

Sam tried to be diplomatic. He'd dealt with this attitude before. "We help local authorities solve a crime. That is all our jobs, right?"

"Yeah, I guess it is. You do know that I didn't want this to be murder. It's Halloween season. Patrol cops are going to have their hands full with corralling a ton of costumed drunks. Now there's a murderer running loose among them."

Sam pictured the boo-hag again from last night.

But no boo-hag had sucked the life out of John Bradbury.

No.

That poor man had been murdered.

Chapter Five

"During the afternoon, the only people here would have been me, Jeannette Mackey, John Bradbury, or Naomi Hardy," Micah told Jenna. "There are deliveries during the day. And when we're not open, the doors are supposed to be locked. Of course, we're open during the day in the afternoons for tours, but only if we have tours. They're by appointment only during October. That's not to say that someone might not have left a door or window open."

"No security cameras or alarm system?" Jenna asked.

"Yes, there's an alarm."

Whoever killed John Bradbury had done so in the afternoon before six o'clock since, by then, the actors and guides had reported and there were people coming and going from the basement. She asked Micah about who might have been at the mortuary that afternoon.

"It should have been locked. The only people there were the usual day workers. That's myself and Jeannette Mackey. During the season, it included John Bradbury and Naomi Hardy. I'm not sure when I first saw Naomi that day, but Jeannette and I both came in around eleven. I didn't see or hear anything. John had talked about taking a day off, so we assumed that he had. To be honest, while we like to be the "real" psychic deal and distance ourselves from

Halloween hokum, it's all a little bit fun. So we like being a part of it. Participating. Watching." His voice drifted off. "We went through all of this with the police that night. They were dumbfounded that so many people who worked here, and then so many attendees went through, before anyone realized that our swinging corpse was real. There was always a corpse there and things are supposed to look authentic."

"And the police have said that you can reopen tonight?" Jenna asked.

He shrugged. "It seems part of the attraction now. You can rent the room in Fall River where Lizzie Borden hacked her stepmother to death. You can rent the room at the Hardrock Hotel in Florida where Anna Nicole Smith died. And someone died, at some time, in a good percentage of the homes in New England."

"I think it was more than two nights after before you could rent either room," she said. "So the people who should have been here during the day were you, John, Jeannette, and Naomi. And there is a security system. So if someone broke in, you should have known it?"

He shrugged a little unhappily. "Probably. But Jeannette and I were getting ready for a meeting of the Salem Psychic Research Society. We did find a college kid walking around, just looking, not doing anything bad."

"But with this hugely popular attraction going on, you have no cameras, no eyes on the crowd anywhere?"

"We have plenty of eyes," he said. "Every room has what Hauntings and Hallucinations calls 'security guides.' Someone not in costume, but in a black uniform, carrying a flashlight, there to help out in an emergency."

"And the police have a listing of these people? Did they interview the 'security guide' working last night?"

"Of course. It was William Bishop, and he was a basket case. The guides are just simple hires, like the kids who go in costume. Most of them are college aged, a few are retirees. Some are just high school students. We comply fully with all labor laws."

"Micah, I'm not concerned with labor laws. A man is dead."

"It's not my fault he killed himself!"

"But the point is, no one saw him do it."

Micah flushed. "I had no idea John was here. I was upstairs. I have some files beneath the dueling skeletons in the tarot room. Our computers and communications are still up in that room too. Jeannette was with me. Like I said, I don't know what time Naomi got here because I just wasn't paying attention. But she was a little distracted because she hadn't heard from John, and assumed he was taking the night off. I told her not to worry, I'd work the ticket kiosk with her if he didn't come in. She told me they were short a few actors, too. Sally Mansfield, a local housewife who does this every year, was sick with the flu. So Jeannette said she'd be happy to be chopped up or whatever."

"I saw Jeannette last night."

Micah looked at her, surprised. "She said she was going home to bed. She was really upset by what happened. We all cared about John. Poor Naomi. She has to keep this going or the monetary loss will be incredible."

"I've seen businesses closed down for weeks after a tragedy like this. But, I guess you're right, the show must go on.

He hesitated and looked at her suspiciously. "Why are you trying to make a bad situation even more difficult?"

"I'm a special agent with the Federal Bureau of Investigation, Micah. This is my job."

She preferred not to be so pretentious, but sometimes she had to be. And with Micah, it worked.

"Of course, I understand," he said. "But it was a suicide, wasn't it?"

"I don't think so."

"Am I a suspect?"

"Actually, you are," she said pleasantly. "So any assistance you can give me will certainly help in eliminating you."

"Whatever you need. But you know that John's personal life wasn't going well. Oh, my. There was a murderer in here with us? But how? When? I don't see how this can be possible. Oh, my God."

He was panicked, of no help any further. So she decided to leave. "Thanks for your help. I'll call you if I need anything."

She turned to head up the stairs, back to ground level, and out through the front. Micah followed.

"Someone could have come in through the back, through the delivery entrance, I suppose, and we wouldn't have known," he said.

"You can't hear. I mean it is a big place."

Outside on the front porch, Jenna noted the quiet location and sad feel to the day. The ticket kiosks seemed cheaply thrown up, the Halloween decorations worn and frayed. Everything was much more magical at night. Naomi Hardy sat at the kiosk, head bowed. Jenna glanced over at the cemetery. Midmorning light was rising, sending streaks of yellow and gold down on the graves. Both the cemetery and house occupied a hill that sloped down to thick forest, the leaves a brilliant collage of orange, crimson, and gold. Past a decaying mausoleum and a weeping angel, she thought she saw something.

A strange flash of darkness and light.

Near the weeping angel and a worn tombstone stood someone in a black cape. Someone with a red face and body. The boo-hag they'd seen the other night. What would someone in costume be doing at the edge of a forlorn graveyard at this time of day, just looking up at the mortuary? She excused herself and headed down the rocky drive toward the cemetery. She leapt over a few tombstones and wove around ancient sarcophagi. But, when she reached the far side and the forest edge, the boo-hag was gone.

She drew her weapon and called out, "FBI. Get the hell out here, whoever you are."

She hadn't really expected a reply, not unless it might come from some holdover partier unsure of where he was from a function the previous night. She moved cautiously into the woods, alert and wary, careful of the leaves and twigs beneath her feet.

And then stopped.

No boo-hag was in sight.

Instead, a woman dangled from a tree limb.

* * * *

"Hanged by the neck until they be dead,'" Detective Gary Martin said, quoting from the death warrants handed down to those executed back in 1692.

Sam watched as a forensic photographer snapped pictures. The victim had been dressed up for display. Their male victim, John Bradbury, had also been decked out in Puritanical garb. Whether this woman often dressed in period clothing for one reason or another, they had no way of knowing. He and Gary Martin had arrived on the scene within minutes of Jenna's call, both on the outskirts of Salem. Once again, Sam was plagued with a feeling of urgency and fear.

The boo-hag.

But Jenna hadn't mentioned a boo-hag. She just said that she'd left the mortuary, come through the graveyard, then walked into the forest, finding a dead woman hanged from a tree. She was calm. No surprise. She was one hell of an agent. She'd touched nothing, securing the scene until forensics and a medical examiner could arrive. They'd asked if Laura Foster might be sent, explaining that they might be looking at a serial killer. He and Martin stood next to Jenna, watching while the crime scene techs did their thing.

"Think this one is a suicide too?" Jenna asked Martin sarcastically.

"Kind of hard to hang yourself from a tree," Martin said. "Unless she climbed up there, then out on the limb, tied the rope, then jumped. Not likely."

Jenna smiled at him. "I'm sorry. I didn't mean to be a pain."

Martin moved around the tree, trying to get a better look at the hanging victim. A large white bonnet hid most of her face and it was difficult—without disturbing the rope—to get a good look at her face.

"It's Gloria Day," Martin said. "She's a big Samhain fest organizer and throws a witches' ball on Halloween. Or it's Samhain, to her, I guess."

"You knew her?" Sam asked.

Martin shook his head. "Not really. I know of her. Her face is on a number of advertisements. This is really going to shake up the community."

Sam and Jenna moved carefully around to where Martin stood to study the corpse too. As they did, the medical examiner's van arrived through the trees. When Laura Foster stepped out, Sam was grateful. They were going to need her on this one. Jenna had not met her, so he introduced the two women and then Laura went to work. Enough photographs had been taken from every angle so the rope was cut and the corpse lowered, laid carefully on a tarp that could be formed into a body bag. A temperature check indicated that the time of death had been somewhere between five and six A.M.

Laura provided as many specifics as she could from a cursory inspection, pointing out the corpse's coloration, the neck had not broken, and she was probably strangled to death, slow and excruciating.

"This is Gloria Day," Laura said.

"Did you know her?" Martin asked.

"I've only seen her. She runs an ad on the local news about her ball every year. She also has a shop and helps promote classes run by some of her coven members. She's kind of a big cheese around here."

"Like John Bradbury?" Jenna asked.

"That's right. But look at the way the rope was tied. It's exactly the same as with Bradbury. When you look at the photographs, you'll see what I mean. I don't believe that either victim tied a rope that way around their own neck." Laura shook her head. "This is going to be one wicked Halloween."

"What about the costume?" Jenna asked.

"She could have worn that herself. She ran the ball, owned a shop, and did some tour guide stuff. I know all that from the ads you can't help but see if you live here. I know she was thirty-eight years old, born in Peoria, Illinois, and a fairly recent transplant to Salem. She arrived in the city in a big way, though her commercial devotion was twitching away."

"Maybe we're looking at a rival coven, or group of covens, or even one of the other sects. Like the voodoo guys, the Haitians, or the Asian-Indians. Maybe I should throw the Catholics and Baptists in there, too," Martin said.

"They're not going to stop," Jenna said.

"Why do you say that?" the detective asked.

She looked up at him. "Someone is trying to recreate the witch craze."

"John Bradbury wasn't a Wiccan," Sam said.

"And neither were any of those executed long ago for signing pacts with the devil," Jenna noted. "People like Bridget Bishop, Rebecca Nurse, Sarah Goode, Susannah Martin—"

"You know their names?" Martin asked.

She nodded. "Elizabeth Howe, Sarah Wilde, George Burroughs, John Willard, Martha Carrier, George Jacobs, Sr., John Proctor, Martha Corey, Mary Eastey, Ann Pudeater, Alice Parker, Mary Parker, Wilmott Redd, Martha Scott, and Samuel Wardell."

"That's impressive," Martin said. "I can add Giles Corey—

pressed to death. Had the reputation of being somewhat of a mean son-of-a-bitch, stuck to his guns. He had that famous line, '*More weight!*'" He studied Jenna. "Were you from here? You've got it down."

"Boston. But I spent a lot of time here while growing up. What I'm afraid of is some kind of large-scale plot, or sick deranged thing going on. They're both dressed. No man was hanged first during the real deal. Women got that honor. But there were men condemned and hanged as witches. From what I understand, John Bradbury had a love of local history, but he wasn't a Wiccan. Gloria Day was a big-time Wiccan, apparently famed for her classes and her ball."

Martin looked at Sam. "Let's get a search grid going."

"Sounds good to me."

Martin let out a whistle. A number of uniformed cops hustled over from the road area, around the outskirts of the trees, keeping their distance from the actual murder site until they were given instructions.

"I'm going back to the graveyard," Jenna said. "That's where I came in from."

Sam frowned at her. What had she been doing running around among the tombstones?

"No problem, whatever you need to do," Martin told her.

"I'll join her," Sam said, following Jenna.

To his surprise, Martin came too, leaving his crew to grid search the crime scene.

"You know," Martin said, "it's a 'graveyard' when it's by a church. It's a cemetery when it's freestanding or planned. Most of the plots have names."

Sam was trying to catch up with Jenna, but she was moving ahead quickly.

"Jenna," he called out.

She heard him and stopped.

He reached her. "Did the ghost of John Bradbury find you? What were you doing here? I thought you were searching the house."

She glanced back. Martin stood close to the edge of the forest. "I think he might have whispered to me down in the basement."

"The winged-death's-head is the most popular art on tombstones around here," Martin called, pausing at one of the graves. "The Puritans didn't want anything to do with icons that might suggest

Catholicism. 'Life is uncertain, Death is for Sure, Sin is the Wound, and Christ is the Cure,'" he read to them. "Pretty succinct."

"That's a common epitaph in this area," Sam called back.

He looked over at Jenna, waiting for more information.

"It was bizarre," she told him, her green eyes intense. "I followed a costumed figure in there."

"But?"

"I came into the woods and didn't see a soul, except the woman hanged from the tree."

"Cigarette butt," Martin yelled.

"Great. Bag it," Sam called back. "Jenna, what happened to the person you were chasing? You think that they might have done this, or do you think it was a spirit?"

"No, nothing like that. And I don't know if they were a possible suspect or not. The guy in costume might have headed straight for the road, while I cut into the woods deeper. And it's Halloween. Finding someone in costume is going to be ridiculously hard. Half the world around here is going to be dressed up."

"What costume, Jenna?" he asked, holding her shoulders and trying not to grip too hard.

"It was a boo-hag."

Chapter Six

They were sitting in a meeting room at the police station when Craig Rockwell called Sam to say that he and Devin Lyle had landed and were on their way. Sam had seldom been more grateful to have other Krewe members around.

Lt. Bickford P. Huntington, Supervisor for the Criminal Investigations Unit, had called a meeting to inform a task force from Salem and the surrounding areas about the two murders and bring them up to speed on what was known. He had Gary Martin speak and introduced Sam and Jenna as representatives from the federal government. Some there were old friends, some on the force new, not around four years ago when the murders had taken place at Lexington House, which Jenna and Sam had worked.

Sam thought Huntington seemed competent as he laid out all of the information they knew. He also provided a good assessment for what they might be looking for. Someone with a deranged historical sense of revenge, or someone with a contemporary sense of it, or someone who just wanted to kill people. Huntington looked over at Sam and suggested that he provide the group his thoughts. Before he could speak one of the officers spoke up.

"This woman you found today, she was a major commercial-style star Wiccan. Does that mean that we're really looking for someone in a coven?"

The answer was probably yes, but Sam was careful with his reply. He couldn't say that a ghost had told a young woman that his killer had been talking about the witch trials and cults.

"It's my understanding that a feud has been ongoing. So I think it's going to be important to discover if there's someone in some kind of an offshoot cult that might be doing this, not necessarily Wiccan. We all know that today's pagan religions, especially here in Salem, believe in treating everyone with love and respect. Murder would be a terrible sin to anyone truly practicing the Wiccan religion. There are many ways to look at this without stereotyping anyone."

"But, the two victims were killed in the same manner as those executed during the witchcraft trials," another officer said.

"You all know your history here. Anything was witchcraft. If you looked into the future, silly girls playing at love potions,· even goodwives trying medicinal herbs, all of that was considered witchcraft. Of course, none of those executed was a witch. It was hysteria, fueled over petty squabbles and simple hatred among the people who lived here then. The pagans, or Wiccans, we have in Salem today have nothing to do with all that. Should we look at strange cults and fundamentalism of any kind, be it Wiccans or another group? Absolutely. Do we need to question people spouting against Gloria Day? Definitely. But the medical examiner's office hasn't even started on the second autopsy yet. Let's see what comes of that."

Jenna was introduced—she smiled and greeted old friends and thanked those she'd worked with before, asking that they be especially vigilant in the areas surrounding the mortuary, graveyard, and forest, and to listen to what they heard around town. "You know Salem. You'll know when something isn't right or when it feels strange. We need to keep a close eye on the mortuary. The first murder apparently happened at a time when those in charge were busy or unaware. And we need to watch out for local situations. Crack pots, cults, culture clashes of any kind."

The meeting ended and Sam and Jenna wound up discussing their next moves in one of the conference rooms while Lieutenant Huntington went on to speak to the press. The community, Sam knew, would be talking about nothing else. But, none of it would stop Halloween or Samhain celebrations. Salem had a life of its own at this time of year. A pulse. A beat. Like a living entity.

Gary Martin was working hard. He hadn't wanted a murder, but he'd wound up with two. His men had retrieved a fair amount of evidence from the forest where Gloria Day's body had been found. All of the cigarette butts, cans, bits and pieces of hair, and everything else would go to the DNA lab. And while TV shows might get their results back in an hour, it would be days, possibly weeks, before these would be ready. Sam harbored no illusions. They were not going to get anything off an old cola can. Their killer wasn't sitting there enjoying a soda before hanging a woman. Results would come from walking and talking and discovering what was going on in the community. Someone had to have seen a car. The hill upon which the mortuary sat alongside the cemetery wasn't in walking distance from town. And Gloria Day's killer had not forced her to walk up the hill then into the forest to be hanged. It made sense that John Bradbury had been in the basement of the mortuary. He worked there. But Gloria Day was another matter. Her shop and school sat in the middle of town, down the street from the Hawthorne Hotel. Had she been lured up there to see something unusual? To participate in some kind of ceremony? Sam was anxious to get to her shop, but he also wanted to know more about the various groups in the community now. And much of it, he thought, needed to be done by himself and Jenna, or Rocky and Devin. The local police were good. But the Krewe team was better.

Alone with Gary Martin and Jenna in the conference room, Sam looked over the files on locals, along with the notes they'd received from Angela Hawkins, Jackson Crow's wife and top assistant. She'd found pages and pages of Facebook, Instagram, Google, and other social media communications that spoke of an all-out verbal war between two factions in the city. Two main rivals were clear. The Coven of the Silver Moon, Gloria Day's group. And the Coven of the Silver Wolf, Tandy Whitehall's people. Each of the two had hives, where the overflow went when there were too many people in a coven. Thirteen was considered the ideal number, but that wasn't etched in stone. Hives, he knew, kept their membership low so as not to become unwieldy, the perfect place for a newly ordained high priest or priestess. Both Day and Whitehall had enjoyed a lot of popularity, their hives numerous and, on occasions like Samhain, they gathered together. In Salem, that usually happened at Gallows Hill, which, frankly, Sam didn't agree with, and for good reason.

Just seemed the wrong place.

"There's been a lot of talk on the web," Martin said, reading through some of the notes Angela had e-mailed. "The word 'bitch' seems overly popular. Gloria Day seems to be accused of being a greedy, manipulative usurper, determined to rule all of Salem. She gives good cause for the world to believe modern-day witches to be old hags with saggy brooms and warts flying across the moon on broomsticks.'" He paused and looked at them. "Now that's just mean. She's old, yes. But certainly not ugly and doesn't have any warts."

Officers had tried to pay a visit to Tandy Whitehall, but she'd not been at her shop, Magical Fantasies, nor at her house. Everyone was on the lookout for her. If she wasn't found soon, sterner measures would be used. Sam believed Whitehall had to know they were looking for her. The media had sniffed out the latest murder with the speed of light. So quickly, in fact, that Jenna had wondered if they shouldn't be looking for someone involved with the media. But Sam kept remembering Elyssa's words. That the ghost mentioned the witchcraft trials and cults. That didn't necessarily mean modern-day pagans. But the well-publicized feud between the two most prominent covens could not be ignored.

Among the information Angela had sent was details on a legend. Sam had specifically asked about the Gullah culture and the boo-hag.

"Listen to this," he said, reading the information.

And he told them about an old folk story and a boy named Billie Bob who just could not find a wife. So his father fixed him up with the daughter of a swamp woman. He was stunned when he met her. She was gorgeous, with dark eyes, dark hair, and a beautiful body. She didn't want to be married by a priest, but was willing to stand before a judge. So they were married and she was the perfect wife by day. But at night she never came to bed. Suspecting the worst, Billie Bob, armed with sugar and honey and all manner of gifts, went to see a local conjuring woman. The old woman told him to pretend that he was asleep, then watch what his wife did. The next night Billie Bob did just that, following his wife up to the attic where she sat at a wheel and spun off her skin. All bloody muscle and bone, she headed out into the night. Billie Bob was terrified, so he went back to the old conjuring woman who told him he had to paint every window and door in the house blue, except for one. She also told him to splash salt and pepper on her discarded skin. He did both, and when she returned home, she found herself trapped, as the blue doors were a weakness. When she slipped back into her skin, the salt and pepper burned her horribly. In a panic, she crashed through an attic window and turned as bright as a falling star, her body exploding into chunks of flesh that were enjoyed by the swamp gators. Billie Bob was sad. The conjuring woman told him that he should not be. He'd had no wife, only a boo-hag. Once she'd tired of him, she would have brought him to her boo-daddy, who would have eaten his flesh, drank his blood, and gnawed at his bones.

"But Billie Bob didn't become chow," Sam said. "It's a bit like a vampire story, or even a story about our old concept of witches, bringing their new recruits to Satan. Their version of a boo-daddy."

"And what does a boo-hag have to do with Salem?" Martin asked.

"What about the Gullah culture up here?" Sam asked.

"We have a few transplants, but—"

A uniformed officer entered the room, escorting Devin and Rocky. Jenna rose to quickly hug and welcome the newcomers. As it turned out, Rocky knew Detective Gary Martin. They explained what had just happened.

"A second murder?" Rocky asked. "People are being killed in period costume. Not to profile anyone here, but—"

"We're looking for the head of the opposing Wiccan coven now," Martin made clear.

Rocky looked at Sam. "Divide and conquer? We've been reading the briefs on the murders all the way here."

"What do you mean 'divide and conquer?'" Martin asked.

"We'll go off and interview members of the opposing team," Devin explained. "The more of us talking to people in a more casual manner, the better."

"And you think—"

Rocky leaned forward, "Gary, these are our old haunting grounds. We've dealt with murder here before. Bad things, involving people we knew. Out on the streets, we can do a lot of good."

Martin nodded. "But I need to be in the loop on everything. I was planning on heading to the mortuary tonight. I want to keep an eye on the place now that it has reopened. Two people are dead either in or near that place. But John Bradbury was no Wiccan."

"No, but he supported Tandy Whitehall," Sam said.

"How did you know that?" Martin asked.

"From hanging out in a bar."

"We don't have any viable suspects," Sam said, "except for Tandy Whitehall. And that's just because she seems to have a motive. She might also have an alibi."

"And unless we get out on the street, we'll have no idea about anything," Rocky said. "Hey, this is Salem. And Salem at Samhain and Halloween? That means hope."

"I'm pretty sure a little nook or hole-in-the-wall bar is where we'll find Tandy Whitehall," Jenna said. "Surrounded by those who'll protect her."

Martin seemed both indignant and worried. "And that could be bad. They could be armed with more than curses. Man kills his wife. Son-in-law kills father-in-law. Junkie kills for drugs. That's the usual things. But these people around here are fanatics. You don't think they'll turn this into a stand-off, do you?"

"This killer doesn't want to get caught," Devin said. "He, or she, or *they*. And as for my real thoughts, I can't help but think that it's not this Tandy Whitehall at all. It's too obvious. We have to be casual. Walk in like customers. Hey, I still own my great aunt Myna's cottage. I'm almost a real live local girl. And Rocky is from Marblehead. Let us do this our way. We'll find what we're looking for."

"I don't have a lot of choice, now do I?" Gary said, an edge in his voice alluding to the influence of the Krewe of Hunters agents. "I'll be watching things over at the mortuary. We'll keep in close contact."

"I'll hang out at the mortuary with Gary," Jenna said. "You guys handle the streets. How's that?"

Sam looked back at her, surprised and annoyed. He didn't like being away from her in Salem. But she was already up, ready to leave with Gary Martin. Sam stood as well, gently laying an arm on her shoulder.

She smiled at him. "I'll be fine."

He accepted that, just as he accepted who she was, what she did, how they were different, and how they were alike. He loved her. And part of that involved letting her be who she was. But there was still the matter of the boo-hag.

"Where are we meeting up? And when?" he asked.

"Last tour at the mortuary is midnight," Martin said. "We can do it then. The next two days promise to be long. The day before

Halloween, then Halloween itself. We need to catch this killer quickly, before this goes any further."

* * * *

Apparently nothing stopped Halloween.

The Mayberry Mortuary was packed, the parking lot full. Jenna and Martin arrived in a police car, uniformed officers everywhere. Two at the entry, two by the ticket booth, one man watching the parking lot.

"I can only imagine the overtime," Jenna said, looking around.

"We don't really have a choice. Salem's economy would be totally in the trash if we had to start closing down things like this. Winter is cold as a witch's tit! Whoops, sorry. I'm sure that's politically incorrect now. But you know what I mean. Christmas is great, New Years, Wiccan holidays, we get people then. Summer is a fantastic time with school kids and families. But we can't lose Halloween. A lot of the locals only survive the off months thanks to what they make at Halloween."

"So the overtime is worth it," Jenna said.

But she doubted this killer intended to strike in the same place twice.

Martin used his phone, checking in with headquarters. Jenna paused in the parking lot, staring out over the cemetery, toward the trees and the edge of the forest. She'd volunteered to come with Martin only because she wanted to get back to the cemetery. She wanted the ghost of John Bradbury to come to her. She also wanted to know why she'd seen a boo-hag heading into the trees moments before she found a woman hanged.

"Still no sign of Tandy Whitehall," Martin said, hanging up. "Your coworkers are out, and we have officers trying to reach her. But she's seen the news by now and has to know we're looking for her. Probably long gone. I'm going in to do a walk-through. You coming?"

"I'll hang out here for a bit. I want to watch some of the people coming and going. I'll be in soon."

He left and she headed over to the busy ticket booth. She saw Micah working, but no Naomi Hardy or Jeannette Mackey. A young woman she'd never seen before sat next to Micah.

"Everything going all right?" she asked, watching him hand out tickets that were available from a pre-sale online.

He looked over at her. "We're sold out. But people get in line for cancellations. We're always crazy, but tonight is extra rushed."

Jenna overheard whispers from the crowd, where some of the visitors were commenting on how they could go to the place where the man's corpse had been hanged.

"You're a creep, Joe," someone said.

"Come on, creepy is fun. Afterward, we can go in the woods and find where that other corpse was hanging. The witch. Yeah, man, they hanged a witch."

Jenna grimaced at the nonsense. "Best of luck," she told Micah, moving down the porch steps, smiling and excusing herself as she moved through the crowd. Her smile faded as she made her way to the cemetery. She hated not being truthful with Sam. She loved him so much. He'd gone through the FBI Academy just for her, becoming a crack shot and a proficient agent. True, he talked to ghosts, and it wasn't a bad thing to be a lawyer who could talk to the dead. He seemed to be really worried about the boo-hag.

She entered the cemetery.

Most ghosts didn't roam around, moaning. Ghosts stayed for a reason, mainly to tell the living what happened to them. She'd seen fathers stay for children, mothers for a family, and children in a sad attempt to ease the pain of their parents. She knew ghosts who'd remained for centuries, hoping to see that history was not repeated. And, yes, she'd met a few in cemeteries. But, usually, they preferred being elsewhere. Tonight, however, one was here, following her. She threaded a path through the tombstones, glancing back to see the glow from the mortuary through the trees. If any of the visitors decided to head into the woods tonight, they'd be in for a surprise. The crime scene from the murder earlier was roped off, two officers watching over it. Finally, she stopped, noting a death's-head on the stone at her feet.

She turned.

John Bradbury faced her, still attired in his Puritan dress.

"We're truly trying," she said to him. "Elyssa tried to repeat what you told her. But we're not sure we understand."

He seemed to waver for a moment, gathering strength. Then he managed a weak smile. "I knew you would come. I tried hard to get someone to see, someone to know. It's not easy. I knew about you from Lexington House."

Jenna nodded. "Tell me exactly what happened."

He was a tall, nice-looking man, big enough that it must not have been easy to get his neck into a noose.

"I was working. Checking the connections on some of our automated monsters, readjusting the props on the embalming tables. I don't know where they came from. I just had a sense that someone was behind me."

"When you say you don't know where *they* came from—did they enter from the house or from the delivery doors? Did you smell something? Was anyone wearing aftershave or cologne? Or as if they hadn't bathed? Did you see their hands or anything about them?"

"I felt like I was hit by a bulldozer. I was standing there, then suddenly someone was behind me. I was slammed against one of the props, then I felt the rope go around my neck. They pulled it tight fast. I was struggling with the noose, trying to get it off. Then I was off my feet, being dragged and jerked. I couldn't really see anything but black. I think they were in costumes. Maybe capes."

"Were they wearing masks?"

"I don't know. But I never saw their faces. I heard them. The one said something giving 'dimension to the witch trials' and the other said 'to shut up.' Then the one who'd spoken first said, 'he's going to tell someone what we were talking about. The Wiccans, the cultists, the weirdos.'"

"That was it?" Jenna asked.

John Bradbury nodded. "They jerked the rope, and my neck snapped. I died. Then I felt like I was drifting, looking on, and I saw people coming through the mortuary. I kept trying to speak, but I realized they didn't see or hear me." He paused, smiling wistfully. "I worked with Elyssa. She had a way about her that reminded me of my oldest daughter. But I also felt that she knew things that maybe even she didn't know she knew. I felt her coming near me. I reached out with my mind. And she must have listened. Everyone else was pretty much just walking by me. She seemed to hear me. So I spoke to her. I then managed to follow her home. But I couldn't connect with her until the following morning. That was strange. But it happened."

"I am so sorry," Jenna said. "We're looking for two killers. But, John, I need you to think. Were they men, women?"

"I don't know. They were whispering. But you mentioned smells. I remember that it seemed absurd, but it was like I smelled a forest. Flowery, like an autumn breeze."

"Anything else?" she asked quietly.

"I was strangling, dying. And the thing is . . . my kids. They have to know that I didn't do this to myself. That I would never have left them, no matter how bad things seemed to be."

Jenna reached out instinctively, but touched nothing but a chilly breath of air. "They'll know. I'll make sure. You do know there was another murder?"

He nodded. "Gloria Day. I didn't like her very much."

"Did she have a lot of enemies?"

"On Halloween night, for years, Tandy Whitehall has been throwing a big gala. Gloria arrives in town and lures away half of Tandy's business. Gloria and I knew one another. We were never friends. She was more a bitch than a witch."

He was quiet for a minute. Jenna allowed him the moment of thought. She wondered what she looked like, standing in the graveyard, talking to herself. A number of family tombs were strewn between her and the mortuary, which probably blocked the vision of anyone who might have casually looked this way. The entire scene was vintage Salem at Halloween, complete with the giant old Victorian house, covered with webs and scarecrows and monsters, caught in an eerie glow that barely reached the cemetery.

"Red," John Bradbury said.

She waited.

"You made me think about that night. What I was feeling and smelling and I suddenly thought about the color red."

Jenna heard Sam from earlier with his story of a boo-hag. A body stripped down to muscle, bone, and red blood.

"Does that mean something?" he asked.

"I followed someone in a red costume into the forest. A red costume beneath a black cape. Does that mean anything to you?"

"What you mean..." a new voice said, "is that you followed someone in red and black into the forest, then found Gloria Day, the wretched bitch witch dead?"

Jenna turned toward the new voice. Female.

"Really, John?" Gloria Day said. "Bitch witch? How rude. I'm dead, too, you know."

The new ghost joined the party, wearing the same Puritan garb in which she'd died, standing with them among the lichen-covered tombstones. She'd been an attractive woman with dark hair, light blue eyes, a heart-shaped face, and a charming smile.

Gloria looked at Jenna. "You will find out who did this to us. And so help me, dead or alive, Wiccan, Catholic, Buddhist, whatever, I'll curse them in a fiery realm of hell where they'll burn for all eternity."

Chapter Seven

"Where would a popular Wiccan head to avoid detection and the press?" Devin pondered, linking arms with both Sam and Rocky.

"Did you know her?" Sam asked Devin.

Sam knew that Devin had not started out as an agent. She'd first been an author of children's books—all based on a witch. She'd grown up in Salem and returned when her Aunt Mina left her a cottage on the outskirts of town. She and Rocky had met when Rocky had come to Salem. The murders they'd solved had traced all the way back to the days when Rocky had been in high school.

When the dead had first spoken to him.

Sam was fond of them both and had been glad when they'd become part of the Krewe. All of them were New Englanders from approximately the same area, hard not to share a few local peculiarities. For one, they all had the tendency to overuse the word "wicked." To a Brit everything tended to be "brilliant." In New England, things were just "wicked."

"I'd say she's hiding in someone's house," Rocky suggested. "The cops have a list of all her followers, so they'll be going door to door."

"Which doesn't mean much. There are no warrants. She's not under arrest, only wanted for questioning," Sam said.

Rocky grinned. "Can't get the attorney out of the agent, huh?"

"Thing is, once we get a murderer, we'd like to see he or she locked up, not free on a technicality."

"I just wish we could find this woman," Rocky said.

"Angela just texted me," Devin said. "There's a little place near the end of the Salem Harbor Walk, owned by a Wiccan woman who is in a hive that's an offshoot of Tandy Whitehall's coven. It's called the Goddess, serves a lot of Paleo foods, vegetarian offerings, homemade wine and beer. It's two blocks from Tandy Whitehall's house. Sounds like a place to start."

"Sound good to me," Sam said.

So far they'd managed to keep themselves out of the news. He and Jenna had been involved in the Lexington House case four years ago. It had been just a little more than a year since Devin and Rocky had met here to solve an old murder, which had been hard on Devin, since it had involved one of her old circles of friends. They needed to maintain their anonymity.

They headed down along the dark streets, avoiding revelers, costumed or not. Sam had loved Salem growing up. True, a lot had gone commercial. But the Peabody Essex museum was wonderful, teaching the history of fear and suspicion and distrust of one's neighbors and what those emotions could do to a community. The people who lived and worked here gave the place a pulse. And yet the old could still be found, along with the new. Quaint stood side by side with fun and the silly. So many restaurants had brought in excellent chefs. The House of the Seven Gables still stood, a testament to the past and a reminder that the past came alive through great literary works. Ships continued to ride high in the harbor, beneath the moon, the water seeming to stretch out forever.

Devin suddenly squeezed Sam's hand. "One way or the other, if we find Tandy or not, you need to tell Rocky and me what's going on with you and Jenna."

He looked at her with surprise. "We're good. We're great."

"You were acting a bit strange. You kept looking at her as if you're afraid you're never going to see her again."

Rocky nodded. "She's right." Then he paused and pointed. "There's our place. Rambling, with lots of rooms. Plenty of hiding places. Angela may be hundreds of miles away from here, but she can track like a bloodhound."

"Let's see what we find before we canonize her," Sam said, grinning.

The bar/restaurant was situated in a house where a plaque on the door informed them that it had been built in 1787. Plain dark wood on both the outside and inside. Booths offered hardwood benches, those along the wall with backs. Doors opened to additional rooms on either side of an oblong bar. Like everything else in Salem, it was decorated. No monsters here, though. Only pumpkins, Indian corn, and all manner of natural fall decoration. The place was busy, but not overcrowded, and a young hostess asked them if they'd like a booth or a table.

They opted for a table. Soon, they were sipping locally brewed brown beer with steaming bowls of chowder before them, listening to the snatches of conversations from those around them.

"Will the gala go on? I mean a woman is dead," a tall blonde at the bar said to her companion.

"Probably. There are sponsors, bands and tickets were sold. They can't cancel it," her male companion said.

"I heard this is a real Wiccan hangout," another girl said.

"Tourists," Rocky murmured, then he looked at Sam. "What's up with you?"

Sam hesitated, but these were his coworkers. They'd worked well together because they were straight with one another, even when it seemed ludicrous.

"Boo-hag," he said.

"What?" Devin asked, a frown furrowing her brow. "That's not like a redneck banshee or something, is it?"

"More like a vampire, a really creepy, ugly one," Sam said. "And we keep seeing one in particular. A boo-hag nearly threw itself on the car when we were driving into town. And Jenna saw one right before she found Gloria Day's body."

"You mean—someone costumed as one?" Devon asked.

Sam smiled. "Sure, what else. And I dreamed about one coming after Jenna. I couldn't get to her in time, and it was going to suck the life out of her. A dream, I know. But boo-hag keeps coming up, and it's bugging me."

"Where would one find a boo-hag in Salem?" Devin asked. "If we find someone in a boo-hag costume on the street, we can't just stop and search him."

"There's a community of Gullah people here who I want to check out tomorrow morning," Sam said.

"Gullah?" Rocky asked.

"It's a blend of different African and island cultures, along with a Creole mix. The culture originally stretched from the coastal areas of the Carolinas to Florida. Now, it seems, they're mostly in South Carolina. The boo-hag is one of the demons, I believe, in their storytelling. It's hideous, shedding its skin, answering only to a boo-daddy."

"Ah, yes," a female voice said.

Sam turned and saw a petite, attractive woman standing behind him dressed in black and wearing a beautiful gold pentagram. Her platinum blonde hair was short and curled around a thin, lovely face.

Tandy Whitehall.

"Young and lovely women meet unwary men," she said. "They seduce them and use them, and, when the time is right, take their husbands or young lovers to their boo-daddy. He consumes them, down to gnawing on their bones. Every society has its monsters. The boo-hag is a bad one." She glanced around the table and smiled, then shook Sam's hand. "Emily told me you three were here. Would you care to come into the back where we can talk in private?"

"Tandy?" Devin said.

"Devin Lyle. You know, I miss your Aunt Mina. She was an amazing friend."

She drifted away from the table. They followed. Which seemed expected. They'd wanted to find Tandy Whitehall.

And had done so.

* * * *

Jenna knew this was her best opportunity to find out the truth.

"The oddest thing is that I don't believe Tandy Whitehall had anything to do with this," Gloria Day's ghost said. "You have to realize that some of the argument between us was all for hype and promo. We go about things differently—*went* about things differently." She looked at John Bradbury. "This is really so unfair."

"Tell me about it. I had children."

"And I'd hoped to have them one day, too," she said. "You didn't like me a whole lot, John. So don't pretend that you do now."

"I didn't like your Wiccan kick against haunted houses," he said. "You, I hardly knew."

Gloria made a face at him. "I just tried haunting the place, but no one could see or hear me."

"Could you two focus on the problem at hand," Jenna said. "We're trying to figure out who killed you, and disprove that it was two suicides."

"Hard to hang yourself over a tree," Gloria said. "You need some help."

"It's like with your death they want us to know a murderer is at work," Jenna said. "That might be because the killers have realized John's death isn't going to be accepted as a suicide."

"Either that," John said, "or someone is going about recreating the deaths of those condemned to hang, and maybe even Giles Corey's death, too. This could get really bad."

"Do they want it to look like a Wiccan war? If so, they missed the debate somewhere along the line. John and Tandy Whitehall were close," Gloria said.

"Gloria, I need to know what happened to you," Jenna said. "You didn't drive yourself out here, somehow make your car disappear, then hang yourself.

She wasn't meaning to be cruel, but Gloria seemed the type who wanted things straight.

And she did.

Gloria arched a brow with a shade of humor and said, "I don't know what happened. I was in the shop, just straightening up, and some kind of a bag was suddenly over my head. I was suffocating and passed out. I came to feeling the roughness of a rope around my neck, then agony and darkness. And I was here. On the other side. I wandered out of the trees and was surrounded by gravestones. I saw the mortuary up on the hill and had no idea how I had gotten here. And then, of course, I realized. I was dead. And I've been trying ever since to find someone who could hear me."

"Any smells?" John asked her.

"What?" she asked, looking at him, a faint wrinkling forming above her brows.

"A smell, a feel, a sensation? Anything?"

"The trees. I remember the smell of trees. Something like a forest."

"I smelled the same thing," he said.

"Did either of you recognize the scent? From a store, a shop, either one of the big department store colognes, or anything more local?" Jenna asked.

"I know where something close can be bought," Gloria said after a minute. "A woodsy scent. At Tandy Whitehall's shop."

"You really think Tandy did this?" John protested. "I'm a big man, and even with a noose around my neck it would take more than a tiny woman like Tandy to take me down."

"We know from what you heard, John, that there were two killers," Jenna said.

"I don't believe Tandy did this to me. I really don't," Gloria said, looking at John. "We had our differences, but I respected her. No, I may be dead, but right is right, and I won't attack the woman, even if I am dead." She seemed to shake off her sadness and looked at Jenna with purpose. "But I know that scent, and it can be bought at Tandy's shop."

"Tandy has disappeared," Jenna said. "She's wanted for questioning. Would she have fled Salem?"

"Never," John and Gloria both said.

Jenna's phone buzzed and she glanced at it quickly.

Sam.

She answered and learned that John and Gloria were right. Tandy was still here, with Sam, Devin, and Rocky, and Sam's assessment was clear. *She's not our killer.* So everyone seemed in agreement, Tandy was innocent.

Jenna looked over at Gloria.

"I appreciate you finding my body," Gloria said. "I could have hung there a long time."

But it had been the boo-hag who led her. Had it intended for her to find Gloria?

She texted Sam.

Check Tandy's inventory. Find out who bought a woodsy scent that she sells. Find out about the Gullah community.

She finished her text and looked up.

"Someone is trying to make this look as if the Wiccans are evil," Gloria said. "As if the community should be hanging us again."

"Or trying to make it look like a feud," John added. "I was killed, so someone from the other camp had to die, too."

"What do either of you know about the Gullah community?"

"I know a number of folks who moved up here who are basically Gullah, but they don't really follow any special practices. There's one church in town that has a Southern twist, but it's basically Baptist. Most of them attend there. They're actually all great people," Gloria said. "Where do they fit in here?"

"I don't think they come into it at all. I think that boo-hag is being used."

"Boo-hag?" John murmured.

"Creepy, soul-sucking yucky demon," Gloria explained. "Gullah. Red. Woodsy. Mortuary."

"Red mortuary?" Jenna asked quickly.

"Maybe it's because you said boo-hag," Gloria said. "But I have an impression of red in my memory. For some reason, I seem to remember a whisper of the word mortuary."

Gloria paused and gazed across the graves to the mortuary on the hill.

John joined her, then glanced at his wrist and shrugged with an unhappy sigh. "I always wore a watch. But it stopped when I died. Go figure. Loyal watch, I guess."

"It's way past midnight," Gloria said. "The lines are gone and people are leaving. They try to have it all closed up by 2:00 A.M."

Jenna looked over at the mortuary, too, which appeared both dead and eerily alive, as if on a plain between the living and the dead. Haunting, opaque, sheathed in garish Halloween décor, in the moonlight it appeared decayed and faded.

Jenna was certain the answers she sought lay there.

"I'm going up there," she said. "Care to join me?"

* * * *

The back room at the bar/restaurant reminded Sam of an old brothel, especially the brocade cushions in gold and burgundy on the sofas and loveseats. Tandy served them an excellent herbal tea and talked about Gloria Day.

"I have to admit some of the bad feelings were jealousy. Every time I looked at her, I thought I should start singing *Memory*. But I actually liked her. We both managed to get people to ball-hop on

Halloween, after the Sabbat on the Gallows Hill, of course. There was plenty here for everyone. So I want you to know that I'm not leaving town. I have no intention of running."

"Tandy," Sam said. "We need a list of people who wear, or have recently purchased a scent you make at your store. It's something woodsy, smells like a forest, that kind of thing."

She found her phone and tapped a message. "I'm getting it for you."

He leaned forward. "And what do you know about the Gullah community?"

"How did you even know we had a Gullah community?" Tandy asked, bemused. "They're usually in coastal South Carolina or Georgia."

"We heard there was a group here," Devin said.

"We do have a group here now. Almost a hundred," she said. "All good people. Some are more conventional; some have converted more or less to the Wiccan religion. They have their own language, a Creole similar to a Krio language spoken in what's now Sierra Leone. Their religion is based on Christianity, but includes a great deal of believing in the spirits of their ancestors. I buy a lot of merchandise from them to sell at the store. Beautiful, hand-crafted masks and totems, and jewelry."

"What about the boo-hag?" Sam asked.

Tandy smiled at that. "What about it?"

"It seems to be a popular costume."

"Wait here," Tandy said.

She rose and disappeared from the room, returning a moment later with a young woman, clad in black, wearing a beautifully crafted pentagram.

"Sissy, this is Special Agent Sam Hall, and Special Agents Lyle and Rockwood," Tandy said. "Meet Sissy McCormick. She's from Gullah country in South Carolina."

"Nice to meet you," Sissy said, joining their grouping by taking the chair Tandy had vacated. "My people are Gullah."

Sissy was striking, her skin coffee-colored, her eyes a soft blue. She had dark hair, queued at the nape of her neck, wearing a black cape over a long black skirt and tailored shirt.

"You've chosen to be Wiccan?" Devin asked.

Sissy nodded. "Something speaks to all of us, and not always what's in our heritage. But, basically, I follow the tenets of almost any creed. Be good to others, care for the elderly, sick, and injured, cherish all children, never offer violence. Be a good human being."

"Nice," Devin said. "Gullah is based on Christianity?"

"Of course, but so is voodoo," Sissy reminded her. "And look, many fundamentalists have caused tremendous harm to others in the name of traditional religions. Every faith out there has those who choose to take it too far, or read into it what isn't there."

"Or use it," Sam said. "Sissy, we're seeing a lot of boo-hag costumes, or at least one boo-hag costume, over and over again. The boo-hag is a Gullah demon, right?"

Sissy nodded. "Some manufacturer came up with that awful costume. Red latex to look like a fleshless body, a horrible demon face. My mother was so upset. She said it's just going to make people anti-Gullah. But it's just part of Halloween. People dress up as crazed movie characters. They know Freddy and Jason and all those fictional killers are just from movies. They'll know that a boo-hag is simply from legend, like a vampire or a werewolf. No true Gullah in this community would ever buy or wear such a costume."

"Here we go," Tandy said, slipping a pair of reading glasses from her pocket to stare at an incoming message on her phone.

Sam's phone rang. He didn't recognize the number, but it was local, so he answered. For a moment, there was nothing. Then he heard something like a snuffled tear.

"Sam?"

For a split second, he was confused.

Then he knew.

"Elyssa?"

He heard a sudden cry.

Then a whispered voice. "You want this one to live? Then get your wise-ass partner under control. All of you back down. Leave this alone. Let these murders go into the great cauldron of unsolved crimes. That is if you ever want to see this kid again. You back off, and she's free on November 1. You keep it up, she dies before Halloween."

Sam forced himself to remain calm, glancing at Rocky, who knew what the look meant. Trouble. So he worked to keep the caller on the phone, as Rocky called headquarters to run a trace through Sam's phone.

"We want Elyssa alive," he said. "But I have to have some kind of assurance that you're not going to hurt her regardless of what we do."

A soft laugh seeped through the speaker. "Trying to keep me on the line? You're on your cell, not at police headquarters. So you'll need some time to run a trace. It was nice that Elyssa kept this number in her phone. You were an attorney, so I would hope you understand the fine art of negotiation."

"So negotiate," Sam said. "I have to know that Elyssa remains alive."

"A call every six hours. But there'll be a new number each time. If I even suspect you're playing me, this pretty little girl will be hanged. Maybe by the witch memorials or the cemetery, right there amidst all the tourist attractions. Or I could find another cool place. So you need to find Jenna Duffy. Actually, I wouldn't mind seeing her hanged either. Now there's a thought..."

"Touch her," he said, "and you'll face hell a thousand times here on earth before going to the real thing."

Laughter followed his remark.

Cocky? Why not? Two people were already dead.

"Sam," the voice said, "I'm disappointed in you. I thought you were a negotiator."

"Okay, let's negotiate and not threaten other people."

He looked at Rocky, who was listening to his own phone, watching Sam with anxious eyes. Rocky nodded. They had a location.

"Okay. I agree. Don't kill anyone else and we'll back off. I'll get Jenna right now, and she'll back off."

"Six hours, you'll get another call."

The line went dead.

Tandy Whitehall seemed oblivious to the tenor of the call. But Sam had risen and stepped back where only Rocky and Devin knew who'd been on the other end of the line. But he was now really interested in that scent from Tandy's shop.

"It's popular with a number of men in town," Tandy said. "And a few women. Here's the list one of my cashiers just sent me. John Bradbury bought that scent, and I guess he suggested it to a lot of his friends and coworkers."

Sam took the phone and looked at it.

"Mortuary? Now?" Rocky asked.

"You got it." And he handed the phone back to Tandy.

"I'll turn myself in to the police now," Tandy said.

"No. Sit tight, right here. You too, Sissy."

"The call came from the mortuary," Rocky said.

He hurried out the door, wondering just which one of the people on the list was now holding Elyssa Adair hostage there. He didn't want Tandy calling the police. Not until he found out exactly who he was dealing with, someone that might even now be stalking Jenna, who may be stumbling into a trap.

Chapter Eight

The mortuary was definitely clearing out. People were leaving in groups and singles. The ticket booth was closed. By the time Jenna walked across the porch and reached the front door, no one was around, the last of the visitors having reached the parking lot. She entered through the front door and no costumed actor greeted her.

"Detective Martin," she shouted.

No answer.

"Micah? Jeannette? Naomi?"

No reply.

The silence gave her a sensation of unease, one that had nothing to do with the fact that she was accompanied by two bickering ghosts. She ignored them, allowing them to follow her as she searched the ground floor rooms, amazed that the actors and staff could clear out so quickly. Also, no one had locked up. She passed through the dining room with its array of skeletal guests. On through the kitchen, where it appeared that a massacre had taken place. Fake blood leaked from a cauldron on the stove top, body parts lay scattered on a table, but no actor-chef or cook standing around with a plastic butcher knife to put chills and thrills into the bloodstreams of attendees.

"Goodnight," she heard someone call from the front of the house. "Last one out, lock up."

Jenna hurried to the front door. But whichever performer had just left had done so quickly. She could just make out a dark form heading to the parking lot. She hustled back to the kitchen.

"There's no one down here," Gloria said, following close behind her.

"We should check upstairs," John suggested.

"We should go to the basement," Gloria said.

Jenna was irritated. "Stop. I'll go up first, then we'll go down."

The stairway up seemed misty in the eerie black lighting used for the haunted house attraction. She moved carefully, unnerved, not wanting to be taken by surprise. One by one, she searched through the second floor rooms. Spider webs, creepy creatures, all manner of frights remained. But no one person. Where the hell was Detective Gary Martin? She heard the sound of movement coming from the back of the house. She hurried across the hall to one of the rooms that looked down over the delivery entrance to the old embalming rooms.

"Basement," she said.

"Told you," Gloria whispered.

"Where is everyone?" John asked.

"Good question. Detective Martin should be here," Jenna said. "Let's see what's down in the basement."

She moved quickly, hurrying down the blackened stairs. Portraits adorned the walls that started off as depictions of the living and changed to rotting skeletons from different perspectives. She ignored them and hurried around to the stairs to the basement. Her phone rang. Sam. She hit the answer button.

John screamed.

She whirled to see why.

A fist came out of the darkness, smashing against the side of her face. Her body crashing down the rest of the stairs, her phone disappearing into the misty darkness of the embalming room below.

Before the world vanished, she heard Sam's voice through the phone.

Calling her name.

* * * *

Sam spotted the mortuary, high on the hill, glowing opaque in the strange mix of moonlight and artificial electric haze. No cars filled the parking lot. The building seemed to be alive, its upstairs windows like soulless eyes. The front door appeared to be a gaping mouth caught in a strange and twisted oblong O of horror.

"Not sure how exactly we should be doing this," Rocky said.

"Maybe call the local police?" Devin murmured.

"No," Sam said. "We handle this ourselves."

The killer had threatened to kill Elyssa and now he probably had Jenna too. No time to wait for the locals.

"No police," he said.

And neither of his colleagues argued since, among those who bought the woodsy scent from Tandy Whitehall's shop was Detective Gary Martin. A cop gone bad? Sam didn't know. Especially since another man associated with the mortuary had purchased the scent, too.

The head of the paranormal research department.

Micah Aldridge.

* * * *

Jenna tumbled down the stairs, feeling every bruise to her body, but managed to roll out on the floor and draw her weapon.

She heard an eerie laugh.

"You have no idea how much trouble you're in," a voice told her in a hoarse, eerie whisper.

Then she heard another voice. Gloria Day. "It's a boo-hag."

Down the steps one came. But no demon. Instead, a living, breathing person in a boo-hag costume, armed with a Smith and Weston pistol gripped by red latex-clad hands.

"Stop," she commanded.

But the costumed person ignored her. "Throw down your gun. Now."

A snap of sound and a system was turned on that offered first eerie music, then the deep, rugged, masculine voice of the attraction's narrator. "And so Proctor died as well, for, as he was supposed to have said, the girls did, in the end, make devils of far too many a man and woman. It was in June of 1692 that the first of the condemned were hanged. Before it was over, nineteen would die in such a manner, and one man, Giles Corey, would be pressed to death."

A sudden flow of light sprang from one of the niches.

She heard a sob of fear and terror.

"Auntie Jenna? Help me. Please!"

Elyssa stood in the niche, supported on a stool, a noose around her neck, a second costumed boo-hag at her side ready to rip away the stool.

* * * *

Sam came through the mortuary front door. Rocky and Devin had slipped around the house, intent on entering the basement via the delivery entrance. He moved with care. What he wanted was to barge in with guns blazing and wrap his fingers around the throat of the killer now threatening Elyssa and Jenna. But he told himself to slow down, use caution. His head pounded, ready to explode. All he could hear was Elyssa's sobbing through Jenna's phone, from four minutes ago.

A lot could happen in four minutes.

He climbed the porch steps and saw that the mortuary's front door hung half ajar. He entered the foyer and looked around, certain from the acoustics and sounds made when he'd called her that the phone had dropped in the basement. He hurried through the garish decorations and around to the stairway.

A body lay on the floor right by the door to the basement stairs.

Not a prop.

Micah Aldridge.

He hunkered down and felt for a pulse. Faint. But there. He found his phone and dialed 911 requesting an ambulance and the police. He'd identified himself and asked for no sirens. His phone blinked for an incoming call. Rocky. He answered and told him the situation and that help was coming.

He left the fallen man and headed for Jenna and Elyssa.

Knowing now who he was about to encounter.

* * * *

"We'd been debating how to handle this, and honestly," the costumed boo-hag said, "you weren't on our original list. But that's okay. We had you running all over looking at Wiccans and talking about the Gullah people, and don't you love our costumes?"

Elyssa was still sobbing, but Jenna realized that struggling just caused the rope around the young girl's neck to chaff more. Elyssa's wrists and ankles were tied. Once the stool was kicked aside, there'd be no recourse for her.

"It's not that I care," the boo-hag said. "I really don't care if the kid—or you—live or die. You couldn't let a damned suicide be a suicide. You just had to turn it into a murder investigation."

"You're so sadly mistaken," Jenna said. "The medical examiner knew immediately that John Bradbury had been murdered."

The boo-hag by Elyssa spoke out angrily, "That's because your good buddy Sam Hall talked the medical examiner into believing that. It could have been left a mystery, accepted as a suicide. But that's all right. Eventually they would have blamed the Gullah people or the Wiccans. But you! Bursting in here, pushing everyone around. Here to pat poor baby cousin on the back. What made you start running around screaming murder anyway?"

"John Bradbury told Elyssa it was a murder and that you would murder more people. Then John found and told me about the way you two attacked him. And yes, you did have us investigating what might be going on in Salem. But this has nothing to do with the Gullah community or the Wiccans or history, except in whatever way you thought you could use it. This is all about greed."

John Bradbury's ghost floated over the niche where he'd been hanged, and where Elyssa was now dangerously close to meeting the same fate, swiping angrily at the air.

To Jenna's surprise, the boo-hag moved back, as if the movement had been felt.

"Don't you understand?" the boo-hag behind Jenna said. "We're in complete control. So I'll only say it one more time. Drop your gun or my pal over there will kick the stool out from under your cousin."

"I don't think so," a new voice suddenly announced.

Sam.

The boo-hag whirled around. "Sam Hall. The great attorney, P.I. No—great FBI special agent now. Have you forgotten all about our negotiation?" stairway boo-hag said.

"Not at all."

The boo-hag beside Elyssa said, "We've still got all the cards, Special Agent Hall. Come down here. Now. Or this girl dies."

Jenna recognized the woman's voice. Naomi Hardy. And she

knew that their suspicions had been right. This had nothing to do with the past, nothing to do with feuds or beliefs. "Naomi Hardy. You did this for a promotion? You killed people—you probably planned on killing more people to create a real Wiccan war and send a Wiccan to prison—all for a promotion."

The boo-hag's head whipped around. "She knows who I am."

"Shut up," the boo-hag on the stairwell said.

"You know, I thought at first that it was either Micah—or even poor Detective Martin," Sam said. "But, Jeannette, you and Naomi have to be the two dumbest murderers I've ever met!"

Of course, Jenna thought. Jeannette Mackey.

"Kill the stupid girl, Naomi. Do it," Jeannette yelled.

"They'll shoot me," Naomi said.

Jenna thrust herself up and burst toward the niche, trying to get to Elyssa. She could make that move because Sam had her back. Luckily, Naomi Hardy stayed hesitant. The boo-hag on the stairwell raised her red latex arm to fire, but Sam slammed his arm down on hers and the weapon went cascading down the stairs.

Jeannette screamed in fury.

Sam and the boo-hag went down.

"Kill the damned girl," Jeannette roared.

Naomi recovered her wits and kicked the stool.

Jenna lunged forward to save her cousin. Arms around the girl, she supported her weight so the rope could not tighten around her neck. Naomi's body began to jerk from side to side, as if being pushed hard. Gloria Day and John Bradbury were trying to have an affect on her, but it was another ghost who managed to stop her. He was in Puritan garb as well, a big man, heavy-muscled, broad-shouldered. He appeared before Naomi, who gasped and backed away.

Rocky burst through the basement door and helped Jenna get the noose down and off from Elyssa's neck. Sam wrenched Naomi Hardy aside. Devin Lyle appeared and cuffed Naomi, telling her that she was under arrest.

Sirens screamed from outside.

Help was coming.

The reign of terror was over.

* * * *

"Naomi Hardy thought that she had a brilliant way to become the head of the company? Get rid of John Bradbury? In the midst of the highest paying time of the year? Really? She did this for a job?" Devin Lyle asked.

"It was a pretty damned good job, from what I understand," Sam told her. "And trust me, I didn't get it until the end. I knew that both Detective Martin and Micah Aldridge had ordered that cologne—Scent of the Pine—Tandy Whitehall sold. And since both of our victims had smelled it, the scent seemed involved. But, as we would have learned had we had time to ask Micah about it, he bought it for Jeannette Mackey, who loved the scent."

They were all at Devin's place, a charming cottage on the outskirts of town. Devin had inherited the house from her Aunt Mina, who remained after death, still watching over Devin when she was in Salem. Mina was with them now, shaking her head over the terrible things an emotion like greed could cause a person to do. She'd done her best to make the ghosts of John Bradbury and Gloria Day comfortable in her house.

"How did she get Jeannette involved?" Rocky asked.

"Jeannette saw herself as a seer, a medium, the rightful agent at the gate. Their agreement was that once Naomi became boss, she'd find another place for the haunted house company to operate. They were so obsessed with what they wanted to do that they were willing to kill," Jenna said.

"And," Sam explained, "Jeannette knew all of the legends about the new local cultures and communities beyond the Wiccans. She also hated both Tandy Whitehall and Gloria Day. What better way to get back at the two women than kill the one and get the other arrested for her murder."

"They planned on killing more people," Elyssa said.

Her parents, overcome with gratitude for Jenna and Sam and the Krewe members, had allowed her to come along with the adults.

"Who was next?" Rocky asked.

"Somebody named Sissy," Elyssa told them. "In case they didn't blame the Wiccans, they'd start looking at the Gullah people. They never intended for any of us to survive the night."

"I'm pretty sure they thought they'd killed both Gary Martin and

Micah Aldridge," Sam said.

Martin had been discovered in the basement, a bad gash to his head. But both men were going to be all right.

"Here's what I understand," Sam said. "They had to kill John and make it look like a suicide. They figured that it might not work, so they planned an elaborate scheme to kill more people and make it look like an inter-Salem cultural war of some kind."

The ghostly presence of Gloria Day said, "So I died because of you, John?"

"It seems so. I'm sorry."

"You didn't die because of John," Auntie Mina pointed out. "You died because of two greedy, sick, demented women."

"Who really thought they could kill me, Sam, and Elyssa, and get away with it," Jenna said. She looked at Sam and smiled. "Thank goodness they underestimated you."

"They underestimated the Krewe," Sam said.

"I don't think Jeannette cared if she died," Elyssa said. "As long as she took us with her. But, you're right. Thank goodness for the Krewe. I think I'd like to be part of this one day." Elyssa leapt to her feet. "Gotta go."

"Where?" Jenna asked her.

"Party. It's Halloween. And I'm rather an important person right now. My guy is here for me. Don't worry, my parents love Nate."

She kissed and hugged them all, thanking everyone profusely, and then she was gone.

"What about us, John?" Gloria asked him. "Shouldn't we be going somewhere by now? Into the light or whatever."

John looked at her. "I'm thinking about sticking around for a bit."

"How lovely," Aunt Mina said.

Gloria reached for John's hand. "If we're going to stick around together, we're going to play give and take. Come on. It's Samhain."

"Where are we going?"

"Gallows Hill, of course."

John Bradbury groaned, then shrugged and took Gloria's hand. "Why not."

They said their good-byes and disappeared.

"I'm curious about one thing still," Jenna said. "There was a third ghost there last night. A powerful ghost. He was in Puritan apparel, big guy, like a hearty farmer type. Then he was gone. Who was he? There's not another victim somewhere, is there?"

Rocky shook his head. "The two women spilled everything at the station. No more victims."

"Big dude, powerful, looked like a farmer?" Mina said. "Might have been John Proctor, sick to death of watching more horror over petty jealousy and greed. Those bitter human emotions might have caused the hysteria once, but he wouldn't want to see it happening again. Could have also been George Burroughs. He was a big dude, too."

"I wish we could thank him," Jenna said.

"I'm sure he feels thanked," Mina said.

"Are we going out for Halloween?" Sam asked.

Jenna jumped up laughing and grabbed his hand. "No. We're staying in. Rocky, Devin, Mina, thank you for your hospitality. We're going back to Sam's house. Uncle Jamie is busy dishing out Halloween treats. We're going to be alone for a while."

Sam jumped up, ready to comply, but noted, "We'll all head back to Krewe headquarters in the morning."

And he told them all goodnight. Outside, the moon had risen over a beautiful, brisk, October night.

Jenna rose on her toes and kissed his lips.

"Trick or treat?" he asked.

"I intend to see that on this Halloween, every move we make is going to be one hell of a treat." She drew a finger down his chest. "Here, there, and everywhere."

He kissed her.

"I shall strive to make this a happy, happy Halloween too."

They drove to his house, and then they were alone.

There were all manner of treats...

And it was a very happy Halloween indeed.

* * * *

Also from 1001 Dark Nights and Heather Graham, discover Hallow Be the Haunt.

Sign up for the 1001 Dark Nights Newsletter
and be entered to win a Tiffany Key necklace.

There's a contest every month!

Go to www.1001DarkNights.com to subscribe.

As a bonus, all subscribers will receive a free
1001 Dark Nights story
The First Night
by Lexi Blake & M.J. Rose

Turn the page for a full list of the
1001 Dark Nights fabulous novellas...

Discover 1001 Dark Nights Collection Four

ROCK CHICK REAWAKENING by Kristen Ashley
A Rock Chick Novella

ADORING INK by Carrie Ann Ryan
A Montgomery Ink Novella

SWEET RIVALRY by K. Bromberg

SHADE'S LADY by Joanna Wylde
A Reapers MC Novella

RAZR by Larissa Ione
A Demonica Underworld Novella

ARRANGED by Lexi Blake
A Masters and Mercenaries Novella

TANGLED by Rebecca Zanetti
A Dark Protectors Novella

HOLD ME by J. Kenner
A Stark Ever After Novella

SOMEHOW, SOME WAY by Jennifer Probst
A Billionaire Builders Novella

TOO CLOSE TO CALL by Tessa Bailey
A Romancing the Clarksons Novella

HUNTED by Elisabeth Naughton
An Eternal Guardians Novella

EYES ON YOU by Laura Kaye
A Blasphemy Novella

BLADE by Alexandra Ivy/Laura Wright
A Bayou Heat Novella

DRAGON BURN by Donna Grant
A Dark Kings Novella

TRIPPED OUT by Lorelei James
A Blacktop Cowboys® Novella

STUD FINDER by Lauren Blakely

MIDNIGHT UNLEASHED by Lara Adrian
A Midnight Breed Novella

HALLOW BE THE HAUNT
A Krewe of Hunters Novella by Heather Graham

DIRTY FILTHY FIX by Laurelin Paige

THE BED MATE by Kendall Ryan
A Room Mate Novella

NIGHT GAMES by CD Reiss
A Games Novella

NO RESERVATIONS by Kristen Proby
A Fusion Novella

DAWN OF SURRENDER by Liliana Hart
A MacKenzie Family Novella

Go to www.1001DarkNights.com for more information.

Discover 1001 Dark Nights Collection One

FOREVER WICKED by Shayla Black
CRIMSON TWILIGHT by Heather Graham
CAPTURED IN SURRENDER by Liliana Hart
SILENT BITE: A SCANGUARDS WEDDING by Tina Folsom
DUNGEON GAMES by Lexi Blake
AZAGOTH by Larissa Ione
NEED YOU NOW by Lisa Renee Jones
SHOW ME, BABY by Cherise Sinclair
ROPED IN by Lorelei James
TEMPTED BY MIDNIGHT by Lara Adrian
THE FLAME by Christopher Rice
CARESS OF DARKNESS by Julie Kenner

Also from 1001 Dark Nights

TAME ME by J. Kenner

Go to www.1001 DarkNights.com for more information.

Discover 1001 Dark Nights Collection Two

WICKED WOLF by Carrie Ann Ryan
WHEN IRISH EYES ARE HAUNTING by Heather Graham
EASY WITH YOU by Kristen Proby
MASTER OF FREEDOM by Cherise Sinclair
CARESS OF PLEASURE by Julie Kenner
ADORED by Lexi Blake
HADES by Larissa Ione
RAVAGED by Elisabeth Naughton
DREAM OF YOU by Jennifer L. Armentrout
STRIPPED DOWN by Lorelei James
RAGE/KILLIAN by Alexandra Ivy/Laura Wright
DRAGON KING by Donna Grant
PURE WICKED by Shayla Black
HARD AS STEEL by Laura Kaye
STROKE OF MIDNIGHT by Lara Adrian
ALL HALLOWS EVE by Heather Graham
KISS THE FLAME by Christopher Rice
DARING HER LOVE by Melissa Foster
TEASED by Rebecca Zanetti
THE PROMISE OF SURRENDER by Liliana Hart

Also from 1001 Dark Nights

THE SURRENDER GATE By Christopher Rice
SERVICING THE TARGET By Cherise Sinclair

Go to www.1001DarkNights.com for more information.

Discover 1001 Dark Nights Collection Three

HIDDEN INK by Carrie Ann Ryan
BLOOD ON THE BAYOU by Heather Graham
SEARCHING FOR MINE by Jennifer Probst
DANCE OF DESIRE by Christopher Rice
ROUGH RHYTHM by Tessa Bailey
DEVOTED by Lexi Blake
Z by Larissa Ione
FALLING UNDER YOU by Laurelin Paige
EASY FOR KEEPS by Kristen Proby
UNCHAINED by Elisabeth Naughton
HARD TO SERVE by Laura Kaye
DRAGON FEVER by Donna Grant
KAYDEN/SIMON by Alexandra Ivy/Laura Wright
STRUNG UP by Lorelei James
MIDNIGHT UNTAMED by Lara Adrian
TRICKED by Rebecca Zanetti
DIRTY WICKED by Shayla Black
THE ONLY ONE by Lauren Blakely
SWEET SURRENDER by Liliana Hart

Go to www.1001 DarkNights.com for more information.

Discover More Heather Graham

Hallow Be the Haunt
A Krewe of Hunters Novella
By Heather Graham

Coming October 24, 2017

Years ago, Jake Mallory fell in love all over again with Ashley Donegal—while he and the Krewe were investigating a murder that replicated a horrible Civil War death at her family's Donegal Plantation.

Now, Ashley and Jake are back—planning for their wedding, which will take place the following month at Donegal Plantation, her beautiful old antebellum home.

But Halloween is approaching and Ashley is haunted by a ghost warning her of deaths about to come in the city of New Orleans, deaths caused by the same murderer who stole the life of the beautiful ghost haunting her dreams night after night.

At first, Jake is afraid that returning home has simply awakened some of the fear of the past…

But as Ashley's nightmares continue, a body count begins to accrue in the city…

And it's suddenly a race to stop a killer before Hallow's Eve comes to a crashing end, with dozens more lives at stake, not to mention heart, soul, and life for Jake and Ashley themselves.

On behalf of 1001 Dark Nights,

Liz Berry and M.J. Rose would like to thank ~

Steve Berry
Doug Scofield
Kim Guidroz
Jillian Stein
InkSlinger PR
Dan Slater
Asha Hossain
Chris Graham
Pamela Jamison
Jessica Johns
Dylan Stockton
Richard Blake
BookTrib After Dark
The Dinner Party Show
and Simon Lipskar